# HELLULAND

BY

## C.R. LINDSTRÖM

A Modern Saga

Interior Illustrations by M. Harris
Original *U-537* log references from *Deutshes U-Boot Museum* archives (1943)
*Bjarni Grimolfsson's* tale from *The Sagas of Icelanders* (Penguin Classics, 1997)

Eerie River Publishing
Box 99900 HP 157 673
RPO Stanley Park
Kitchener, Ontario, N2A 0H1
Canada
eerieriverpublishing.com
Literary representation by MBE Media (UK)
info@mbemedia.co.uk

ISBN: 978-1-990245-95-4



modernsagas.com

*To our mother,
and the beautiful way
she saw the world*

CANADA
Cambridge Bay
Gjoa Haven
Resolute
Repulse Bay
Pond Inlet
Baffin Island
Iqaluit
BAFFIN BAY
BAFFIN BAY
Qaanaaq (Thule)
ELLESMERE ISLAND
Alert
ARCTIC OCEAN
North Pole
SEVERNAYA ZEMLA (Russia)
FRANZ JOSEF LAND (Russia)
Nord
80
Longyearbyen
SVALBARD ISLANDS (Norway)
GREENLAND (Denmark)
DAVIS STRAIT
Sisimiut
Ilulissat
Nuuk
Ittoqqortoormit
GREENLAND SEA
BJØNØYA ISLAND
NORWEGIAN SEA
Jan Mayen (Norway)
Narvik
FINLAND
Tasiilaq
Qaqortoq
LABRADOR SEA
ARCTIC CIRCLE
Reykjavik
ICELAND
SWEDEN
Vaasa
FAROE ISLANDS (Denmark)
Tórshavn
NORWAY
Stockholm
Bergen
Oslo
NORTH ATLANTIC OCEAN

*From the fury of the Northmen, good Lord deliver us.*

– Medieval English Prayer

THE
ARCTIC REGIONS
OF
NORTH AMERICA
BY
EDW. WELLER. F.R.G.S.
PARRY ISLAND
PRINCE PATRICK ISLAND
MELVILLE ISLAND
BATHURST Isd
CORNWALLIS ISLAND
North Cornwall
Grinnell Land
BANKS LAND
Melville Sound
Pr of Wales Land
Som
Pr Albert Land
Banks Strait
Minto Inlet
Victoria Land
Pr Albert Sound
Wollaston Land
Boothia
King William Land
Great Bear Lake
Arctic Circle

# PROLOGUE



A horn blast distracted Liam from his grim task. He paused to look at the old icebreaker. It rested at anchor several hundred yards from the rocky beach where he sat. The in-shore waters were calm, a few northern birds flying low across the surface. A lone iceberg drifted in the distance. The sky was clear, offering no hint of the severe weather approaching from the west. The ship's signal was a warning it would depart within the hour.

An Atlantic puffin landed near the rusted antenna. Liam watched the bird bounce about the derelict weather mast, slowly swaying in the wind. He had never seen an auk this close before. Its courtship colours had faded, a sign autumn would soon arrive. The bird's plumage stood in contrast to the barren Arctic surroundings. Snow still dusted the smooth rocks of the ancient inlet, even in late summer. The puffin perched itself atop a shattered barrel, dried battery acid cementing the canister to the ground. It watched the young researcher intently through dark eyes. As the bird flew away, its wings brushed the dead sailor's body, bringing Liam back to reality.

He examined the corpse with morbid fascination. While the back appeared well preserved, the front was a frozen mess of torn flesh, slashed fabric, and protruding ribs. The sailor's face stared at the northern sky through hollow eye sockets. Its lower jaw jutted sideways at an awkward angle, the man's teeth exposed behind leathery curled lips. Both arms were stiff by its side, as if at attention, as were its legs. A faded eagle and swastika dangled from the tattered wool uniform. Liam imagined the submariner howling a last cry before the awful end. Spent shell casings littered the ground surrounding the remains.

"Liam, where are you?" a familiar voice called out from the rocky shore.

"Over here, Professor," he replied, standing up beside the body. He pulled his wool hat down over his ears. Even in late August, the daytime temperature this far north was only slightly above freezing. Professor Barbara Douglas, wearing a red hooded jacket, approached with a sombre face.

"I found three more over the ridge," she said quietly. "We knew they landed here during the war, but not that they suffered casualties."

Liam watched his professor while contemplating the tragic scene before them. This was not what he had expected from his summer internship. Liam Holstrom was an environmental science sophomore from the University of Minnesota. He had landed a dream summer placement as a research assistant, part of a joint American-Canadian Arctic expedition. They were searching for a rumoured German weather station, abandoned in the far north during the last war. The evidence came from the archived logbook of a *U-boat* tasked with delivering the clandestine equipment sometime in 1943. Deployed in remote northern locations, the devices were designed to give *U-boats* an advantage over allied convoys. The Third Reich's naval logic had been ruthless in its simplicity. If they could accurately predict the weather, they could estimate the probable sailing routes of allied ships, and sink them.

Another horn blast echoed across the bay. The icebreaker's captain was getting nervous about the weather. Dr Douglas ignored the warning, her demeanour sullen. She coughed loudly, courtesy of an addiction to cigarettes. Liam tried easing the tension.

"How do you think they died, Professor, an air raid?"

Dr Douglas quietly stared at the sight before her, trying to comprehend what the evidence presented.

"Unlikely," she said, her breath visible in the cold air. "There are no apparent entry wounds, only... exit wounds."

The academic shook her head before continuing. "And look at this," she pointed at the charred ribs covered in ice. "These are burn marks, but not from a flash burn or explosion. They seem very precise, almost surgical, even after forty years."

Liam examined the dead sailor's blown-out ribcage. The frozen chest cavity was devoid of any internal organs. All he could see was a scorched cavern where the man's lungs and heart should have been.

"Maybe it was a lightning strike, especially this close to the weather antenna?"

Professor Douglas lowered her head, deep in thought. She had no idea how this could have happened, but felt there must be a rational, scientific explanation.

A third horn blast from the old ship meant it was time to leave.

"I want to check the other bodies I found before we go," the professor said with a sense of urgency.

"Shouldn't we head back to the ship?" Liam protested. "That storm front will be here soon."

"Then we'll have to be quick."

Liam was unsettled by his mentor's request. He was studying to be an environmental scientist, not a student of forensics. With some trepidation, he stumbled up the icy ridge to where Dr Douglas had found the other three sailors. They all lay face down, frozen into the ground. The wind was picking up as the two academics knelt over one of the deceased. At the professor's insistence, they tried rolling over frozen remains not disturbed in four decades.

*Did your family ever know what had happened to you?*

Liam grunted trying to lift the dead sailor. After five minutes of effort, they were only able to free the submariner's right arm and shoulder, lifting both just enough for Dr Douglas to peer underneath. As she lay beside the body, the professor fiddled in her pocket for a cigarette lighter. She reached under the sailor's chest and tried sparking the flint in order to see. The wind kept blowing it out. Finally she succeeded, holding the open flame under the frozen chest for a brief instant.

"It appears to be the same kind of wound..."

Before she could finish, a flash of blue flame ballooned out from under the dead man's exposed ribcage. Both researchers scrambled back from the small fireball, which dissipated as quickly as it had appeared. Neither spoke as they sat on the ground opposite each other, the dead German again face down between them. Dr Douglas let out a gentle grunt as she brushed the soot from her face. The sudden fireball had singed her eyebrows.

"Now that was a rookie move," she allowed, looking over at her pupil.

"What just happened?" Liam asked, his voice nervous.

"Probably a pocket of methane gas trapped within the chest cavity. A by-product of slow decomposition and the ice forming an airtight seal." The professor stood up. "Nothing to worry about."

Liam had had enough, and his teacher could tell. She gestured that it was time to go. As historically significant as their find was, they needed to heed Mother Nature's warning and leave before the northern blizzard arrived. Professor Douglas had no intention of ending up like the permanent residents of the abandoned weather station. The pair hastily walked across the smooth pebble shoreline towards an awaiting powerboat.

"Liam, when we get to Pond Inlet, remind me to request a copy of the logbook for *U-537*. That's the submarine these sailors belonged to. I think I now understand the German archivist's hesitation at showing us the original entries."

"Will do," Liam said, his teeth chattering from the cold. "You're hoping it will mention what happened to the four we found today?"

The professor nodded and carried on towards the rubber craft with its trio of coast guard sailors.

A glint of metal caught Liam's attention off to his right. He walked a few paces and crouched down to find an object in the shape of a teardrop, no larger than the palm of his hand. At the bottom was a square-shaped piece roughly the size of a quarter, with comb-like teeth extending downward. Its intricate design seemed strangely out of place for the Arctic. Whatever it was, it looked beautiful and old, very old.

Liam placed the item in his pocket and walked off to join his professor, who was already seated in the powerboat. He promised himself he would properly catalogue the artefact once they reached Pond Inlet.

# The Weekly Sagas

THE
ARCTIC REGIONS
OF
NORTH AMERICA
BY
EDW. WELLER, F.R.G.S.
PARRY ISLAND
PRINCE PATRICK'S LAND
MELVILLE ISLAND
BATHURST Isle
CORNWALLIS ISLAND
BARROW
BANKS LAND
MELVILLE SOUND
Pr. of Wales Land
Melville Sound
Pr. Albert Land
Pr. Albert Sound
Wollaston Land
Victoria Land
King William Land
Banks Strait
Minto Inlet
Baring Ld.
Franklin
Great Bear Lake
Arctic Circle

# CHAPTER 1

EARLY SUMMER
ONE YEAR FROM NOW

Erika gazed wearily out the cabin window. A cluster of raindrops pooled at the bottom of the circular glass. Across the harbour, a majestic skyline rose from the water. Low storm clouds masked the tallest skyscrapers. The concrete buildings looked cold and grey. Their stark appearance added to Erika's sense of emptiness, her thoughts consumed by recent events. The young woman rested her forehead against the window frame. Condensation from her breath clung to the worn glass. She closed her eyes, willing away another bout of tears. The cause of her anguish replayed in her mind. First there was the funeral, then the condolence letters, and finally the cremation.

"Flight attendants, please be seated for take-off."

The propeller engines of the commuter plane accelerated to full power. The rain-soaked runway rushed by. Erika was gently pushed back in her seat as they climbed out of Toronto's island airport. She had passed through the city several times, but only for connecting flights. Today was no different, not that it mattered. She felt utterly detached from reality, her usual love of flying lost to a deep sorrow. The sooner she reached her destination, the better. Erika's pain was more than anyone her age should have to endure. Mercifully, the seat beside her was empty.

"Ms Holstrom, would you like something to drink?"

The flight attendant startled Erika. The airline was one of the few that served free alcohol domestically. Though not yet eighteen, like any self-respecting high school graduate, Erika had fake ID.

"I'll take a tea please," she said softly, "with milk, no sugar." There would be no drowning of sorrows today. Not yet anyway.

The aircraft shook as it flew through a pocket of mild turbulence. The subtle cabin movement knocked Erika's leather purse onto its side. As she reached down to pick it up, she noticed that a small gift box had fallen out. Her father had given it to her as they said goodbye that morning. An early birthday present, she was not to open it until she turned eighteen next month. That suited her just fine.

For almost an hour, Erika silently watched the clouds below. Her smartphone lay on the seat beside her, the airline's complimentary Wi-Fi of no interest. Her thoughts turned inward. The puffy white clouds reminded her of the first time she'd been swarmed near her home. It had been winter, the snow several feet high. Her tormentors had been young, but their words still stung. Erika had learned over the years to handle being ridiculed for her fashion, or the music she liked, but not her roots. She could never get used to that. Her escape from the taunting growing up had been to excel in sports, especially ice hockey. This passion had recently taken her senior girls' team to the state championships, losing in overtime to a club from Minneapolis. Though upset by the loss, her individual skills had not gone unnoticed by the varsity scouts present.

The pilot announced their descent into Burlington. Erika again glanced out her window while the flight attendant passed down the aisle. She figured the large body of water below was Lake Champlain. Erika knew the airport was east of her destination, so the structures suddenly passing underneath must be downtown. Two large football fields were visible, one with a giant *V* in the centre. North of the fields was a rectangular building with a curved roof Erika recognised from photos as Gutterson Fieldhouse. Known as *The Gut*, it housed one of the largest varsity ice rinks in the north-eastern United States. This would be her home away from home for the next four years.

The aircraft gently touched down, the plane soon stopping in front of a small terminal building. Erika was the last to leave, her favourite leather purse slung across her chest as she emerged onto the tarmac. The weather was warm with the sun shining in the late afternoon sky. The airport didn't strike her as a busy place. Once inside the terminal she proceeded to U.S. customs. As a dual citizen, Erika had both American and Canadian passports. Today she was going to be an American.

Her father had always said, when passing through border control, reveal only what you are asked, no more, no less. She was through customs in less than three minutes. Turns out her dad had given good advice.

"You must be Erika Holstrom?"

An older woman walked over, dressed in a green sweatshirt and grey jeans. "The hockey bags were a bit of a giveaway," she said with a laugh.

Erika allowed an awkward smile.

"Forgive me, I'm Nancy from the University of Vermont's athletics program, and your assistant coach for the summer. Congratulations on earning your sports scholarship with us, well done. I'm here to take you to your residence and get you settled. Let me help you with your stuff."

The short drive to the main campus lasted ten minutes. After filling in some routine paperwork, Nancy escorted Erika up the second floor steps of her new residence building. She opened the door to room *207* and placed the oversized luggage on the floor.

"Your roommate must be out at the moment, but I'm sure she'll be back soon," Nancy said while handing Erika a binder. "Why don't you get settled? If you need anything, just text or call my number at the bottom of your registration forms. Your first hockey practice is tomorrow at eight in the morning. All the info you need is in your welcome package." Nancy waved and gently closed the door, leaving Erika alone for the first time in days.

Her new home was a standard-sized residence room with two single beds and a kitchenette in the corner. She could see her roommate had occupied the left side of the room, leaving Erika to claim the rest. Most of her sports equipment was in a single hockey bag she left on the floor. The other duffle bag contained her personal items, which she slowly unpacked. Clothes, books, toiletries, and a few framed photos she placed on the windowsill by her bed. The first picture was of her father as a young man, standing by an old weather station in the Arctic. Erika's parents had had their daughter later in life, so she had only ever known her dad as a kind, middle-aged professor. He had told her the story behind the photo a few times, but the details no longer registered. She liked the image because it showed him as a young man with the same boyish face her mother had fallen in love with. The second picture was of her family taken last fall, before her mother's diagnosis. Her parents were both smiling with their daughter in the centre, holding up the latest hockey trophy she had won. Erika's eyes welled with emotion.

*Why did you have to leave?*

Just then the residence room door burst open, causing Erika to jump. An athletic figure with a dark complexion walked in. The woman's arms were full, with a case of beer in one hand and a bundle of groceries in the other. She placed the items by the kitchenette.

"Hi, I'm Sandra Bruster," Erika's new roommate announced. "Really good to meet you." She offered her hand, which the newest occupant of room *207* accepted. They were both equally tall, though Sandra had broad shoulders and braided long black hair. Erika preferred a short pixie cut for her own appearance. It made getting in and out of her hockey helmet easier.

"So what position do you play?" Sandra asked while unpacking her groceries.

"Centre. You?" Erika said, feeling a bit shy.

"Goal, where all the action is!" The response came with a boisterous laugh. It brought a small smile to Erika's face. Her father had often joked that she had inherited her mother's intuition. Of course he was just telling fairy tales, but it showed he cared. Regardless, Erika somehow felt she was going to get along with her new roommate.

"Want a beer?" Sandra asked, opening up a bottle for herself.

"Not yet..." Erika said, sitting down on her bed.

"I spent my gap year playing hockey in Oregon, where the local lumberjacks got me into craft beer. I got a cute senior from the men's team to buy these for me. So where are you from?" Sandra asked.

"Duluth."

"Where's that?"

"Northern Minnesota, on the border with Wisconsin."

Sandra seemed to think for a second, as if checking a mental map. By her accent, Erika could tell she had grown up in New England, probably Massachusetts or Rhode Island. Sandra wore a plaid shirt with the sleeves rolled up. Her wrists were covered in bracelets, some homemade, others store bought. They included a Jamaican flag, one for breast cancer awareness, and a Pride rainbow. As Erika sized up her new roommate, she noticed a series of jagged scars across Sandra's forearm. She looked up at the goalie with concern.

"Don't mind them," Sandra said with a reassuring smile. "Let's just say junior high school wasn't exactly fun, but I made it through, thanks mainly to my folks, and hockey. You like it there, in Duluth?"

"Sometimes. It's quiet, and my mother taught me to love nature, which Minnesota has plenty of, especially bald eagles."

"Really? That's cool. Are you and your mom close?"

"We were, but she's gone now." Erika looked at the floor. Her fingers traced the imprint carved on her leather purse, resting on the bed. Erika's loving, smart, beautiful mother named Star, born and raised in the high Arctic, had taken her last breath ten days ago. Since then, Erika's world was numb. Star had lived long enough to see her daughter graduate, but by the following weekend the ravages of her cancer were too much. With her husband Liam by her side, she whispered a final northern poem and died in the family home. Erika and her father had cried uncontrollably for hours.

"Oh man, I'm so sorry," Sandra said, visibly shocked. "That really sucks." After a pause, she gently continued. "Did your mom give you that purse?"

Erika nodded, cradling the leather satchel for comfort.

"It's beautiful. Where did she find it?"

"Nunavut."

Sandra's expression was blank.

"It's in the Arctic."

Still nothing registered.

"Never mind..." Erika breathed, looking away.

Sandra sensed a subject change was needed. "You have a boyfriend?"

Erika was taken aback. She had never had a boyfriend. In fact, she couldn't remember the last time the thought of finding one had crossed her mind. She shook her head.

"Me neither, so let's make the most of this summer!" Sandra said with a smile. She finished her beer and moved towards the door. "Hey, wanna go eat? I found this great local café. We have to get up early tomorrow for our first practice, and I always play better going to bed on a full stomach. I can save my groceries for later in the week."

Suddenly Erika felt very hungry. Only then did it occur to her that she hadn't eaten since five in the morning, and then just a bowl of her father's Nordic porridge. She gestured to Sandra that she would come along, opening her leather satchel to make sure she had her wallet and mobile phone. Inside her purse, she found the small gift box her dad had given her to open on her birthday. She placed it on the windowsill by her bed and promptly followed her new roommate out the door.

Erika had not noticed the ambient heat gently radiating from the gift box.

# CHAPTER 2

**M**agnus prepared himself for another difficult day. The Dane stood quietly, scratching at his greying beard. Using binoculars, he could see what was left of the fishing trawler's stern. The wooden hull fragment gently bobbed up and down in the half-metre swells of the open ocean. He tried reading the vessel's name etched across the floating wreckage, but his ship was still too far away.

"Watch officer, bring us to a full stop," Magnus ordered from his central position on the bridge. "Prepare to launch the *SB90* powerboat configured for search and rescue. Also inform the maritime coordination centre that we've found debris."

Lieutenant-Commander Magnus Jakobson was captain of the Arctic patrol ship HMDS *Knud Rasmussen*. Named after the early Danish surveyor of Greenland, the *Rasmussen* had sailed the previous day from its summer anchorage at Nuuk. Its mission was to search for a fishing trawler reported missing in the Davis Strait two days earlier. Magnus was certain the stricken vessel had been absent for much longer. Since it was likely involved in illegal fishing activities, its owners had been hesitant to raise the alarm. As a result, precious days of searching the frigid waters had already been lost.

*The greedy corporate fools should be brought up on charges*, Magnus vented to himself. After three decades in the navy, most served in northern waters, he knew how treacherous the Arctic could be. If the wreckage proved to be the missing fishing trawler, it would be the third such hapless vessel they had discovered since the late spring. During the two previous incidents, the *Rasmussen* had come across bits of floating debris and the occasional life preserver, but no crew. Not even a distress signal had been sent. It was only after the ships were overdue to return to port that the alarm had been raised. If today proved to be a similar experience, Magnus knew their efforts would be focused on recovery rather than rescue.

"Sir, the SAR boat is away," the watch officer reported.

From the bridge's port window, Magnus observed the speedboat race off to investigate the wreckage. The small craft used a water jet propulsion system instead of propellers. This allowed it to move close to shore or launch up on ice floes, ideal for operating in Arctic waters. Today, as part of its search and rescue configuration, it carried a crew of three: a pilot and two medics.

Magnus confirmed the *Rasmussen's* position as forty nautical miles west of Sisimiut, off Greenland's west coast. Normally this part of the Davis Strait should be filled with massive icebergs, but not lately. The climate of the planet was changing and nowhere was it more evident than in the north.

The radio crackled to life. "*Rasmussen,* this is SAR one, over?"

Magnus reached up and keyed the handset dangling from the roof. "Search and rescue one, this is *Rasmussen*, send."

"SAR one, I have visual confirmation of the vessel's name and hull registry, prepare to copy."

The watch officer moved next to the captain, pen and notepad ready.

"*Rasmussen*, send," Magnus responded.

Both men made note of the vessel's name and registration number as they were transmitted. *L'Étoile Bretonne* was listed as a fishing trawler from the small French islands of Saint-Pierre and Miquelon, south of Newfoundland. The islands were the last remnants of France's once-vast North American possessions, lost to the British in the eighteenth century. In modern times, they had become a focal point for North Atlantic fishing efforts from the Grand Banks to the Arctic Ocean. With fish stocks declining, sailors had been venturing further from their traditional fishing grounds, sometimes into areas that were off limits. The *Bretonne* had a crew of five, all French nationals.

"*Rasmussen*, SAR one, we've found a body, VSA."

Even through the radio static, Magnus sensed the apprehension in the pilot's voice. All present on the bridge knew VSA stood for vital signs absent.

"*Rasmussen*, roger, can you bring it aboard?" Magnus said in a reassuring tone.

"SAR one, affirmative. Returning now."

The captain peered through his binoculars as the rescue boat crew hauled a bloated shape onto their small vessel. As soon as the fisherman's remains were aboard, the nimble craft returned to its mother ship.

"Watch officer, please ask the ship's doctor to meet me in the sick bay," Magnus instructed and headed below deck.

Like any modern warship, the *Rasmussen* was a maze of grey angles and hallways, covered in pipes, wires, and metal doors running every which way. Magnus navigated the inside of his ship like a pro, knowing when to duck under some unusually low steam pipes. The SAR boat was being recovered in the rear docking bay when the captain came across the ship's medical expert, Doctor Rikke Larsen. Though Rikke worked for the Danish navy, she was a civilian, assigned to the *Rasmussen* for the short Arctic summer months. Magnus understood that the rest of the year she practiced medicine in Roskilde, a town in Denmark made famous by its Norse ship museum. Rikke had told Magnus that she'd once worked at the facility while a student, learning ancient languages as a hobby.

"Good to see you, Captain," Rikke offered.

Magnus nodded back quickly, then gestured for them to enter the sick bay. The two medics from the search and rescue boat had already entered the room carrying a stretcher. Their orange immersion suits were covered in frigid saltwater. A waterproof blanket had been placed over the fisherman's body, both out of respect for the dead and to spare the Danish crew an upsetting sight. Rikke asked for a moment while she prepared her instruments, a signal for Magnus and the others to move into the waiting room. He looked up at the three members of the SAR boat, who appeared shaken. Assessing their discomfort, the captain spoke calmly.

"What did you find? Was it the same damage as the other two fishing boats this spring?"

"Aye, sir," the pilot said, "but there's more. What was left of the hull had precision burn marks. Long and deep, like a thermal cut."

The young sailor went on to explain that it was clear *L'Étoile Bretonne* had exploded, but not from an engine fire. The piece of floating debris was the aft section, which contained the fishing boat's power pack. Unlike the outer hull, the engine was intact with no sign of combustion damage. Explosions on small vessels were rare, but not unheard of, and almost always the result of an engine fire igniting fuel lines. Magnus had learned over the years that many strange things happened in these waters, with most incidents explained away as random accidents. While the first two ship losses were unfortunate, this latest tragedy demonstrated a pattern. All three of the doomed fishing vessels the *Rasmussen* found that year had been destroyed by a similar massive explosion, which now seemed to originate from an external source.

*They couldn't have been attacked by smugglers,* the captain thought sombrely, *not this far north.*

"Well done," Magnus said, placing his hand on the pilot's shoulder. "Get cleaned up and prepare your report after you've had some warm dinner."

Just then Rikke emerged from the sick bay's operating room, motioning for the captain to join her. Magnus placed latex gloves on his hands and followed the ship's doctor to where the fisherman's body lay under a white sheet. Recovery at sea was an uncomfortable business. After a few days, a drowning victim's remains would begin to decompose, filling with water and gasses that bloated a corpse to twice its original size. Sadly, given his line of work, this was not the first time Magnus had witnessed such a grisly sight. Rikke slowly removed the white sheet from the upper torso.

The dead fisherman on the metal gurney appeared average in height. Magnus could see the doctor had cut away the sailor's waterproof overalls, leaving only rubber boots on the victim's swollen feet. The body's arms were straight by its side, despite the enlarged mid-torso. The chest cavity was splayed open, charred ribs pointing towards the ceiling. Magnus assumed Rikke had already begun her autopsy since the victim's chest was cut open.

"Forgive me, Rikke, you do fast work," Magnus commented with genuine respect. Like most officers, he only used the doctor's first name when they were alone. Maintaining the appearance of professionalism was vital for the sake of discipline on a warship.

Rikke seemed confused, then shook her head. "I haven't begun my post-mortem, Magnus. This is how they found him."

The captain watched in silence as the doctor began her inspection. Magnus saw she had a small camera attached to her headlamp as she worked. After several minutes she looked up.

"His internal organs are gone. Somehow blown out of his chest."

"What?" Magnus said, surprised. "How?"

They both leaned over the fisherman's exposed chest cavity. The blackened cavern had been subjected to extreme heat. Magnus could see right through to the sailor's spine and back muscles, which appeared intact. Something with enough force to blow out a man's chest would surely leave a visible entry wound, but there was none to be found.

"Could this be the result of electrocution?" Magnus asked.

"I don't think so. There are no burn marks on the legs or hands," she replied.

"How about an orca or shark feeding on the remains?"

"No, there are no bite marks, and the wounds are too precise... almost surgical."

"A grenade?"

Rikke looked up dismissively at this last question. Magnus shrugged back. He was at a loss. In all his years at sea he had never witnessed such a peculiar way for a sailor to die, and he had come across many: boats capsizing, collisions, drowning, and engine explosions, to name a few. He'd even heard of a poor kayaker, crushed by an overly amorous whale as it breached during mating season. The captain shook his head.

"Look at this," Rikke gasped. She was examining the neck of the dead sailor, between the jaw line and shoulder. "Are these markings?"

She gestured for Magnus to come round the gurney and inspect what she had discovered. He peered at the sailor's pale neck to see what appeared to be two triangles on their side, the lower points connected at the base. It reminded him of a jagged letter *B*. At first Magnus dismissed the find as merely a fisherman's tattoo. Seafarers had been inking their skin since the dawn of navigation; how was this any different? When he raised his observation to Rikke, she asked him to examine the symbol again. She then pinched the surrounding skin with her latex gloves.

"Magnus, these have been burned into the skin. And look at the surrounding flesh, there is no scarring. This was done after death."

The captain stared long and hard at the ship's doctor, letting her words sink in. Rikke glanced back at the precisely etched symbol, just as the intercom came to life.

"Captain to the bridge, Captain to the bridge, please."

With a brief nod to Rikke, Magnus left to climb the three levels back up to the ship's control room. As he made his way through the grey metal corridors, he could hear the SAR boat departing. The senior duty officer must have found more wreckage worthy of inspection, and ordered the launch. As Magnus emerged onto the bridge he noticed additional crew were now present, obviously curious. The earlier clear sky had become overcast and dark despite the Arctic's twenty-four hour sunlight.

"Report," he instructed.

"Sir, there appears to be a floater off the starboard quarter, roughly two hundred metres away," the first officer said, handing a pair of binoculars to his captain. Magnus observed the rescue boat personnel first circling, then hauling up another bloated corpse from the frigid water. As soon as the body was retrieved, the nimble craft raced back towards the *Rasmussen*.

"First officer, you have the ship," Magnus ordered as he walked outside onto the railing behind the bridge.

The fastest way to the *Rasmussen*'s rear docking bay was via the exterior stairs, but it was cold and often dangerous due to ice build-up. Magnus held onto the railing with both hands as he climbed down the rear ladder, onto the empty helicopter deck. From there, he re-entered the ship's aft compartment, emerging in the rear-docking bay just as the second body was being removed. He walked up to the stretcher being carried by his crewmates and lifted back the blanket covering the victim's upper torso. Still wearing latex gloves, he canted the fisherman's head to the right, inspecting the area behind the ear.

Burned into the pale skin were two identical triangles, linked at the base.

# CHAPTER 3

Erika was body-checked hard into the sideboards. She felt her lungs compress as she collapsed to the ice. The Delaware enforcer that hit her took possession of the puck. Erika shook her head, trying to catch her breath. She watched from all fours as her opponent, the number *19* emblazoned on her back, cleared the puck back into the Vermont zone.

"C'mon, Ref, open your eyes!" Nancy yelled from the home bench.

Erika slowly got up, wiping blood from her lip onto her green and white jersey. She'd been winded, but not badly. She inhaled three times before skating towards the UVM bench, motioning for her coaches to swap her for another player.

"27, you're up. Holstrom, you OK?" Nancy bellowed, her chewing gum visible.

Erika raised her right glove with a thumbs up, then sat down amongst her teammates. The University of Vermont women's summer hockey camp was into its third week, and Erika was exhausted. Back in Duluth, she had been at the top of her game, one of the oldest on her team and a captain. Here she was just another first-year rookie, looking to prove herself among the more experienced varsity players. Though only an exhibition game, today was the first time the newest additions to the UVM squad joined their older teammates in competition.

"That was a rough hit, Holstrom. Their number nineteen came at you like a sledgehammer." Seated to Erika's right was Nicole Gibson, one of the assistant captains. A third year engineering student, hockey was her way of rebelling against her socialite parents. The rumour was she had once ditched her debutante ball for a Stanley Cup game at Madison Square Gardens. Now in her early twenties, she was experienced and dependable on the ice. Nicole handed her new teammate a water bottle, which Erika squirted into her mouth.

"Thanks, I'm good..." she exhaled, before spitting blood onto the floorboards.

"That doesn't look good," a soft voice observed to Erika's left. She turned to see Michelle Lavoix staring back through the cage of her hockey helmet. Michelle was a biology major and local to Vermont, her family equestrians of early French ancestry. She didn't say much, but of all the older players, she had been the most kind to Erika.

"Oh no," Nancy yelled, standing behind the Vermont bench. Michelle and Erika followed their coach's gaze to centre ice. Three Delaware players charged with the puck against a single UVM defender. Number 19 was among them. The trio easily out-skated their lone opponent and barrelled towards the Vermont net. Sandra Bruster stood ready in goal. One of the Delaware players feigned a slap shot and with the flick of her wrist, passed the puck to number 19. Erika could now see how large the opposing player was compared to the others on the ice. Number 19 sliced across the rink with the puck, controlling it with ease. To the goalie's left, she wound up for a shot, sending the puck sailing towards Sandra at phenomenal speed. Michelle, Erika and Nicole all leaned over the side railing to catch a glimpse of the amazing shot.

With the speed of a professional, yet the grace of a dump truck, Sandra nabbed the inbound projectile with her oversized glove. The Vermont bench roared. Moments later the arena buzzer went off, signalling the end of the second period of play. Sandra smiled to herself as the Delaware players swooped behind her net, cursing madly as they went by.

"All right ladies, it's an exhibition game, so we've only got ten minutes before the last period," Nancy explained. "Everyone to the locker room."

It occurred to Erika that ever since she had met Nancy, her assistant coach had only ever worn the same green UVM sweatshirt.

"Did you see that?" Sandra exclaimed, the saved puck still in her glove.

"Yeah, you were awesome," Erika said with a smile.

"Wow, what happened to your face?"

"Delaware."

Both players smirked as they hobbled on their skates to the locker room. Of everyone Erika had met at hockey camp, Sandra was by far her favourite. She felt very lucky to have her as a roommate and new friend. Inside the dressing room, Nancy arranged several folding chairs into a circle for the players to sit on. Once the team had settled, she moved to the middle of the group with a handheld whiteboard.

All at once, Erika felt the sensation.

Just like a handful of times before, the hairs on the back of her neck stood up. Her eyes blinked rapidly, and she was overcome by a calm sense of *déjà vu*. She looked about the room to see if anyone had noticed, then focused on Nancy.

*You're going to tell Nicole to attack towards the right side of the Delaware net in order to favour her slap shot.*

"Now Gibson, you've got a strong right handed slap shot, so I want you to try and come at the Delaware net from the right," Nancy instructed. Erika leaned back in her chair and closed her eyes.

*Sandra, well done in net, keep doing what you're doing.*

"And Bruster," Nancy continued, "well done in net, keep up the good work and don't change a thing."

The assistant coach slapped her white board three times in encouragement, then told everyone to stay hydrated and be back on the ice in five minutes. Erika shook her head, as though trying to clear a fog. Perhaps it was just a coincidence. She'd been around hockey long enough to know most pep talks sounded the same. Back in Duluth, she'd made bets with her teammates about which clichés they'd hear from their coaches. This was different. She could *feel* it was different.

"Hey, Holstrom," Sandra yelled so everyone could hear. "Isn't your birthday in a few weeks?" Erika nodded her agreement. "And how old will you be?"

"Eighteen."

A number of the players looked at each other, then back at Erika before hollering in unison, "MONTREAL!"

She looked at Sandra, confused.

"Montreal, dude. The legal age in Quebec is eighteen. You can get into bars and dance clubs no problem. We'll get a bunch of the girls together and do a road trip. Maybe even meet some cute French boys," Sandra laughed, then looked about the room. "Hey Lavoix, you speak French, right?"

Michelle glanced up coyly at Erika from re-lacing her skates. "Mais oui."

The rest of the players gossiped about a weekend in Canada as they made their way back upstairs for the third and final period of play. The score was 0-0. As this was an exhibition game, there would be no over-time, and with both teams defending well, it looked likely to end in a draw. Erika sat back on the bench, watching players from both teams circle their various end zones on the ice. The University of Vermont feline mascot was skating about with a giant UVM flag, even though the stands were mostly empty. The academic school year would not begin for another eight weeks.

The sensation Erika had felt earlier was gone, having dissipated as quickly as it began. She watched Nicole take the face-off for Vermont, skilfully managing the puck towards the opposing net, before a Delaware player snatched it away. Number 19 was at it again.

The final period of regulation play passed with neither team scoring. With only two minutes left, Erika was thinking about what she'd do after the game when Nancy tapped her helmet.

"Holstrom, you're up."

Erika turned to see Michelle coming off the ice with a broken hockey stick. She entered the Vermont bench via the side door as Erika jumped over the boards onto the ice. She quickly took her bearing, realising the momentum was in Delaware's favour. Just then, the arena's buzzer and bell went off together. A goal.

Erika glanced down the ice to see Sandra standing in net, her goalie helmet bowed. In front, the Delaware players converged on their triumphant teammate. It was number 19. She had just made the game 1-0 with only ninety seconds left to play. The referee blew a whistle to set up for the face-off. Nicole again took the puck for Vermont, but lost it to an opposing player.

The sensation returned.

Erika froze at centre ice, staring detachedly at the organised chaos surrounding the Vermont net. She closed her eyes. In the distance, what seemed like miles away, she could hear Nancy yelling at her to get back in the game. Erika's eyes opened. She quickly skated in the opposite direction of everyone else, towards the Delaware net. At precisely that moment, an accidental ricochet off the sideboards sent the puck sailing down the ice, directly at Erika. Somehow she knew it would. Without stopping, she raised her stick, smashing the puck in a new direction as it passed by. Caught unprepared, the Delaware goalie could only watch as the dark object flew over her shoulder and into the back of the net. The buzzer and bell rang simultaneously.

The Vermont bench erupted. Erika's fellow players circled her on the ice, each taking turns to bang their helmet against hers in congratulations. After a few more pats on the back, she skated back to the home bench. Soon after, the buzzer sounded signalling the end of play and a 1-1 score.

Back in the locker room, Erika's teammates lovingly teased her about being a secret superstar. *Holstrom the slash!* She took it in her stride. This was the best part of the game for her. Sharing a room with her comrades after a hard game on the ice, even if it was a tie. As an only child, this was the closest thing she had to sisterhood. The Vermont players stripped off their skates and uniforms while chatting away. Some, like Nicole, headed straight for the showers, while Sandra preferred to soak in the hot tub first. Not Erika. Her paternal grandmother was from Finland and had instilled in her a love of the sauna. Luckily, for all its utilitarian appearances, the Gutterson Fieldhouse had a small cedar steam room where she could escape.

Erika entered the wooden sanctuary wearing a white sports towel. She checked to make sure there was water in the pail located on the bottom shelf. Seeing she was alone, she removed her towel and sat on the top bench, letting the dry heat sink into her skin. Using a ladle, she scooped up some water and threw it onto the sauna stove. The hissing sound of steam rose from the hot oven rocks. Erika closed her eyes and laid down on the bench. Sauna time had always been important in her family. It allowed for reflection and meditation, as the humid heat cleansed the pores. She knew most northern cultures enjoyed something similar. For Erika, this was a moment of pure bliss.

Someone was approaching.

She sat up as the sensation returned. Erika could already feel a presence in the room before anyone had arrived. The sauna door gently opened and Michelle leaned into view.

"Mind if I join you?" she asked quietly.

"Please, there's plenty of room."

In her short time at UVM, Erika had grown used to having the sauna all to herself. Most of her teammates didn't like the heat. She watched as Michelle removed her towel, setting it down on the lower bench. Like many of her fellow players, Erika could see that Michelle was fit, yet feminine. She was two years older than Erika, with a mild collection of ivy tattoos. Both women sat on the top bench as the younger of the two threw more water on the hot rocks. The soothing steam washed over them.

"That was a really amazing goal," Michelle said after several minutes of silence. "You really have a hidden talent."

"How do you mean?"

*Has she noticed something about me?* Erika thought apprehensively.

Michelle looked over with her green eyes. "It's as though you knew exactly where to be to intercept that puck. Like it was your pet, running directly to its master."

Erika sat still. What was Michelle getting at? Was she thinking that Erika was somehow different? She didn't even understand the premonitions she was experiencing, if that's what they were. How could Michelle?

"So, do you have a partner?" Michelle asked, catching Erika by surprise.

"What, like a boyfriend? Nah, no time. I've been too busy with hockey, and then with my mom's illness..." Erika paused, not wanting to seem too emotional in front of her new teammate. "Anyway, boys were a bit of a distraction. Besides, all the good ones were taken."

It was clear that Michelle wasn't buying it.

"OK, I kinda had a crush on one of my cousins when I was fifteen." Erika felt she was starting to sound like an idiot. "But I never told anyone because it seemed weird." Thankfully Michelle just looked on calmly, the humid air causing drops of sweat to glisten over her body.

*Why are you staring at me like that?*

Suddenly the sauna door swung open, Sandra's dark frame blocking the light from outside. Erika could see she was already dressed.

"Would you two put some clothes on and hurry up. It's half-price chicken wings at the student centre and this girl is hungry!"

The two women took their cue from Sandra and collected their towels. They showered in silence, then got dressed as several other players still milled about. Erika tried to break the awkward quiet between them.

"You going to join us for wings?"

"No, I'm good," Michelle replied, her face neutral. "I need to head home. My folks are out of town so I have to take care of the horses."

Erika always forgot her teammate was from Vermont, and not living in residence.

"Go along with the others," Michelle said as she grabbed her hockey bag and walked towards the door. "You can plan your birthday trip to Montreal with everyone." Before exiting, she looked back at Erika with a sly grin. "Just make sure I'm invited."

THE
ARCTIC REGIONS
OF
NORTH AMERICA
BY
EDW. WELLER. F.R.G.S
PRINCE PATRICK ISLAND
PARRY ISLAND
MELVILLE ISLAND
BATHURST
Isld
CORNWALLIS
ISLAND
Melville Sound
Pr of Wales
Land
BANKS LAND
Pr. Albert Land
Prince
of Wales
Land
Banks Strait
Minto Inlet
Pr Albert Sound
Wollaston
Land
Victoria
Land
King William
Land
Boothia
Great
Bear Lake
Arctic Circle

# CHAPTER 4



"**U**jurak, where the hell are we?"

Eleanor could barely see her guide through the Arctic fog. She removed her protective eyewear, the lenses covered in perspiration. Major Eleanor Matthews, top graduate of the academy and hardened veteran of Afghanistan, was well and truly lost. All her navigational tools, as well as twenty years of military experience, were failing her. Solar flares had charged the ionosphere, disrupting any satellite signals and rendering her GPS useless. Given their proximity to magnetic north, her compass just spun in circles. She couldn't use the stars to navigate, thanks to the twenty-four hour summer daylight, while the unseasonal fog made line of sight triangulation impossible. Eleanor lifted her hand through the frigid mist, glancing at her palm. On her glove was the unmistakable sight of ice melting. Yet when airborne, these same particles formed moisture more akin to a southern rainforest than the Arctic tundra.

Over the past few days, Eleanor's local guide Ujurak had bemoaned his changing homeland. From melting pack ice to starving wildlife, the face of the north was changing at a dramatic rate. Just last month, three homes in his community of Pond Inlet had been lost to mudslides. The permafrost underneath the structures had dissolved for the first time in living memory. Then there were new phenomena, such as the gradually lifting Arctic fog that surrounded them.

Slowly, Eleanor started to see the rest of her organisation stretched out in a long green line. The young men and women were part of an Arctic infantry company, currently deployed on southern Baffin Island. As the officer commanding the company, Eleanor's mission was to conduct sovereignty patrols in the far north. Essentially reinforcing, through their presence, Canada's claim to this vast territory. The Americans did the same in Alaska, as did the Danes in Greenland, with all three nations providing exchange personnel to one another. Eleanor's troops had flown up from the south ten days ago, moving out of Iqaluit to their current location over the past week. All had been going well until the Arctic fog set in three days earlier. To everyone's relief, it finally appeared to be lifting.

"Major Matthews," a French-accented voice called out. It was the Company Sergeant Major, Luc Bernard. He moved up the line of soldiers towards his boss. "Ma'am, the fog is dissipating, so we should be able to move off soon." His comments were more a wish than a statement of fact.

"Understood, where is our second-in-command?" Eleanor asked.

"Captain Simmons is on her way now from behind our third platoon."

"Merci, CSM," Eleanor looked in the opposite direction. "Ujurak!"

A tall man emerged from the fog. Eleanor guessed he was in his early fifties. He wore a traditional parka and modern windproof pants, a *Lee Enfield* rifle slung over his shoulder. His name meant *rock*, and that he was: solid and reliable.

"Signaller," Eleanor called out.

"Right here, ma'am," her young radio operator replied.

Eleanor looked at him hopefully. "Have you been able to raise anyone other than our three platoons?"

"Negative, ma'am," the signaller sighed in disappointment. "I've tried everything; UHF, short wave, even the satellite phone, nothing,"

Eleanor nodded her understanding as their second-in-command arrived. An exchange officer from Alaska, Captain Janet Simmons was very familiar with operating in the north.

"Ma'am, some of one platoon's personnel are reporting unidentified noises to their front," the captain said. "It's probably two hundred metres out. We can't see anything using the thermal sights."

Eleanor keyed the handset of her own radio, tuned to the company frequency.

"One-one, this is one-niner, send SITREP," she requested.

Several British Commonwealth armies used numeric call signs over the radio. The first number indicated a company, the second a platoon. One-one therefore represented the lead company's first platoon. As the officer-in-charge, Eleanor was given the leadership number nine, thus one-niner.

"One-niner, one-one, situation report," the lead platoon commander responded. "We are currently deployed in an extended line roughly seventy-five metres to what I believe is your east. Lead scouts are reporting unknown sounds to our front, like a low growl or rumbling, over."

Eleanor looked up at her sergeant major. He'd been following the radio chatter.

"What do you think, CSM?"

"No idea, ma'am," he said. "Visibility is about fifty metres now, so I recommend we move off slowly. The danger of walking off a cliff has diminished somewhat."

The sergeant major was half-joking, but moving effectively blind in the Arctic fog held serious risk. Eleanor knew there was a shoreline to their north, but which way was that? Before the fog rolled in, they had been navigating a horseshoe-shaped inlet with land on three sides. With the limited visibility and useless navigational tools, simply finding open water was not enough to confirm where they were. Eleanor turned to her guide.

"Ujurak, the shoreline must be close," she said, "and with the fog lifting, we should be able to see it soon. But how do we navigate around here if we can't use GPS or a compass, there's no visual references, the stars are gone, and the sun just spins above our heads?"

The guide replied after a pause. "Icebergs."

"What?" Eleanor smiled.

"Icebergs. In this part of the basin, the water currents flow west to east."

Ujurak let his words hang in the air. Both Captain Simmons and the sergeant major looked stumped. Eleanor closed her eyes, deep in thought.

*Icebergs. If the current flows west to east, then an iceberg floating from left to right means we're facing north. But if its right to left then we must be facing...*

"South!" She called out as if to say *eureka*.

Eleanor engaged her radio. "All call-signs one, this is one-niner, prepare to move off in company arrowhead formation, one platoon has the lead, two platoon left rear, and three platoon right rear. One-one, move off in the direction you are currently facing. As soon as you see a shoreline, start looking for any signs of icebergs. All call-signs acknowledge receipt, over."

The platoon commanders confirmed their understanding, though Eleanor was sure the iceberg bit had them confused. This was the north after all.

"Major Matthews, just a thought," the sergeant major grinned. "Should we be looking for the *Titanic* as well?"

*Smart ass.*

Eleanor didn't mind the banter. It meant their morale was still good. The key leadership moved off to begin the advance. Eleanor placed herself with Ujurak, directly behind the lead platoon. Captain Simmons and the sergeant major fell back in between the two trailing platoons, some seventy-five metres behind. Normally they wouldn't move this close to one another, but with no imminent threat and only slightly improved visibility, this configuration was safer.

The company had been advancing for ten minutes when a piercing sound echoed about them. It soon dropped to a deep growl. It was the same noise the forward scouts had heard earlier. Over the radio, Eleanor instructed her troops to halt in place. She then moved forward with Ujurak towards her lead platoon. She noticed the troops had instinctively crouched down on one knee, their weapons resting on their thighs. This was standard procedure for a short halt. If the pause lasted more than five minutes, they would lay down prone.

The sound was distinct, and directly to their front. It kept shifting from a threatening growl to a high-pitched whine. Ujurak stopped.

"Nanuk," he said softly.

Eleanor raised her rifle, hearing her guide mention the Inuktitut word for polar bear. Ujurak rested his hand on the barrel of her weapon, gently lowering it back to the ground.

"You won't need that. It's too late for this one."

Eleanor and Ujurak moved forward cautiously. As they advanced, the white fur of the Arctic's legendary guardian came into view. It lay close to the ground, staring at the two approaching humans. Eleanor saw the animal attempt to raise its hind legs, but collapse in place. It let out an awful cry. On closer inspection, she could see how emaciated the bear appeared. Its ribcage was visible against its fur, while its normally powerful legs were practically skin and bones.

"It's starving," Ujurak sighed. "With the ice gone, there are few seals for the bear to hunt. It will not be long before this young one passes."

He explained to Eleanor that the animal was likely an adolescent, perhaps two years old. Sadly, this was not the first time he had come across such a tragic sight. The two lingered by the bear, both knowing what needed to be done, but neither wishing to act first. It was only then that Eleanor realised the unwelcome fog had lifted. The Arctic inlet they sought was less than a kilometre to their north. Far from shore, an iceberg floated by from left to right.

Ujurak dropped to his hands and knees, catching Eleanor by surprise. She watched him move his ear close to the rocky ground.

*Maybe this is some sort of ritual*, she thought, *before you kill a bear.*

Now Eleanor felt it. Very faint at first, then building into a low rumble. She glanced about, trying to determine what was causing the ground to vibrate. It couldn't be an earthquake. Ujurak stood up, peering south. Eleanor followed his gaze to the horizon.

It moved.

Eleanor was certain it wasn't an optical illusion. The southern horizon resembled a long brown line that shifted back and forth. She ascertained distinct movements within the mass, like little ants bobbing up and down. From this distance, the skyline appeared to grow branches, all bouncing in unison. Gradually, the shifting horizon revealed patches of white among its dark shapes. The vibrations were now far more noticeable. It was then that Eleanor caught the unmistakable sight of antlers. She shot a look at Ujurak.

"Run!" he yelled.

Eleanor and Ujurak dashed back towards the lead platoon as fast as they could, covering the distance in no time. She frantically keyed her radio.

"All call signs one, this is one-niner. Take any cover you can find, we have a stampede of caribou approaching from the south. Move now."

She was on her feet again, encouraging the soldiers about her to head north as though their life depended on it, which it probably did. Eleanor glanced over her shoulder. The solid wall of hooves and antlers, at least a hundred metres wide, was heading straight for her. Though still two kilometres away, she knew it was only a matter of time before the caribou were upon their position.

"Can we shoot them?" Eleanor panted heavily. "Make explosions to scare them in a different direction?"

"There are too many," Ujurak hollered back. "We need to find higher ground."

Caribou migration patterns stretched from Alaska to Baffin Island. Masses with thousands of beasts instinctively crossing rivers, valleys, and forests, just like their cousins the reindeer in northern Siberia.

*Great*, Eleanor thought dryly, *I'm going to be killed by Rudolph.*

"There," Ujurak pointed, "that crest, it might be high enough to drive them away!"

Both yelling and using the radio, Eleanor directed her now terrified troops towards a low rise off to their left. The thundering brown wall closed in behind them. She heard gunshots. Someone had panicked and was shooting at the herd in a useless attempt at self-preservation. Eleanor was one of the first to reach the hilltop. She turned around to see the mass of animals barrelling towards them.

"All call-signs ceasefire," she ordered across the radio. "I say again, ceasefire."

The bulk of the first and second platoons were now up the hill, but most of the third was still exposed, several of its solders firing into the stampede. Eleanor could see the occasional animal fall amongst the masses, but hundreds, perhaps thousands more kept coming. Then the galloping beasts did something unnatural. They slowly shifted their direction towards the soldiers firing at them. Ujurak looked alarmed. Caribou herds moved en masse, but in very linear directions. Only a large physical feature like a hill or river would redirect them, and even then they usually barrelled through. This was different. The wall of animals was turning towards the gunfire, specifically focusing on the desperate soldiers blasting away at them.

"Binos!"

The out of breath signaller threw Eleanor the binoculars. She peered anxiously at her stricken troops, then at the front of the massive animal formation. From her hilltop vantage point not two hundred metres away, she could see the front row of charging beasts. Their eyes were bloodshot red, while they foamed at the mouth. The heads of the caribou were lowered, their antlers bent forward like a wall of spears about to do battle. This made no sense.

Sergeant Major Bernard and Captain Simmons had just joined their boss when the charging wall collided with the soldiers trapped in the low ground. Eleanor watched helplessly as bodies were tossed in the air like bundles of rags. The entire hill shook while the awful sight unfolded before them.

As quickly as the stampede had collided with the exposed troops, it moved off into the distance, leaving behind a scene of carnage. With the sounds of the caribou herd fading, the screams of anguish began.

The leadership of the Arctic company sprung to life. Eleanor requested situation reports from her platoon commanders across the radio, while the sergeant major raced to set up a casualty collection point. The company medic had been with Captain Simmons. Both moved forward with a dozen soldiers from the second platoon to assist their comrades. As they ran off, the company signaller kept trying to raise someone, anyone, on the UHF and short wave radio. The satellite phone still had no signal. Eleanor couldn't see where Ujurak had gone, but she had more pressing matters.

"One-niner, this is one-niner alpha, CASREP." It was Captain Simmons calling in a casualty report from what was left of the rear platoon's position. "We have three times priority one, four times priority two, and two VSA including one-three sunray, over."

*No.*

Eleanor felt the awful burden of command weigh down on her. Two of her soldiers, including one of her platoon commanders, had no detectable vital signs. They may already be dead, apparently killed by a freak accident of Mother Nature.

"Ma'am, ma'am," the signaller yelled. "I've got a ship! Thirty clicks east of our location."

Eleanor grabbed the radio handset.

"Unknown call sign, this is one-niner. We are a military land unit in need of immediate medical assistance. We believe we are centred in the area of Cape Mercy. Please identify yourself." She pulled out her map, trying to get a visual bearing now that the fog was gone.

The response was immediate. "One-niner, this is the Danish warship *Knud Rasmussen*. Roger your last transmission. We are notifying the joint search and rescue centre immediately and altering course to your position's nearest coastline. Please maintain comms on this frequency and we will send further instructions."

Eleanor acknowledged the ship and glanced about the controlled chaos before her. The scene reminded the major of her worst days in Afghanistan. She was moving towards the casualty collection point when she noticed Ujurak kneeling, his massive hands cradling a white bundle of fur. She saw it was the starving young polar bear they had found before the stampede. It had been trampled to death.

As Eleanor walked over, Ujurak silently showed her the small burn mark on the animal's hide in the shape of two linked triangles. There was no scarring, nor dried blood surrounding the marking.

# CHAPTER 5

Hello, cub
Mother?
They need you
Mother, is that you?
Help them rest
Mother, wait, help who?

"Erika, Erika, it's OK, it's just a bad dream!"
She awoke in a pool of sweat, her roommate Sandra by her bedside, trying to calm her. Erika stared at Sandra, confused for an instant, then looked about. Their residence room was dark, the pre-dawn glow not yet seeping through the curtains. Erika sat up and looked at the clock radio on her windowsill, 04:56. She swung her legs out from under her sheets as her roommate went back to bed.

"You all right?" Sandra asked, concerned. "That's the third night in a row you've been yelling in your sleep. I figured it must be something related to your mom..."

Erika looked up at her.

"Hey, I'm sorry," Sandra pleaded. "I didn't mean anything... Look, I'm going to try to get some more sleep. You should do the same. We've got a big weekend coming up for your birthday."

Erika managed a brief smile for her roommate, who looked relieved. She watched as Sandra replaced her earplugs and eye mask, then curled back under the covers. Erika paused, slowly got up, and made her way quietly out to the hallway and the residence restrooms. She didn't turn the lights on as she entered the first bathroom. The ambient light from outside filled the linoleum chamber with a yellow aura. Erika turned on the sink and splashed cool water on her face, then looked up in the mirror. She appeared tired. Between the last few training days at UVM, mixed with the sleepless nights, she was not her normal self.

*Happy birthday*, Erika thought, still shaken from her most recent nightmare. She'd been having bad dreams since arriving in Vermont. Initially, she chalked them up to anxiety at being alone and in a new place for the first time. Lately, however, her dreams had grown in their intensity. They now even included her late mother. It all seemed so real, and unlike most dreams, her thought patterns were not random. Instead, it felt like the same recurring dream, becoming more vivid as the nights went by. To add to the confusion, Erika had continued experiencing premonitions while awake. It sometimes genuinely felt as though she could see the future just before it happened, like during the last exhibition game versus Delaware.

She turned off the tap and walked back to her room. As she entered, the mild snoring told her Sandra had fallen back asleep. Erika wished she could do the same. The clock now read 05:10 as she crawled into bed. Luckily there were no hockey events that weekend. Erika would try to sleep in, before her teammates dragged her off to Montreal for a much-touted birthday road trip. She reached up to reset the alarm clock from eight to ten, when she noticed her father's small gift-wrapped present on the windowsill. Erika decided she would open it later, and curled up under her comforter.

"Play something else," Sandra demanded from behind the steering wheel. To her right, Nicole Gibson sat in the passenger seat fiddling with her smartphone. She found a tune that met with the driver's approval, and all was good in the world. Erika sat behind Nicole in the back seat, with

Michelle Lavoix beside her. The two had not spoken much since their awkward exchange a few weeks back in the Fieldhouse sauna. She wasn't sure if Michelle was embarrassed or upset, since the third year student maintained a perfect poker face. She was still pleasant to Erika, especially during hockey practice, but somehow things now felt detached.

The birthday girl let her thoughts wander as she glanced out the used minivan's window. It was a sunny July day. They were travelling north on Highway 89 towards the border between Vermont and Quebec, having just passed the town of Swanton. Erika had her favourite leather purse by her side. She heard the distinct ping of her phone, and reached inside the satchel. It was a message from her father, Liam.

> Dearest Erika.
> Happy 18th birthday to our beautiful daughter. Know that we are so very proud of you and please have a safe birthday. We're looking forward to seeing you later this summer in Pond Inlet. Enjoy your little gift.
> Much love, Dad

As hard as the loss of her mother had been, Erika had known the end was coming. She had desperately wished it were otherwise, but the type of cancer Star had meant a slow, inevitable goodbye. From her father's use of the plural in his text, it was evident Liam was still in denial over the loss of his life partner. She suddenly missed both her parents very much, and felt her eyes swell. Michelle must have been quietly watching. She discretely handed Erika some tissue paper so their friends in the front seat wouldn't notice. The two passengers shared a kind look, then went back to their respective thoughts.

"Border with Canada coming up, ladies," Sandra announced.

The three other UVM players reached for their documentation as their driver eased her minivan into the two-car line up at Canada customs. Soon they were waved forward, a tall border agent in his mid-thirties greeting them in both French and English.

"Bienvenue au Canada, welcome to Canada, passports please," the officer requested. With a huge smile, Sandra handed him three American and one Canadian passport. Today, Erika would be from her mother's homeland. After a few brief questions about firearms and tobacco, the border agent prepared to wave them through, when he glanced again at Erika's credentials. He then leaned into the open back door window.

"Happy birthday, Miss Holstrom, have a good day."

The eruptions of laughter and teasing continued all the way to Montreal.

"I've got us rooms on the main McGill University campus, right downtown," said Sandra. "The residence is super cheap because it's summer and the Canadian dollar is really low right now, compared to the greenback. Yay for us!"

Though Sandra was officially a first year student, it was obvious she had been on her own a couple years after high school before returning to university. Whatever the circumstances, Erika knew she was going to benefit greatly from her roommate's prior experiences.

As the four women drove into the downtown core of their new twenty-four hour home, Erika got the sense of a city that had come to life in the 1970s. Most of the skyscrapers had the drab concrete feel of decades gone by, while the road network everywhere seemed under construction. Regardless, the city had a reputation for some of the best nightlife this side of Chicago, and the legal age was eighteen. Sandra found the McGill campus with ease and the women were soon showering and getting ready for their night on the town.

Erika didn't feel well. She leaned against the mirrored wall that surrounded the dance floor and tried to keep her balance. Around her, dozens of bodies gyrated to the latest dance anthems being spun by one of Montreal's hottest DJs. On entering the club, Sandra had announced Erika's birthday to the bartender. This led to her first three drinks being free. It had been Nicole's idea to try something called *Sambuca* shots. That felt like ages ago, Erika's sense of time now a blur. She looked around in a daze for her friends.

Both Sandra and Nicole were on the dance floor, moving about with two French-Canadian college boys they'd met. Erika had been introduced to them but couldn't remember their names. Her head began to spin. She started to see stars from the corner of her eyes, each movement slightly delayed. Erika felt the mysterious sensation again, though dulled by alcohol. Michelle appeared to Erika's right. She was wearing a one-piece dark catsuit, with a black blouse over top. Strobe lights twinkled in her eyes. In her hands she had what appeared to be a cocktail, and a glass of water. She placed the water on a small ledge beside Erika.

"Here, drink this," Michelle yelled over the booming bass sounds. "Water will do you good."

"I'm fine," shouted Erika, aware that she'd dragged the "f" long enough to suggest she wasn't.

She drank the liquid greedily. Erika hadn't realised how thirsty she was until now. *How can drinking too much make you thirsty?* The water helped, refreshing her inside. She looked up at Michelle as if to say, *Can I have more?* Her friend took the hint, heading back to the bar for a jug of water, leaving Erika to take in the sights before her.

*So this is adulthood*, she thought. She'd been tipsy before, but nothing like how she felt now. Erika adjusted the strap of her leather satchel, and forced herself to stand up straight when Michelle came back into view. She swayed her hips a little to the music, though dancing had never been her thing. Michelle poured the jug of water into Erika's empty glass, who drank it quickly, keen for refreshment. Michelle watched, her eyes seeming to glow under the club's flashing lights.

"You good?"

"I'm great." Erika replied, part-truth, part-bravado.

Michelle nodded. She moved in closer, so that she could speak into Erika's ear without shouting.

"You are," she said. "I actually think you're awesome."

Then the third year student took Erika's face into her hands. Michelle looked into her eyes, as if asking a question, then leaned in and kissed her on the lips. Erika froze. She suddenly felt very aware as Michelle's tongue gently entered her mouth. She had never kissed anyone before, let alone a girl. It felt different, yet intimate and warm. She slowly moved her lips as she'd seen on TV, trying to match the sensual motions of Michelle's mouth. She closed her eyes, as thoughts of both bewilderment and pleasure swirled in her mind. Before she knew it, Michelle had taken her lips away.

"You OK?" Michelle asked, looking at Erika.

"Yes. I've just... I've just never kissed anyone before."

"How does it feel?"

"Actually, really good."

"Wanna dance?"

"I'd love to."

The pair made their way to the lit-up floor, soon finding themselves near Sandra and Nicole. The four women bounced about, the euphoria of the deep bass beats taking over.

Erika moved to the music, allowing the rhythm to guide her. She watched Michelle from the corner of her eye, trying to process what had just happened and how she felt about it.

*Danger.*

Erika hesitated while the others kept dancing. Something terrible was about to happen, but what? She scanned the room. Erika could see Sandra and Nicole had moved towards the corner of the dance floor with their French-Canadian boys. She looked up to see a giant speaker hanging from the ceiling by silver chains. Erika desperately tried to clear her head. She shuffled towards Sandra, Michelle following her with a dance move.

*Danger.*

Erika's senses honed in on the speaker chains. They were going to give way. She had to act now. Masking her actions as a drunken stumble, she slammed into Sandra, sending them both into a row of chairs beside the dance floor. As they hit the ground, the chains holding the dangling speaker broke, sending the huge piece of equipment crashing to the ground. Sparks flew from the massive box. Several people nearby screamed, pushing themselves away from the electrical calamity. The music stopped.

From her position under a pile of chairs, Erika could hear Michelle calling out to Nicole. "Gibson, where are Holstrom and Bruster?"

The club lights came on. Erika's face was embedded in Sandra's midriff. Slowly they untangled themselves and got to their feet.

"Damn, Erika, that hurt," Sandra complained as she rotated her right shoulder. "For a package your size you feel like a freight train."

Erika smiled, her earlier alcohol-induced confusion replaced by the clarity of adrenaline. "Sorry, Sandra, I tripped. Too many birthday shots I guess."

"Hey, no apology needed," replied the goalie, looking amazed at the shattered speaker box.

*What just happened?* Erika thought, before catching Michelle's eye, whose expression seemed to say the same thing.

One of the club bouncers ran up, asking in French if everyone was all right. Michelle explained in her second language what had occurred, while Nicole helped her friends dust off their clothes and check for bruises.

"Where's Jean-Pierre?" Sandra exclaimed while scanning the room.

By now, other bouncers were herding the club patrons to the various exits. Sandra and Nicole's dance partners were nowhere to be found. They had apparently bolted after the speaker drama, leaving the women to it. Sandra shrugged as their foursome, shaken but unhurt, moved towards the exit.

Erika walked ahead with Sandra, partly to make sure her roommate was OK, but mostly to avoid Michelle's inquisitive looks.

Erika leaned her head out the front passenger-side window of the minivan. She had a splitting headache, the result of last night's festivities. It didn't help that her friends had convinced her that greasy pancakes with scrambled eggs was a good remedy for a hangover. Sandra patted her roommate's arm in sympathy, while Nicole and Michelle sat in the back seat, quietly nursing their own hangovers. It had certainly been a memorable night. After filling in a brief statement with the Montreal police about the speaker accident, the friends had returned to McGill University for the night. Erika was not at all clear what had occurred the previous evening, except of course, that she'd saved Sandra.

*Did Michelle really kiss me?* she thought to herself, confused.

"How come the U.S. border agents aren't as friendly as the cute Canadian guy we had yesterday?" Sandra asked rhetorically.

They had decided to return to Burlington via Highway 87, crossing the border north-west of Lake Champlain. After a few probing questions, their mini-van had been subjected to a random inspection by the American customs agents. Since marijuana was legal in Quebec, a van full of college-aged women was instantly suspicious. They laughed to themselves at the notion of being drug runners. There was a positive outcome to their short border delay: the agents found one of Sandra's favourite lost earrings from under the back seat. In her typical irreverent style, she had the lone earring dangling from her lobe with pride. Erika smiled at Sandra as the road slid away behind them; the painkillers she had taken earlier were slowly having an effect.

*Stop the van.*

"Stop the van!" Erika called out.

Sandra looked sideways at her.

"You OK?"

"I'm gonna be sick."

Sandra quickly turned on her hazard lights and pulled over to the side of the forested highway. There were very few vehicles about this early on a Sunday. Just as Sandra brought the vehicle to a complete stop, a massive female moose burst out of the tree-line ahead, running at full trot across the highway. No sooner had the cow passed by, then a lone calf followed. As quickly as the one-ton animal and her offspring had appeared, they were gone again into the woods opposite the empty northbound lanes.

"Holy shit, did you see that?" Nicole exclaimed from the back seat. "Sandra, if we hadn't pulled over to let Erika puke, we would have hit that thing at seventy miles an hour."

The van fell silent. Even to the inexperienced, it was evident what a moose strike would have done to the vehicle and its occupants. They had cheated death a second time in twenty-four hours. Sandra and Nicole laughed nervously at their luck, before slowly continuing the drive south towards Burlington. No one in the van had realised that Erika hadn't actually been sick, except Michelle.

# CHAPTER 6

"No luck, my Captain," the chief of the boat reported in Russian. "We've reduced the reactor's output to fifty percent and still the vibrations continue whenever we move."

"Thank you, Chief," Captain Sergei Egorov responded. "Please, carry on."

The submarine's senior enlisted member acknowledged the two men seated in the captain's cabin, and departed. Sergei looked to his first officer, Lieutenant-Commander Dmitri Lebedev. The younger man was busy studying schematics of the submarine's nuclear propulsion system. Dmitri shrugged his shoulders.

"Sir, I think it's best that we remain stationary until we can ascertain what is causing the vibrations within the reactor coolant pumps. If we start sailing again in our current condition, the American anti-submarine efforts out of Thule will most certainly detect us."

Sergei felt frustrated but knew his first officer was right. The *Volkov* was the newest *Yasen*-class nuclear attack submarine within the resurgent Russian navy. Designed to move quietly and very deep, the boat had only joined the fleet last year. To demonstrate the *Volkov's* capabilities, the senior leadership of Russia's northern fleet had come up with an audacious plan. For the first time since the end of the Cold War, a Russian submarine would try to sail undetected beneath the polar ice cap, then navigate the tight narrows of the Davis Strait between North America and Greenland. The *Volkov's* orders were first to conduct a deep sonar analysis of the continental shelf that ran from northern Russia, under the Arctic Ocean. The region contained a wealth of underwater minerals and resources that would likely become accessible in the coming years due to the changing climate. The sonar pictures obtained by the submarine would be used to justify Moscow's international maritime claim to the region. Following these surveys, their task was to observe military and commercial shipping in Baffin Bay, before sailing south-east to the North Atlantic and eventually home. A straightforward if not risky plan, it depended on the Russian submarine's ability to move silently while submerged. The problem was that currently the *Volkov* was anything but quiet.

The submarine's passage from northern Russia under the North Pole had been uneventful. It was only in the last twenty-four hours, upon entering the Davis Strait, that a vibrating sound had begun somewhere within the *Volkov's* nuclear propulsion system. Try as they might, the engineering officer and his chief could not isolate the origins of the noise. It also didn't seem to matter at what speed they travelled, the cursed rattling persisted. Sergei shook his head. Here he was, captain of the most advanced submarine in his nation's arsenal, arguably in the world, and he was essentially a sitting duck. The only solace Sergei took from their current predicament was that as long as they remained submerged and stationary, they were silent.

"It's not the steam condensers," Dmitri said. "That we were able to visually confirm. The primary drive shaft and noise isolator are also intact. It must be something in the main reactor coolant pump. Perhaps a foreign object accidentally sucked in from the ocean?"

The introduction of ocean pollutants into the primary pumps was a remote, but still plausible theory. Modern oceans were littered with millions of tons of discarded waste and plastics, everything from miniscule exfoliating shampoo beads to massive truck-sized sea containers. As society's addiction to plastic continued, floating islands of trash had begun to form in the Atlantic and Pacific oceans, courtesy of the prevailing currents. Not only was this devastating to marine wildlife, it was also a serious hazard to navigation. Even in the high Arctic, discarded waste could be found from as far away as South Africa.

The first officer sighed in defeat. "I don't think there is much else we can do, Captain. If the problem truly is inside the main reactor coolant pump, then we'll have to return to home port in order to carry out repairs."

"Thank you, Dmitri," his captain replied. "Please head back to the control room and let me know if we are tracking any surface or sub-surface sonar contacts. If we have to head home making all this racket, I want to at least try and get a head start before we're noticed." Dmitri acknowledged his superior, then left Sergei alone in his cabin.

*Dammit*, he thought. *Volkov* meant wolf in Russian. An appropriate name for an attack submarine, though at the moment Sergei felt the title *goat-with-a-bell* more fitting. Just then, the intercom in his cabin came to life.

"Captain, engineering," the voice reported.

"What is it, Chief?" Sergei replied into the small microphone.

"You need to see this for yourself, sir. Please hurry."

The engineering chief signed off before his captain could respond. This was out of character for a man Sergei had known for years. He switched a dial on the intercom and called the *Volkov's* control room.

"Conn, Captain," Sergei said. "Mr. Lebedev, I'm making my way aft to engineering in case you need me."

"Aye sir," Dmitri responded.

Sergei opened a small desk drawer and pulled out a mini-flashlight and the radiation dosimeter he was supposed to wear at all times, but didn't. He figured he had surrendered his long-term health to the navy the day he agreed to work on nuclear submarines. Still, Sergei believed in leading by example, so whenever he moved about the *Volkov*, he made sure the dosimeter was visible for his crew's benefit. He left his cabin and began navigating aft through the tight spaces of the submarine.

By any measure, the *Volkov* was a massive vessel. Only 8,500 tons on the ocean's surface, it displaced nearly 14,000 tons submerged. Its maximum speed under water was thirty-five knots, while some ninety officers and sailors called the cigar-shaped tube their home. With a length of over one hundred metres, it took Sergei several minutes to make it to the rear compartment. Just before he entered, he grabbed a pair of protective goggles and gloves from a wall rack. Inside he found the chief of engineering crouched down under a series of large pipes, surrounded by three young sailors. Sergei could see they had removed several floor grates in order to access the various tubes underneath. The chief had a large power tool in his hands and was trying to unscrew a side panel attached to the inner hull. The only noise was the slow release of steam coming from the reactor room located a few metres away.

"What have you got, Chief?" Sergei's tone was confident but friendly.

The older man crawled out from under several pipes, and showed his gloves to the captain. Sergei was taken aback. The fabric was covered with green and brown mucus, similar to what a snail might leave in its wake. To emphasise how odd their find was, the chief opened his fingers as if signalling the number five. Sergei watched in amazement as the slime clung to the digits of his colleague's glove.

"I have no idea what this is," the chief said, "but it seems to be originating behind this panel." He pointed back to the metal plate he had been working on.

"Is it hazardous, or radioactive?" Sergei said with concern.

"No sir," the older man shook his head. "We checked with our Geiger counter and it's well within safety limits, which means it's not from the reactor, nor the coolant pumps." He tried to wipe the residue from his gloves. "It almost looks organic."

Sergei watched as the veteran submariner crouched down again to try to remove the panel from where the mucus was oozing. Two sailors assisted by pushing aside several unneeded tools. The chief removed the last of the screws securing the panel, then slowly lifted it away to peer at the cables underneath. To everyone's astonishment, they moved. Sergei watched dumbfounded as hundreds, perhaps thousands of finger-sized reddish worms fell from the open panel. They slithered about helplessly as the sailors quickly backed away from the disgusting sight.

"What the hell are those things and how in God's name did they get on my submarine?" Sergei demanded.

The rest of the men in engineering were equally mystified. The chief picked up one of the squirming creatures.

"They look like sea worms, but much bigger," he said. "The same type that can wreak havoc on a wooden ship's hull over time, but not metal. How did they get in here?"

The intercom sounded in the engineering room. It was Dmitri's voice.

"Captain, Conn, we have a possible sub-surface sonar contact bearing two one zero, range eight thousand."

Sergei acknowledged the report from the control room. He then instructed the chief and his men to clean up the mess they'd found, before heading back towards the front of the *Volkov*. Sergei moved as quickly as he could, trying not to knock over any of his fellow submariners in the tight corridors. He entered the control room to find Dmitri standing by their two sonar operators, all closely monitoring the screens before them.

"Sir, take a look," Dmitri offered his captain. "The contact is currently running parallel to our position at roughly five knots and submerged. At first we thought it was a pod of orcas or narwhal whales, but the signal is too dense."

Sergei looked over to Dmitri. "Is it an American sub, perhaps a new one that emits a distorted sonar picture?"

Dmitri again shook his head. "No sir, there are no cavitations, nor any vibration sounds. Unless you order otherwise, we were going to hold in place and allow the contact to pass. What did you find in engineering?"

Sergei looked at his first officer with a special glance the two had rehearsed that meant; *Go to my cabin now.*

"Officer of the watch, you have the Conn," Dmitri ordered, and followed Sergei to the confined privacy of the captain's quarters.

"We have an infestation of sea worms in engineering," Sergei said dryly.

"Sea worms?" Dmitri protested. "How is that even possible?"

The captain shrugged, then pulled over the schematics of the *Volkov* they had been reviewing earlier. The chief's unusual find was located along the inner wall of the engineering compartment on the starboard side. There did not appear to be any imminent danger to the electronics or the pressurised hull. Apart from the less-than-appealing sight of the worms, at the moment they appeared harmless. Which still did not explain how they got on board an airtight submarine in the first place.

"Captain, Conn," a young voice spoke over the intercom, "sonar contact has altered direction to course one four zero, and is maintaining a steady speed of five knots submerged."

The contact's new course would bring it much closer to the stationary *Volkov* than anticipated. With a roll of his eyes, Sergei again made his way back to the submarine's control room, his first officer in tow. This was, so far, proving to be the strangest week of his naval career.

The control room was now a whispered hive of activity as the captain entered, the mood visibly tense.

"Conn, sonar," the operator reported in a hush. "Contact has split into three similar-sized targets, all bearing zero nine zero, depth one five zero, speed steady at five knots." Sergei moved into the small sonar cubicle beside the control room, while Dmitri took his position near the helm operators.

"Show me," the captain ordered quietly. The young sonar operator wiped the condensation from his screen and pointed out the three contacts. Sergei watched as the three shapes suddenly changed direction and accelerated to over forty knots, heading directly towards the *Volkov*. There was barely any time to react.

"All hands, brace for impact!" Sergei yelled into the submarine's intercom, just before the speeding sonar signals on the monitor merged with his own vessel.

Nothing happened.

Sergei paused. The targets, whatever they were, should have slammed into the side of the *Volkov's* hull by now. He looked down at the sonar operator's screen, the young sailor trembling. The monitor was clear. According to the submarine's instruments, they were the only contact above or below water for at least fifty kilometres.

The monitor flickered. The sonar operator tried adjusting the screen. It flickered again. With a bright flash, the sonar screen started projecting various shapes and symbols, randomly appearing in rapid succession. Vertical lines with diagonal cross sections came and went as Sergei tried to comprehend what he was seeing.

*Maybe the software had malfunctioned*, he thought. *A computer virus?*

A deep howling noise echoed throughout the submarine, a ghostly sound that Sergei felt was coming from inside the *Volkov*. The lights in the control room blinked as the intercom system turned on. A deep, haunting voice started projecting words in an unknown language. It sounded like a distorted version of Norwegian or Icelandic to the utterly confused captain, but he couldn't be sure. Clearly the Danish or American navies must be playing some sort of terrifying joke on their Russian counterparts.

The submarine rocked violently to port. Any personnel not seated were thrown to the ground, including Sergei. The *Volkov* lurched just as quickly to starboard, its bow being forced forty degrees down towards the sea bottom. The submarine started descending rapidly, as if a giant hand was pushing it nose first.

"Conn, all engines full reverse," Sergei yelled over the chaos. "Full up angle on the dive planes!"

It was no use. The submarine continued to sink towards the depths.

"Conn, read me the depth gauge, now!" Sergei ordered, crawling along the floor against the submarine's sharp angle of descent.

"Depth reads five three seven and descending rapidly by the bow," Dmitri yelled.

"Blow the main ballast tanks," Sergei called out towards the front of the control room. "Helm, make your depth zero five zero."

"Sir, helm not responding," came the panicked reply. "We have no horizontal, nor vertical pitch control."

"Blow all tanks," Sergei ordered in desperation. "Surface the boat, emergency surface." Again there was no response to any of the submarine's controls.

"Depth six five zero and descending," Dmitri screamed. "Captain, approaching hull crush depth!"

Sergei knew if they went below seven hundred metres, they were doomed.

The green translucent forms entered the control room through the grated floor, appearing to rise from below. Sergei watched in disbelief as the ghostly figures floated about the control room, petrified sailors scrambling to get away. He was able to discern what appeared to be arms, adorned with unfamiliar designs and bracelets. In one hand, Sergei saw what he thought was a blade, or sharp weapon. He watched in horror as Dmitri's body was raised into the air among the haunting figures. With a gut-wrenching sound, the first officer's chest blew out into an explosion of red mist and internal organs, the officer's entrails falling to the deck below. A young sailor to his right screamed in terror before he too met the same fate.

Sergei scrambled behind the periscope console in the centre of the control room, as the apparitions decimated more of his crew. The agonizing screams continued. He glanced at the passageway that led aft to the submarine's reactor and engineering room. The *Volkov's* rescue capsule was located near the galley, one floor above. Just before Sergei made a run for it, he noticed one of the apparitions hovering over his first officer's eviscerated body, Dmitri's empty eyes staring at the ceiling. A grossly deformed green arm held out what Sergei swore was a sword. Its tip was molten red as it carved a symbol into the first officer's neck.

It was the last thing Sergei ever saw.

The *Volkov* was well below its assigned crush depth when the hull finally buckled. Under enormous external water pressure, the submarine's compartments telescoped into each other in a split second with pulverizing force. A massive air bubble rose to the frozen ocean surface as the shattered hull fragments imploded. Death was instantaneous for all aboard, except the sea worms found in engineering that wiggled among the debris, slowly sinking to the ocean bottom.

# CHAPTER 7

**M**ichelle Lavoix watched from the Vermont bench with a mixture of awe and envy as Erika scored her third goal against Colgate University. The team from upstate New York was supposed to be formidable, yet halfway through the second period, UVM led by an impressive 7-2. Michelle knew that as a summer exhibition game, not all of Colgate's star athletes were in attendance. Still, the teams should have been more evenly matched. The rookie from Minnesota was again proving to be the decisive factor for Vermont's success. The whistle blew, launching another face-off at centre ice. While all other eyes were on the hockey puck, Michelle focused on Erika.

Since their road trip to Montreal, Michelle had observed many odd quirks about her new friend. Somehow Erika consistently seemed to know where the puck would end up, as opposed to where it currently was on the ice. Then there was the speaker accident that had almost crushed their goalie, Sandra; never mind their potentially fatal highway encounter with a moose. Michelle was not a religious person, nor superstitious, but there appeared to be something extra-sensory about Erika. It was as though she possessed an undefined sense about future events that beguiled Michelle. To her, Erika was magnetic.

Michelle had been raised on a horse farm outside of Burlington by French-American parents. Growing up, they let her experience all that rural life had to offer, and in adulthood, accepted her for the partners she chose to love. Michelle wished deeply that Erika would respond to her advances. Despite what had seemed like a mutual flash of passion in Montreal, Erika had been neutral towards Michelle ever since. Not unfriendly, and it still felt there could be some latent chemistry between them, but nothing approaching a repeat of that moment. It was frustrating.

Michelle was startled from her thoughts by the sight of Erika getting slammed into the sideboards by a pair of Colgate enforcers. She watched with dismay as the stick end from one of the opposing players wedged itself inside the helmet cage protecting Erika's face. She dropped like a stone to the frozen ground, as Nicole Gibson lunged towards the offending Colgate players. Before Nancy could protest, the other Vermont members on the ice converged against the aggressive Colgate duo. This in turn spurred the rest of the on-ice visitors from New York to join the fray. Before long, there was an all-out team brawl at centre ice.

"Don't even think about joining them, ladies," Nancy hissed at her Vermont players still stationed on the home team bench.

Michelle noticed the rest of the off-ice Colgate players also stayed seated while the melee of green against burgundy hockey jerseys continued. It took all three referees and two UVM officials to finally break up the shoving match. As the players dispersed, Nancy urgently called for Vermont's medical trainer.

On the ice, Erika lay motionless near the visiting team's blue line.

Erika sensed she was outdoors. There was a body of water nearby, which felt much larger than a lake. She sat up among a field of tall grass, swaying from side to side in the warm summer breeze. In the distance, she thought she saw the ocean, and what appeared to be icebergs. She walked towards the shore, the grassy field under her feet replaced by the smooth stones of a pebble beach. She could smell the distinct scent of wood burning. It reminded her of the fireplace at her family cabin on Lake Superior. As the waves slowly rolled up against the rocky shore, she could see a low-lying thatch hut in the distance. She seemed to float towards the structure built of natural peat and mud, its roof covered in straw. A lone opening at the centre of the roof emitted a constant plume of white smoke. The occupants had a fire burning within their home.

Someone moved. Erika glanced over to see a young girl, perhaps eight years of age with long braided hair, run behind an overturned rowboat. She wore a long, single-piece garment that came down to her knees, tied at the waist by a rope. The little girl was barefoot, a small necklace dangling under her chin.

"Hello?" Erika called out, approaching the overturned boat. The craft was not a design she was familiar with from growing up along the Great Lakes. The small girl peered out at Erika from behind the boat, her blonde hair blowing against her face. Erika smiled at the dishevelled child. As she approached the little girl, the young one crawled under the overturned boat, her long hair still visible. Erika could also see the girl had dropped her necklace. The shape of it seemed familiar. It was then that she noticed the wooden hull of the rowboat. The nails that fastened the vessel's planks together appeared very large and square-shaped. Erika was no sailor, but even her inexperienced eye could tell the marine construction was rudimentary, and old.

"*Skraeling!*" A voice called out in alarm behind her.

Erika turned to see an adult woman wearing the same clothing as the little girl, standing in the doorway of the thatch hut.

"*Skraeling!*" the woman called again. She disappeared inside the doorway, to be replaced by a large, bearded man with long blonde hair. He was a giant. Erika could see his exposed arms were covered in dark tattoos and several scars. His wrists were wrapped in leather bracelets, while in his right hand was a two-sided...

...*Axe!* Erika thought in a panic.

The man ran at Erika. Without a second thought, she was on the move, running as fast as her legs could carry her. She dashed back towards the rocky shore, away from the hut and overturned rowboat. Erika was moving so quickly it was hard for her to keep balance along the pebble beach. The enraged man was gaining on her. She could hear him yelling at her in an unknown language. Erika didn't understand him, but could tell by his dark demeanour it wasn't anything good. Her right foot caught under a large stone. She slammed down against the rocky beach with a gasp. She rolled over just in time to see the bearded man raise his two-sided axe and swing it towards her heaving chest.

Erika screamed so loudly that the medical trainer tending to her jumped back with a fright. She blinked multiple times, trying to process where she was and what was going on. She looked out from her caged helmet to see women in either Vermont or Colgate hockey uniforms, all watching her from a safe distance. Erika's back was cold. Actually, it was freezing. It dawned on her she was lying down on the ice. The medical trainer came back into view.

"Holstrom, can you hear me?" he asked. "Can you tell me where you are?"

Erika looked at the bright ceiling lights and curved roof of Gutterson Fieldhouse. She then glanced over at her teammates, most looking back at her with concern. Erika recognised Sandra from her goalie equipment, as well as Nicole by the *A* on her assistant captain's jersey. In her mouth was the distinct, salty taste of fresh blood. Again, the medical trainer asked if Erika knew where she was.

"I'm lying on my back inside the *Gut* arena, freezing my ass off."

The other players laughed quietly as Erika was helped into a sitting position. She felt a bit faint, but after a few moments, was able to stand up. She slowly skated back to the Vermont bench while players from both teams banged their hockey sticks in a show of solidarity. The blood was freely flowing from Erika's nose, both down her face as well as the back of her throat. Once seated, a medical assistant with a towel wrapped in ice pressed it against Erika's face. She took off her helmet and leaned her head forward, applying the towel against her nose. It didn't feel broken, which was good. She spat out several mouthfuls of blood onto the wooden floor.

"All right, Holstrom, no hero antics for you today, my friend," Nancy ordered. "Time to get you to the medical centre."

Erika knew better than to protest as she was helped up from the Vermont bench and back towards the locker room. With the first aid drama over, the exhibition game resumed. The Colgate enforcers were banished to the penalty box as a new group of players took to the ice. Just before Michelle skated to join them, she discreetly mopped up some of Erika's blood from the floorboards with a handkerchief. No one noticed her place the bloodied material inside the pocket of her hockey pants.

Later that evening, Michelle walked up the steps of the Marsh Life Sciences Building, located in the middle of the UVM campus. The three-story structure housed an impressive assortment of scientific lecture halls, laboratories, and a library. As a third year biology major, Michelle knew the Marsh building and its facilities well. She was also aware that at this late hour, she'd have to sweet talk the on-duty security guard to gain access. Even though it was August, there were a few summer courses being run inside the building. That would be her ruse.

"Evening, Tony, how are you?" Michelle asked the uniformed guard at the front desk. She smiled broadly at the young man, who instantly blushed. Michelle looked on amused as he awkwardly tried to regain his composure.

"Hi, Michelle, I hope you're not going to ask me to give you access to the DNA lab again," he said hesitantly.

She looked directly into his eyes. "That's exactly what I'm going to do, Tony." Again the man went red.

"You know I'm not supposed to let people in after hours, unless its exam time, or they have special permission."

"You can give me special permission," Michelle responded with a sly look. "I only need access for an hour or so, to confirm my findings before I hand in my paper."

Tony nodded, and went behind his desk.

"I'll need you to sign in though," he said, fumbling with a form for her to complete. She smiled at the nervous man and jotted down her particulars. In the background, she noticed a TV set was on in the front foyer. The news anchor was reporting something about a missing Russian submarine in the Arctic. Michelle handed the notepad back to Tony.

"What's your paper about?" he asked sheepishly.

"Whether the fragmentation of the genome by restriction enzyme cutting is a better alternative than shattering it through sonication," she said, quoting one of her first year papers. The baffled security guard was left speechless as Michelle walked into the building, and up the stairs to the DNA lab.

*Men*, she thought wryly.

The modern process for DNA testing was developed in the mid-1980s and had fascinated Michelle since junior high school. The idea of capturing an individual's genetic fingerprint through a hair follicle or saliva, drove her imagination. Far more complicated than how it was depicted in most crime dramas, Michelle's recent area of study was the use of DNA sequencing to determine an individual's genetic background. Essentially discovering where they came from in the form of an evolved DNA family tree. Tonight she would focus on the profile of Erika Holstrom from Minnesota. She knew that since Erika had no idea this was being done, her efforts were at worst illegal, and at best unethical, if not borderline creepy. She could have easily asked Erika her background, but where's the intellectual fun in that? Michelle outwardly justified her actions as scientific curiosity. Her suppressed inner guilt, however, knew she had ulterior motives. Michelle craved to know the origins of the first year hockey player that so dominated her thoughts. She knew there was no logic to it. Yet Michelle wondered if understanding what *made* Erika might help her understand how Erika's mind worked. And from that, perhaps...

She turned on the laboratory's florescent lights, then donned a white lab coat hanging by the entrance. She walked to her assigned workspace, complete with an enhanced microscope and processor designed for short tandem repeat analysis, or STR. Next Michelle removed from her pocket the bloodied handkerchief she'd taken earlier in the day, following Erika's hockey injury. Wearing latex gloves, she placed some of the dried blood onto a laboratory slide and inserted it into the electron microscope. Once the display showed the sample was ready for analysis, Michelle hit *enter* on her keyboard and sat back. The process could take a while, which didn't bother her, despite the late hour. Within twenty minutes, a completed X-ray film of the test results was displayed on the screen.

Michelle looked on in fascination. This was the best part of the process for her. She saw Erika had 2% Neanderthal DNA, which was no great surprise as most people of European and Upper Asian descent had this same genetic characteristic. Michelle continued reading; 48% Nordic, including traits found in modern day Norwegian, Finnish and Icelandic genetic groups. She then paused. The majority of the remaining DNA belonged to Dorset and Thule groups.

*Who are they?*

She turned to the laptop on her desk and quickly surfed online for various key words. Michelle went on to read they were a *paleo-inuit* group that predated the modern day Inuit, which she also searched. She sat back in her chair and smiled. The impossibly fast, young, first year rookie who so captivated her, was part Inuk. Satisfied, Michelle cleaned up her work-station, placing the slide with Erika's DNA into the mini-refrigerator located under her desk. She convinced herself she was not a bad person, just a bit infatuated. She then turned out the lights and left the room.

Had she looked at the slide through the microscope, she would have noticed that, as the temperature dropped, Erika's dehydrated cells slowly began to reanimate.

The sun was still rising when Erika's phone rang. Sandra had already left to get her morning bagel and coffee, leaving her roommate alone to answer.

"Hi, Dad," Erika said in a stuffed-up voice, courtesy of the two cotton swabs in her nostrils. Her mouth felt dry, having slept with a blocked nose.

"Hey, I heard what happened from your assistant coach," her father said in a concerned tone.

*Thanks a lot, Nancy*, she thought to herself.

"Why didn't you call or text me to let me know what happened?" Liam asked, a bit offended.

"Sorry, Dad, I didn't want you to worry," Erika said. "Besides, it's nothing. No concussion, and no broken nose. I think I ruined one of my jerseys, but that's all."

"If your mother was here she'd..." Liam's voice trailed off.

Erika's eyes instantly swelled at the mention of her mother. She realised it had been several days since she had thought of her. After a long silence, her father changed the topic.

"Did you open the birthday gift I gave you?"

Erika had totally forgotten.

"Oh God, I'm so sorry, Dad! Hang on, let me put you on video and open it now."

Erika propped her smartphone on the windowsill and pressed the video icon. Soon Liam's gentle but tired face filled the little screen.

"Hey cub, you look like shit," he said with a dry smile.

"Dad!" Erika exclaimed, rolling her eyes. She reached for the small gift box on the windowsill. Erika noticed it was warm to the touch, which she attributed to the sun's rays. She slowly unwrapped the box, holding it up so her father could watch, then gently lifted the lid. It was beautiful. Erika couldn't explain why, but she loved it immediately. The teardrop-shaped ornament was the size of a rose petal, with comb-like bristles at one end. It was made of a metal alloy that seemed to twinkle in the sunlight.

"Dad, it's gorgeous," Erika said. "Where did you get this and what is it?"

"I'm not sure what it is," Liam shrugged on camera. "I found it up in the Arctic around the time I met your mother. It reminded me of her, so I figured it was time for you to have it. Use it as a good luck charm. You can bring it with you to Pond Inlet next month when you fly up for the memorial service."

Erika wanted to cry. The object in her hand unleashed a wave of emotion, from joy to anguish. She so missed her mother, especially now. Trying to maintain her composure, she decided to shift the conversation.

"Dad, what does *skraeling* mean?"

# CHAPTER 8

"Engines at eighty percent, Commander, and we are rolling," the co-pilot announced.

Lieutenant-Commander Emma Gonzalez glanced down at the snow-covered runway, then back at her instrument display. She pushed the throttle forward, bringing her aircraft's twin turbofan engines to full power. Her co-pilot informed the control tower of their take-off run, while Emma focused on the increasingly blurred runway before her. The fog caused by the unseasonably warm Arctic weather had lifted, but there was still the usual concern of stray birds flying into the aircraft's path. Despite all the advances in modern aerodynamics, airplanes continued to be most vulnerable during take-off.

"Passing ninety knots airspeed," Emma confirmed. "Rotating now." She eased back on the aircraft's yoke, lifting the forward landing gear off the ground. Emma did a final inspection of the horizon immediately to her front, then leaned back as the rear wheels lifted off the icy runway. Her grey P-8 *Poseidon* climbed with the lumbering grace of a passenger jet. Though based on the famous civilian Boeing 737 design, there was little commercial about her aircraft. Emma's plane was a hunter, primarily designed to find, target, and if necessary, sink a hostile submarine.

"Blue fox four-two-niner, wheels up Thule," the co-pilot calmly radioed to the control tower. "Passing through angels one thousand and climbing."

Emma watched as they flew over Saunders Island. Named after British navigator James Saunders, the ice-covered slab of rock was located due west of Thule. Even with clear skies and the beautiful twenty-four hour summer sun, Emma knew the Arctic weather could change unpredictably in a matter of minutes. This was a far cry from her home in Jacksonville, Florida, where her anti-submarine squadron was stationed. Known as the *Blue Foxes*, they provided the navy with anti-submarine aerial surveillance, as well as search and rescue support, up and down the American east coast. As such, their aircraft was uniquely qualified for their current mission, locating a missing Russian nuclear submarine in the Davis Strait off Greenland.

The airframe shuddered as they passed through some turbulence. The picture of Emma's family taped to the forward console shifted slightly. She looked at the image of her two young daughters. The girls' father had long-since been out of the picture, both literally and figuratively. Luckily she had met a fantastic man in Florida who relished being a domestic step-dad. Emma loved her family deeply, but she loved flying just as much. The naval aviator revelled in her role as an eye-in-the-sky. Looking for a submarine among the vast waves of the Atlantic was akin to finding a needle in a haystack. This reality made a successful mission all the more satisfying for Emma and her *Poseidon* crew. Though her plane could carry a sizeable arsenal designed to sink a submerged vessel, their role today was purely humanitarian. Regardless of the strained politics between Washington and Moscow, ninety Russian families deserved to know what had happened to their missing loved ones on the *Volkov*; never mind what the sub was doing in North American waters.

Emma was responsible for a crew of seven on today's search mission. She and the co-pilot were located in the flight deck, while five radar and sonar personnel worked the sensitive instruments in the encased rear fuselage. They had been together six months and were already a cohesive team, having recently flown a dozen surveillance missions in the Western Pacific. Instead of submarines, their points of interest had been Chinese industrial construction efforts on remote coral reefs. Though a tedious assignment, it had the perk of being based on the tropical island of Guam.

"Pilot, sonar two," a young voice from the rear of the aircraft reported. "I have confirmation of a surface contact bearing three two zero, sixty nautical miles. Friendly beacon identified as the Danish warship *Knud Rasmussen*."

Emma acknowledged the sonar operator then glanced at her altimeter, which showed an altitude of ten thousand feet. She had already met the captain of the *Rasmussen* on a few occasions, and they regularly communicated via radio when airborne. There were not many international military units stationed in the north, which meant professional acquaintances were easier to establish than down south. Emma asked her co-pilot to change their radio frequency to a maritime UHF channel. She then brought her aircraft slowly down to five thousand feet.

Emma keyed her headset. "Warship *Rasmussen*, this is U.S. naval aircraft blue fox four-two-niner, message over."

A familiar Danish accent replied. "Blue fox four-two-niner, *Rasmussen*, good to hear your voice again."

"Roger, same to you, Magnus, we will be on station for the next ten hours operating in the north-eastern quadrant of the international search zone. Have you got any traffic you can send our way?"

Emma was hoping the *Rasmussen* had discovered a sub-surface sonar contact on the seabed that the *Poseidon's* advanced sensors could decipher. The *Rasmussen's* captain replied negative, then sent his American counterpart the coordinates they had already searched for the missing submarine. Emma acknowledged the Dane, while bringing her aircraft down to a lower altitude. She passed near the *Rasmussen* at eight hundred feet. Emma skillfully dipped the *Poseidon's* wings in an internationally recognised sign of salutation, before climbing back to her pre-assigned cruising altitude. She could never get away with flying like this over the crowded skies of eastern Florida.

"Pilot, sonar two, I have multiple translucent surface contacts to our north-west, bearing three four zero."

Emma thanked the sonar operator, then checked the electronic tablet strapped to her thigh for the latest sea ice conditions. Icebergs, as massive as they could be, were still only frozen water. They were visible to most modern sensor instruments, but did not have the density of a metallic surface such as a ship or submarine. Emma's co-pilot looked in awe at the white horizon before them. The young man had grown up in Louisiana, so seeing Arctic pack ice at such a low altitude was a first for him. Their interest today, however, was what might lie beneath the ice. It was this aspect of the search, and the challenge the frozen formations presented, that most perplexed Emma.

Up until the introduction of the *Poseidon*, American anti-submarine aircraft had been equipped with a magnetic anomaly detector or MAD. Encased in a long metal rod that protruded from the aircraft's tail, it could detect the magnetic signature of a submerged vessel. The system had been replaced on the *Poseidon* with modern sub-surface sensor arrays and software that were supposedly superior to the MAD. Emma was not convinced, especially when trying to *see* through ten-metre thick Arctic pack ice. No matter, they would have to make do with what they had.

"Pilot, sonar two, I have what appears to be a surface contact directly to our front, range twenty nautical miles."

Emma looked at her ice chart, then out the aircraft's window at the wall of frozen sea below them.

*That doesn't sound right*, she thought.

"Confirm you have a surface and not a sub-surface contact?" Emma requested from her operators in the belly of the *Poseidon*. They responded that they were tracking a solid contact on the ocean surface in the middle of the massive sea ice.

"Could the *Volkov* have surfaced through the ice?" the co-pilot asked.

Emma nodded in slight agreement. Depending on the thickness, modern nuclear submarines routinely surfaced through the polar ice. It was possible the Russian vessel had done the same. Perhaps they had a communication failure, which is why they weren't able to signal their superiors in Moscow. For once there might be a happy ending to an Arctic search and rescue operation. Then again...

"Sonar, pilot, what's the estimated length of the surface contact?" Emma requested.

"Roughly thirty to thirty-five metres, ma'am."

The pilot and co-pilot looked at each other confused. The *Volkov* was at least one hundred and twenty metres long, unless the surface contact wasn't the Russian submarine.

*What could it be in the middle of solid pack ice?* Emma felt unsettled, imagining pieces of a shattered submarine hull. She shook the thought from her mind, bringing her aircraft into a slow descent towards the frozen sea below.

"Flight crew, pilot, we will circle over the surface contact in order to attempt a visual identification," Emma ordered. "Observers, to your stations please."

In the back of the *Poseidon*, two crewmembers moved to the lone bubble windows located at the rear of the fuselage, one on each side. The aircraft levelled off at one thousand feet. Though authorised to fly lower, Emma knew the jagged ice below could suddenly protrude several hundred metres skyward.

Both pilots glanced out their windows as they received confirmation that they were over the surface sonar contact. All they could see was the vast expanse of a frozen white ocean. The visual monotony was occasionally broken by pockets of open water, courtesy of the above average temperatures. Emma gently turned the aircraft in order to take another look. She engaged her headset.

"Sonar, pilot, transfer your current image to the flight deck for simultaneous tracking."

The pair of aviators soon saw the same pixilated image the technicians in the rear compartment were observing.

*What is that?* Emma thought. A long, thin object was visible on the monitor. It had wedged ends and a likely width of five metres.

*It must not be on the ice, but trapped in it.*

Whatever it was, it probably wasn't from the missing Russian submarine. Emma instructed her crew to make note of the location, then prepare to launch a homing beacon onto the frozen surface. Sea ice could move very quickly depending on ocean currents and the prevailing winds. She brought her aircraft around for another pass.

"That's beautiful," the co-pilot observed. "I've never seen the northern lights before."

Emma looked at the horizon to see a flood of long green lines dancing about. The waves of energy seemed to fill the entire sky, blocking out the sun.

"It's pretty, but very unusual," she allowed. "It's August, the sun is up, and it's the middle of the day. We shouldn't be able to see them."

"Pilot, crew chief, beacon away."

Emma switched her monitor to the bottom fuselage mounted camera, facing aft. This allowed her to watch the homing beacon's small parachute deploy as it slowly descended.

The green bolt of energy seemed to originate from the horizon, obliterating the homing beacon in a flash of sparks. Before Emma could react, three more energy beams slammed into the side of the aircraft. They caused vibrations ten times worse than any turbulence she'd experienced.

"Lightning strikes," the co-pilot warned over the intercom. Emma increased the *Poseidon's* engines to full throttle. She pulled back on the yoke in order to climb above the clouds, and the danger of the apparent electrical storm. Two more waves of energy bounced around the airframe, causing the digital instrument panel to flicker.

"Five thousand and climbing," the nervous co-pilot announced. "Today's cloud ceiling should be eleven thousand, ma'am."

Emma nodded as her aircraft lifted away from the immediate threat of the surprise electrical storm. It was only then that she noticed there were no clouds. With the exception of the northern lights, it was a clear day.

*Then where is the lightning coming from?*

The plane shook again as more electric bolts struck. Green waves of energy cascaded about the flight deck's windows in branch-like patterns. Emma watched in fascination at the awesome spectacle surrounding them. A bright flash. More shaking. Another bright flash. This time the green energy seemed to linger outside the window just long enough for Emma to see... a face?

"Jesus Christ," she gasped, blinking several times. She looked again, but saw only green static energy waves. Once more the instrument panel flickered.

What could best be described as a green fireball rose up from the ice below, flying directly into the turbofan of the *Poseidon's* starboard engine. The nacelle shifted violently, the engine straining at the sudden spike of heat and energy.

"Fire in number two engine," the co-pilot yelled.

"Extinguishers," Emma ordered, then keyed her headset. "Pan, pan, pan, Thule control, this is blue fox four-two-niner declaring an in-flight emergency. We're currently caught in an electrical storm at angels ten thousand and have a fire in our number two engine."

The sole response they received was static.

Emma relayed the message a second time, only to be met by a garbled background noise. Soon a different sound filled her headset, a deep metallic tone that gave off a pulsating distortion. It increased in intensity as alarm bells continued ringing about the flight deck. The distortions started to sound like someone's voice; a deep, haunting voice. It spoke in a language she did not understand. Emma tried to communicate with whomever she had reached.

*Might that be the Rasmussen? Could the voice be Danish?*

The number two engine exploded into a ball of molten flames. Hundreds of fan blades from the disintegrating motor flew in every direction at the speed of sound. At least a dozen pierced the *Poseidon's* hull, leading to immediate cabin depressurisation.

"Masks on, now," Emma called out, grabbing the rubberised oxygen mask located over her left shoulder. Though only at ten thousand feet, she wasn't taking any chances. "Mayday, mayday, mayday, this is blue fox four-two-niner calling Thule control, we need vectoring to the nearest airfield immediately, over."

More static, and again the deep, almost taunting voice filled Emma's headset. It was a relief when the unknown language was replaced by the familiarity of the *Poseidon's* crew chief. He reported there was extensive damage to the rear fuselage, but all personnel were uninjured. She then directed her co-pilot to find the nearest airport. They were beginning to lose altitude and Emma had no idea how badly the destruction of the number two engine had damaged the starboard wing.

More violent energy bolts struck the plane. The sky outside was now entirely green. All at once, the digital monitors on the *Poseidon* started displaying unidentified symbols. They reminded Emma of stick figures, or a simple version of ancient hieroglyphics.

"I can't access any of the navigational data to pull up an electronic map," the co-pilot announced in a panic.

For the first time in her naval career, Emma swore loudly at a subordinate, before continuing. "Use the paper nav charts in the pocket behind your seat. Plot us a manual course to the nearest airfield. I don't care if it's a dirt strip."

The co-pilot frantically complied as Emma peered through the green haze outside. She saw land, shaped like an inlet.

"Based on where we were before the instruments went down," the co-pilot reported, "the nearest airstrip is at Pond Inlet on Baffin Island, but it's gravel and only twelve hundred metres."

*It will have to do*, Emma thought and eased her plane down, increasing the throttle of her remaining port engine.

The *Poseidon* burst out of the green energy clouds that had intercepted the aircraft over the icy ocean. Emma fought the shuddering of the plane's yoke, trying to keep the wings level. Directly to her front, she could see a small village nestled against an inlet, the lone gravel airstrip visible to the west of the town. She had given up trying to radio their predicament to anyone, focusing instead on the emergency landing procedures.

"Auto spoilers," she ordered.

"Auto spoilers armed," the co-pilot confirmed.

"Flaps."

"Flaps down thirty degrees."

"Landing gear."

"Landing gear is down and locked."

Emma instructed her crew to brace for an emergency approach, then levelled her wings just over the rooftops of the northern community below. The control column vibrated viciously, forcing her to rely on the foot pedals that controlled the aircraft's tail. She angled her right wing slightly to avoid a radio tower, easing back the throttle of the remaining engine. She fought against the plane's desire to roll to the left, calling out to her co-pilot to read her the altitude.

"Two hundred, one-fifty, one hundred..."

The young man deliberately calmed his voice, allowing his training to take over. The gravel airstrip was now directly in front of them as they rapidly descended.

*No.*

There was a single engine floatplane parked at the end of the runway. It was too late to abort now, not that Emma's plane had the power to climb anymore. She thought of her daughters as the co-pilot read out the last altitude readings, "twenty feet, fifteen, ten, five, wheels down!"

*Here we go.*

The P-8 *Poseidon* slammed onto the dirt airstrip at twice its normal landing velocity, immediately buckling the landing gear which dug into the gravel. A dozen sirens and alarm bells rang throughout the flight deck. The aircraft's port engine twisted violently as it filled with dirt before being ripped away by the force of the forward momentum. Emma applied the airbrakes and reverse thrusters out of instinct, even though there were no longer any engines left to command. The plane slid forward at a thirty degree angle, its right wing becoming entangled in the small airport's perimeter fencing. *Please don't let it end this way*, Emma begged as she was thrown about her seat from the bouncing and shuddering of their crash landing. Then, less than twenty metres from the parked floatplane, it was over. The plane stopped in a cloud of dust.

Emma paused, then looked at her co-pilot who was bleeding from the forehead. She unstrapped herself, placed one of her gloved hands against the man's head, and keyed the intercom.

"All personnel, evacuate, evacuate, evacuate!"

She pulled a lever that blew the roof-top escape hatch wide open, then assisted her co-pilot as they awkwardly climbed out. Using an extended emergency harness, the two naval aviators dangled down the side of the airframe until they hit the damp, fuel-covered gravel. The pair quickly scrambled away from the wrecked *Poseidon*, watching as the rest of the crew escaped out the back of the mangled fuselage. Soon they were all some fifty metres from the wreckage; exhausted, frightened, but alive.

It was only then that Emma noticed the large markings burned into the side of the aircraft's grey hull, just above the wings.

THE
ARCTIC REGIONS
OF
NORTH AMERICA
BY
EDWD WELLER, F.R.G.S.
PARRY ISLAND
PRINCE PATRICK ISLAND
MELVILLE ISLAND
BATHURST ISLE
CORNWALLIS ISLAND
BANKS LAND
Melville Sound
Pr. of Wales Land
Pr. Albert Land
Minto Inlet
Pr. Albert Sound
Wollaston Land
Victoria Land
King William Land
Franklin
Great Bear Lake
Arctic Circle

# CHAPTER 9

Erika felt the dark cloud of depression descend across her thoughts. She'd experienced bouts of sadness as a teenager, particularly when taunted by nasty school peers, but this was different. As she sat on a quiet bench among the trees and campus buildings, Erika was overcome by an unbearable wave of sadness. The tears freely flowed down her face, the sunlight glinting against her moist cheeks. She was tormented by her dreams, and confused by the inexplicable premonitions that beset her when awake. Though they had saved her friends from several nasty situations, she was still left filled with anxiety. Erika was desperate for some maternal wisdom. She longed for her mother, Star, aching for her guidance and the warmth of her embrace. After nearly two months in Vermont, the full weight of Erika's loss finally crashed upon her like an emotional tidal wave. It was agony.

She cried uncontrollably. Her sobs mixed with gasps of air echoed across the empty park. Erika's only companion was a cluster of small birds chirping among the leaves. She wiped her eyes and nose with her shirt sleeve, but to no avail. The steady stream of tears continued. The full reckoning of her mother's loss had arrived, and it was unbearable. She swatted away a curious fly, then felt her smartphone buzz in her pocket. The message was from her roommate, Sandra: *Where are you?* She ignored it. Though her new friends were proving to be the best part of her time at

UVM, at the moment she craved solitude.

*Pain is approaching.*

Erika instinctively slammed her hand down on the wooden park bench. She lifted her palm to find a crushed wasp, its wings still vibrating as the signals from its nervous system faded. She stared at the offending insect.

*I knew you were coming*, she thought. *I knew you were going to sting me.*

This was the most unnerving aspect of her summer in Vermont. The premonitions. They were becoming more regular, and easier to sense. Her nightmares were growing in their intensity as well, but she didn't understand what they meant. This only added to her confusion, all of which contributed to her current mood. Something was fundamentally wrong with her, but she had no idea what it was. Erika felt she could literally *see* danger just before it occurred. She didn't understand *how* any more than she understood *why*, never mind her graphic dreams of axe-wielding barbarians.

Star had warned Erika she was special, but every mother says that of their child. During their northern visits, her grandparents would encourage her to close her eyes and peer into tomorrow. To a child it all seemed like a game, but now as an adult it felt ridiculous and superstitious. Yet the accuracy and prescience of her foresight was undeniable.

*Am I a freak?* She brooded. Perhaps it wasn't all that bad. If she did possess some kind of sixth sense, it seemed to improve her hockey game, which had certainly made her popular amongst her new teammates. This in turn had helped her to develop some genuine friendships. For the first time in her life, Erika felt she had peers who truly cared about her. So maybe there were some benefits. Again she rejected the thought. If she was so special, why hadn't she predicted the arrival of her mother's illness?

She felt a warmth against her chest. From under her shirt, Erika lifted the old amulet her father had given for her birthday. It was beautiful, but today the piece of ancient art only reminded Erika of her loss. She held the jewellery in her hand. It felt warm to the touch. Not a burning sensation; more like a metal object left in the sun. This was yet another occurrence she could not explain, nor did she want to. Somehow the unique warmth of the necklace brought comfort to her soul, which had been a rare feeling of late. Another ping from her smartphone signalled that Erika's friends were looking for her. There was yet another house party this evening, which she wanted no part of.

The cancer that took her mother was insidiously cruel. Known as glioblastoma, it's web-like tumour spread through a victim's brain, slowly shutting down bodily functions. Since it manifests itself in brain tissue, it is often only discovered in the disease's late stages. Treatment options are primarily palliative, with less than 4% of diagnosed patients living five years or more. Star didn't even survive half that time. She didn't have a chance, and knew it the day her doctor revealed the life-shattering news. Erika hated the name glioblastoma. It sounded like a deformed beast from a badly made horror film. An evil ailment brought on by a malevolent wizard, designed to torture, before it killed its victims. Now her mother was a pile of ashes in a ceramic jar, waiting to be disposed of in the community of her birth, far from civilisation.

*Stop it.*

Erika looked up, suddenly apprehensive. Did she hear something?

*Take meaning from this.*

Erika turned her head about quickly, scanning the empty park. She sensed she wasn't alone, but found no evidence of another person. A slight breeze had picked up, but that was it. She noticed the amulet around her neck was getting warmer, almost uncomfortable against the skin of her chest. Again she pulled it out and examined the piece.

*You need to prepare yourself.*

Now Erika was standing. She swore she had heard another voice just now. She held the jewellery in her right fist, close to her chest. It somehow provided a sense of reassurance. Erika felt she recognised the voice, perhaps from a dream.

*Mother?* She thought, then quickly dismissed the notion. Then who, or what? After a few tense moments standing by the park bench, a small sparrow landed by Erika's feet. It curiously canted its head up at her. The sight of the innocent creature calmed her. She sat back down, again cradling the amulet in her hand.

"Holstrom!"

This voice Erika definitely recognised.

"C'mon, Holstrom, we know you're around here. Your phone GPS tag says so."

Erika watched her roommate Sandra round a copse of trees and walk towards the park bench. She waved at the goaltender, but Sandra did not respond.

"Hey there," Erika called out, her voice cracking, but nothing.

Sandra walked right past Erika seated on the bench, passing by only a few yards.

*Why can't you see me?*

Erika looked down at the jewellery she still held in her hand.

*Are you doing this?*

She decided to stay quiet to see how long it would take for Sandra to notice her. The burly goalie kept looking at her smartphone, glancing about to confirm her location was correct.

"Holstrom, quit messing around, where are you?"

Erika released the amulet her father had given her. She tucked it back in her shirt, and stood up.

"I'm right here, I just needed some time alone."

Sandra spun around with a fright. "Dude, you scared the crap out of me," she glared, catching her breath. "You can't do that to somebody!"

"Sorry?" Erika said meekly. "I thought you'd notice me sitting here."

Sandra looked at the park bench behind Erika, then back at her roommate. After a few moments, Sandra shrugged her shoulders and offered to sit with her friend, who had clearly been crying.

"Listen, the girls and I have been talking," she said.

"Which girls?" Erika interjected.

"Who do you think?" Sandra looked back amused. "Nicole and Michelle."

Erika listened as her roommate explained in great detail that her friends knew she was in a difficult place because of the loss of her mother. Sandra continued that they were there to help her "no matter what", and said that if there was anything she needed, to let them know right away. Though Sandra's words intended empathy, they instead sounded like empty clichés. The kind of thing people feel they are supposed to say when dealing with an uncomfortable topic such as death. She found her mind wandering as Sandra went on. It wasn't that she didn't appreciate the effort. Erika just felt so detached from reality there was little her friend could do to cheer her up.

*Take them with you.*

Erika froze. "What did you just say?"

Sandra paused, looking a little confused. "I was saying that my aunt had a cousin who knew a guy who had dealt with some real bad stuff in his life..."

Again Sandra's words were lost to Erika as she scanned the empty park. She felt as though someone was trying to tell her something. She closed her eyes, thinking of Star as her friend rambled. Erika's thoughts jumped to memories, first of her mother, then her father Liam. She remembered the cottage of her paternal grandparents. The old log cabin by the lake in Minnesota with its wooden bunk beds and traditional wood-burning sauna. How she had loved running in and out of the sauna as a child, jumping in the cold lake, often with nothing on. She was lucky to have had such good grandparents in her life. Salt of the earth people who took care of her, nurturing her intellectual curiosity while supporting her winter sports. They were proud of their son Liam, and more importantly, the granddaughter he and Star had produced. She missed them.

Sandra continued her well-intentioned diatribe.

From the nostalgic shores of Lake Superior, Erika's thoughts turned to Star's parents, both of whom were still alive and well in Pond Inlet. She imagined their pain. How fundamentally unfair it must be to outlive your own child. Though she did not know them well, Erika's childhood memories of her northern grandparents involved endless sunlight. This was the result of her only ever visiting them in the summer, when the Arctic experienced twenty-four hour daylight. Grandpa was a trapper, while grandma acted as a guide for the increasing number of tourists visiting the north. She had tried to teach Erika how to sing with her throat. A deep, guttural sound that when performed in unison, produced a melodic, chanting rhythm. Star used to explain that the tradition of Inuit throat singing went back centuries, if not thousands of years. Liam would lecture in his academic way, that there was medieval lore of early Norse seafarers being hypnotised by young female throat singers, luring them away from their ships. As far back as a millennium, early European sailors may have even reached the far north and been enchanted by the magical throat sounds, explaining why so many never returned. The clarity of what she needed to do was immediate.

"Come with me," Erika blurted out, interrupting her friend.

"Come with you?" Sandra asked, even more confused than before. "Where?"

"Come with me to Pond Inlet. My mother's memorial service is next week and we have a break in hockey camp, so you won't miss anything." Erika's sullen demeanour was now alight with excitement. "Please. It would mean so much to me. In fact, let's invite Michelle and Nicole as well."

Sandra examined Erika's expression. "Where's Pond Inlet?"

"Baffin Island."

"OK, and where's *that*?"

"North. Way north. Its where my mother's family is from."

"You mean up in the Arctic?"

Erika nodded emphatically. "Near Greenland, yes."

"Look, I like you Erika, I really do, and I know you need emotional support, but I can't afford a plane ticket right now, let alone hotel costs. Even with the hockey scholarship, I still need to save for the autumn semester..."

"I'll pay for you," Erika insisted.

"What? How?" Sandra snorted.

"When my mother passed, we got some life insurance that covers various costs, including bereavement travel for family and friends. I can take up to three people with me."

Erika's roommate looked down at the ground, mildly ashamed. "I know you need the support, but I don't want you wasting money on me. What about your high school friends? You must have somebody your age that knew your mother back home. Wouldn't it be more appropriate to invite them?"

Erika grew dour. "I don't have any friends back home."

"C'mon, what about all the girls you played hockey with in Duluth?"

As much as Erika had adored growing up in Minnesota for its nature and her family, she hadn't fit in well with her high school peers. No matter how hard she tried, she often felt judged and belittled. The anonymity social media afforded her classmates had only emboldened their taunting. Her solution had been to excel in sports and academia, but that meant alienating herself from the usual teenage cliques. She did have two close friends from her former hockey team, but they were both now playing in North Dakota. Regardless, Erika felt closer to her new Vermont teammates, whom she'd only been with for two months, than people she'd known back home for years. Though still confused by her emerging senses, she felt she belonged with Sandra and the others. They made her feel safe, and appreciated. The very fact Sandra was sitting beside her proved it.

"Sandra, you're my best friend at UVM," Erika said, "and Nicole is solid and reliable as anything, even if she has some latent mommy issues. Even Michelle is awesome, in a really weird way, though I think she's trying to get down my pants."

Both women giggled lightly as Erika continued.

"Besides, nothing would be wasted money as you'd be my emotional support. We can stay at my grandparents' lodge. It's big enough. They could sure use some friendly company right now. I can show you where I spent some of my summers as a kid. We can go kayaking, watch narwhals, go fishing for Arctic char..."

Erika hesitated.

"What is it?" Sandra asked as her friend trailed off.

"Nothing, I thought it might still be polar bear mating season, but we're good."

"Polar bears!" Sandra rolled her eyes in disbelief. "Are you for real?"

"Forget I said anything. In fact, they hardly come into the community. Besides, most people up north have guns, but rarely need to use them."

"Sounds like Texas."

Both girls smiled.

Sandra took a moment to think about it. Subtlety was not one of her attributes.

"Screw it, I'm in!"

"Really? You're awesome!" Erika shrieked as she jumped up to hug her roommate, nearly knocking the two off the park bench.

"BUT..." Sandra said after a brief moment, "I'm not eating any seals, or whales, or reindeer..."

"Caribou," Erika corrected.

"You know what I mean," Sandra insisted lightly.

"This is so great," Erika rejoiced. "I'll let my dad know we're coming. He's already up there. We can book our flights through the university travel app. Hey, let's go find Nicole and Michelle."

Sandra held back her friend's enthusiasm for an instant. "We should probably tell Nancy, just in case there is an unplanned exhibition game."

She glanced at Erika, who spoke with a wistful look on her face.

"My mother had an awesome sense of humour. She used to say things about her illness like, *if we can't use the disabled parking spot, then what's the point of having cancer anyway?* What she really meant was, always try to see the positive in everyday life, no matter what. Seize the day, that sort of thing."

The two looked at each other, before blurting out in unison: "We don't need to tell Nancy."

After more laughter, they got up and started walking back towards their residence.

Sandra glanced over at Erika. "How'd you sneak up on me so easily, anyway?"

"I didn't," Erika said innocently. "I was sitting on the bench the whole time. You walked right past me."

Sandra shook her head. "Maybe I need glasses."

"The way New Hampshire scored on you during our last game, you definitely need glasses."

As the pair walked off, Erika allowed herself a bit of inner peace. It was as though the voices she had sensed earlier were satisfied, for now.

# THE DAILY SAGAS

THE
ARCTIC REGIONS
OF
NORTH AMERICA
BY
EDW. WELLER, F.R.G.S.
PRINCE PATRICK ISLAND
PARRY ISLAND
MELVILLE ISLAND
BATHURST ISLAND
CORNWALLIS ISLAND
BANKS LAND
Melville Sound
Pr. of Wales Land
Pr. Albert Land
Prince Albert Sound
Victoria Land
Wollaston Land
Minto Inlet
Baring I.
Booth
King William Land
Franklin
Great Bear Lake
Arctic Circle

# CHAPTER 10

The latest Arctic naval intelligence report was placed in front of Brigadier-General Katherine Tremblay. It rested within a red envelope marked *secret*. She glanced up from reading an encrypted tablet at her American intelligence officer, known as a J2. The man looked exhausted as he spoke.

"This is the latest correlation of the data analysis you requested, General. It includes a triangulated overlay of the various significant incident reports we've been tracking this summer in the north between Canada, Greenland, and the United States."

Katherine nodded and took the heavy file folder into her lap. "Anything of substance from the Russian defence attaché?" she asked the J2, who shook his head.

"No, ma'am. Colonel Borishov insists they have no additional information on the *Volkov's* last known whereabouts."

The general looked across the room at the uniformed Russian officer seated on a folding metal chair and scowled.

*What I really want you to tell me,* she pondered accusingly, *is what the hell your sub was doing in our waters, not to mention how much radiation might now be contaminating the surrounding seabed.*

Katherine knew Colonel Oleksandr Borishov was probably a member of Russian military intelligence, otherwise known as the GRU. It was no mystery that Moscow routinely sent such agents as attachés to their diplomatic missions abroad. Still, the chances he actually had any insight into highly classified Russian nuclear submarine movements was likely zero.

"Thank you, J2, please carry on," Katherine acknowledged.

The general had been due to relinquish her command of Canada's northern military headquarters this past July. Based in Yellowknife, her HQ was responsible for a vast geographical footprint. It stretched from the western Yukon border with Alaska, to the frigid waters separating Canada from Greenland. After twenty-four months commanding in the Arctic, Katherine and her family had been looking forward to an exchange posting in North Carolina. These plans were now on hold, following a string of unfortunate events beginning this past spring.

Including the *Volkov's* loss, the human toll in the north over the past four months had risen to almost 150 souls; a tenfold jump from all of last year. With the increased effects of climate change taking hold, the melting sea ice meant vessels of all types were now sailing into waters previously thought unreachable. It appeared that weather conditions, inexperience, or just bad luck had led to half a dozen tragic incidents, primarily in the vicinity of the Davis Strait. Katherine's military bosses were concerned. So much so that they had extended her time in the north, while establishing a temporary headquarters in the remote community of Pond Inlet, where she now sat.

Katherine paused before opening the J2's latest report. All around her, a mixture of uniformed and civilian personnel moved about, getting ready for the daily commander's update briefing, or CUB. It was to be delivered for her benefit at 08:30. The Pond Inlet community centre had been transformed into a beehive of sophisticated electronics, satellite communications equipment, and flat-screen monitors. From the small gymnasium floor, Katherine and her staff were able to *see* their entire northern area of responsibility, as far away as Iceland. In the centre of the gym, collapsible wooden tables accompanied by folding metal chairs had been placed in a large horseshoe shape. Listed in alphanumeric order were assigned seating locations and laptops for some twenty staff officers and officials from a dozen different departments. American, Canadian,

Danish, and French personnel moved about with increasing urgency as the bottom of the hour approached. Though the community centre was now technically a secure facility, Katherine had permitted the Russian defence attaché to attend the morning updates. She did this out of professional courtesy more than anything else. After all, it was Colonel Borishov's government that had to explain to its citizens why ninety of their young sailors had likely perished in North American waters. For a leader who promoted himself as a competent defender of the motherland, the president of Russia would not be pleased with this latest international incident, and, as the expression suggests, *shit rolls downhill.*

Katherine noticed a familiar face enter the room. She made eye contact with Major Eleanor Matthews and motioned her over. Eleanor was still wearing her beret, so quickly saluted the general, before relaxing her posture. Back when Eleanor was a young platoon commander, Katherine had been her first commanding officer.

"How did things go down south?" Katherine asked gently.

"Fine, ma'am. The battalion CO and chaplain took care of the next-of-kin notifications, with both funerals taking place in Ontario. An assisting officer will continue to be assigned to each family until the last of the death benefits are released."

Katherine loathed the term death benefits, for obvious reasons. More troubling, she knew Eleanor and her troops were still coming to terms with the freakish way their colleagues had perished. Could a migrating herd of caribou really *attack* a group of soldiers? Even members of the local hunters and trappers association had never heard of such behaviour.

"I'm glad you're back, Eleanor. Let's chat some more after the CUB."

The major nodded and moved over to her assigned seat beside the captain of the Danish Arctic patrol ship *Knud Rasmussen.* Katherine knew the *Rasmussen* was the only vessel that summer to find any trace of the missing fishing trawlers that had failed to return to port. She had read the Danish ship surgeon's autopsy report on the ghastly condition of two missing French sailors pulled from the sea in June. Katherine had yet to be presented with a reasonable explanation as to how the deceased members from *L'Etoile Bretonne* had been surgically eviscerated. She shuddered at the thought.

A few seats down from the Danish contingent sat U.S. navy pilot Lieutenant-Commander Emma Gonzalez. She had recently performed a miraculous emergency landing following a severe electrical storm. What was left of Emma's P-8 *Poseidon* still sat at the end of Pond Inlet's only runway. Katherine understood the aircraft's black box data and voice recorders had been retrieved and deciphered. The American aviation crash inspectors were to share their initial findings with their international counterparts that morning, which would make for an interesting CUB. Across from them sat Dr Liam Holstrom, an Arctic research professor from the University of Minnesota and trusted advisor to Katherine's predecessor. He was already in Pond Inlet visiting family when the general and her headquarters arrived. Well respected in academic circles for his studies into the north and its history, the professor had conducted research in the area most summers since the 1980s. She knew he'd lately experienced some form of personal tragedy, but couldn't remember exactly what had happened. Finally, seated beside the professor, were Colonel Borishov and his newly arrived aides from the Russian embassy.

*Great, more GRU.*

Katherine watched as her chief of staff, an air force colonel, walked by a series of large flat-screen monitors at the front of the room, and faced the audience. Normally the introductory remarks would fall to a young duty officer, such as an army captain or naval lieutenant, but not today.

"Bonjour, Brigadier-General Tremblay, ladies and gentlemen, welcome to the morning commander's update brief for Operation *Northern Wolf*, the international search effort for the missing Russian nuclear attack submarine *Volkov*. As a reminder, the use of smartphones and wireless communication devices is prohibited during the CUB. Today's briefing is rated as unclassified."

Katherine shifted uncomfortably in her seat. Given the amount of sensitive items in the room, including the protected documents before her, the CUB should have been classified. However, in order for the Russians to participate, certain exceptional courtesies were being extended. Katherine knew that once Operation *Northern Wolf* came to a close, Colonel Borishov would be writing a lengthy report for Moscow on her team's tactics, techniques, and operating procedures. As a small measure, the various satellite communication terminals and secret level computers had been wheeled into another room for the duration of the CUB.

The J2 intelligence officer replaced the chief of staff, as a large three-dimensional map of the north-eastern Arctic appeared behind him, centred on the Davis Strait.

"Good morning, ma'am, no change to last night's weather forecast for today. Overcast with a high of fourteen Celsius, or fifty-seven Fahrenheit. Lows will be twelve Celsius or fifty-three Fahrenheit. Full daylight will occur from 04:23 to 22:00, with a nautical twilight of 00:40 to 01:49. There continues to be no true darkness at this time of year."

*Those temperatures should be at least five degrees cooler*, Katherine thought to herself with resignation. The J2 continued.

"General, the Davis Strait maritime search area continues to be divided into four sectors, each centred on one surface asset and two aircraft. Beginning in the top left corner of the map, the Canadian icebreaker CCGS *Jean Goodwill* is operating in the north-west search area. Sector north-east is being monitored by the Danish Arctic patrol vessel *Knud Rasmussen,* while the American guided missile destroyer USS *Samuel Ronaldson* is in the south-west sector. The south-eastern quadrant is currently being serviced by the French frigate *Forbin*, though it will be relieved on station by HMCS *Margaret Brooke* in the coming days. The at-sea replenishment duties are being shared by the Canadian auxiliary vessel MV *Asterix*, and the American tanker USNS *Laramie*. In addition, maritime patrol aircraft from several nations are operating out of both Goose Bay, Labrador, and the American airbase in Thule, Greenland."

Colonel Borishov raised his hand, causing the J2 to pause.

"If I may, General, we are pleased to report the Russian frigate *Nikolay Khabalov* will soon arrive in the region following a courtesy visit to Venezuela. With your kind indulgence, it will assist in the search efforts."

Katherine nodded politely to her Russian guest. She had known for days through American sources that the *Khabalov* was currently sailing up the eastern U.S. coast, arriving within forty-eight hours. When the search operation was first launched, someone higher up the chain-of-command had resisted allowing Russian military vessels into North American waters. Katherine understood the security logic behind such a decision, but knew it was morally wrong. Political leaders in Washington, Ottawa, and Copenhagen had quickly intervened, allowing for Moscow's naval participation. This reversal was partly due to mounting public pressure, led by the families of the missing sailors. In reality, the Russian northern fleet probably had at least two additional submarines already operating in the region, searching silently below the Arctic waves. Regardless, Katherine knew their collective chances of finding the *Volkov* any time soon were slim.

"J2, please carry on," she gestured.

The morning update lasted another fifteen minutes, with the American intelligence lead handing over to the J3 operations officer for the remainder of the briefing. Various coordination efforts were synchronised, primarily de-confliction of search areas and flight routes for patrol aircraft. Katherine was pondering what little new information had been disclosed, when the operations officer finished his remarks.

"This concludes the unclassified portion of the morning CUB, ma'am. Are there any questions?"

The general looked about the room. None of her staff moved. Their anticipation for the upcoming classified portion of the CUB was too great to be delayed by questions.

"Very well," Katherine said. "Colonel Borishov, thanks to you and your colleagues for joining us this morning. Our duty officer will kindly escort you out, and we will see you tomorrow unless we have any additional news in the interim."

The Russian attaché and his party stood and politely nodded towards the Canadian general, then exited. As much as Operation *Northern Wolf* was a humanitarian mission to find lost souls, there was still the need for security. This was particularly important given the tense state of affairs surrounding Russian activity in Eastern Europe. On cue, the chief of staff gave permission to wheel back in the various pieces of secure communications equipment. At the same time, Lieutenant-Commander Emma Gonzalez moved to the front of the room. She was joined by several members of the P-8 *Poseidon* crash investigation team.

"Good morning, ma'am," Emma started. "Normally as the pilot involved in a crash investigation it would be inappropriate for me to comment publicly on the incident before the formal investigation has concluded. Having said that, the audio and visual information contained in the retrieved aircraft black box is too important to wait."

Emma had succeeded in grabbing Katherine's undivided attention. As she continued, the crash investigation team projected their findings onto three screens. The first monitor showed what the instruments inside the *Poseidon's* flight deck had displayed for the final fifteen minutes before it crashed. The second screen had typed transcripts generated from the crew voice recorder, presented in unison with the actual audio feed. The third TV projected rotating angles, taken from the on-board external cameras of the ill-fated flight, both above and below the fuselage.

"Our aircraft, call sign blue fox four-two-niner, lifted off from Thule airfield at approximately 08:23 local time on day fourteen of Operation *Northern Wolf*, climbing to our pre-assigned altitude. Our mission was to patrol the north-eastern sector of the international search area in support of the *Knud Rasmussen*." Emma gestured towards the Danish captain, Lieutenant-Commander Magnus Jakobson, who nodded in support. She continued. "With the exception of some unusual daylight aurora borealis activity to our north, the initial search mission was uneventful." The images on the three screens, which were paused until now, began to play at half-speed. The room was eerily quiet except for Emma's narration of events.

"At approximately 10:16, our surface sonar operator detected a solid object, roughly thirty to thirty-five metres in length, some twenty nautical miles to our front." There was slight murmuring among the audience. Most realised that Emma's search area that day had been covered in pack ice, thus the intrigue at finding something on the frozen water.

"We circled the potential surface contact, but could not make a visual confirmation. At approximately 10:33, I ordered the release of a parachute homing beacon onto the sea ice, so we could carry on with the rest of our search mission. Then, this happened."

Katherine watched in amazement as the slowed imagery from the underbelly camera showed a green bolt of energy obliterate the descending sensor.

"As soon as we lost the beacon, our aircraft was hit by a series of apparent lighting strikes. This occurred despite the absence of any significant cloud cover or storm front in the area." The tense room watched in awe as wave after wave of jade coloured energy beams impacted the beleaguered *Poseidon*. It was apparent from the recorded imagery that the bolts of lightning originated from the frozen ocean, and not the sky. Emma paused the footage.

Katherine looked over at her intelligence officer.

"Energy weapon?" she asked him with concern. He shrugged, at a loss for words. Had the *Volkov* been equipped with a new form of energy weapon designed to imitate lighting strikes? This, coupled with some kind of experimental stealth technology, could explain why they had not been able to locate the missing Russian submarine.

*Perhaps it wasn't missing after all*, Katherine thought wryly.

Emma sensed what the military trained minds in the room were likely deducing from her presentation and interjected. "Ma'am, before we assume this is some kind of new Russian weapon, there's more."

Katherine watched in silence as Emma slowly moved her presentation forward, frame by frame, until she stopped at what appeared to be a dark green cloud with two blackened ovals. The swirling mist was visibly different from the surrounding background. Emma digitally enhanced the picture's resolution, while adjusting the contrast of the image. Katherine strained her eyes to make sense of what she was being presented. As the picture came into focus, she was visibly startled by what she saw.

"Freeze imagery," she snapped. "Which camera took this shot?" the general demanded, now standing. One of the crash inspectors indicated the dashboard camera, mounted in front of the pilot's position. Katherine looked over at Emma, who bowed her head apprehensively, fearful her colleagues would not believe her version of events.

"Chief of staff, secure the room please," Katherine ordered firmly, "no one goes in or out. J2, this briefing is now rated secret. I want a log of all persons in the room including service numbers and ID of visiting personnel. Duty officer, turn on the emission control scrambler." She watched as a young captain engaged the device that jammed any wireless devices within a fifty-metre radius.

Katherine then addressed the audience members sternly. "I want to make it crystal clear everyone present is subject to both our respective national and NATO level secrecy acts. What we will see and hear in this room today stays in this room, understood?" Using her best command presence, Katherine went around the room, verbally receiving individual acknowledgements from each member present that they understood her direction. She then stopped in front of Dr Liam Holstrom, who appeared visibly out of place.

"Professor," she sighed, "please tell me you have some form of security clearance?"

Liam looked up at her and lied through his teeth. "Yes ma'am, I have level two, secret."

The general peered down at Liam, not quite convinced, but equally anxious to see the rest of Emma's footage.

"You know we will check, Dr Holstrom," she said, glaring at him. Liam nodded his understanding, while Katherine returned to her seat.

"Please, carry on Lieutenant-Commander," she reassuringly instructed Emma.

For the next thirty minutes, the leadership of the Arctic headquarters watched in fascination as Emma reviewed the rest of the imagery from her beleaguered flight. They listened to audio of the haunting tones the black box voice recorder had captured. Deep reverberations that occasionally sounded like words from an unknown language. Emma then outlined the rudimentary hieroglyphics her crew had witnessed on their in-flight monitors. An assortment of bisecting vertical and horizontal lines, arranged in linear rows that kept flashing across their displays until the *Poseidon's* power supply failed on impact with the ground. Finally, Emma clicked on a split-screen photo of two identical markings, one taken from an aircraft monitor, the other somehow burned into the side of the crashed fuselage.

Had anyone been paying attention, they would have noticed the brief look of recognition on Liam's face.

THE
ARCTIC REGIONS
OF
NORTH AMERICA
BY
EDW? WELLER, F.R.G.S.
PARRY ISLAND
PRINCE PATRICK ISLAND
MELVILLE ISLAND
BATHURST ISLAND
CORNWALLIS ISLAND
Melville Sound
BANKS LAND
Pr. of Wales Land
Pr. Albert Land
Pr. Albert Sound
Wollaston Land
Victoria Land
King William Land
Boothia
Arctic Circle
Great Bear Lake

# CHAPTER 11

"Oh man, I'm gonna puke!"

Erika watched as her roommate pulled an airsick bag from the seat pocket. Sandra leaned forward and hyperventilated into the paper bag, Erika reassuringly rubbing her back. The turbulence was unlike anything she had experienced in the Arctic. Erika was used to small northern bush planes being bounced around by rough weather, but not like this. The 1970s vintage *Twin Otter* turbo-prop aircraft they flew in had the capacity for two crew and nine passengers. Seated behind Erika and her very ill roommate were fellow Vermont teammates Nicole and Michelle. Nicole looked uneasy, while in contrast Michelle appeared completely calm, offering a reassuring nod to Erika. She smiled back then returned her attention to Sandra, who needed another airsick bag.

Most communities in the far north were only accessible year round by air. Interstate roads did not exist, while coastal hamlets could occasionally be replenished by ship from July to September. Though the effects of climate change were opening up new summer sea routes, the long polar winters still ensured a frozen, impassable wasteland for much of the year. Summer or not, the flying conditions that day were treacherous, even by Arctic standards.

Erika sat up in her seat and yelled forward over the roar of the propeller engines. "How much longer to Pond Inlet?" she bellowed. The *Twin Otter's* interior was an open cabin, meaning there was no physical separation between the pilots and their passengers. The co-pilot raised his left hand and gave a V sign with two fingers, then made a fist. Erika knew he was indicating *two* and *zero*, signalling twenty minutes left. She looked about the aircraft's small cabin. The noise of the engines, enhanced by the windblast outside, meant everyone was forced to wear earplugs.

An unusual sight for any seasoned air traveller was a shotgun strapped to the back of the pilot's seat. This was needed for northern flying in the event of an unplanned weather landing, the weapon designed to fend off any curious polar bears looking for an easy meal. Between the two pilot seats, Erika could see a bright yellow nylon bag with the words *Rescue/ Sauvage* emblazoned in red. Before leaving Iqaluit on the last leg of their journey north, the pilot had demonstrated how to don the emergency wet suits within the rescue bag. Her father routinely reminded her to avoid the frigid Arctic waters at all costs, given that most people survive less than ten minutes if they fall in. This made Erika smile as she remembered the number of times her grandfather had secretly snuck her fishing in his rowboat. If only mother had known. She stared out the cabin window as thoughts of her grandparents morphed into memories of her mother, Star. Erika shook her head quickly to ward off yet another bout of tears.

"Is that normal?" Nicole called out from the rear seats. Erika followed her friend's gaze out the window. The weather conditions were clear, without a cloud in sight, making the unwelcome turbulence all the more confusing. In the distance, Erika could see the horizon glowing, the Arctic sun enhancing green curtains of light that danced about the sky.

"It's probably the northern lights," Erika yelled reassuringly, "the aurora borealis." Nicole nodded nervously while Michelle, seated beside her, had dozed off. The youngest of the bunch smiled. Despite the bumpy ride, Erika knew they were in no danger. After a summer experiencing various premonitions, she was learning to interpret her visions, or at least understand when there were no threats about.

The pilot pointed downwards.

Nicole nudged Michelle awake while Erika peered out the window, poor Sandra still nursing an airsick bag. Their destination was located in an inlet along the northern tip of Baffin Island. Nestled between a rocky shoreline and northern brush, the community of 1,600 was named after the English astronomer John Pond, though many locals preferred the name *Mittimatalik*. Across the water to the north, Erika could see the mountainous peaks of Bylot Island, a vast migratory bird sanctuary covered in green lichen. Memories of Star teaching her the different types of avian eggs found on the island flashed through Erika's mind. The plane lurched yet again, then banked slowly to the left as the pilot lined up for their approach into Pond Inlet's airport.

It was then that Erika noticed the usually empty inlet waters were cluttered with at least six large grey ships. As they descended, she could see small boats dashing between the vessels and the town docks, presumably loading and unloading supplies. A bright red helicopter took off from one of the ships at anchor, carrying a huge net of oil drums under its airframe. Further in town, Erika observed a number of olive drab trucks and all-terrain vehicles, neatly parked in rows behind the community centre.

*Must be some training exercise*, she thought. Erika knew the military routinely operated in the north during the milder summer months. Just then the pilot raised his hand and made a circular motion with his finger.

"What does that mean?" Nicole asked apprehensively.

"It's ok," Erika reassured her. "It means we have to circle around and make another landing attempt."

Erika looked down to see the gravel runway below them rush by, as well as... *is that a crashed airplane?*

By now, all four Vermont students were staring out their windows at the mangled remains of a grey Boeing fuselage, resting against one end of the runway. Its engines had clearly been torn away from its wings.

"Now that's reassuring," Michelle said dryly.

Dr Liam Holstrom sat in the Pond Inlet airport terminal, flipping through an old hardcover book. Terminal was a generous term for the facility. In reality, it was simply a large cement room with a few chairs and a lone vending machine in the corner. Liam was the only occupant, waiting for the arrival of his daughter and her three university friends. The next few days were likely to be very emotional for Liam and his family, given the upcoming memorial to his late wife, Star. At the moment, however, family was the last thing on his mind. He flipped through the pages of a 1980s archaeology textbook he had found at his in-laws' house. *Archaeology and the Ancients* had been Liam's go-to literature during his graduate student days. The book was a guide to everything from the early Mesopotamian civilisation that had surrounded the Persian Gulf, to the fourteenth century Aztec and Inca empires of Central America. He had left a crate full of his academic works in Pond Inlet years ago, with the intent of keeping a stock of primary sources handy for his annual summer research expeditions. Despite the arrival of the Internet and its magical wonders, his father-in-law had kept the crate of books safe. With no cellular coverage at the moment in Pond Inlet, likely due to lingering atmospheric interference, uncovering his old textbooks was proving helpful and timely.

*Where is it?* Liam wondered as he read through the index. Ever since yesterday's confidential military briefing, he had been obsessed with uncovering what the intricate symbols were he had witnessed. The professor flipped to a series of hieroglyphics from ancient Egypt and slowly ran his fingers over each translated meaning. None triggered his memory. Next it was on to the Greeks, then the Byzantines, but still nothing. Liam placed the book down in frustration. His instincts told him he was chasing a fantasy. Despite how fascinating yesterday's presentation on the *Poseidon* crash was, there had to be a reasonable explanation for what brought down the $200 million dollar aircraft.

*Maybe this is just an elaborate Russian psychological ruse after all,* Liam thought. It made the most sense and all the motives fit: a desire to test Russian stealth technology while embarrassing the West, all for the sake of enhancing Moscow's prestige abroad. Even the idea of a missing submarine could be a hoax, or a deliberate cover story. A means to justify moving multiple Russian warships into North American waters, under the guise of a humanitarian search and rescue operation. If this were a trick, it would explain the unknown energy weapon that apparently brought down the navy plane, especially if fired from a submerged platform like a *Yasen*-class attack sub. And yet, that symbol somehow carved into the crashed fuselage. That familiar symbol which Liam sketched onto a napkin for the tenth time that morning.

"What are you, my friend?" he sighed to himself. Liam knew it was only a matter of time before Brigadier-General Tremblay, or one of her staff, discovered that his security clearance had long-since expired. Until then, he would continue to attend the daily commander's update briefings; all in the hope of ascertaining more information about yet another unexplained event, during an increasingly peculiar Arctic summer.

Liam was startled from his thoughts by the roar of two turbo-prop engines reverse cycling outside the terminal window.

The *Twin Otter* came to a halt in a cloud of dust next to the Pond Inlet airport building. As the engines throttled back, two local ground crew personnel placed wooden chocks against the airplane's giant rubber tyres. The dust had not yet settled when the rear hatch opened, the inner doorframe dual purposed with a set of folding stairs. Erika was the first to emerge, followed by Sandra and the others. They each took out their earplugs and made various yawning gestures to alleviate the pressure in their auditory canals.

"Welcome to Pond Inlet," Erika exclaimed with a grin. The response was less than enthusiastic.

"Who's that?" Nicole asked, pointing at the terminal doorway.

"Dad!"

Without hesitation, Erika ran towards her father, her arms flung wide open. A slightly taller man, Liam embraced his daughter as her head buried itself against his chest. Suddenly overcome with emotion, she began to cry. He held her close for a good minute, gently whispering in her ear. "It's all right, cub, I'm here now."

Erika pulled away slightly and looked up at her father through tear-soaked eyes. She did not realise how much she had missed him all summer until this very moment. It was as though all the pain of her mother's loss, which she'd tried to suppress while in Vermont, now boiled to the surface. She hugged her dad again, holding him as tight as she could.

Liam glanced up to see three very fit varsity athletes looking back at him rather awkwardly. "Cub, maybe you should introduce me to your friends?"

"What?" Erika looked up. "Oh gosh, of course."

She grabbed her father's hand and brought him over to meet her teammates. Three selfless women who had travelled with Erika for seventy-two hours, in four different airplanes, all for her emotional support.

"Dad, this is Nicole Gibson from New York. She's a junior at Vermont and is our team's assistant captain. And this is Michelle Lavoix. She grew up near UVM in Burlington and speaks fluent French."

Liam shook hands with the pair, while Michelle glanced at Erika, mouthing the words, "Your Dad's kinda cute."

Erika glared at Michelle, who shrugged while raising an eyebrow.

"And Dad, this is my roommate and our team's amazing goalie, Sandra Bruster."

Sandra extended her right hand towards Liam, but quickly covered her mouth before dry heaving towards the tarmac. Erika again rubbed her back.

"Sorry, Dad, the flight was a bit bumpy."

Liam smiled gently. It was clear his daughter had become the social glue for her new set of friends. This was a welcome change from her painful high school years.

"Dr Holstrom, what happened over there?" Nicole asked, pointing towards the wrecked navy plane at the end of the runway.

"It was hit by lighting during a search and rescue flight," he said. "There aren't any cranes big enough to move the wreckage so it will have to sit there, probably until next summer. Don't worry though, everyone made it out safely. And you can call me Liam."

Michelle perked up at the professor's lack of formality. She moved closer towards him with an inquisitive gaze.

"What were they searching for, Liam?" Michelle asked, pausing deliberately before saying his name. Erika rolled her eyes.

"A missing Russian submarine," he said.

"Seriously?" Nicole asked, turning away from the downed *Poseidon* wreckage. Until then, Nicole's only exposure to the navy had been shunning the advances of drunken sailors during New York's fleet week. "When did it go missing?"

"A few weeks ago," Liam said. "Well, if it's actually missing. Look, we should get you to my in-laws' house. They are anxious to see their granddaughter, and meet you three. They don't get many visitors up here, so it'll be nice to have company that can distract them from..." His words trailed off.

Erika picked up on her father's sudden anguish and moved in for another hug. Her friends also read his body language and gestured towards the terminal building. Their luggage was now sitting on a cart by the entrance. Liam regained his composure and offered to help with their baggage. Michelle swooped in and looped her arm through Liam's in an effort to distract him further from his wounded thoughts.

"Your daughter tells me you're a history buff." She batted her eyes as the group moved to the terminal. "I loooove history."

Erika stopped as the others went inside.

Something was watching her. She could feel it. Something ravenous. She glanced about in all directions, looking first past the parked *Twin Otter*, then towards Pond Inlet in the distance. Erika's eyes then fixed on the grey fuselage of the downed *Poseidon*. She took a few steps towards the smashed aircraft, before her instincts told her otherwise.

*I know you're watching me*, she thought slowly. *I can feel your hunger.*

The hairs on the back of her neck stood up as she felt a warm sensation against her chest. To her mild surprise, the ancient amulet around her neck started to glow. She gently pulled it out, letting it dangle over the top of her sweater. She sensed the air was heavy, her own adrenaline flowing through her veins. Again she moved towards the mangled grey fuselage. Slowly. Deliberately.

*I'm not afraid of you.*

Erika was learning to trust her emerging senses. She refused to call them powers since it sounded ridiculous. Yet there was no denying she had abilities. She felt it, and so did whatever was out there, watching her. Stalking her.

Erika's eyes caught the side of the shattered flying machine. Long gashes burned into the width of the plane started to gently glow green. She canted her head sideways to make out the symbols. It didn't trigger any recollection in her mind, and yet seemed familiar. She then sensed that the presence, or whatever it was, felt uneasy, unsure of what to make of her. This was something new for Erika. Up until now, her feelings and premonitions had only manifested themselves in times of danger, or extreme physical activity, like on the hockey rink. Now she felt she could read emotions being projected.

"What are you?" she breathed, her fists tense.

"Erika," a voice behind her called out. "We gotta go!" It was Sandra calling from the terminal building. "Your Dad is waiting with the others in his truck."

"Ok, I'll be right there," she yelled back, eyes still fixed on the crash site.

Erika scanned the scene before her one last time before turning and running in the direction of the building entrance. She sprinted towards the door. It reminded her of how as a child, she hated going into the basement of the family home. Dark and damp, she always took two steps at a time when climbing back upstairs from fetching something in her parents' pantry. *No boogieman is going to catch me*, she'd convinced herself at the time. That was how she felt now. When she reached the doorframe of the building, she glanced back one last time at the airfield tarmac. The sense of foreboding was gone. The glass door closed behind her as she ran to join the others.

In the distance, something slipped back into the shadows.

# CHAPTER 12

Katherine hung up the encrypted satellite phone with a sigh. Her bosses in Ottawa and Washington were coming under increasing pressure to show results. The search for the missing submarine *Volkov* was already several weeks old with nothing found, a fact Moscow was keen to exploit for its propaganda purposes. When Russian military assets were prohibited from joining the initial search in North American waters, the Kremlin liberally painted the rescue effort as a fiasco. This narrative was successfully reinforced with daily images of grieving widows in Murmansk, home port of the missing submarine. Katherine knew the *Volkov's* clandestine reasons for being in the Davis Strait were now irrelevant to public opinion. What mattered was that human lives had likely been lost, and the blame was increasingly being pointed at her.

"I don't buy it," her J2 intelligence officer protested. "General, it just doesn't make any sense." Most of the key headquarters staff in Pond Inlet had been on the call with their commander.

"If the *Volkov* sank," the J2 continued, "we'd have surely known about it. Between the shallow depth of the Davis Strait and the sensitivity of our underwater sonar network across the North Atlantic ocean floor, we'd have heard any anomaly."

"Anomaly?" Katherine raised her eyebrow.

"Yes ma'am, the sound of a submarine imploding or its hull impacting the seabed would leave a seismic signature loud enough for us to detect. It's how we eventually found the USS *Scorpion* in the sixties, and the Russians located the *Kursk* back in 2000."

Katherine looked over her American counterpart with scepticism. He was nothing if not tenacious. "What are you saying, J2?"

"General, I'm saying the Russian sub is still out there, and I bet it was the *Volkov* that brought down the P-8 *Poseidon* Lieutenant-Commander Gonzalez was flying."

Katherine listened patiently to her intelligence officer, who continued while laying out a maritime navigational chart on the folding table before them.

"Look at the evidence. The Russians lost contact with their sub somewhere in this location," he circled an area in the north-eastern search sector. "It's the same area where all those French fishing vessels went missing this past spring. Then look at this…" The American drew a red line across the map outlining the flight route of the downed P-8 aircraft from Thule. He continued, using the navy plane's call sign. "Blue fox four-two-niner picked up a surface contact here, roughly the same spot as the *Volkov's* last known position according to Moscow. We've reviewed the flight data records multiple times and there was definitely something on the water, according to the *Poseidon's* sensors. The camera angles all confirm nothing was visible on the frozen surface, which means the contact must have been inside or under the ice, just before the crazy electrical storm started."

Katherine looked up at the American pensively. "You don't think it was a crazy electrical storm, do you?"

"No, ma'am. We know the Russians have been investing heavily in cyber technology, artificial intelligence, and even energy weapons. They can't beat us in a conventional fight, so it makes sense they'd focus on hybrid capabilities that make attribution difficult. Since we can't prove with certainty it was them, all they have to do is deny their involvement and offer a believable counter narrative. It's what they did in both Georgia and Ukraine a few years back."

"What about the images from the *Poseidon's* monitors," Katherine interjected, "or those voices captured by the flight data recorder?"

"Ma'am, with all due respect, listen to yourself. The Russian mind games have clearly worked, since we're actually considering the possibility of ghosts bringing down a state-of-the-art surveillance plane. Do we really believe Casper and his buddies did this?"

Katherine looked back at her J2, somewhat annoyed. He had made his point, but didn't need to be patronising about it. Despite the pilot's sworn testimony, it was more probable the Russians had managed to hack the *Poseidon's* in-flight systems, while bombarding it with energy pulses from a submerged platform. It was increasingly evident to Katherine that her headquarters was the likely victim of an elaborate Russian deception campaign. The general was not pleased. She turned to her chief of staff and J3 operations officer, who'd both been seated quietly next to her.

"J3, I want to mount another search of the area outlined just now by the J2. Use any air assets we have that can put an insertion team on the ice. Major Eleanor Matthews and her Arctic troops should be available. Liaise with the Danes since it's in their sector. Make sure that Eleanor reviews the rules of engagement with her personnel."

The J3 acknowledged his commander and scurried off. Katherine then looked over to her chief of staff.

"COS, would you be so kind as to invite the Russian defence attaché, Colonel Borishov, to my office. I'd like you and the senior military police officer on duty to join me."

Acting Captain Ivan Egorov cursed at his watch. They were already twelve hours behind schedule, with more delays expected due to increasing sea ice, this despite the warmer temperatures. The Russian frigate *Nikolay Khabalov* had been on a tropical deployment to Venezuela when word arrived from Moscow of a missing *Yasen*-class attack submarine near Greenland. Shock had turned to frustration as the *Khabalov* was forced to linger off Cuba, waiting for various governments to make up their minds about allowing the Russian warship to sail into North American waters. Sensible diplomatic voices had prevailed, and for the last four days the Russian frigate had been racing north up the U.S. eastern seaboard. It was only once the *Khabalov* rounded the northern tip of Newfoundland that their progress had slowed to seven knots, due to the prevalence of massive icebergs.

By all accounts, the *Khabalov* was an impressive ship. The newest *Admiral Ghorshkov*-class frigate, it boasted a deadly arsenal of anti-ship missiles and high-speed torpedoes, all supported by a sophisticated array of sensors and radar. It also carried a single Ka-27 anti-submarine helicopter, which was currently airborne twenty nautical miles ahead of its mother ship, searching for a path through the growing ice floes. As a result of its lightweight construction, the frigate's two diesel engines burned less fuel than earlier Russian warships. This allowed the vessel to stay at sea at least a month without resupply. At only 5,400 tons, the *Khabalov* was also fast, able to sail in excess of thirty-five knots. For all the ship's capabilities, Ivan still shook his head.

*What good is a sports car when you're stuck in rush hour traffic?*

The acting captain's mood was grim, and had been for several days. If word of a missing Russian submarine had come as a rude shock for Ivan, the news that it was the *Volkov* was a punch to the gut. His older brother and hero, Sergei Egorov, was the *Volkov's* captain.

Sergei and Ivan were one year apart and had grown up near St Petersburg. Born in the dying days of the Soviet Union, they had come of age during the humiliation of the late 1990's Russian economic collapse. Ivan remembered clearly their unemployed mother sending the two brothers to fish for their dinner in the local stream. Their father, once a proud physicist in the Soviet space agency, had been reduced to scrubbing floors at a metro station by the turn of the millennium. His humiliation compounded his need for alcohol, a liquid escape he could also no longer afford. Eventually the need for vodka gave way to other chemicals, mainly cheap and industrial. Ivan and Sergei's father had been found dead behind an abandoned metal factory, his liver destroyed by years of substance abuse. When it came time shortly after for the boys to undertake compulsory military service, first Sergei, then Ivan, joined the navy. They both figured it was their best hope for a steady income, however meagre, and a chance to escape the depression of home. While Ivan became a weapons officer on warships, Sergei embraced the underwater fleet, finding his niche with fast-attack submarines. He rose through the ranks quickly, with the pinnacle of any naval career being command of a ship. In Sergei's case, he was rewarded twice. First with command of a refurbished *Kilo*-class attack submarine in the Black Sea, and more recently, the *Volkov*. Ivan and his brother were at the sharp end of Russia's re-emergence as a world naval power. Propelled by its lucrative oil and gas economy, their homeland would once again be respected as an equal among superpowers. Their fellow officers had collectively made a pact to never again relive the agony of the 1990s, Russia's own decade of darkness. Ivan swore to find out what had become of his beloved brother and the *Volkov's* crew, no matter what the cost.

"Bridge, CIC, air contact bearing zero three zero, range thirty nautical miles, altitude eight hundred."

Ivan acknowledged the report from the combat information centre's duty officer and moved to the air search radar terminal in the centre of the bridge. The monitor allowed the *Khabalov's* acting captain to see the same images being tracked in the CIC. With the ship's actual captain back in Russia on compassionate leave, the ultra-modern warship was Ivan's to command.

"Helm, increase speed to ten knots, bearing zero three zero," Ivan ordered. "Inform the Ka-27 of our course change and vector the helicopter accordingly."

All personnel on the bridge gently leaned forward to compensate for the increased speed of the ship under their feet. The churning sound of twin, diesel-electric engines deep in the *Khabalov's* belly were joined by the occasional bump of floating ice fragments grazing the frigate's hull. Ivan ordered additional personnel onto the forward deck to watch for icebergs. Even in the constant summer sunlight of the Arctic, he was taking no chances.

The intercom crackled to life. "Bridge, CIC, acoustic signature of the air contact denotes a rotary wing asset, likely an MH-60 *Seahawk*."

*That makes sense*, Ivan thought. He had read in both media reports and messages from Russian naval intelligence that the *Arleigh Burke*-class guided missile destroyer, USS *Samuel Ronaldson,* was taking part in the *Volkov's* search. It could carry at least two *Seahawk* helicopters if needed. Despite the technological leaps his own navy had made over the past twenty years, he still seethed with envy at his American counterparts.

*Keep it cool, Ivan. Don't do anything rash just yet. Not until we find out what happened to Sergei.*

"Bridge, CIC, we're beginning to detect significant atmospheric disruption to our north, which is affecting our air search radar," the voice across the intercom reported. "We still have positive contact with the Ka-27 and the *Seahawk*, but their signals are intermittent."

*Could they be jamming us?* Ivan thought. If that was the case, these Americans sure had some nerve. After all, the *Khabalov* was coming to help in the search for their own countrymen. They were no more a threat than the pod of pilot whales they had passed earlier in the day. Damn the Yankees and their superiority.

Ivan was the first to notice the green flashes on the horizon.

He grabbed his binoculars and moved to the bridge's forward windows, straining to look north. Several of the ship's company did the same. It was only then he noticed the distant skyline had taken on an olive glow. More green flashes, then a visible explosion along the horizon.

The intercom switched on. "Bridge, CIC, we've lost contact with the Ka-27. I no longer have radar, nor voice communication."

Ivan took the headset dangling from the roof.

"CIC, bridge, confirm you have lost contact due to atmospheric interference affecting the radar?"

"Negative, the Ka-27 no longer appears on any of our sensors, nor is the *Seahawk* visible on radar."

Ivan moved back to the air search radar monitor. Though the display was clouded with static, he could still see the pixilated image ahead of his ship, which was now empty.

*A mid-air collision*, Ivan thought in despair. *Those damn hot-headed Yankees and their cowboy flying.*

Tensions between the United States and Russia had been mounting since what Ivan's president called the "reunification of Crimea" in 2014. Long-range reconnaissance flights, abandoned by both sides after the Cold War as a peace dividend, were once again occurring in the Arctic. In addition, near collisions between warships and *unprofessional* flying by Russian and NATO fighter jets operating in close proximity, had taken place several times across Eastern Europe. It was only a matter of time before someone made a mistake.

"Helm, maintain current speed and heading," Ivan ordered, and then pulled the intercom close. "All hands, action stations, prepare for deployment of the search and rescue boat. Medical personnel to the sick bay."

For now, Ivan would do the right thing.

Katherine was staring down the Russian defence attaché when her intelligence officer burst in the room. Realising Katherine was not alone, the J2 covered his mouth while whispering to her. "General, the USS *Samuel Ronaldson* is reporting they've lost contact with their helo."

*Damn.*

"Colonel Borishov," she breathed, "you'll have to excuse me for a moment." The attaché started to protest before Katherine closed the door behind her, leaving the Russian with her chief of staff.

The Arctic headquarters in Pond Inlet's community centre was already alive with activity. Katherine took her position at the head of a series of flat screens and looked to her J3 operations officer. "Report, please."

"Ma'am, at approximately 20:44 Zulu, the USS *Samuel Ronaldson*, operating in the south-western search zone, dispatched one of its helos to act as overwatch due to deteriorating sea ice conditions." The J3 pointed to the electronic map to his front. Katherine mentally deducted five hours from the reported time, since *Zulu* was based on Greenwich Mean Time, or GMT in England. The operations officer continued. "General, roughly thirty minutes later the Russian frigate *Nikolay Khabalov* entered the *Ronaldson's* search area from the south and dispatched its own helo."

Katherine's face was tense. She could tell where this was leading, but hoped she was wrong. The J3 pressed on.

"Though there was considerable electronic interference at the time, at roughly 21:20 Zulu, radar contact was lost with the *Khabalov* and *Ronaldson* helos. From what we gather, they were both within the same grid square when this occurred. Ma'am, at this point we are assuming a mid-air collision between the helicopters. The *Ronaldson* has undertaken its search and rescue procedures, and we believe the *Khabalov* is doing the same."

Katherine looked about the room. All eyes were on her.

"Any survivors, J3?" she asked quietly.

"Unknown at this time, ma'am, though no emergency beacons have been detected."

Katherine pulled a notepad from the right cargo pocket of her pants and scribbled down several points before directing the operations officer. "Engage the search and rescue protocols if not already done, and request SAR aircraft to support us from Goose Bay and Thule. Open up a secure line to both Ottawa and Washington."

The headquarters staff started carrying out her orders when Katherine glanced grudgingly at her closed office door.

"J3, please ask Colonel Borishov to join me. He deserves to know what has happened."

Lieutenant Evans clambered out of the frigid water onto the windswept ice floe. He was already shivering uncontrollably as he hauled the emergency Arctic survival kit up beside him. The orange rescue bag was attached to his waist by a nylon string, which he quickly cut loose with a multi-tool. His flight suit was drenched, but he dare not take it off yet as it temporarily provided some insulation. He hacked at the rescue bag's frozen zipper, but to no avail. Using his multi-tool, the young American navy pilot cut into the survival bag's thick nylon, spilling some of its contents onto the ice. He quickly took off his flight helmet and replaced it with a warm wool hat. It instantly made a difference, even with his wet hair. Next he pulled out the one-piece immersion suit and winter boots, both wrapped in waterproof plastic. He could barely feel his fingers as he cut away the laces of his frozen footwear, replacing them with dry wool socks. Next he slithered out of his wet flight suit, groaning as the bitter wind stung his exposed flesh, and pulled on the orange overalls lined with a fleece interior. With this task accomplished, he laced up the dry pair of polar boots and donned two oversized mittens.

He was alive. The young pilot was in shock and suffering from hypothermia, but he was alive. He looked about the floating sheets of ice where he now found himself. In the distance, he could see bits of his helicopter still smouldering among the Arctic waves. The tail rotor had disintegrated, probably from a lightning strike, causing the *Seahawk* to spin violently as the machine lost torque control. His co-pilot had screamed upon impact with the water, as green energy pulses electrocuted the man he'd known since flight school. Evans barely made it out of the front cabin before the *Seahawk* slipped under the surface, taking their trapped crew chief in the rear compartment to the bottom. Slowly he tried to piece together what had happened as he dug in the survival kit for the emergency beacon. The shock and cold were playing tricks with his mind, the clattering of his teeth echoing about his head. His movements were becoming more deliberate, almost lazy. Evans knew he needed to be rescued, and soon, if he was to survive. He had to find and activate the emergency beacon.

The noise behind him sounded like footsteps.

He paused, concentrating as hard as he could through the confusing effects of the cold. It was definitely footsteps. Two sets, no three. Their pace was slow and methodical, but footsteps nonetheless. Had rescue arrived already? Evans again tried to focus. He knew from his training that hallucinations were an early symptom of hypothermia. Could he be imagining a rescue party that wasn't there? He turned about. To his delight, he noticed three large figures slowly moving towards him across the ice. They appeared to be on the adjacent ice floe, a small body of water separating Evans from his would-be rescuers. Still they approached. The pilot waved.

*I'm here*, he thought, too cold to yell.

Evans knew he must be in severe shock since the three figures appeared to float directly across the open ocean to his ice shelf. Clearly, the cold was taking its toll. As they came closer, he was able to make out their clothing. Brown and grey rags, interlaced with various straps that appeared to be leather belts. Evans couldn't yet see their faces, but he could tell all three had long, ragged beards that fluttered in the Arctic wind. The one on the left appeared to wear some form of metal helmet, while the other two had on brown hats made of animal hide. Evans was down-wind and caught the first scent of his rescuers. It was putrid. He instantly began to dry-heave at the stench. Covering his mouth with a scarf, he looked back at the approaching figures and noticed long metal objects in their hands. A spear perhaps, maybe even a sword. Were these Inuit hunters? At this point, it didn't matter who his saviours were, as long as they were friendly.

The rusted blade from the lead figure cut the pilot in half, leaving his steaming remains scattered about the windswept ice.

# CHAPTER 13

Erika sat with her mother on a grassy hilltop, looking at the old settlement below. It was summer and the westerly wind was warm against her skin. She knew they were somewhere up north, the puffins flying nearby gave it away. Erika gazed past the settlement at the deep blue ocean. Waves slowly lapped against a pebble beach. She could see the occasional iceberg lumbering by, surrounded by smaller pieces of floating ice. The village to her front was made up of several longhouses covered in natural thatch roofs. Erika could tell the inhabitants were home by the smoke rising from the stone chimneys. There were half a dozen dwellings in sight, with salted fish hanging from multiple ropes tied between the homes. Along the shoreline, Erika could see a collection of wooden boats resting on makeshift berms of dried mud.

This place felt like home. In fact, the more Erika studied the shoreline, the more it seemed familiar. Across the water, she was certain she could see the mountains of Bylot Island. Even the hill they sat on tweaked her memory, but instead of being covered by pebbles and sand, the land was lush with green grass and wild wheat. She knew this was a dream. The presence of her mother, Star, proved it, but no matter; for the first time in weeks, Erika felt calm, warm, and safe.

A small blonde girl ran out from one of the longhouses. Erika recognised her from earlier dreams. She was still wearing a long brown sack as clothing, tied off at the waist with string. A second child emerged and gave chase to the first. Their laughter carried up the side of the hill to where mother and daughter sat.

*Is this Pond Inlet?* Erika thought.

*Perhaps*, she sensed her mother respond, *in another time.*

*How are you here, mother?*

Star turned towards her daughter. *It's your dream, my dear.*

They both smiled quietly.

Erika rested her head against her mother's shoulder as they watched the two children chase each other about.

*What are skraeling? I asked father, but he never answered.*

*We were, supposedly. In ages past.*

*Says who?*

Star gestured at the settlement.

*And who are they, mother?*

*Some called them kavdlunait, from away.*

Both women watched a bear of a man dressed in leather emerge from one of the longhouses and yell at the children. His words immediately sent the youngsters scurrying back inside. The man walked over to a small fire pit filled with red embers. His long hair was braided at the back, while his blonde beard appeared recently trimmed. From their vantage point, Erika and her mother could see the man pull a long iron rod from the embers, its tip molten hot. He placed the rod against a large stone and began pounding it with a hammer. Each hit sent red sparks flying in the air. His blows were steady and consistent. Thump, thump...

*I miss you, mother.*

Thump, thump, thump...

*I know, cub.*

Thump, thump, thump...

Erika awoke in the bunk bed of her grandparents' guest room.

Outside, a tremendous noise was vibrating the wooden cabin walls. A deep, steady rhythm that sounded like a hundred drums beating in unison. She noticed Sandra in her pyjamas, already awake and looking intently out the window. Erika clambered down from her perch and cozied up beside her roommate. She looked outside, past the back deck to see what Sandra was watching. In an open field sat two massive cigar-shaped helicopters painted olive drab, each with a pair of powerful rotor blades spinning impossibly fast. They both looked to be the size of a school bus. The flying machines faced away from the lodge, allowing Erika to see their giant rear ramps, lowered to the ground.

Out of nowhere, a tall woman in a camouflage uniform ran up to one of the open ramps. She was wearing a backpack and carried some sort of object that appeared to be a weapon. A man in a grey flight suit emerged from the rear of the thundering beast and proceeded to exchange hand signals with the woman. She then turned about and waved towards the bushes off to Erika's left. Dozens of uniformed men and women burst out of the scrub, racing for the thundering green machines. Once all were onboard, the tall woman climbed the rear ramp last as it closed. The roar of the engines increased to an oppressive volume. Slowly, the two behemoths rose from the ground, large black tyres hanging from their flat underbellies. As soon as the massive flying machines lifted off they were gone, the steady *thumping* of their rotor blades echoing against the distant mountains. Within a minute all was quiet again, save for a few dogs barking in the village.

"Cool," Sandra said with a smile. "I wonder where they're going?"

Erika shrugged and looked at her childhood cuckoo clock on the wall, which showed just past five in the morning. Her thoughts were still in a haze after being awakened from such a deep sleep. She started remembering bits and pieces of her dream. Erika so wished to fall back asleep, even if only to spend a few more moments with her mother. Later that day was to be Star's memorial service. It would be a celebration of her life, overlain with the poems she used to compose. As with many in the community, the lingering negative effects on her parents of the abandoned Canadian residential school system had left a bitter taste in Star's mouth. Created in the late 1800s to forcibly assimilate generations of indigenous children, the last institution had mercifully been closed in the 1990s. In Star's mind, organised religion was to blame. Despite all this, she had indeed been spiritual, having embraced the teachings of her elders, but always on her terms. Star had instilled the same belief system in her daughter. A natural respect for tradition and the environment, mixed with a healthy scepticism of modernity.

Erika was distracted from her daydream by the gentle sounds of Sandra snoring. She was constantly amazed how quickly her roommate was able to fall asleep. Making sure not to wake her slumbering friend, she slowly made her way back to the top bunk. As Erika pulled the covers over herself, she noticed her amulet necklace dangling from the bedpost. As always, it was comfortingly warm to the touch.

Erika's maternal grandparents gently helped each other down from the podium. Her grandfather had delivered a moving eulogy about their daughter. His wife had then offered her own thoughts about Star, before ending with a poem. Erika sat in the front row of the hall, beside her father. In recent years, larger funeral services normally took place in the Pond Inlet community centre instead of a church. As this was not possible due to the current military presence in town, the local hunters and trappers association building was a worthy substitute. Erika looked about the room. She recognised a few familiar faces from her youth, mainly childhood friends of her mother. The mayor was seated across from Erika and her father, along with several elders dressed in mourning clothes. Her three university friends sat behind her in solidarity, each quietly wiping away tears.

Unlike most modern funerals, Star had requested her memorial be incorporated into a five-day mourning period called *naasiivik*. At the end of the five days, a crystalline flint known as a firestone would be thrown against the ground in order to create a mass of sparks. This gesture would symbolise the end of *naasiivik*, and was intended to provide emotional closure for the bereaved. Instead of a burial, Star had chosen cremation, with her ashes to be sprinkled in the nearby Arctic Ocean.

Liam gently nudged his daughter, signalling that it was her turn to speak. Erika looked up at her father who attempted a brave smile. He had already made the decision not to speak, his current emotional state too painful for words. Erika gripped his hand firmly, then glanced over to her now seated grandparents. They nodded towards her in support. She was dressed in black, a long sweater overtop a pair of dark jeans. Around her neck hung the ancient amulet her father had given her, while in her hands she gripped a series of folded papers. She proceeded to the podium at the front of the hall, and with all the courage she could muster, turned to face the audience.

"Mom," she said through tears, "you were everything to me. You were my mother, my mentor, my best friend." She briefly pulled back from her notes, heaving to catch her breath before continuing. "And you were my hero."

Erika spoke eloquently about her late mother for ten minutes, though it felt like an eternity. She reminisced about her earliest memories playing with Star in Minnesota, and had the audience laughing over the pranks they'd played against Liam. She spoke of her mother's determination to raise a strong and independent daughter, free of any self-created barriers or psychological walls. Erika moved the crowd with the intimacy of Star's love for Liam, while acknowledging the difficulty of their initial long-distance relationship. She thanked all assembled for attending, especially her teammates from Vermont. Finally she looked over through tears at her father and grandparents.

"Lastly, I want to thank my grandparents for raising the wonderful woman that was my mother. For encouraging the love affair that became my parent's marriage, even if it meant Star would move away forever. In closing, I'd like to speak directly to my father, Liam. Dad, Mom loved you with every ounce of her being. You two were soul mates with a passion and respect for each other I can only hope to find some day. We will get through this together as a family, and I love you dearly." Erika then turned to the audience. "My mother was sixty-three years old, and she was still too young to die. I love you so very much."

Erika collapsed against the podium, her last bit of emotional stamina now drained. The tears rolled down her face as Liam stood, easing her back to her seat. The audience quietly applauded out of respect. Once seated, Sandra reached forward and gently squeezed Erika's shoulder in support. Delivering the speech had been one of the most difficult moments in Erika's life, but she had performed admirably with quiet eloquence and determination.

Her mother would have been proud.

The community members filed out of the memorial service, under the glow of the Arctic summer sun. The weather over the last few days had improved. Even so, the persistent green aurora borealis lingered along the northern horizon. Erika walked arm-in-arm between her grandparents, her father trailing quietly behind. The older couple didn't say much, but Erika could tell from their expressions they deeply mourned the loss of their only daughter. Erika's grandmother patted the young woman's arm. She acknowledged how difficult it must have been for Erika to deliver such moving remarks about Star. She then placed a small firestone in her granddaughter's hand. Erika nodded her understanding at the gesture, and placed the flint in her leather purse. The elderly couple both gave Erika a hug before proceeding towards their wooden lodge at the edge of town. The plan was to sprinkle Star's ashes from their motorboat in a few days' time, but for now, the two needed to rest.

"You did really well, cub," Liam said softy.

"Yeah, that was really powerful," Sandra offered as she walked up to Erika, Nicole and Michelle with her. "Is there anything you need or want? Are you hungry? Maybe you want a drink?"

Erika shook her head gently. She acknowledged the kindness of her friends' presence, but admitted she was in no mood to be indoors. Somehow being outside and breathing the crisp Arctic air calmed her nerves. She looked over at Liam.

"Dad, if it's okay with the girls, I'm going to go with them for a small walk down by the docks. I could use some sisterhood at the moment." Her three friends nodded their approval.

"Of course, cub," Liam replied. "I'm going to head over to the community centre and see what the military types have been up to. It will be good to get my mind off things." Erika gave her father a hug then moved off with her friends in the direction of the harbour, some ten minutes away. They passed several homes, many in various states of disrepair. As they walked, Erika explained the socio-economic realities the remote community faced. She suddenly stopped in her tracks.

*Someone is in pain.*

She looked past the confused faces of her teammates, towards a schoolyard.

*Please don't be sad, I'm on my way.*

Erika moved in the direction of the schoolyard, with her friends following. As they approached the academic building, they could see a group of young boys no older than ten playing ball hockey. Two nets sat at either end of the playground, with the youngsters slapping a rubber ball using wooden hockey sticks. In the corner of the yard, Erika noticed a young girl seated alone on a bench, crying. She walked up to the girl dressed in a hooded parka and sat down beside her.

"Hey there, why the long face?" Erika asked the girl, who appeared to be the same age as the boys. The child rubbed her nose with her sleeve, answering Erika and her friends through sobs.

"They won't let me play."

"Why not?" Sandra asked as she joined Erika on the bench.

"Because I'm a girl," she protested. All four women looked at each other. They could instantly relate to how the young one felt, based on their own experiences growing up playing hockey.

"Well, we'll have to fix that, won't we?" Michelle said encouragingly.

The little girl looked up at the foursome around her.

"What's your name?" Erika asked.

"Amber," the girl said softly.

"C'mon, Amber, we'll show these boys a thing or two," Nicole said triumphantly, and marched over to the group of youngsters playing. One of them slapped a ball towards the net but overshot, sending the rubber object directly at Nicole, who caught it mid-air.

"You boys up for a game of twenty-one?" She bellowed at the dozen or so young boys before her. They looked at each other, before their apparent leader walked over to Nicole.

"The four of you want to play against all of us?" he asked bemused.

"Not four, five," Erika declared, their new young friend running up beside her. The boy looked back at his teammates who egged him on. He gave his approval.

"There's one condition," Michelle interjected. "If we win, Amber gets to play with you from now on." The boy smirked, nodding his head in agreement.

The group of women walked over to a large garbage can filled with hockey sticks and selected their weapons of choice. Sandra set herself in front of the net while Erika and Nicole took up forward positions, with Michelle and Amber in defence. The boys outnumbered their opponents almost three to one, with every one of them on the field. The instant the lead boy dropped the rubber ball in the centre of the yard Erika was on it like a flash. She ran past her opponents, stick handling the ball with ease. She glanced over her shoulder to see Nicole racing up the left side of the yard and passed the ball over, through the legs of at least four boys. Nicole easily directed the pass into the opposing team's net, the goal marked by a cheer from the women present. Michelle looked over at Amber who was grinning from ear to ear.

It took less than thirty minutes for the Vermont players to reach a score of twenty-one. The boys did put up an impressive fight, scoring at least eight times against Sandra, much to her frustration. Even young Amber earned four points. The losing team reluctantly acknowledged their defeat, offering praise for Amber's skills. As agreed, she was invited to join the boys' team, with the two groups forming lines to shake hands.

*Danger.*

The mass of white fur bolted past the hockey players in a blur, taking Amber with it. Erika watched in horror as the young girl dangled by her parka hood from the massive beast's mouth. Amber screamed hysterically as the creature stopped by the schoolyard fence, cornered. It turned around and rose onto its hind legs. The animal stood at least three metres in the air, huge paws by its side. Erika recognised it to be a mature female polar bear, as did the local boys, who scattered behind her in a panic.

*Stop it.*

Erika stood her ground.

*Put her down.*

The polar bear dropped back down onto all four legs as Erika calmly approached the animal. The massive white beast released Amber's hood, allowing the girl to scramble away towards her new found friends.

"Holstrom, what the hell are you doing?" Nicole demanded.

"It's okay," Erika said, her eyes fixed on the polar bear. "I think I know a trick."

"You *think*?" gasped Michelle, her usually calm voice now filled with concern.

"Be cool," Erika urged, as much to herself as anything else.

She felt the warmth of the amulet against her chest while her heart raced. She continued towards the beast, which started to instinctively sway its head from side to side in a defensive gesture. She ignored the animal's physical warnings and forcefully walked up to the bear. It stopped its motion and stared at Erika.

*I know you're hungry.*

The bear whimpered. The changing climate was making it harder and harder for these northern predators to find their traditional prey, leading to unwanted forays into urban areas.

*I'm going to open the gate. There are seals down by the water.*

Erika tried hard to visualise the seals, projecting their presence into the bear's mind. The thought of their salty blubber made the predator's mouth water. It gave a warm growl. Erika gently rubbed the bear's snout. She could see it had a yellow tag clipped to its ear, no doubt placed by some well-meaning conservation officer. Erika walked past the animal to a metal gate and opened the latch. The polar bear hesitated, before slowly moving past her and trundling off into the shrubs that surrounded the schoolyard. Soon its white fur had disappeared in the direction of the ocean, as the glow of the amulet against her chest receded. Erika closed the gate behind her before starting back towards her shocked teammates.

Sandra was the first to speak. "Holstrom. What the hell?"

Erika shrugged. "My grandfather taught me. I guess it worked."

She felt guilty about her fib. It was the only thing she could think to say, short of the truth. Sandra seemed impressed while Nicole looked stunned. Michelle, however, hands on hips, raised an eyebrow.

"Incredible," she said flatly, the double meaning hard for Erika to avoid.

THE
ARCTIC REGIONS
OF
NORTH AMERICA
BY
EDW? WELLER, F.R.G.S.
PRINCE PATRICK ISLAND
PARRY ISLAND
MELVILLE ISLAND
BATHURST ISLAND
CORNWALL ISLAND
BANKS LAND
Melville Sound
Pr. of Wales
P? Albert Land
P? Albert Sound
Wollaston Land
Victoria Land
King William Land
Minto Inlet
Franklin B?
Great Bear Lake
Arctic Circle

# CHAPTER 14

The pair of *Seahawks* raced low across the frozen surface. From a distance, the grey helicopters resembled giant insects darting between jagged outcrops of snow and ice. The high-pitched whine of the rotor blades indicated the pilots were manoeuvring their machines at full throttle. They were roughly thirty minutes south-east of Pond Inlet, heading towards the open ocean of the Davis Strait. Flying conditions were slightly overcast, but nothing unusual for this time of year, except for the green glow of the northern horizon. The helicopters climbed rapidly to avoid a protrusion of ice that rose several hundred feet in the air. The pair descended just as quickly back to their original altitude. Though both aircraft were *Seahawks*, the lead helicopter had Danish markings, while the second was American.

Katherine sat in the back corner of the first *Seahawk*. She tried tracking their progress on the map feature of her tablet, but to no avail. The persistent atmospheric interference was scrambling the on-board navigation system. The pilots were essentially flying by dead reckoning, occasionally triangulating their direction via radio signals transmitted from their destination. Seated beside Katherine was the executive officer, or XO, for the USS *Samuel Ronaldson*. The Danish vessel *Knud Rasmussen* had earlier found the remains of a naval aviator from the XO's ship, which he now had the grim task of identifying. Katherine looked away.

*So much death*, she thought.

The apparent mid-air collision of an American and Russian helicopter two days earlier was still top of the international news headlines. While politicians in both Washington and Moscow beat their chests for the cameras, the incident was being treated locally as an unfortunate accident. The presence of the Russian defence attaché, Colonel Borishov, seated across from Katherine, was a testament to this prevailing viewpoint.

"General, the American helo will soon break away to conduct its re-supply task," the Danish pilot reported.

Whenever possible, helicopter crews liked to fly in pairs, especially in the Arctic. If one aircraft experienced a mechanical issue or had to ditch, the second was close by to assist. Katherine watched out her window as the trailing grey flying machine banked off to the left. In the distance, she could see its intended landing point, marked by a cloud of red smoke. She knew Major Eleanor Matthews and her Arctic troops had been down on the floating pack ice for at least forty-eight hours. Their mission was to locate the unidentified object several sonar scans had detected hidden somewhere on the ocean's frozen surface. Katherine thought back to the *Poseidon* pilot's testimony. She pondered at what they might have discovered, just before the surreal events that brought down their airplane.

*Maybe it was the missing Russian sub after all, using some kind of energy weapon. Then again...* Katherine looked off at the green sky to their north.

An alarm rang inside the cabin, signalling the helicopter's air defence sensors had been triggered. Katherine adjusted her headset and keyed the intercom, while Colonel Borishov looked about, confused.

"Pilot, report."

"Ma'am, we're being painted by a surface-to-air radar," the pilot said calmly. "It has a good lock on us."

Katherine looked over at Colonel Borishov, annoyed. The only non-NATO vessel in the region with the capability, and more importantly the gall, to target them was the Russian frigate *Nikolay Khabalov*. She signalled for the defence attaché to put on his headset while asking the pilot to open a channel to the *Khabalov*.

"Colonel Borishov, would you be so kind as to tell your naval colleagues to stop threatening my helicopter with their air defence radar?"

The man sheepishly complied and radioed in Russian to the *Khabalov*. As soon as he completed his transmission, the alarm bells inside the *Seahawk* stopped.

"Spasiba," Katherine thanked the colonel.

The Danish aircraft overflew the *Khabalov* a few minutes later. Katherine knew from intelligence reports that one of the ship's senior officers had a close family connection to the missing *Volkov* submarine. That same individual had a reputation for reckless behaviour, both on and off duty. She looked down at the brown and grey-hulled warship below. Its forward deck was sleek, occupied by a single auto cannon and vertical missile tubes. In contrast, the rear flight pad was cluttered with pieces of deformed metal. Katherine assumed the mangled wreckage was from the *Khabalov's* downed Ka-27 helicopter. The sight of two body bags next to the ship's hanger door confirmed her suspicion.

"General, fifteen minutes to the *Rasmussen*," the pilot indicated. Just enough time for Katherine to compose a personal note for her daughters, though how to describe a day like today. The more these puzzling events occurred, the harder it became to explain them. She was a rational commander, grounded in evidence-based thinking, but even her sensibilities were a bit creeped out as of late. Perhaps she would simply tell her young children how beautiful the Arctic water appeared under a near-constant sun, even if it was glowing green. The senior flag officer and mother of two began to write her letter.

The remains of the young American pilot were gently lowered onto a metal gurney. Doctor Rikke Larsen read the name *Evans* on what was left of the aviator's identification tags. On first inspection, the severe trauma to his body suggested he died during the actual helicopter crash, but Rikke knew better. The search party found what was left of him dressed in a survival suit, his flight uniform discarded nearby. Not only had he survived the crash, he'd managed to get onto the ice and change into warmer clothes. As to what happened next, that remained a mystery.

Rikke was keenly aware she did not have much time. While she worked in the *Rasmussen's* sickbay, a military aircraft from Pond Inlet was en route to their ship. Its passengers included the general overseeing the missing submarine search efforts, as well as a Russian defence attaché. The powers that be were working with the theory that the late pilot's helicopter had collided with a similar aircraft from the nearby Russian frigate *Khabalov*. Once Rikke's preliminary examination was complete, an American officer would try to identify the pilot, then transport the deceased back to the USS *Samuel Ronaldson*.

Something behind the pilot's ear caught Rikke's attention. Using her latex gloved hands she gently turned the aviator's head for a closer inspection. Her eyes widened. Just behind the left ear lobe were two vertical triangles burned into the skin. Rikke stepped back. It was the same mark she'd recently found on a pair of dead French fishermen. She ensured the mini-camera on her protective glasses had a good shot of the symbol. As with the French sailors, there was no apparent scarring, indicating the mark was made post-mortem. She then examined the gaping wound across the pilot's mid-torso. The aviator had essentially been cut in half, so Rikke had a clear view inside the frozen remains. It appeared a blade of some sort was responsible for the damage, but not from a propeller. As she slowly rubbed the edge of the wound, small orange flakes fell into her gloved hand. She held the thin particles up to her glasses.

*It's rusted metal, but from what?*

She placed the orange bits in a plastic bag, marking it with the pilot's name and date. Rikke would have to examine the metal pieces later. Outside the ship's hull, she could hear the vibrations of an approaching chopper.

The Danish pilot flared his helicopter, angling its nose with the *Rasmussen's* rear-landing pad. The seas were relatively calm, with the *Seahawk's* wheels touching down on the first attempt. As the aircraft powered down, several sailors pushed open the side doors, allowing the passengers to disembark. Katherine stepped out first, followed by Colonel Borishov and the *Ronaldson's* XO. The ship's captain, Lieutenant-Commander Magnus Jakobson, greeted Katherine and her party with a salute.

"General, it's a pleasure to see you again and welcome aboard. If you don't mind, we'd like to provide you a quick update before we see Doctor Larsen in the sickbay."

Always the empathetic commander, Katherine turned to the American XO, ensuring Magnus' timetable worked for him. Within seconds of the man's approval, they were all scampering up an external ladder towards the bridge. Colonel Borishov trailed behind them in a huff. On entering the ship's primary control room, the visitors removed their waterproof jackets and huddled around a maritime chart in the centre of the bridge. Nicknamed a bird table in the military due to the vantage point it provided, the one on the *Rasumssen* depicted most of the Davis Strait. A young Danish sailor handed Katherine a freshly made café Americano, which caused her to smile.

*Only a warship built in Europe would have an espresso machine.*

"General," Magnus started, "this information is current as of 14:35 local time, on day twenty-three of Operation *Northern Wolf*. At present, we are on station in the centre of the north-east search sector, with the Russian frigate *Admiral Khabalov* some thirty nautical miles west of us. Ma'am, your Arctic troops are currently on the pack ice north-west of our position, proceeding towards the last known location of an unidentified sonar contact spotted on day fourteen of the search." Magnus paused. No one needed reminding of what had happened to the airplane that made the discovery on day fourteen.

He continued. "The *Ronaldson* is now back on station in the south-west sector and we are making arrangements for the recovered remains of the deceased pilot to be returned to the American frigate, pending a proper handover." The Dane gave a respectful nod to the *Ronaldson's* XO, who stood motionless.

"And what of the Russian recovery efforts?" Colonel Borishov demanded. Katherine was annoyed at the outburst, but let it pass.

Magnus answered. "Colonel, my understanding is that the bulk of the Ka-27 wreckage and two deceased aviators have been recovered by the *Khabalov*, but we'd be pleased to confirm that for you."

The Russian attempted to look important by writing the information down. Katherine tried not to look dismissively at Colonel Borishov, but it was hard. Everything Magnus had mentioned was already being reported by the international news media, including in Moscow.

"Anything else, Captain?" she asked.

"General, we are still experiencing considerable atmospheric interference, which is affecting our onboard navigation and communication equipment, but apart from that we are provisioned for another three weeks at sea. It goes without saying, we have found no evidence of the missing *Volkov*, nor its crew."

"Thank you Magnus," Katherine acknowledged, "now let's please proceed to the task at hand in sickbay."

With that, the group slowly made their way below deck.

Major Eleanor Matthews covered her face against the icy downwash of the resupply helicopter as it took off. The grey *Seahawk* was soon speeding north-west while her troops loaded the newly delivered supplies onto their sleds. The three platoons of Eleanor's Arctic infantry company were in an arrowhead formation, facing west. Each half-section of four soldiers was responsible for a cargo sled that contained an Arctic tent. This they dragged behind them using harnesses when on the move. Even though they were under near twenty-four hour daylight, Eleanor would stop for the evening in a few hours. Their progress was painfully slow, covering some three nautical miles of jagged pack ice a day. As a result, her troops were exhausted. In hindsight, the soldiers should have been equipped with cross-country skis instead of snowshoes, but no matter. Like her sergeant major would say, *It is what it is*.

As with any detective story, no matter how significant the clues, ultimately someone still needs to physically collect the evidence, or catch the culprit. For Eleanor, this meant locating what was probably a very large piece of the *Volkov* submarine, trapped in the floating sea ice. Eleanor was not one for conspiracy theories. As far as she was concerned, her summer tour in the Arctic had already cost her the lives of two soldiers, and the sooner they got back south, the better. If that meant digging out a chunk of Russian naval hardware from the frozen ocean, so be it.

"Two platoon has the lead on the advance, one platoon left rear, three platoon right rear," Eleanor yelled, followed by three whistle blasts. They had given up using their personal radios days ago due to the constant electromagnetic interference. In the twenty-first century, she was leading her troops with technology from the Napoleonic era.

"We're being tracked," their guide Ujurak reported quietly. "Male polar bear, probably an adolescent."

Eleanor looked back at him in total amazement.

"Ujurak, how do you know that, and how do you know it's an adolescent?" she half-protested.

"Because if it was an adult, we wouldn't know it was following us until it was too late," the guide grinned at her knowingly. "Teenagers have no patience."

He then moved off behind number two platoon, leaving the major speechless.

"Sir, we have an infestation of sea worms," the chief engineer reported to Acting Captain Ivan Egorov, who looked back confused.

"What did you just say, Chief?"

"Sea worms." The older petty officer removed the lid from the metal pail he'd placed on the floor. Ivan peered in to find dozens of dark red worms slithering overtop each other.

"Where were they?" he demanded.

"In engineering, sir, along the main drive shaft for the propellers."

Ivan's initial frustration turned to mild alarm. "Have they affected the propulsion system? Can we still make way?"

"Yes Captain," the chief nodded, "as far as we can tell, nothing is damaged."

Ivan ran his hands through his hair several times, trying to collect his thoughts. It was bad enough they had lost their only helicopter and crew to an accident with the reckless Americans, now this. He thought back to his early days fishing with his brother Sergei near St Petersburg.

"I thought sea worms only fed on organic material, like wood?" he asked. The chief nodded his concurrence.

*Then how the hell did they get on my ship?*

The intercom system buzzed. "Bridge, CIC, we have a sub-surface sonar contact bearing one one zero, approaching from the south-east, ten nautical miles and closing."

Ivan knew the combat information centre could normally detect approaching vessels at ten times that distance, but due to all the cursed atmospheric interference, this contact was practically on top of them.

"Action stations?" the chief asked Ivan, who shook his head.

"Stay at defensive watch until we ascertain what it is," he ordered. "No sense getting all excited if it turns out to be a pod of beluga whales again." Besides, Ivan suspected the only country that likely had submarines in the area, was his.

"Bridge, CIC, sub-surface sonar contact continues on same bearing, speed roughly twelve knots."

Ivan keyed the roof-mounted intercom. "CIC, bridge, any acoustic signature or cavitations? Is it organic?"

"Unknown sir."

Ivan contemplated the situation for a moment. His ship was sitting in the middle of an international search effort for his brother's missing submarine. He was surrounded by pack ice to his north, warships to his east and west, and now an unknown submerged contact approaching from the south-east. The propeller shafts were somehow hosting a colony of sea worms, while the persistent green aurora borealis and its electromagnetic field were still playing havoc with his instruments. Even if he sent a signal to Moscow, there was no guarantee it would be received.

*Maybe that's not such a bad thing*, Ivan smirked to himself.

"Bridge, CIC, contact now five nautical miles and closing. No change to speed or bearing."

The sudden high-pitched sound was ear-splitting. It radiated from everywhere, yet nowhere at the same time. Any crewmember standing instantly collapsed to the floor due to the horrendous ringing in their ears. Ivan was on the deck in a foetal position, covering his bleeding ears when the noise just as abruptly stopped. He clambered up the captain's chair to find the bridge monitors displaying different angled symbols and shapes, a deep baritone humming coming from the speakers. About him, other sailors were regaining their senses, some also wiping blood from their ears. He took a handset from the roof console and boosted the sound to full.

"CIC, bridge!" he yelled, not realising the volume of his own voice. "Where is the sub-surface contact now?"

After a moment, "It's gone sir."

Just then Ivan noticed every monitor now displayed the same cryptic image.

The beauty of being assigned to an Arctic patrol vessel was that the ships were equipped with multiple pieces of research equipment not normally carried in the south. Some of this was due to the remoteness of their operating environment, but also the fact that much of the region had yet to be thoroughly explored. It was not uncommon for several discoveries to occur each summer, from new plant species to the remains of ancient indigenous campsites, all preserved by the cold. The most famous recent Arctic discoveries were the sunken wrecks of HMS *Erebus* and *Terror*. Found by a Canadian research team, the two ships were from the lost nineteenth century Franklin expedition. Neuron microscopes, a DNA reader, and radiocarbon dating equipment were all standard issue on the *Knud Rasmussen*, a fact Dr Rikke Larsen was currently taking full advantage of.

The machine Rikke fiddled with was known as an accelerator mass spectrometer or AMS. It was carried on board the *Rasmussen* to determine the age of any archaeological artifacts the ship might come across during its northern travels. They had already used it once that summer to date an abandoned Thule dwelling in Greenland to the mid-fourteenth century. The AMS determined the age of a sample by counting the amount of beta radiation emitted from decaying atoms. The older the sample, the less detectable the carbon atoms became, thus its age could be determined.

Brigadier-General Tremblay and her party had already departed the ship, taking with them the remains of the downed American pilot. Rikke had been contemplating a radical theory since she'd performed the young aviator's initial autopsy earlier in the day. As far-fetched as it sounded, she could come to no other conclusion based on the evidence. For starters, the American had the same surgical burn marks on his neck as the deceased French sailors she'd examined earlier that summer. Second, all had died incredibly gruesome deaths, with wounds far too precise to be accidental. Lastly, Rikke had found rusted metal shavings within the dead pilot's wounds, likely caused by a worn-down blade, which could only have been wielded by a human. Whether it was the twisted actions of a lone fisherman, or someone else, Rikke was convinced a murderer might be operating in the high Arctic. Maybe even a serial killer. Sadly, if this were the case, it would not be the first time in the region.

Rikke sat alone in her lab adjacent to the sickbay, as she gently placed the rusted metal flakes onto a sample tray. Whoever this psychopath was, they seemed to prefer using an old, worn-down weapon. If Rikke could determine the age of the blade, it would assist the police in narrowing down a suspect. The northern populations were very small, and local fishermen tended to use the same tools for decades. Even if the AMS machine came back with a thirty-year old reading, it would still be a significant lead for local law enforcement. Rikke closed the lid of the carbon dating machine and went to fetch one of the *Rasmussen's* much loved espressos while the system analysed the contents.

She returned a few minutes later, warm coffee in hand, to see what the analysis indicated. She assumed a reading as far back as the early 1990s was plausible. Her coffee cup fell to the floor, spilling its contents as Rikke read the year listed on the small screen: 996 CE.

# CHAPTER 15

Erika awoke from yet another nightmare. She sat up in the top bunk, curling her knees to her chest. From the bottom bed she could hear Sandra snoring away as usual. A glance at the clock revealed it was 03:58, the Arctic sun already poking through the curtains. She reached for her precious amulet and slipped the necklace over her head. The ambient warmth it somehow gave off calmed her racing heart. Erika was getting pretty fed up with axe-wielding crazy men invading her dreams. She gently climbed down the bunk bed ladder, careful not to disturb Sandra, and made her way to the hallway.

Erika's grandparents had owned their lodge since before she was born. Built mainly of wood with a stone floor, it resembled a giant *H* with four separate bedrooms joined in the centre by an open kitchen area and living room. In the middle of the main chamber was a large cast iron fireplace, surrounded by limestone. From within, smouldering embers gave off a reassuring glow. Erika took a fresh log from a pile beside the fireplace and gently placed it on the warm coals. Soon the log was alight, filling the room with the scent of burning wood. The aroma took her back to her youth and the time she'd spent along the shores of Lake Superior. Erika curled up onto a beat-up old couch adjacent to the fireplace and looked about the room. Various soapstone carvings made by her grandmother lined the shelves, while the wall art consisted of large tapestries and photos. In the corner, a grey and white caribou hide served as a carpet, while in the adjoining kitchen the floor was covered by a polar bear rug. She took a moment to examine the photos on the wall. There was a faded black and white picture of an elderly couple holding an infant, the baby one of Erika's grandparents. Beside it was a picture of her parents Liam and Star as young adults, her father's bushy haircut denoting it was taken in the early 1980s. Yet another photo on a table beside the couch showed the pair several decades older, with young Erika in Star's arms. She traced the outline of the picture frame with her finger as the amulet around her neck started to glow. Next to the photo, surrounded by flowers, sat a blue and white urn with her mother's name. Later that day, using a pair of small fishing boats, her family would sprinkle Star's ashes into the ocean.

"You all right?" a voice whispered.

Erika turned her head to find Michelle standing in the open kitchen. She was wearing green University of Vermont flannel pants and a white tank top. Several multi-coloured tattoos covered her exposed shoulders. Her short hair was dishevelled, while her eyes were puffy with fatigue.

"I got up to use the bathroom and heard someone by the fireplace," Michelle gestured. "Mind if I sit with you?"

Erika motioned for her friend to join her on the couch, which she did. Michelle eased herself beside Erika.

"You thinking about your mom?" she asked.

"Sometimes," Erika said. "But lately I've been having these awful nightmares."

She described to Michelle the recurring dreams she had of a warm coastal village inhabited by a blonde haired family, whose father seemed to have a rather violent disposition. Erika explained that sometimes her mother joined her in these dreams, but usually she was alone. They often ended the same way, with her about to meet an untimely demise just before she awoke. The longer she described her nightmares, the more heat the amulet under her pyjama shirt emitted, a sensation she hid from Michelle. Erika continued that the location in her dreams seemed familiar, but she didn't know why. As she explained, her friend listened closely, only responding with the occasional nod. Eventually Michelle shifted her position to face Erika, and moved to take her hand.

"It must have been hard for you growing up," she said softly, "not sure where you fit in?"

The younger of the two glanced at Michelle, who had moved noticeably closer on the couch.

"How do you mean?" Erika asked.

"Did you identify as an American or a Canadian?" Michelle asked. "Or were you Scandinavian or were you Inuit, or both?"

Erika couldn't remember ever telling Michelle her family heritage, at least not like she had to Sandra, but no matter. Perhaps Liam had blurted something out in recent days to stop her from constantly flirting with him. Erika smiled, realising what Michelle was subtly up to. Under normal circumstances, Erika would have been flattered by the attention, even welcomed it, but these were far from normal times. As much as she found herself drawn to Michelle, her instincts told her now was not the time.

"My mother made my childhood really amazing and loving," she said, then looked at her friend. "I like you, Michelle, I really do. Maybe even more than I want to admit. I'm just not ready to be with anyone right now, especially not in a relationship. I'm sorry."

Michelle released her hand.

Erika could tell from the pained look on Michelle's face her words had hurt. She instantly regretted being so blunt, as her companion rose from the couch with a sigh. Michelle raised her arms in a long stretch, her tank top lifting just enough to reveal her pierced naval. She then bent down and lightly kissed Erika's forehead before whispering.

"Whoever said I wanted a relationship?"

She then silently returned to her room and closed the door.

Erika looked at Michelle's door and shook her head, realising she'd probably sounded too harsh, which had not been her intent. Maybe she'd misunderstood her friend's motives, shooting Michelle down when perhaps she was just being friendly. Come to think of it, try as she might to remember, it wasn't clear in Erika's mind who had kissed who back in Montreal.

*Way to go Holstrom, you dummy.*

Erika stirred on the living room couch to the sound of a kettle boiling. She glanced up to find her grandmother dressed in ceremonial clothing, making tea for Erika and her friends.

"You need to hurry, cub," the elderly woman urged. "We should be down by the docks in thirty minutes."

Erika shot up and looked at the stove clock: 09:27. Her mother's ash sprinkling ceremony would begin at ten.

*Shit.*

She burst into her bedroom to find Sandra awake and dressed, fiddling with her smartphone. "Is there ever a cell signal up here?" Sandra demanded. Erika just shook her head and scrambled to gather her clothes and toiletry kit. Soon she was outside the bathroom door, waiting for the occupant inside to finish. She could tell by the noise of a hair dryer it was probably Nicole Gibson, and banged on the door. It swung open.

"Sorry, I was just doing my hair," Nicole apologised.

Erika didn't have the heart to mention her friend's immaculate coif wouldn't last five minutes on the open ocean, but no matter. Nicole gathered her things and left the bathroom to Erika, who quickly stripped down and turned on the shower. Her pixie cut meant very little maintenance was required. As soon as she was finished rinsing away her shampoo, the water was off and the shower curtain flung open. Erika paused as she caught sight of herself in the mirror. She looked thin, but that wasn't what drew her eye. As she moved closer to the reflection, she noticed the amulet around her neck had lightly burned the skin at the centre of her chest. She dismissed it as a rash, covering it with a medical dressing from a first aid kit in the bathroom closet.

In less than ten minutes, Erika was showered, dressed, and in the kitchen gulping down a bowl of cereal. Her grandparents stood in the living room, along with her father, Nicole, and Sandra. She noticed Star's urn was missing from the small table covered with flowers.

"Where's Mom?" Erika blurted out, her mouth still full. The conversation in the room stopped as everyone looked towards her, confused. It was only when she pointed at the table that Liam understood what his daughter meant.

"The urn is outside," he said. "Michelle is watching over it for now."

Erika stopped chewing and looked back at her father. *That's a little weird*, she thought, before placing the empty cereal bowl in the sink.

"I'm all set, Dad."

Erika emerged outside to find a small collection of people in front of the lodge. The sky continued to have an olive green tinge, turning the sun into a jade oval. Among the gathering, she could see young Amber, who appeared happy despite her recent near miss with a polar bear. Michelle was standing at the corner of the crowd, cradling Star's urn, which she let Amber touch. Suddenly Erika became very territorial, and moved quickly towards her. Without saying a word, she gently but firmly freed the urn from Michelle's grasp, who looked up surprised. She was about to say something to Michelle when a familiar deep voice behind her spoke.

"Hi, Erika. Remember me?"

She turned to find a tall, dark-haired man no older than twenty staring back at her. Despite it being over a decade, she instantly recognised him as her childhood friend Jordan, a local from Pond Inlet.

"I'm sorry for your loss," he said shyly. "I also wanted to thank you for saving my little sister."

Erika looked confused until Amber wrapped her arms around her big brother's leg. She remembered Jordan as a kind boy who would walk her home as a child. Though now very tall and handsome, she could still detect a boyish tenderness in his gaze. In spite of the sad occasion, Erika's body language towards Jordan spoke volumes, a fact not lost on Michelle.

"Shouldn't we get going?" Michelle commented dryly at the reunited friends.

Jordan looked over as Liam approached, shaking the professor's hand.

"I understand you'll be handling one of our boats today for the water ceremony?" Liam asked, to which Jordan nodded, Erika smiled, and Michelle rolled her eyes. With that, the group made their way towards the town docks, Erika leading as she carried her mother's urn.

The pair of small powerboats were dwarfed by the massive warships at anchor in Pond Inlet's harbour. As Erika and her entourage walked onto the narrow dock, a helicopter flew overhead heading east. Liam followed the aircraft with his gaze for a few moments, trying to determine its markings. The military presence was far more pronounced than in previous summers, no doubt due to the ongoing search efforts. Still, Erika was convinced her father knew more than he was letting on. Over the years, she was used to her dad disappearing for weeks at a time to attend various northern training events, while she stayed with her grandparents. Erika knew not to complain, for it was these same government-sponsored activities that allowed Liam and his family to regularly travel north at no cost. After all, it had been an official research expedition that had brought Liam to the Arctic years ago, allowing him to meet Star. Erika cradled her mother's urn in her arms a little tighter.

Despite the large numbers gathered on the dock, only a few in the group would actually venture out on the open water. The first powerboat was a wooden design belonging to Erika's grandfather. Joining him would be his wife, Liam, Erika, and Sandra. The second boat, made of modern aluminium, would act as a safety craft and carried Nicole and Michelle, with Jordan at the helm. As they donned their life preservers, Amber ran up and asked Erika if she could join her brother Jordan for the ceremony. Erika glanced over at Liam who smiled, passing his floatation belt to the little girl. With a huge smile, she climbed into her big brother's craft. After a few kind words from the various well-wishers, the two boats cast off from the dock and gently navigated their way among the towering naval vessels.

"What are all these ships doing up here, Professor Holstrom?" Sandra asked from the front of the boat, pointing at a ship flying the national flag of France.

"There are more of them out at sea," Liam replied. "They're still looking for that missing submarine I mentioned at the airfield the day you arrived."

"I can't remember, was it one of ours?" Sandra said, wiping saltwater spray from her face.

Liam shook his head. "No, Russian."

Once past the last of the warships at anchor, both powerboats increased speed, causing them to bounce along the subtle wave-tops. They headed north towards Bylot Island, a favourite summer sanctuary for Star, and the place she had asked her ashes to be sprinkled. Erika closed her eyes as she felt the ocean wind in her hair. She loved being outdoors and could not think of a better send-off for her beloved mother. To her left she could see Jordan's aluminium boat keeping pace with hers. She smiled quietly at the sight of Nicole, her hair already a complete mess courtesy of the sea spray and ocean wind. She even caught the eye of Michelle, who offered a tight smile in return. Erika reflected on their earlier conversation. *I like you, Michelle, I really do. Maybe even more than I want to admit.*

The boat veered to the right, Erika's grandfather avoiding a minor iceberg. As they came round the other side, they caught sight of several harp seals slumbering on the floating ice. The old man gently reached under his seat to ensure his hunting rifle was available if needed. Where there were seals, there were bound to be polar bears not far away.

The two boats came to a stop roughly three hundred metres from the southern shore of Bylot Island. Several birds from the nearby sanctuary flew by at low altitude. The waves had died down, allowing Liam to stand slightly in the lead boat. He offered a few words of remembrance about his beloved wife, Star. He'd been unable to do so at her memorial earlier in the week, his pain too raw for a public gathering. This, however, was different. Here, out on the ocean, in the high Arctic, with Star's parents and his daughter, he could let his emotions run free. Liam tried muddling his way through a local poem, then took the urn from Erika and opened its lid. He eased the contents of the ceramic container into the sea, a grey cloud of dust rising as the ashes fell towards the water. Erika closed her eyes, trying to feel for her mother's presence. Instead she felt only emptiness. She watched as the last of Star's ashes were consumed by the sea.

A squeal off to the right caught everyone by surprise. The two boats floated silently on the water, their occupants searching for the origin of the high-pitched noise.

"There!" Amber called out, pointing behind her.

On the glimmering surface, a bright yellow object the size of a basketball appeared, then quickly dove under water. Erika's grandfather sighed and reached for a fishing hook attached to a long pole. The yellow item surfaced again, this time much closer to their boat, letting off another painful squeal. Again it submerged, as Erika's grandfather stood up. As soon as the yellow object re-emerged from the depths, the old man used the fishing hook to rip a plastic bag off the head of a bewildered seal. The freed mammal bobbed on the ocean surface a few seconds before diving away. Erika looked at her grandfather as he held up a bag branded with a grocery store logo from Virginia. Nothing more needed to be said about the current state of pollutants in the world's oceans.

*Danger.*

Erika felt her senses awaken.

Why would she sense danger? The water was calm. She glanced about slowly, trying not to look alarmed. The occupants of both boats appeared lost in their respective thoughts, either regarding Star's ceremony or the harp seal.

*Danger.*

Erika leaned towards her grandfather, whispering firmly. "Grandpa, I'm ready to head back now."

He didn't hear her. She could tell something ominous was approaching. It was a rare natural phenomena, but dangerous nonetheless. They were attracted to her boat. Her *wooden* boat.

"We need to go back," she insisted, catching her grandfather's attention.

They were now under her craft, rising to the surface.

"Grandpa, we need to head back to Pond Inlet, now please."

The old man looked at his granddaughter knowingly, and started fiddling with the outboard motor.

"What is it, cub?" Liam asked, almost losing his footing. He regained his balance and looked down at the floorboards. They were covered in red slime.

"Grandpa, please, we need to leave here now!" Erika demanded.

Now Sandra was getting nervous as the powerboat's motor refused to turn over. A few metres off to their left, Jordan idled his engine, Michelle, Nicole, and Amber looking on with concern.

*Movement.*

Erika looked about frantically. Something bad was already happening, but she couldn't see where. She urged her senses to reveal what the imminent danger was. Nothing. Then she noticed the floorboards. They moved.

With a shriek, Erika lifted her feet onto the centre bench. Soon dozens, then hundreds of red worms were wiggling about the floor of the wooden craft.

"Sea worms," the grandfather warned. "Cursed things, they're eating out the hull of the boat. The keel was fine when I checked it last week." He tossed Sandra and Liam an oar each. They both looked at each other, and began paddling frantically.

"No, no," the old man yelled at the pair of would-be rowers. "Hit the damn things and scoop them out of the boat!"

It was too late. Water started shooting up from a dozen small holes created by the ravenous worms. If the passengers fell into the frigid water, they'd survive ten minutes at the most. Michelle sprang into action in the aluminium craft.

"Jordan, get us alongside," she ordered. "Nicole, help me bring the others aboard. Amber, I need you to sit quietly, ok?"

The child nodded, as Jordan brought his boat beside the sinking wooden vessel. By now, the stricken boat was ankle-deep in salt water and writhing worms. Her grandmother was the first across to Jordan's craft, followed by herself and Sandra.

"Dad, c'mon," Erika called urgently.

Her father held the two boats together as her grandpa jumped across. Liam was about to leave, when he lost his footing, falling back into the mass of slithering sea creatures, disappearing completely in the frothing water. Amber was wearing his life belt.

"DAD!" Erika yelled.

Before anyone could stop her, she was back across in the sinking wooden boat. Her arms frantically reached into the frigid, slimy pool of slithering worms, desperate to locate Liam. As the seconds went by she became panicked.

*Had he fallen through the hull?*

The amulet around her neck started to glow fiery red. It burned a hole through the front of her shirt, exposing the skin under her life vest. Erika didn't notice as she dug, elbows deep, through the disgusting mass.

*What was that, an arm?*

With an enormous heave she lifted her father's upper torso out from the frigid goo. Nicole and Michelle helped her move Liam into the safety of the aluminium boat. Erika jumped back over, landing beside her unconscious dad.

"Jordan, go!"

Within seconds, they were racing away, the beleaguered wooden boat splitting in two as it sank below the surface. A few of the slithering sea creatures had fallen aboard during the evacuation, which Amber gleefully stomped.

"Dad," Erika called out, slapping her father's face. "Dad, wake up."

She held her ear next to Liam's mouth, but over the engine noise she couldn't tell if he was breathing. She was about to begin mouth-to-mouth resuscitation when Liam coughed loudly, projecting globs of red slime across his daughter's face. Everyone on the boat gave a collective sigh of relief as Erika wiped the ooze from her cheeks. Liam sat up, coughing up more slime and salt water, before regaining his composure.

"I need to get back to the lodge," he blurted out.

Erika looked back at him confused. "No, Dad, you need to see a doctor," she protested.

"Cub, I'm fine," he proclaimed. "The sea worms, of course, of course!" He turned to Erika, his body already shivering.

"I think I know the language of those symbols."

She stared in confusion at her father as their crowded aluminium boat sped back towards Pond Inlet.

*What symbols?*

# CHAPTER 16

Liam bolted from the aluminium boat before Jordan had a chance to tie it to the dock. His teeth chattering from mild hypothermia, Liam sprinted towards the same cluster of well-wishers that had seen his family off in the morning. With looks of bewilderment, they parted in two groups, permitting the slime-covered widower to run between them. He continued up the gravel road, towards Pond Inlet. Just as they came back together, the group quickly broke ranks again to allow Liam's daughter passage. Erika was running as fast as her legs could carry her in order to catch her father. A few calls of enquiry from the crowd followed her up the hill, but she didn't have time to answer. Next came Nicole and Michelle, sprinting in unison through the gathering of people, then up the same gravel road. Finally there was Sandra, huffing under the weight of young Amber, who was riding on her piggyback. With the aluminium boat finally tied down, it was left to Jordan to escort Erika's grandparents past the silent collection of locals.

"They're from the south," the elderly grandmother remarked with a shrug to the dockside crowd. All present nodded their collective understanding with a few smirks. Southerners were always in such a hurry.

"Dad, wait!" Erika protested as she threw off her life vest, trying to keep up with her father. For an older gentleman, Liam was still in excellent shape, especially when it came to running. She had almost caught her father when she accidently barrelled into a well-dressed officer coming out of a café, knocking him over along with his coffee. Erika apologised profusely as she helped the uniformed man to his feet, allowing Nicole and Michelle to catch up.

"Holstrom, WTF?" Nicole panted, her long hair a complete mess. "What were those things out on the water, and what's gotten into your dad?"

Erika raised her hands in ignorance. "Dude, I have no idea, but he said something about symbols, and understanding what it all meant? I don't know..."

The women all looked at each other, then Michelle pointed at Erika's chest. "Check out your shirt."

Erika looked down and noticed a fist-sized hole had been burnt through the centre of her top, exposing her dangling amulet and surrounding skin. She quickly covered the opening with her hand, more to hide the glow emanating from her precious artifact than any sense of modesty. Just then, the uniformed officer Erika had knocked over interjected.

"I take it you're Dr Holstrom's daughter?" he asked with an accented voice.

Erika nodded quickly before running off after her father, her friends in close pursuit. Colonel Borishov's eyes followed the sprinting women until they were out of sight. Based on what he'd just overheard, the Russian attaché made a mental note to review Dr Liam Holstrom's academic area of expertise. Perhaps the Arctic professor's research could help explain what Washington and Ottawa were not willing to share. He was about to return to the café when a woman with a young girl on her back appeared from around the corner.

"Which way... did they... go?" Sandra huffed.

The colonel pointed her in the right direction, and carried on with his day.

Liam burst into the front entrance of his in-laws' lodge. He didn't bother removing his slime-encrusted boots as he moved to the kitchen sink, quickly rinsing the mucus from his mouth. Next, he made his way to the building's main hallway and glanced up at the ceiling. Clearly visible above him was the outline of a trap door, which he jumped up and pulled down. The door opened to reveal a folding ladder and passageway to the dwelling's attic. Liam scrambled up the steps, emerging into a dark rectangular room with old pieces of furniture scattered about, most covered in white bed sheets.

"Where is it?" he sighed, his teeth no longer chattering thanks to the body heat produced by his run. He moved aside several chairs, allowing sunlight from a lone window to glint through newly disturbed dust.

There you are.

Along one of the attic walls sat a Depression-era travel chest, its external colours long-since faded. Slowly Liam crouched beside the old case and opened the front latch. The hinges creaked when he raised the chest door, revealing a mound of discarded paperwork from his days as a research assistant. He leafed through several photos and yellow-stained essays about his time in the north, all written on a long-since discarded typewriter. Liam stopped when he eyed one of the pictures among a pile of photos. It was an early Polaroid of him and Star, taken soon after they met. They looked so young. He smiled quietly, then resumed his search. Next, Liam uncovered a thick, legal-sized envelope addressed to him but sent to his in-laws' Pond Inlet address. The postage was from September 1984, while the return address listed Dr Barbara Douglas as the sender. Liam thought for a moment, trying to reconcile the dates. His mentor had passed away from lung cancer in January 1985, meaning Dr Douglas had mailed the package after her diagnosis. A heavy chain smoker, Liam remembered his professor still being stunned at the news of her medical condition. He inspected the envelope and noticed it had not been opened. Judging by the delivery date, he had probably left for Minnesota before it arrived, leaving Star's parents to file it away. Either that, or the loss of his academic hero was too painful at the time to bother reading whatever she had sent him. Liam shook his head and placed the package aside.

"There it is," he breathed with quiet satisfaction. Liam pulled out a dusty book, titled *The Sagas of the Icelanders*. Printed in the mid-nineties, it was an English translation of various Old Norse oral histories passed down through the generations. The original prose had been committed to paper sometime in the thirteenth century. Though anecdotal in nature, they did describe several aspects of early Scandinavian life a thousand years ago, including travel routes, cultural customs, and language.

"Dad!" Erika exclaimed from the top of the attic ladder. "What has gotten into you? We need to get you to a doctor."

Liam waved her over without saying a word. With a deliberate sigh, she crawled to her father's side. He was still a dishevelled mess as he spoke.

"Those sea worms triggered my memory from an early European history course I studied back in university. In ancient mythology, their presence was often interpreted as a symbol of moral judgment."

Erika stared at her father blankly.

"What?" he asked innocently.

His daughter was incensed. "Dad, you could have drowned out there on the water. In fact, for a second I thought you were dead."

"Cub, I'm fine," he reassured her.

"But I'm not! I've already lost one parent this summer, I couldn't stand to lose you..." her voice trailed off as she buried her face in her hands and sobbed. Liam put down his book and quickly moved to hold his daughter. The trauma of the morning's ocean encounter was finally dawning on him as well.

"I'm sorry, cub," he whispered, gently swaying with Erika. "I'm not going anywhere. I've been so preoccupied by everything that's been going on up here, between the military stuff, and your mom's memorial. I guess the way I'm coping with all this is to bury myself in what I know best, which is my research and..."

Erika gently cut him off. "Dad, I'm not a science project. I'm your only daughter and I just need you to tell me what's going on."

Liam paused before explaining what he knew, about the missing Russian submarine, the lost fishing vessels across the Arctic that summer, and the unknown symbols he'd been exposed to by the military a few days earlier. He told his daughter that the government, both American and

Canadian, routinely sought his Arctic expertise, but that a series of un-explained events over the past few months had stumped even him. Liam explained in detail about the American navy plane that crashed, and the markings carved into its fuselage. He mentioned the old German weather station discovery he'd been part of in his youth, but spared Erika the gruesome details. Finally, he showed her the Icelandic book he'd retrieved and turned to a chapter titled *Erik the Red Saga*, Verse 13. They both read the passage, father and daughter seated closer to each other than they had been for a long time.

13. Bjarni Grimolfsson and his group were borne into the Greenland Straits and entered Madkasjo (Sea of Worms), although they failed to realise it until the ship under them had become infested with shipworms. They then discussed what to do. They had a ship's boat in tow, which had been smeared with such tar made of seal blubber. The majority proposed to set as many men in the boat as it could carry. When this was tried, it turned out to have room for no more than half of them.

Bjarni then said they should decide by lot who should go in the boat, and not decide by status. Although all of the people there wanted to go into the boat, it couldn't take them all. So they decided to draw lots to decide who would board the boat and who would remain aboard the trading vessel. The outcome was that it fell to Bjarni and almost half of those on board to go in the boat.

Those who had been selected left the ship and boarded the boat.

Once they were all aboard the boat one young Icelander, who had sailed with Bjarni, called out to him, "Are you going to desert me now, Bjarni?"

"So it must be," Bjarni answered.

He said, "That's not what you promised me when I left my father's house in Iceland to follow you."

Bjarni answered, "I don't see we've much other choice now. What would you advise?"

He said, "I see the solution – that we change places, you come up here and I'll take your place there."

"So be it," Bjarni answered, "as I see you put a high price on life and are very upset about dying."

They then changed places. The man climbed into the boat and Bjarni aboard the ship. People say Bjarni died there in the Sea of Worms, along with the others on board his ship. The ship's boat and those on it went on their way and made land, after which they told this tale.

Erika looked up at her dad. "Is this true?"

Liam flipped to the back of the book as he answered her. "Who knows? Like any ancient text, they were passed by word of mouth for centuries before someone bothered to write it down. A lot of broken telephone can happen over a few hundred years."

"Who was this Bjarni guy, and Erik the Red?" Erika asked. "He sounds like the name of a craft beer."

Liam raised an eyebrow at his daughter, wondering why she would equate medieval Norse sailors with a pint of ale. No matter, she was now playing hockey at the varsity level, with all the adult life experiences that brought.

"In their time, they were known by the people of the Arctic as *Kavdlunaits*, or those who came 'from away'. They sailed the oceans of the northern hemisphere for centuries, bringing both innovation and terror, depending on who they encountered."

Erika was enthralled by her father's description. It took her back to the childhood fables he'd tell her at bedtime of trolls and witches, princes and fairies, all living in a magical time.

"They mainly came from western Scandinavia," Liam continued, "but their travels took them across Europe, the Middle-East and North Africa, and maybe even different parts of North America."

"Really, when?"

"About a thousand years ago."

"At school they taught us that Christopher Columbus was the first European to reach North America?" Erika protested, to which her father grinned.

"Nope. Your ancestors on my side of the family were visiting these shores five hundred years before Columbus showed up. There's even an archaeological site in Newfoundland called L'Anse aux Meadows with remains of Norse longhouses from the turn of the last millennium."

Erika's interest was piqued as she thought of her recent nightmares.

"Can you describe a longhouse to me? What were they made of?"

Liam was a bit puzzled by Erika's enquiry, but like any good academic he couldn't resist a question on his specialist subject.

"It's assumed they were made of peat moss and mud for walls, with straw or thatch for a roof." He drew a rectangular shape in the air with his fingers. "They could probably house a dozen people, maybe two or three families."

"Would they have a fireplace in the centre?" Erika asked.

Liam nodded.

"And were these houses usually built near the coast?"

"Mostly. The Norse were a seafaring people, whose lives, culture and beliefs were entwined with sailing the ocean."

"What did you call them again Dad? Kavd..."

"*Kavdlunaits* or Norse people, but you would probably know them by their warrior name."

"And what's that?"

Erika looked up at Liam as he replied.

"Vikings."

Michelle and her friends could hear Erika and her father chatting in the attic and decided it was best to leave them alone. Their recent episode on the water had been intense, and all agreed they needed time to chill. Nicole was warming herself up in the shower while Erika's grandparents were away, comforting themselves with a group of elders. Sandra said goodbye to Jordan and Amber as they left. She then proceeded from the front door to the kitchen and grabbed a hot cup of coffee brewing on the counter.

"Oh, that's good java," Sandra exclaimed. She moved to the living room to find Michelle seated on the couch, still covered in her outdoor clothes. "That Jordan guy's cute," Sandra said, hoping to elicit a response from her friend.

Silence. Michelle's expression said it all.

"Hey, what's wrong?" Sandra asked.

"I'm so selfish," Michelle replied, shaking her head. "She asked us to come here to support her during her mother's memorial, and all I could do was feel sorry for myself."

Sandra was confused. "Sorry for yourself? About what?"

Michelle looked over at her with a pained expression, which Sandra understood. She leaned over and rubbed her distraught friend's arm.

"Look, I get it. Erika is an awesome and good-looking woman, and super-fast on the ice. I just get the sense she's got too much going on to even think about relationships. Which totally makes sense given everything she's been through."

"I know." Michelle breathed heavily, throwing her head back against several couch pillows. "I just wish things were different, but they're not. Still, I should have shown more empathy towards her this morning. It was her mother's ash-laying ceremony, and all I could do was wallow in self-pity and envy at the way she looked at..." Michelle made a mocking expression. "...Jordan."

Sandra interrupted her as only she could. "Hey look, if I was into girls, you'd be the first person I'd get busy with!"

Michelle looked at her for an instant. They both burst into laughter that lasted long enough to untangle any anxieties they felt.

"What's going on?" Nicole asked as she emerged from the steaming bathroom, one towel wrapped around her body, the other over her hair.

"Nothing," Michelle snorted through giggles. "Sandra was just offering to be my consolation prize in bed."

Nicole paused awkwardly, before politely excusing herself to get dressed.

The emotional tension of the past few days now broken, the two women continued laughing even harder than before.

Liam flipped to the back of the *Icelanders* book, looking for the pages that detailed the early Norse language and lettering. Erika was now just as consumed as he was at being a history sleuth. He drew the unique symbol he'd witnessed at the military headquarters using an old pencil from inside the storage chest.

"The lettering they had was very basic," he explained. "And what has survived is generally carved into metal or rocks called runes. The Old Norse writing was called *futhark* and consisted of straight angles and lines, sort of like stick figures. Given the tools back then, a straight line was easier to carve into stone or wood than a curved shape."

His words trailed off.

Erika looked up at her dad, then at the page before him. There it was. Mixed in among several other shapes were two vertical triangles, joined at the bottom.

"What does it say?" she asked.

Liam looked puzzled. "Birch," he said simply.

His daughter sat up, disappointed. "That's it? Birch? As in a birch tree?"

He looked over apologetically. "I guess so."

Erika let out a sigh. "Well that was anti-climactic."

From downstairs the two heard laughter, meaning the rest of Erika's friends were home. She glanced at her smartphone to check the time, her device now nothing more than a glorified clock. For some reason, there continued to be no cellular or Wi-Fi service anywhere in Pond Inlet. The pair had been in the attic at least an hour. Both agreed they should get cleaned up, while Liam returned his books and paperwork back into the chest. He held on to the old envelope from his late professor as the two climbed down the stairs, closing the trap door behind them.

Silence.

After several minutes, the attic air stirred.

The latch of the chest unhooked.

The storage container eased opened, revealing the *Icelanders* book the two humans had been reading so intently. The pages slowly flipped on their own, pausing at diagrams of Norse sailing vessels, and a sketch of an early aboriginal hunter. For a brief instant the room filled with a translucent green mist, before the lid of the chest gently closed once more.

The book inside was left open to a faded map of a place called *Helluland*.

# CHAPTER 17

Erika rested her head on her grandmother's lap, the reassuring heat from the fireplace radiating over them. Across from where they were on the couch, Liam sat reading an old atlas. In the kitchen, Sandra made herself a midnight snack. Everyone else had already retired for the night. The Arctic sun was low on the horizon, but still visible despite its green atmospheric glow. It had been a long and exhausting day.

"Grandma, what was Mom like as a child?" Erika asked.

The elderly woman looked down at her granddaughter. "She was a lot like you. Smart, feisty, and curious." Erika's grandmother looked at the photos on the wall before she continued. "You look very much like her, especially when you smile."

Erika nuzzled herself closer to her grandma.

"Did she ever get sent to a residential school?" she asked, looking up.

Liam put down his atlas and glanced over at his mother-in-law before she answered, rather firmly. "Absolutely not. After what your grandfather went through, we kept and raised her right here in Pond Inlet."

"Grandma, do you ever feel... different?" Erika asked quietly. She felt her grandmother's leg muscles tense before answering.

"How do you mean?"

"I don't know. I guess maybe a bit weird, like the feeling that something was wrong with you, or you didn't fit in?"

"I know what that's like," Sandra interrupted from the kitchen. Everyone looked over at her. "Hey, you try being the first black girl in a mainly boys junior hockey league in Rhode Island. I was a minority within a minority. Only way to fit in was to make myself indispensable, that's why I became a goalie. Can't play a game without me!" Sandra raised her arms in triumph, to which the others smiled. "Anyway, I'm gonna call it a night. Been a crazy day." Midnight snack in hand, she made her way to the guest bedroom. Once the door was closed, Liam propped himself up.

"I like your friends, cub," he said in a hush. "Especially Sandra. You've done well to surround yourself with such good people."

"It's your doing, Dad," Erika said. "You and Mom raised me and got me into hockey. That's how I know them all."

He nodded gently, before adding, "Sports can be a great unifier."

Liam stood up and wished his mother-in-law and daughter a good night, then retired to his room.

Now alone, Erika sat up and looked directly into her grandmother's eyes.

"Can you see the future?"

Again, the older woman tensed. "Can you?"

Erika looked down, pondering how to answer. "I'm not sure. Maybe it's just coincidence, or a bad case of *déjà vu*, but there are times when I can feel something bad is about to happen. Like today on the boat, I could sense we were in danger just before those sea worms showed up. And it's not the first time..."

"Go on," the elder encouraged.

"I felt it all summer long playing hockey in Vermont, like I could anticipate events just before they happened. Then when we landed here at the airport, it was like someone... something was watching us."

"Spirits?" Grandma asked.

Erika paused, not understanding what she meant. "What, you mean like ghosts?"

"Not exactly, more like restless souls needing to breathe. Some call it part of *anirniq*. When an animal is killed for food, its *anirniq* is released. It's all part of the circle of life, and should be respected. Some are said to be able to harness the power of the *anirniq,* to use their wisdom and guidance."

Erika wasn't sure what to make of her grandmother's description, but decided she had nothing to lose. "Grandma, what's a *seeress*?"

"That comes from your father's Scandinavian culture. It means a woman who can see the future."

"And what are *skraeling*?"

"That's a medieval word for the Thule or Dorset peoples, the ones that lived here before the Inuit. It can mean savage, or dried skin. It's what the ancient sea raiders called us. Either way, it's not very nice."

"By ancient sea raiders you mean the Vikings, right?" Erika insisted. "Vikings called us *skraeling*?"

"So the stories go, yes." Grandma answered. "But there is no proof they ever made it this far north, so they likely used it against the indigenous peoples of Greenland or Newfoundland."

Erika hesitated, not sure if she should tell her grandmother what was racing through her mind. The incident with the polar bear was foremost, but how to describe it without sounding stupid, or ridiculously irresponsible? The more she pondered the event, the more she tried convincing herself the encounter had been a fluke. Her thoughts again circled back to her mother. Could she really be communicating with Star through her dreams? It made no sense. Yet so much of what her grandmother was saying resonated with her. She felt she had nothing to lose.

"Mom told me about the *skraeling*."

"When was that, dear?"

"A few days ago."

Liam adjusted the night lamp beside his bed, using a pillow to help him sit up. The king-sized mattress originally purchased for him and Star now seemed far too big for its remaining occupant. He could still smell his wife's scent on her old clothes in the closet. He rubbed his tired eyes, and donned a pair of reading glasses. Liam picked up the faded envelope from his late professor and opened the seal. After forty years sitting in an attic, the paper was dry and brittle, tearing easily. He pulled out a stack of photocopied pages, all stapled together. The original text appeared to be typed in German, with English translations scribbled beside each phrase, or in the margins. He read the cover sheet, suddenly fascinated with what he'd discovered.

Geheim / Secret
Kreigstagebuch / War Diary
des UnterseeBootes U-537 / of the submarine U-537
Kommandant: Kapitänleutnant / Commander:
    Lieutenant-Commander Peter Schrewe
Begonnen / Started: 18 September 1943
Abgeschlossen / Completed: 8 December 1943

Liam turned to the next page, which listed the submarine as a German navy Type IXC/40. It had carried a complement of four officers and forty-four enlisted sailors as well as two civilian scientists. Its mission that fall was to transit the North Atlantic undetected and install a *Wetter-Funkgerät Land (WFL) 26* along the remote Arctic coast of North America. Liam scratched his head.

*Why is WFL-26 familiar?* he thought to himself, then had a revelation.

"It's the weather station!" he blurted out, before lowering his voice.

Liam realised he was reading the actual logbook entries from the German submarine that installed the weather station he and the late Dr Douglas had discovered back in 1981. His mentor must have received the copy from what was, at that time, the West German naval archives. Liam paused, wondering why his professor would have sent it to him, apart from the fact she was dying. The discovery of WFL-26 had been a defining moment in his young adult life. It was what eventually drove him to focus his studies on northern history and the environment. More importantly, it was how he met his wife, whose empty bed he now occupied. Liam settled into a comfortable position and began reading various excerpts from the war diary.

*18 Sep 1943 – Winds Calm – Departed Kiel, Germany under tug escort en route to Bergen, Norway with provisions for ninety days of sea operations. A low weather depression should keep enemy long-range aircraft away from the Jutland Strait and Norwegian coast. In addition to the regular crew compliment, two civilian meteorol-*

*ogists are aboard: Dr Kurt Sommermeyer and Walter Hildebrant.
They will install WFL-26, which has been nicknamed "Kurt" after
Dr Sommermeyer. All systems functioning well and crew morale is
good.*

Liam went on to read how *U-537* had an uneventful passage to what
was then Nazi-occupied Norway, where additional fuel and provisions
were taken aboard at Bergen. Dr Douglas had placed yellow sticky notes
on certain pages in the log, denoting significant dates that needed attention. The next major entry he read listed the submarine's planned North
Atlantic route.

*<u>30 Sep 1943</u> – Winds NW – Departed Bergen, Norway on the
surface, heading SSW towards the Scottish-Iceland gap with the intent to sail south of Greenland before making landfall along the NE
coast of Labrador. Lookouts are currently deployed in the conning
tower. Atlantic transit will be in isolation under radio silence. Enemy vessels are not to be engaged until after the delivery of weather
station Kurt. Morale continues to be good courtesy of several days of
shore leave in Norway.*

With a grimace, Liam tried remembering his war history, particularly significant events in Europe during the fall of 1943. Like most people
in the twenty-first century, he would normally turn to his phone or the
Internet to search for the answer, but not this evening. The atmospheric
interference from the green aurora borealis persisted. This left ultra-high
frequency and short-wave radio as the only means of communication to
and from Pond Inlet. He figured Brigadier-General Katherine Tremblay,
and her signals team at the temporary Arctic headquarters, were tearing
their hair out in frustration by now.

*<u>14 Oct 1943</u> – Winds gale force – The submarine was caught
broadside by a rogue wave during gale force winds while running
on the surface SE of Greenland, causing serious damage. The vessel's only anti-aircraft canon was lost overboard by the wave strike,*

*while the lead engineer Günter Cräser reports minor flooding along multiple hull points. The U-boat is currently running defenceless on the surface, unable to submerge. The other watch officers concur the best course of action is to press on to the Labrador coast and effect repairs during the delivery of weather station Kurt. Given the remote northern location, enemy ship activity is unlikely.*

The tone of the next several log entries was tense, but brief, as *U-537* sailed on the surface into hostile Arctic waters. Liam remembered the sight of the fallen German sailors he and Dr Douglas had located in Martin Bay. He wondered if any of the names he read in the war diary belonged to the dead sailors they'd discovered four decades later. *They must.* He recalled one of the bodies likely belonged to an officer. As there were only four on the sub including the commander, it narrowed the names down to three. Liam shuddered and turned to the next log entry marked with a sticky note.

*<u>22 Oct 1943</u> – Winds calm – Arrived at dawn to Martin Bay, Northern tip of Labrador, SW of Home Island at coordinates 60°5'0.2"N 64°22'50.8"W and dropped anchor. Following an initial reconnaissance, Lieutenant [name blacked out] will lead a shore party of ten, plus Dr Sommermeyer and his assistant to set up weather station Kurt. Lead engineer Cräser and his team will examine the external hull damage by day, working to fix the minor internal leaks by night. It is hoped repairs can be completed in twenty-four hours, focused on regaining the ability to submerge. At time of writing, shore sentries have been dispatched to provide overwatch. Nearest settlement is 50 kilometres NW from current position. No enemy activity detected.*

Liam wondered why the officer leading the shore party had his name blacked out, unless it meant he didn't survive. A dark thought entered his mind as he recalled the state of the deceased Germans they'd found in 1981. Reading the log entries made him feel part of a real-life jigsaw puzzle, trying to connect enough pieces to form a clearer picture of what had actually transpired. Liam's curiosity was dashed as he turned the page to the next day's entry. With the exception of the date, 23 October 1943, everything else was blacked out. The daily entry appeared to be three pages long, all covered in dark ink. He held one page up to the night lamp in the hope of seeing through the blackened passages, but quickly dismissed the idea. He was reading a photocopy of a photocopy, meaning there was no way to capture the original text underneath. In fact, there were no uncensored log entries until 26 October 1943, and even then it merely listed the letters NSTR for nothing significant to report.

Liam flipped through the rest of the logbook. *U-537* went on to conduct an unsuccessful combat patrol in the area of the Grand Banks, finding no convoys to target. He read how the submarine was attacked no fewer than three times by allied aircraft in the North Atlantic before departing for occupied Europe. After seventy days at sea, the vessel reached Lorient, France on 8 December 1943. In the patrol summary annex he noticed the Germans had lost six sailors at Martin Bay, with all the deceased names purged from the crew manifest. Liam had never read a military war diary, so he had no idea if censoring names and events was standard practice for incidents where colleagues perished. He stretched both his arms, realising it was well past midnight, and he needed to get some sleep. After a few days away for his wife's memorial, Liam was due back at the community centre in the morning for the daily commander's update briefing. That was assuming no one had discovered his security clearance was expired.

Liam turned on his side and placed the stack of photocopied log entries on the nightstand. As he reached for the bedside lamp, he noticed a small letter-sized envelope had fallen to the ground from somewhere in between the logbook's pages. He reached down and read the front, which only had his first name written on it. He sat up and opened the envelope to find a cover letter addressed to him, attached to three additional pieces of paper. The letter was virtually a time capsule, penned by his mentor, Dr Douglas, over forty years ago.

13 September 1984 – Minneapolis

Dear Liam,

As you've heard by now, my prognosis is not good. I wanted you to know I have enjoyed very much working with you these past five years. You are a bright young man and your field of research is fascinating. One of my deep regrets is that I will not be around to see you earn what will be a very well deserved doctorate.

Please find enclosed the redacted copy of the German submarine U-537's logbook from 1943. Don't ask me how I got it, just know a special colleague in West Germany owed me a favour (long story). This is the same submarine that set up the weather station we found during the summer three years ago. As you'll read, the names and key dates of the events surrounding the crew's time ashore in Labrador is blacked out. I have not been able to secure an uncensored version, and in fact it may not exist. I was, however, able to find an autopsy report from the personal medical notes of U-537's on-board surgeon, Dr Wolfgang Hegler. He performed the procedure on a deceased sailor 25 October 1943, three days after whatever occurred at Martin Bay. A copy of the autopsy report is attached to this letter. I have no idea what to make of it, but the torch is now passed on to you to figure out.

Thank you for all the laughs and for being such an amazing student. I wish you a long and happy life wherever your adventures take you. You're a good man and deserve as much happiness as this world can offer. Please give my best to your wonderful fiancé, Star.

With much love & affection,
Barbara
P.S. Don't ever start smoking!

Liam wiped a solitary tear from his eye. The only word that came to mind was *surreal*. He turned over the cover sheet to find a three-page autopsy report including a full-body sketch, as well as one depicting an upper torso. The deceased sailor's name was removed, but his death date was listed as 23 October 1943, while his age was twenty-one.

*So young.*

According to Dr Hegler's translated notes, the young man's body had been brought aboard along with another deceased sailor, while the remains of four other crewmembers were abandoned ashore. It did not say why they were left behind, but Liam assumed this meant the submarine had left in a hurry. He had always believed an allied patrol or air attack must have surprised them, though Dr Douglas insisted otherwise.

He went on to read that the extremities of the body were unremarkable. There was some surface scarring around the knuckles, likely caused by a bar brawl when in port. Both legs and arms were intact, as was the head. The cause of death was listed as extreme trauma to the central cavity. Liam turned to the second page of the autopsy report, which listed the state of the internal organs. The findings came as a shock. Heart: missing. Lungs: missing. Liver: missing. He went on to read the victim's kidneys, esophagus, and stomach were also gone. The chest cavity of the deceased had been torn open from within, showing severe signs of thermal combustion. Dr Hegler was unable to find a rear entry wound that would correlate with the large exit wound on the chest. His report went on to explain that the back muscles and spine were all intact, with little visible scarring or trauma, except for the upper muscle layers that had been closest to the internal organs.

Liam thought back to the gruesome condition of the dead German sailors he and Dr Douglas had discovered in the early eighties. Apparently they also met the same fate. He vividly remembered how unsettled he was at the sight of their mutilated bodies. Liam went on to read Dr Hegler's autopsy summary, which was inconclusive. The cause of injury was listed as unknown. Liam was startled as he turned to the last page of the report. There, in the centre of the yellow sheet, was a sketch of the now-familiar symbol found behind the fallen sailor's left ear.

THE
ARCTIC REGIONS
OF
NORTH AMERICA
BY
EDW. WELLER, F.R.G.S.

PARRY ISLAND
PRINCE PATRICK ISLAND
MELVILLE ISLAND
BATHURST Isle
CORNWALLIS ISLAND
BANKS LAND
BARROW
Melville Sound
Pr. of Wales Land
Pr. Albert Land
Pr. Albert Sound
Wollaston Land
Victoria Land
King William
Minto Inlet
Booth
Arctic Circle
Great Bear Lake

# CHAPTER 18

"Quick reaction flight scramble!"

Kendra dropped the newspaper and bolted from her chair. With the loudspeaker announcing instructions, she ran from the lounge down a corridor to the locker room. Kendra and her wingman entered the dressing chamber at the same time through opposite doors. They acknowledged each other with a nod. Already wearing their flight suits, they quickly donned their pilot helmets and gloves. Kendra placed a small logbook in her trouser pocket, then slammed her locker shut.

"Is this a drill?" her wingman asked as they emerged outside.

"No idea," she replied, "but get airborne as soon as you can."

The pair sprinted across the airfield towards two awaiting Eurofighter *Typhoons*, their canopies gleaming under the Arctic sun. Several ground personnel urgently prepared the aircraft for take-off as Kendra reached the side ladder of the lead plane.

"Ma'am, the auto start-up sequence has been initiated," a flight sergeant reported in a Welsh accent. "All pre-flight checks are green and your weapons load is armed."

Kendra acknowledged the young man, then clambered up the ladder and jumped into the Eurofighter's cockpit. She quickly scrolled through an abridged departure checklist, turning on several instruments and monitors in the process. Her inspection complete, she glanced down at her flight sergeant with a thumbs up. He responded with the same gesture, indicating she was clear for final engine start up. Using two fingers, Kendra engaged the Eurofighter's ignition. With a tremendous roar, the aircraft's twin turbofan engines thundered to life, causing several birds in the distance to scatter. She moved the flight yoke in the centre console back and forth, then left to right, causing the flaps and forward canards to swivel. After doing a similar test with the foot pedals, she snapped an oxygen mask over her face and keyed the radio.

"Keflavik tower, this is lion flight leader requesting a priority take-off pattern and vectoring to pre-assigned scramble altitude."

The response was immediate. "Lion flight leader, Keflavik tower. You have take-off priority on runway two zero south. Once wheels up, your assigned heading is west south-west at a bearing of two four zero, set altitude at angels forty. You will be handed over to the combined air operations centre once airborne for vectoring to intercept." There was a brief pause. "This is not a drill."

The tower's message infused Kendra with a shot of adrenaline. After weeks of rehearsals, this was evidently the real thing.

"Roger, Keflavik tower. Lion flight rolling now."

To her right, Kendra could see her wingman's Eurofighter mirroring her aircraft as they taxied towards the runway. Once both planes were in position, she lowered her canopy shut, the name *Squadron Leader Kendra Livingstone* stencilled across the bottom. In unison, the two Royal Air Force warplanes raced down the tarmac and up into the skies over Iceland.

A distant relative of the famed nineteenth century explorer Dr David Livingstone, Kendra had thus far led a charmed career. She'd graduated from the British fighter weapons school in the top third of her class, qualifying initially on F3 *Tornado* interceptors before switching to the Eurofighter *Typhoon*. Her first operational assignment had been for half a year at Mount Pleasant airfield in the Falkland Islands. Since the brief but vicious 1982 conflict with Argentina, the British had sizably built up their defences on the South Atlantic territory. This included stationing interceptors and their flight crew in the Falklands as an air deterrent. Kendra enjoyed her time at Mount Pleasant, though arguably she'd learned more about sheep farming during her stay than air tactics.

Her first combat experience was with the NATO air mission over Libya in 2011, where she conducted ground attack sorties in support of rebel forces near Benghazi. Kendra wasn't exactly sure what her efforts in North Africa had achieved towards regional stability, but they did earn her a promotion. A few years later she was part of the international air coalition over Syria and Iraq, targeting various religious cults. It was claimed the precision bombs she'd dropped had achieved the desired effect of helping neutralise a vicious foe, but how to be certain? Regardless, her actions had earned her yet another promotion and her latest assignment as part of NATO's air policing mission in Keflavik. Since Iceland had no air force of its own, it relied on various allied nations to provide airborne surveillance and intercept capabilities over its skies, usually on a four to six month basis. Coordinated through the NATO combined air operations centre in Germany, Kendra was currently part of a British contingent of five Eurofighter aircraft and personnel. Their area of responsibility was considerable, extending thousands of miles from the eastern Canadian Arctic to just west of Scotland. Courtesy of intelligence reports and the media, Kendra was aware of the on-going atmospheric disruptions west of Greenland, but until now they had not affected her. This was about to change.

The squadron leader eased back on the flight controls, bringing her aircraft to a cruising altitude of forty thousand feet. At this height, the nimble fighter jets would avoid most commercial airline traffic, though they were already far from the nearest civilian routes. Over her right shoulder, Kendra watched her wingman close in alongside her Eurofighter. He kept a slight distance in the event they needed to suddenly manoeuvre.

"Lion leader to lion two," she instructed, "come right to heading two four zero and maintain current speed and altitude."

"Roger lion leader," came the calm reply.

Kendra looked down at her control console, as well as her digitised helmet visor. Despite her years of flying warplanes, she never lost her wonder at what these marvels of modern technology could do. The radio crackled to life.

"Lion flight, this is air ops control. You are to vector north on a bearing of three three zero and rendezvous with a *Voyager* tanker for mid-air refuelling and onward intercept task. Transmitting coordinates now."

The air navigation systems on the Eurofighter were a work of art. Without touching a dial, Kendra sat back as her onboard computer received the automated coordinates from the air operations centre. Once the new heading was uploaded, the two Eurofighters banked in unison to the north on autopilot. Both pilots knew their jets burned the most amount of fuel during take-off, and needed to be topped up before they could carry on with their assigned mission.

The pain in Kendra's lower stomach was immediate. The slight gravitational pressure exerted by the plane's right turn sent a stabbing sensation throughout her abdomen. For a few seconds, the pain was so intense she thought she would pass out. Kendra had felt the discomfort a few days earlier, but dismissed it as either cramps or indigestion. Her workout routine hadn't changed, so she was sure it wasn't a sports injury. As soon as her aircraft levelled off, the pain was gone. Kendra promised herself she'd visit Keflavik's infirmary once her current sortie was over.

After an uneventful fifteen minutes, a lone RAF *Voyager* transport plane appeared. It cruised slightly below Kendra and her wingman. Based on an Airbus A330, this particular aircraft was equipped with internal fuel bladders. Using dangling wingtip drogues, military aircraft could fill up mid-flight. Essentially a flying petrol station, the *Voyager* was able to stay aloft for hours supporting dozens of smaller, gas-guzzling fighter jets. Once Kendra established communication with the tanker, she brought her Eurofighter under the port wing of the larger airplane. Her wingman did the same along the *Voyager's* starboard side. She gently eased the fuelling rod on the nose of her aircraft into one of the tanker's dangling drogues, which resembled an enlarged badminton birdie. Soon, both fighter jets had full fuel tanks and were on their way further north, awaiting their next assignment.

Again the pain. This time Kendra winced aloud as her right hand pressed against her stomach. Her wingman heard the squadron leader's heavy breathing across the radio and chimed in.

"Lion leader, lion two, you all right?"

Kendra blinked repeatedly. The pain seemed to ebb and flow between slight throbbing to sharp, knife-like bolts of anguish.

"Lion two, lion leader, roger, all good."

Slowly, as it had earlier, the pain subsided until it was barely noticeable.

*I know I'm not pregnant*, she wondered, *maybe my appendix?*

"Lion flight, air ops, tasking," a German-accented voice announced.

"Lion leader, send," Kendra replied.

Over the next few minutes, the two Eurofighter pilots were briefed on an unfolding situation that began off the coast of Norway. Earlier in the day, a Russian long-range reconnaissance aircraft had entered Scandinavian airspace, before continuing west across the North Sea. Russian surveillance flights over northern Europe were nothing new, but usually they stayed in international airspace. If the intruder maintained its current heading, it would fly directly across Greenland, past the American airbase at Thule and towards the Davis Strait. Given the heightened tensions with Moscow over its missing submarine so close to North America, any intentional over-flight of alliance territory could be interpreted as an act of aggression. Kendra's orders were simple: Intercept the Russian aircraft and escort it away from NATO airspace.

Kendra increased her aircraft's speed while engaging its forward radar array. Within minutes, her system had picked up one large contact, trailed by two lesser signatures. The smaller contacts were *squawking* a friendly signal, identifying them as a pair of Norwegian fighter jets, while the larger aircraft had its flight transponder turned off.

"Orland flight, this is lion leader," Kendra radioed. "We are approaching your location from the south-east and are prepared to take over escort duties from you."

A female Norwegian voice responded, acknowledging the British squadron leader and her intentions. Kendra and her wingman approached the three aircraft formation from the rear and slightly above their cruising altitude. As the formation came into view, she could see the silver airframe of a massive Russian Tu-95 *Bear* bomber, trailed by two Norwegian F-35 *Lightning* interceptors. One of the friendly fighter jets was alongside the Russian's port wing, while the other was behind its tail, maintaining an excellent firing position if needed. Kendra eased her Eurofighter alongside the lead F-35, while her wingman replaced the aircraft flying behind the *Bear* bomber. She glanced over at the cockpit of her Norwegian counterpart, who gave a slight wave before radioing.

"Lion leader, Orland leader, good to see you."

"Lion leader, roger," Kendra said. "Anything unusual about our guest this morning?"

"Orland leader, everything," came the response. "We have been unable to raise the *Bear's* crew on any frequency." Kendra knew that in itself was not unusual, especially since the Russian plane was flying with its transponder off. The Norwegian continued. "Nor have we been able to detect any pattern of life since the aircraft left European airspace."

"Is it a drone?" Kendra asked.

"Negative, we could clearly see crew movement in both the *Bear's* flight deck and tail observation pod over the North Sea until..." the Scandinavian's voice trailed off.

"Until what?"

"Until the green energy surge."

Kendra listened in fascination as her Norwegian counterpart explained how energy bolts appeared to surround the Russian aircraft east of Jan Mayen Island. This was followed by bright green flashes, which emanated from the flight deck. The spectacle lasted less than a minute, but since then the *Bear* had maintained the same altitude and heading for almost three hours.

*An onboard electrical fire?* Kendra thought to herself. It would explain an incapacitated crew.

"Orland leader, lion leader, roger your last and we'll take it from here," the squadron leader confirmed. "You must be approaching bingo fuel, so best be off and many thanks."

The two F-35s gently banked up and away from the huge Russian plane, leaving the pair of British fighter jets to carry on the escort mission.

Kendra took in the sight before her. A relic of the Cold War, the

*Bear* bomber was powered by four massive, counter spinning turbo-prop engines. The wingspan was some fifty metres across, while its red star emblazoned tail rose twelve metres above its airframe. The nose consisted of a giant refuelling probe at the top, and a white chin-mounted radar dome underneath. Other markings on the flying machine consisted of various Cyrillic lettering, as well as the *Bear's* home unit, the 184th Guards Heavy Bomber Regiment, indicating it was from Engels airbase in western Russia.

Kendra used her aircraft's side mounted high-resolution camera to zoom in on the *Bear's* flight deck. Through the bomber's enormous front windows, she could clearly see its primary controls and two empty pilot seats. She panned the camera lens back along the length of the airframe, occasionally pausing to peer inside several bulbous windows that dotted the silver fuselage. It was when she reached the rear tail gunner windows that she paused.

*Is that blood?*

She glanced down at the zoomed-in image on her monitor, then out her canopy at the back of the Russian plane. Though difficult to distinguish at first, on closer inspection it was clear the *Bear's* rear-facing windows were splattered with a crimson liquid.

"Lion two, we're approaching the eastern coast of Greenland," her wingman reported. In the distance, Kendra could see the snow-covered peaks of the Danish territory. Even though the Russian plane was about to violate sovereign NATO airspace, the British pilot was convinced it was the result of a tragic on-board accident.

"Lion leader, roger, I'm going to call this in," Kendra confirmed. "Air ops, lion leader, situation report, over?"

Static.

"Air ops, lion leader, radio check, radio check."

More static.

"Lion two, can you raise air ops on your radio?"

"Stand by," came the response. "Negative, lion leader."

Kendra started using multiple frequencies trying to reach her higher headquarters, but to no avail. She even tried various commercial channels, again without success.

"Lion leader, lion two, one of the *Bear's* engines is failing."

Kendra eased her Eurofighter slightly above the Russian aircraft just as one of its in-board engines sputtered and stopped. Even with its three remaining engines running, the *Bear* gently started to lose altitude.

"Lion leader, lion two, it can't be running out of fuel, can it?"

*That depends*, Kendra thought. She had no idea how much fuel the *Bear* was actually carrying, or whether some onboard technical issue was to blame. Either way, when fully fuelled, the Russian plane should have been able to reach California with no issues.

"Lion two, engine one is now going."

She watched as a second set of the massive propellers came to a halt, further decreasing the *Bear's* altitude. Again Kendra tried to raise someone on the radio. It was then that she noticed the horizon to her front had taken on a deep green hue. She dismissed the sensation as the northern lights and turned her attention back to the descending Russian bomber. With two engines gone, the *Bear* had already dropped from forty to thirty thousand feet.

"Movement," her wingman called out. "Tail gunner's window."

Kendra quickly angled her Eurofighter alongside the silver plane's massive tail. Through the *Bear's* darkened rear window she saw a human form pull itself towards the dome-shaped glass. The young aviator looked dishevelled, perhaps even in shock. She could see he was not wearing his flight helmet and that his hair appeared matted to his head, likely with dried blood.

"Engine three is out," Kendra's wingman announced.

The *Bear's* rate of descent was now more pronounced, which the British pilots matched. Though still reasonably level in appearance, the Russian plane's loss of altitude had brought it below twenty thousand feet. Kendra looked back at the tail section of the bomber just as the trio of aircraft crossed over Greenland's east coast.

*Get out of there*, she beckoned in her mind. *You're over land, you can bail out.*

"Lion two, lion leader, what's the average height of the mountains below us?"

"Lion two, stand by." After a few moments, "We're over Greenland's north-east National Park, which shows the highest peaks at roughly ten thousand feet or just over three thousand metres."

Kendra did a quick calculation in her head. Based on the *Bear's* current rate of descent, the bomber and its only living occupant had less than ten minutes. She frantically waved her hand, hoping to get the surviving Russian's attention. She saw the young man's face look back at her, opening his mouth as if to yell. He looked alone and scared.

"Fifteen thousand feet and dropping."

Kendra dangled her fingers downward, hoping to simulate a parachute. The Russian just stared back.

"Fourteen thousand."

Again Kendra keyed her radio, trying frequencies assigned to Russian forces, though she knew it was no use.

"Lion two, engine four is out."

*No.*

The enormous wingspan of the Russian bomber was now the only thing keeping it aloft. Like a giant glider, the *Bear* gently arced to the right, ever so slightly.

"Twelve thousand. Lion leader, you need to climb to avoid the mountains."

All around her the sky was a foreboding green, yet Kendra stayed focused on the young Russian trapped in the tail section. Politics aside, this was a human being all alone in an unimaginable situation.

But he was not alone.

Kendra watched in disbelief through the *Bear's* rear window as a second figure, hideous and covered in scars, seemed to rise up behind the trapped crewmember. Even with the confined space inside the bomber, the green-glowing creature towered over the terrified Russian. The tail canopy was suddenly covered in fresh blood, as Kendra looked on helplessly.

"Lion leader, pull up, now!"

Kendra was so mesmerised by the shocking events unfolding in the *Bear's* rear window, she hadn't noticed her in-flight speakers blaring *ter-*

*rain* warnings at her. She pulled back on the flight controls. Her Eurofighter climbed out of danger just as the belly of the Russian plane glanced across an ice-covered peak. The jagged rocks ripped open the aircraft's bomb bay doors, sending snow and boulders tumbling down the latter side of the mountain. The *Bear* continued in the air past the first peak, before banking to the right and slamming into the side of a snow-covered ridge. Kendra watched the entire tragedy unfold from her new vantage point several thousand feet above. It was only then she noticed the pain in her lower stomach had returned.

# CHAPTER 19

The incessant knocking at the door woke Katherine from a deep sleep. She lay for a moment inside her army-issued sleeping bag, gathering her thoughts.

"What is it?" she groaned, still groggy from her slumber. Through the wooden door she could hear the muffled voice of her J2 intelligence officer.

"General, very sorry to disturb you, but a Russian patrol aircraft has gone down over Greenland."

Katherine let the man's comments sink in. "I'll be right out, give me ten minutes."

"Yes ma'am, we'll be in the operations room when you're ready."

The general listened as her colleague's footsteps faded. She looked down at her watch. It read 04:10, almost two hours before the official wake up time known as *reveille*. Katherine unzipped the upper portion of her sleeping bag and sat up. Her bed was a folding metal cot, while her room was nothing more than an old storage closet in the Pond Inlet community centre. The cramped space had been her chief of staff's idea for privacy sake, as opposed to sleeping alongside the headquarters personnel. She clicked the light switch, suddenly filling the confined room with an oppressive florescent glow. As her eyes slowly adjusted to the glare, Katherine noticed several mops and a used cleaning bucket in the corner of her abode.

*Oh the privileges of rank*, she thought, light-heartedly. Then, like so many commanders through the centuries before her, Katherine crawled out of her sleeping bag far earlier than she would have liked, and got dressed.

Her eyes still red from the premature wake up call, Katherine entered the temporary operations centre of her northern headquarters. A young Danish corporal handed her a cup of coffee while a Canadian sergeant gave her a copy of the latest Arctic naval intelligence report. The message was incomplete, sent during one of the rare moments Pond Inlet was able to establish a secure satellite link with the outside world. Katherine sipped her coffee as she skimmed the list of events from the past eight hours.

*A Bear bomber*, she read to herself. *Moscow isn't going to like that one bit*.

The J2 walked over to his commander, handing her another folder, this one marked *secret*. Katherine looked down at the envelope, then at the intelligence officer.

"Just tell me what I need to know, J2," she quietly ordered.

"Yes, General. Yesterday at roughly zero five hundred Zulu time, a single Tupolev Tu-95 *Bear* long-range aircraft departed Engels airbase near Saratov in western Russia. Its task was an apparent polar reconnaissance mission, perhaps in support of the *Volkov* search. The plane's flight path took it north to Murmansk, then west over the Barents Sea where it violated NATO controlled airspace on at least three occasions, before heading out over the North Sea."

*That's a bit audacious*, Katherine thought, *even for the Russians*.

"The *Bear* was then intercepted by two Norwegian F-35 jet fighters, which shadowed the aircraft as far as the eastern edge of Iceland's aircraft identification zone." The intelligence officer adjusted a map of the North Atlantic on a handheld tablet, and showed his boss. "After roughly three hours of flight, the intercept mission was handed over to a pair of British Eurofighter *Typhoons* operating out of Keflavik. They in turn followed the contact west over Greenland where it appears to have run out of fuel and crashed roughly two hundred nautical miles east of Thule airbase. There is no evidence of survivors."

Katherine took the tablet from the American and enlarged a blurred satellite image of a blackened debris field, angled into the side of a snow-covered valley.

"What's been the Russian response?" she asked.

"Ma'am, our communication with higher headquarters is still very poor, but as far as we can tell, Moscow is demanding an explanation from Washington and London. Several conspiracy sites are also spinning a narrative that the *Bear* was deliberately brought down by us."

*Of course they would.*

Katherine looked down at the grainy imagery. This had been the worst summer on record in the Arctic for atmospheric interference. The inability to maintain reliable radio and satellite communication in the north had become so poor, the Federal Aviation Administration had closed all commercial polar flight routes to Europe. Instead, airliners had to use the central Atlantic air corridors. This had increased time and fuel costs while wreaking havoc during the summer's peak travel season. As inconvenient as the situation was for thousands of European vacationers, it was the least of Katherine's concerns.

"What has the Russian military response been?" she asked.

The J2 answered apologetically. "Unknown, General."

"Unknown because they have not responded, or unknown because we can't reach anybody worth a damn outside of Pond Inlet?" The sharpness in Katherine's tone belied her own frustration. She composed herself and put a reassuring hand on the intelligence officer's arm.

"Thank you, J2", she smiled. "As soon as the Russian defence attaché shows up for the morning briefing, please have him come see me. Things could get rather interesting."

Liam left his in-laws' home before anyone else was up. He walked down Pond Inlet's central dirt road, past several mobile homes and closed storefronts. The early morning air was cooler than the past few days, but still several degrees above normal for this time of year. The northern sky continued to glow a deep hue of green. Under his arm he carried *U-537's* logbook and the German autopsy report the late Dr Douglas had sent him, so many years ago. He was still piecing together in his mind how he would explain his discovery to Brigadier-General Tremblay. Even Liam was baffled by what he'd read. He found it difficult to comprehend how deceased remains of people who died eighty years apart, could end up with identical post-mortem markings burned into their skin. This, combined with his interpretation of the symbol's ancient Norse meaning, raised more questions than answers.

As Liam passed Co-Op Street, en route to the community centre, he noticed a lone woman approaching from the direction of the airfield. She was in her early forties, dressed in jeans and a Danish naval overcoat. Her blonde hair was tied in a ponytail under a baseball cap with HDMS *Knud Rasmussen* stitched across the front. She looked to be in a hurry, carrying a reinforced briefcase under one arm. They were the only two people about this early in the day.

"Morgen," Liam called out in his broken Danish.

"Hey," she responded with a sudden smile, "hvordan går det?"

"Uh, you've got me there," Liam replied, a bit embarrassed. "You're asking me how I'm doing, I think?"

She let out a friendly laugh and walked over.

"Your pronunciation was so good, I thought you spoke Danish." The woman looked up a Liam with a smile. "My name is Rikke, pleased to meet you."

"I'm Doctor Holstrom," he said before pausing. "My name is Liam."

The Dane smiled again and extended her hand. "Since we're being formal, I'm Doctor Rikke Larsen, medical physician from the *Rasmussen*. I just arrived on the morning helicopter run from my ship. Do you live in Pond Inlet?"

"Yes, well sort of. My in-laws live in Pond Inlet, but I live and work at the University of Minnesota."

"Your in-laws live in Pond Inlet, which means you're married?"

Liam bowed his head. "I'm recently widowed."

"Oh, I'm so sorry," Rikke said, quietly taking a step back. "Forgive me, I had no idea. There I go, always putting my foot in my mouth... wait a minute, did you say your last name was Holstrom?"

Liam nodded.

"*The* Professor Holstrom who wrote the ground-breaking United

Nations report on the effects of climate change in the Arctic?" she asked, genuinely impressed.

"That's me."

"Your findings have been required reading at the Danish maritime academy for several years now. You must be going to attend the morning military briefing at the community centre?"

"Yes, you?" Liam asked, welcoming the change in conversation. Rikke gestured back positively as the front door of a café behind them opened, its owner emerging to place deck chairs on the patio.

"We have a few minutes, want to grab a coffee?" she asked.

With that, Liam and Rikke entered the small restaurant, the pressing need to attend the morning briefing temporarily set aside for a more human moment.

"Clean up that signal!" Ivan ordered angrily. The acting captain of the Russian frigate *Nikolay Khabalov* pressed the radio headset against his ears, closing his eyes in concentration. Several sailors vainly tried adjusting the satellite communication equipment before them, as Ivan keyed his microphone.

"Fleet control, this is *Khabalov*, say again all after hostile, over?"

Following a brief pause, a garbled response came across the radio.

"*Khabalov*, fleet control [*static*] posture [*static*] aircraft loss [*static*] hostile act ...-stroy."

"Dammit," Ivan cursed, "I can't hear a bloody thing they're saying!"

He threw the headset at the communication room console and stormed back onto the ship's adjacent bridge. As he appeared, any non-essential personnel quickly made themselves scarce, leaving only the frigate's pilot and chief petty officer at their posts. Ivan punched the back of his chair. His ship was effectively blind, sitting among floating sea ice, with no means to reach anyone from home.

Ivan took a deep breath and tried to compose himself by reviewing what he knew so far. His brother Sergei's submarine *Volkov* had now been missing for a month, yet Moscow was refusing to declare the vessel lost, preferring the term "overdue". The only justification for this, he thought, was that the *Volkov* was in fact not missing, or the GRU were playing yet another cynical deception ploy against their western counterparts. Either way, the *Khabalov* had no means to confirm with its higher headquarters what was actually going on due to the cursed electromagnetic interference. Though his ship could still manoeuvre, the propeller shafts were somehow infested with a freakish type of aquatic worm. Add to that the loss of the frigate's helicopter and crew to an apparent mid-air collision with the Americans, and the ship was unable to scout for over-the-horizon pack ice while navigating. Now, he was receiving garbled reports of a Russian aircraft being lost over Greenland with NATO aircraft in pursuit. Had it been shot down? If so, was he to engage the North American warships in the vicinity as reprisal? Was it an accident? Finally, there were the sonic energy waves they'd been exposed to a few days earlier. Who or what was responsible for that? The lack of information was aggravating beyond words.

He walked over to the primary chart table in the centre of the bridge. The ship's chief joined him. The *Khabalov* was roughly three nautical miles south of a massive floating ice shelf, several hundred square kilometres in size. Within a few hundred metres of the ice shelf's southern tip, closest to the frigate's current position, were a collection of American and Canadian soldiers. Ivan knew the Arctic troops were on the ice looking for something. They had been dropped off several days earlier by two large helicopters, proceeding on foot in a westerly search pattern ever since.

*Had they found the Volkov trapped in ice?* Ivan seethed, before his mind went to a darker place. *Had they found pieces of the Volkov's wreckage?* He quickly dismissed the thought. To the west, just over the horizon, was the guided missile destroyer USS *Samuel Ronaldson*, while to his east sat the Danish patrol ship *Knud Rasmussen*.

If the Americans and their allies knew where the *Volkov* was, they'd have to tell Moscow. This was a search and rescue operation after all. Ivan refused to use the term recovery, given its implications towards the fate of his beloved brother Sergei. And what of the downed reconnaissance aircraft from his homeland? Ivan looked over at his chief.

"What's our current weapon disposition?" he asked quietly.

The older man looked at him before answering.

"Sir, we're carrying sixteen *Kalibr* surface-to-surface missiles in the vertical launchers, twelve anti-submarine torpedoes, and full ammunition stocks for the forward deck canon and the two anti-missile miniguns."

"Thank you, Chief," Ivan said, looking out at the green sky.

*If it does come to blows, dear brother, we'll have a fighting chance to avenge you.*

The young soldier tasked as a runner arrived panting beside Eleanor. His home platoon was currently some four hundred metres ahead of Major Eleanor Matthews and the rest of her Arctic infantry company. Eleanor's sub-unit was spread out over a thousand metres, tasked with searching the southern-most section of floating pack ice in the Davis Strait. As the troops in her organisation slowly pushed west, engineers with metal detectors had been deployed ahead of the formation. They were looking for an elusive sonar contact detected weeks before in the area, that some felt might be the missing Russian submarine *Volkov*. The runner was needed to relay messages since their issued personal radios continued to prove useless.

"Ma'am, the sappers ahead of one platoon have found something," the runner reported. "The Lieutenant requests you please come forward and have a look."

Eleanor acknowledged the young man and sent him on his way, then called over her sergeant major, the company second-in-command Captain Simmons, and her signaller. The three formed a circle around their commander. Eleanor reflected how they looked like puffy white snowmen in their winter parkas, mukluk boots, and snowshoes.

"The engineers up front have picked up something in the ice with the metal detectors," she explained. "Sergeant Major Bernard, I want you to join me with my signaller and Ujurak, as we move forward. Captain Simmons, you've got the rest of the company until we return. Have the troops pause in location for now. They can set up their Arctic tents for warmth if we halt for more than fifteen minutes."

"C'est bon," her sergeant major bellowed in French, before moving off with their guide Ujurak, Eleanor and the signaller.

The sun was high in the east, casting a jade-coloured glow across the ice before them. Up ahead, Eleanor spotted the tail end of the lead platoon, its personnel still in their sled harnesses, ready to manually tow their toboggans like human horses. She rendezvoused with the platoon commander to receive a brief situation report, then continued west with her four-person headquarters team.

"Over here, ma'am," a voice called out.

Eleanor adjusted her snow goggles in order to see the two combat engineers, known as sappers, to her front. A female engineer was holding a plotter map in both hands, while her male colleague had a circular metal detector on a long pole held out in front of him. Normally used for locating land mines, today the device had identified something much larger. Eleanor walked up towards the pair, the ice under her snowshoes making a cracking sound as she approached.

Suddenly she was falling.

Eleanor reached out her arms, frantically trying to grab at the icy walls racing by. With a crash, she lurched to a halt and became inverted. She dangled upside down as her signaller landed below her, face-down with a grunt, his rifle and radio impacting beside him. The man didn't move. Eleanor looked about, trying to deduce what had just happened. She was hanging upside down, several metres above the ground. It was hard to tell from her position, but it looked like they'd fallen about fifteen metres. Her snowshoes were caught between two jagged ice ledges, inside an apparent cavern. They must have walked across a pressure ridge and fallen through the thin layer of frozen snow covering the top. The surrounding pack ice was easily a thousand years old, meaning this icy cavern could have existed for centuries.

"Calice de tabarnak, Major, are you all right?" Sergeant Major Bernard hollered from high above. Eleanor quickly inspected her arms and legs while still dangling upside down.

"I'm OK," she yelled towards the surface, "but my signaller isn't moving."

"Roger, we'll get you out. Just stay put!"

Eleanor could hear the sergeant major high above, swearing madly in French. She looked back down at her signaller on the floor below, still motionless. It was then she realised he had landed on a wooden floor. She tried adjusting her eyes to the darkened shadows of the ice cavern. Eleanor took off her tinted goggles and rifle strap, allowing both to fall two metres to the bottom. She then pulled herself up, as if doing a sit up in mid-air, and unbuckled the harness attaching her boots to her trapped snowshoes. She landed beside the signaller with a thud, scrambling over to the man and gently turning him on his side. He was breathing but unconscious. Eleanor quickly performed a tertiary pat down of his extremities, making sure they were not damp with blood. All seemed ok.

"Don't worry, brother, help is on the way," she whispered. Next Eleanor pulled a headlamp from her parka and placed it over her wool hat. She turned on the light and scanned about the cavern. Her signaller was lying across a series of long wooden planks. Nearest to them, the boards were covered in snow, but became exposed as they extended deeper into the dark tunnel. The air smelt dank and stale. She stood up and adjusted the headlamp to her front. The timbers creaked under her weight as she advanced deeper into what resembled an enormous glacial cave. Eleanor looked down at the wooden planks, which she noticed were held together by square nails. The boards were covered in what appeared to be miniscule insect trails, likely the residue from a long-ago infestation. She walked further along the planks until they dropped off, revealing a square wooden pit about the size of a small car. Within the pit she could see large barrels, bits of cut-down lumber, and several bags made from a rough woollen material. The sub-zero temperatures must have preserved the site.

*What the hell is this place?*

Past the pit she identified a very large wooden pole rising several metres from the floor, before disappearing into the frozen cavern's roof. As Eleanor adjusted her headlamp upwards, she could see another wooden beam, bisecting the much bigger pole by ninety degrees. Swathes of coloured fabric dangled horizontally from the decaying spar. At the base of the primary pole, she noticed what looked like a metal storage chest. She hesitantly approached the box, shining her light across its rusted surface. The old chest was the size of a large suitcase. It was covered in intricate line markings she did not recognise. Eleanor tried opening it, but to no avail.

She then noticed an antique lock on the front of the container, which could probably be opened with a key. Whether made of lead or primitive steel, the beat-up trunk was most likely what had set off the metal detectors above. She took some photos and video with her smartphone of the sea chest, as well as the other contents in the storage pit. Everything else around her seemed to be made of wood, save for the square nails.

*Where am I?* she thought in awe, moving back towards the cavern entrance and her injured colleague. She tripped over something and lost her balance. Her clumsiness was rewarded with a painful face-plant onto the frozen timber floor. Eleanor regained her composure, shining the headlamp towards her feet to see what she'd fallen across. Within the beam of light she was amazed to find several enormous and very well preserved rowing oars.

# CHAPTER 20

"How do we know you didn't shoot it down?" Colonel Borishov demanded, slamming his fist on the desk. "You have yet to provide us with any credible proof this was an *accident*."

Katherine looked back at the fuming Russian defence attaché from across the map table. Though her headquarters was filled with forty personnel, the room was dead quiet. The general knew her counterpart's bravado was partly a reaction to his own frustration at the lack of information surrounding the latest Arctic *incident*. If Katherine was unable to reliably reach anyone with her state-of-the-art communications equipment, she was sure Colonel Borishov couldn't either.

"Colonel, we understand your concern," she said in a conciliatory tone, but was immediately cut off by the Russian.

"No, you don't! How dare you feign empathy. Over a hundred of my countrymen have likely perished in the last two months, yet you share nothing with us. Now *two* aircraft have been lost and still no sign of our submarine. If this had happened in our waters, we would have immediately engaged you for assistance."

Katherine knew that was a bit rich. When the nuclear submarine *Kursk* sank in 2000 due to an onboard explosion, it had taken the Russian fleet days to request underwater assistance from the outside world. In the end, it proved too late to save the trapped submariners. Still, her own political masters had similarly hesitated before allowing Russian military assets into the Davis Strait to join the current *Volkov* search.

*If it was in fact missing*, she reflected quietly. Katherine's American intelligence officer and his colleagues were convinced the *Volkov* was still lurking about. Just then, Dr Liam Holstrom and Dr Rikke Larsen entered the operations centre.

Colonel Borishov vectored his anger towards the newest arrivals.

"They know what's going on," he bellowed at Liam and Rikke. "I heard your daughter the other day explaining what you were up to, Dr Holstrom. What you know about these so-called symbols. It's all an elaborate deception operation, admit it!"

Now Katherine was intrigued, as Liam stared back stunned at his Russian accuser. The two civilians quickly moved over to the general's side, as if for protection. They were obviously at a loss regarding the tense situation they had suddenly stumbled upon. Liam was about to answer the defence attaché when Katherine raised her hand.

"Colonel Borishov, we understand your frustration," she allowed. "Believe me, we feel it as well. We are only able to get two, maybe three messages out a day due to the relentless atmospheric interference. The only thing we ask is for your patience, out of professional courtesy, if nothing else."

The Russian glanced at the faces about the room, before storming off. "To hell with you," he murmured on his way out, just loud enough for a few bystanders to hear.

Katherine dropped her head, then looked over at Liam and Rikke with a reassuring glance. "Don't worry," she said. "That was just as much bluster on his part as it was substance. Though I genuinely sympathise with his frustration."

She glanced at her communications officer as if to say *got anything yet?* The man just shook his head quietly in the negative. She looked back at her guests, her demeanour now noticeably stern.

"Well, Dr Holstrom, I'm not sure what our Russian friend was insinuating, but evidently, you're not allowed to be here."

Rikke looked over at Liam, whose shoulders sank. He knew he was caught.

"You lied to me, my friend," Katherine continued. "Your security clearance expired years ago." Before he could protest, two military police constables appeared beside him. "Gentlemen, please escort the good professor outside."

"General, wait," Liam pleaded. "We have to show you something, it's very important. We think the downed American helicopter pilot may have been murdered."

"Murdered?" Katherine scoffed. "You lied to me once, professor, why should I believe you now?"

"I know it sounds far-fetched, but we think the same person killed several French fishermen earlier this summer."

"What are you suggesting, Dr Holstrom? That some kind of serial killer is operating in one of the most inhospitable places on earth?"

Liam nodded, though the general's tone made him question his reasoning.

"Let me guess," Katherine continued. "This same individual also knows how to bring down a multi-million dollar surveillance plane, correct? Hard to believe, professor."

Before Liam could respond, Katherine ordered the MPs to take him outside, leaving Rikke alone in a visibly suspicious room.

"Easy now, troops," Eleanor yelled encouragingly against the deafening noise. Four soldiers carefully carried the stretcher with her unconscious signaller inside the awaiting *Chinook* helicopter, its twin rotor blades beating about the frigid air. Once the casualty was onboard, two more personnel hauled up the decorated sea chest Eleanor had found earlier in the pack ice. The helicopter's crew chief strapped the metal container down securely, using hooks embedded in the cargo bay floor.

Eleanor turned to her second-in-command, Captain Janet Simmons, leaning forward to yell in her ear. "All right, sister, you've got the company until I get back."

The American gave her the *okay* symbol, as Sergeant Major Bernard and Ujurak joined them.

"Be sure you get yourself checked out as well, ma'am," the sergeant major encouraged. "That was a hell of a fall."

"I'm good, Sergeant Major," Eleanor replied, feeling somewhat guilty at having to leave her troops behind on the frozen ocean. "Just make sure the ice cavern entrance is secure, and no one goes down there."

Sergeant Major Bernard nodded back while Eleanor handed her rucksack to the awaiting crew chief. As much as she wanted to stay, what she'd accidently discovered within the sea ice was far too important. With their communications equipment still down, the daily helicopter resupply run was the only sure way to let her commander in Pond Inlet know what they'd found. Eleanor shook hands with her colleagues, then boarded through the helicopter's rear ramp, while the others moved away. Soon the massive aircraft lifted off the floating ice shelf, and headed west.

As the noise from the rotor blades faded, CSM Bernard looked towards their guide, who was staring at the darkened cave opening.

"What do you think, Ujurak?" he asked. "Ever thought you'd find a boat trapped in the ice? What do you figure, a nineteenth century whaling ship?"

The guide took a moment before answering the sergeant major, his eyes still fixed on the frozen cavern entrance.

"No," Ujurak said apprehensively. "I fear it is much older."

Ivan watched through his binoculars as the olive drab flying machine rose above the sea ice. From the bridge of the *Nikolay Khabalov* he was able to see the American and Canadian troops load something into the helicopter, but wasn't sure what. It had to be from his brother's missing submarine. What else could they possibly have found frozen and floating in the middle of the Arctic Ocean? He watched the *Chinook* as it flew west towards Baffin Island, tracking it until it disappeared over the green horizon. The chief of the boat joined the *Khabalov's* acting captain, following his gaze.

"Report," Ivan said quietly under his breath.

"Sir, the infestation of sea worms has spread slightly," the chief remarked. "They seem to be moving along the twin propeller shafts. We've tried what little pest control poison we have on board, but it has had limited effect."

"Can we still make way?" Ivan asked.

"Yes sir, they have not reached the main engines, but I strongly recommend we leave the area soonest and put into the nearest port to effect repairs. Nuuk in Greenland would be the closest..."

Ivan cut an ice-cold stare at the man.

"Chief, this ship is going nowhere," he hissed.

*Not until I know what happened to you, dear Sergei.*

"Keep an eye on their progress and keep me informed," Ivan ordered. "In the worst case, we do carry *other* poisons we could use."

The chief petty officer went white. He leaned forward, urgently whispering to Ivan. "Sir, with all due respect, we are only allowed to use *those* poisons in time of war. Even then, it would be a violation of the Geneva Convention, never mind the serious risk to the crew..."

"Captain, Captain!" A young sailor interrupted, emerging from the communications room. "We've received a message from Fleet headquarters. It was garbled, but we managed to get most of it."

Ivan took the printed communiqué from the excited sailor and skimmed through its contents, before handing it to his chief to read.

"Sir, what does this mean?" the older man asked confused.

Ivan rolled his shoulders, trying to relax his tense muscles before answering.

"It seems Moscow would like to send a rather stern message to our North American friends in the form of a *White Swan*."

The two men silently peered out the bridge windows at the bleak seascape of open water and floating icebergs.

"Squadron Leader Livingstone, I'm afraid you have kidney stones."

Kendra looked at the Keflavik base doctor surprised. "I'm sorry, Doctor, I have what?"

"Kidney stones. Small calcium deposits that have built up in your kidneys due to bouts of chronic dehydration. I see it in fighter pilots all the time. You don't drink enough water when you fly, in order to avoid the urge to urinate. After several years, this is what can happen."

"But, the pain was in my stomach area," Kendra complained. "Aren't the kidneys in your lower back?"

The doctor read over her notes as she replied. "Actually, when they form in your kidneys, they're usually quite painless. It's when they pass through your urinary tract that they hurt. The really big ones can require surgery."

"Surgery?"

"Sometimes, yes. In the meantime, you'll need to start drinking plenty of water. We'll also get you in for an ultrasound next week." The doctor scribbled some notes in Kendra's medical file. "And I'm afraid you'll need to be grounded until this is resolved."

"What?" the fighter pilot protested. "Why?"

"It's for your own safety. If you're in the air when an enlarged kidney stone suddenly tries to pass, it may get stuck, which will lead to a whole series of dangerous complications if not treated right away. Besides, what if the pain becomes so debilitating you pass out?"

Kendra just looked at the doctor in stunned silence.

"Don't worry, Squadron Leader Livingstone, it's not that bad. As long as you're on the ground and near medical help, you're safe. Now, here's a prescription for you in case the pain comes back, as well as your ultrasound appointment time for next week. Have a nice day."

Kendra quietly exited the smiling doctor's office without a word. *Have a nice day*, she thought, defeated. She emerged outside and walked back towards her barracks, located next to the active airfield. Kendra lived to fly. It was the whole reason she'd joined the Royal Air Force. She was still trying to process the tragedy she'd witnessed over Greenland. The image of the young Russian aviator, trapped in the tail of his aircraft, haunted her thoughts. It was bad enough her commanding officer was sceptical of what she'd witnessed. Her in-flight camera had only captured static. Now she was about to be grounded.

"Quick reaction flight scramble!" The base loudspeakers blared.

That meant her.

*But I'm not officially grounded yet*, Kendra rationalised, running towards her locker room.

Within twenty minutes she had linked up with her wingman, started her Eurofighter *Typhoon*, and taken off from Keflavik airfield. As the two British fighters reached their pre-assigned cruising altitude of thirty-seven thousand feet, Kendra's wingman signalled over the radio.

"Lion leader, lion two, so what did the Doc say?"

"It's a woman thing," she replied, knowing her little fib would politely shut down the man's curiosity. Just then, the in-flight computers on both Eurofighters began receiving electronic orders from the air operations centre in Germany.

The two pilots took several seconds to read their newest instructions.

"Lion leader, lion two, this must be an exercise, correct?"

Kendra scanned the incoming message on her monitor a second time to make sure she understood it correctly. The text was plain and direct, as only military orders could be.

"Lion two, lion leader, we will proceed to the pre-assigned coordinates for intercept. I confirm, if the unidentified contact violates sovereign NATO airspace, our signal is buster; I say again our signal is buster. Confirm my last, over?"

After a pause, her wingman responded. "Roger lion leader, I confirm, our signal is buster."

The pair of fighter jets banked north under the glare of the summer Arctic sun while Kendra engaged the on-board weapon system. Based on a fusion software suite, it synchronised the homing radars of the six *Meteor* air-to-air missiles her Eurofighter carried under its wings. Though Kendra had dropped several bombs in anger during her military career, she'd never had to shoot down an opposing aircraft. She hoped she wouldn't have to today either.

"Lion leader, lion two, I have positive contact with two bogies bearing three one zero, angels forty-five, range one hundred. Their transponders are off."

"Lion two, lion leader, roger, climbing now."

Within ten minutes Kendra and her wingman had closed the distance towards the two radar contacts. The pair of unidentified aircraft to their front flew in formation, heading north-west, but stayed away from Greenland's eastern airspace.

*Good*, Kendra thought.

The pain shot through her abdomen again. In her rush to get airborne she hadn't taken any of the prescribed painkillers she'd been given. The nose of her fighter dipped slightly as she fought the urge to pass out.

*Oh God, make it stop.*

"Lion leader, lion two, are you all right?" came the concerned call from her wingman. Kendra steadied her Eurofighter as the pain subsided, just as quickly as it had appeared.

"Roger... roger, all good, lion two. Closing on contacts now."

Kendra looked up to see the sleek white wingspan of two enormous swing-wing aircraft take shape in her heads up display. The pair of high-speed bombers were flying roughly eighty metres apart as the British jets took up their escort positions.

"Ops centre, lion leader, contact identified," Kendra reported. "We have a positive tally of two times Russian *Blackjack* fast-attack bombers. Angels are forty-five thousand feet with a cruising speed of five hundred knots, roughly two hundred nautical miles east of Greenland."

Known affectionately as *White Swans* by their flight crews, the Tupolev Tu-160s were the largest fast-attack bombers in the world. Capable of reaching speeds in excess of Mach two, they could carry dozens of cruise missiles within their rotating internal bomb bays. Their presence, given recent events in the area, was a direct escalation. Moscow was apparently trying to send a message that they were displeased. For now, however, the two Russian behemoths and their trailing British escorts remained safely in international airspace.

Erika sat on the porch of her grandparents' lodge with Jordan. Her childhood friend had stopped by with his little sister Amber earlier in the day. The pair watched the young girl quietly as she played a game of hopscotch on the gravel road with Sandra. Inside the lodge, Nicole and Michelle were helping her grandparents prepare an early lunch.

"When do you head back south?" Jordan asked softly.

Erika looked down, tracing the carvings on her leather purse with her finger. "We're supposed to fly back in a few days," she said. "The fall hockey season starts next week, and school the week after that."

"That's too bad," he sighed. "It's been good having you around. You make my sister very happy."

Erika sensed what Jordan was really trying to say and smiled. She looked at the little girl laughing with Sandra, then over at Jordan. She was impressed with who the young man had become. Following a life of substance abuse, his father had finally taken his own life when Jordan was twelve, leaving him and his grieving mother to raise Amber. He could have wallowed in self-pity, or worse, run away from the sudden responsibilities he'd inherited, but he didn't. Jordan became a positive male role model in his sister's life, a position left vacant by their father's suicide. He had confided in Erika how lucky he felt that Amber was too young to have any memories of their abusive dad. "It's probably for the best," he'd say. She knew behind her friend's dark brown eyes were family secrets too painful to reveal. Though only twenty, Jordan sometimes sounded twice his age. Erika rested her head on his shoulder, wrapping her arm around his.

"Hi, Doctor H." Sandra waved as Liam walked up the street, dejected.

"Hey Dad, what's wrong?" Erika asked as she stood up to meet him. Liam shook his head in defeat.

"It's nothing, cub. Your Dad has done a dumb thing, but it will be all right." He looked over at Jordan, then back at Erika with a soft smile. "I guess I'll leave you two alone."

The thumping noise originated from the eastern horizon. The massive olive drab helicopter slowly appeared just above the rooftops as it approached. Its flight path would take it directly over the lodge, as it did almost every day at this time. Suddenly Erika felt something move against her chest.

She paused.

The ancient amulet her father had given her was not only radiating its comforting warmth, it was now also vibrating. The pendant lifted up against the inside of Erika's sweater. Both Liam and Jordan watched in amazement as the outer fabric of her garment moved back and forth on its own. The sight reminded Liam of an old science fiction movie he'd watched in his youth, about sinister aliens bursting out of a victim's chest.

"What's going on?" Jordan asked, alarmed.

"I don't know," Erika said nervously, trying to prevent the amulet under her sweater from moving. "It's doing it on its own!"

Just then, the enormous twin bladed aircraft soared overhead as it returned from its resupply mission. The ancient artifact around Erika's neck shot out of her clothes, hovering in mid-air towards the passing helicopter. The only thing preventing the amulet from flying away was the necklace attaching it to Erika's neck. She held onto the thin jewellery chain with all her might.

"Dad, it wants to go where the chopper is," Erika yelled, the chain cutting into the back of her neck. Liam couldn't believe what he was seeing.

"Cub, if this is some kind of practical joke, it's not funny."

"Dad, I swear it's not. Jordan, help me!"

The younger man grabbed Erika's hands, trying to keep the amulet from soaring aloft.

The sensation returned.

*Let it guide you.*

Erika froze.

*It will lead you.*

She gently took Jordan's hands away from hers, leaving the amulet to hover in mid-air at the end of her necklace. Then she was off running, heading in whichever direction the artifact guided her. Liam and Jordan looked at each other, then took off after Erika. Amber and Sandra continued to play hopscotch, oblivious to what was going on.

The sensation in her body was the strongest she had ever felt.

Erika let herself go as she ran, the amulet instinctively leading the way. She sprinted through the open gates of the small airport, just as the giant flying machine was powering down. Erika stopped some twenty metres behind the mighty *Chinook*. She watched as several ground personnel carried a stretcher-bound soldier to an awaiting ambulance. Erika stood motionless, her hands by her side. The sensation she felt was intoxicating. A wave of euphoria hypnotised her senses. The piece of jewellery around her neck continued to hover, pointing at the helicopter's open ramp. Two aircrew carried off a large sea chest, covered in rust. They placed it on the ground then joined a female officer near the rear of the *Chinook*. Erika had never felt such clarity of thought in her life. Somehow she knew exactly what needed to be done, what the amulet *wanted* her to do.

Erika was startled by Liam's hand on her arm. He looked at his daughter, desperately concerned.

"Cub, what is it?" he pleaded. "What's going on?"

She glanced over at her father, just as Jordan arrived out of breath.

"It wants to be with the sea chest," Erika said calmly.

"What do you mean *it*?" Liam exclaimed. "What wants to be with whom?"

Without another word, Erika removed the necklace from around her neck. As if in a trance, she walked over to the intricately carved container sitting on the tarmac.

*You are strong and wise.*

She looked over briefly at the female officer who was distracted, speaking with two pilots.

*You know what is needed.*

Erika leaned down beside the chest. She inserted the amulet into the rusted lock on the front of the container. It fit perfectly. Next she turned it like a key, unlocking the chest with a single click.

# THE HOURLY SAGAS

THE
ARCTIC REGIONS
OF
NORTH AMERICA
BY
EDWD WELLER. F.R.G.S
PARRY ISLAND
MELVILLE ISLAND
BATHURST Isld
CORNWALLIS ISLAND
Melville Sound
Pce of Wales Land
Pce Albert Land
Pce Albert Sound
Wollaston Land
Victoria Land
King William Land
Booth
Banks Land
Minto Inlet
Baring I.
Arctic Circle
Great Bear Lake

# CHAPTER 21

Erika stood quietly with her mother in the corner of the large room. She sensed they were inside one of the earth-built longhouses from her dreams. The air was scented with charcoal. A thin layer of smoke from an unseen fire pit curled up against the thatch roof. There were no windows, the only natural light coming from a small doorway on the far side of the chamber. The dirt floor was covered in a series of long wool carpets, while deer or caribou hides hung along the walls. In the centre was a wooden table upon which rested a motionless figure, covered in white linen. The sight of the body caused Erika to reach for her mother's hand.

*Who is it?*

*Someone's father.*

The two watched as a pair of middle-aged women entered the room, both carrying copper pots filled with warm water. The women wore heavy dresses, covered by long grey aprons. They gently removed the linen from the dead man's body, revealing a naked figure with ghost-white skin. Using a damp cloth, one of the women caringly washed the upper torso and shoulders of the body. The other woman turned the man's head in order to braid his flowing blonde hair. Erika instantly recognised his face as the axe-wielding lunatic from her nightmares. Now, however, he looked peaceful. His enraged features replaced by the calm stillness of death.

*How did he die, mother?*

Star paused, sighing quietly.

*Skraeling.*

Erika looked over at her. Even in the dimly lit room she could read the anguish on her mother's face. Star seemed to foresee a painful moment was approaching. Her daughter was about to ask what troubled her, when two young children were brought into the room. The boy and girl from Erika's dreams stood silently beside the table, tears rolling down their faces. One of the middle-aged women nudged the grieving pair forward, but they refused to move. The small blonde girl looked in Erika's direction, seemingly making eye contact, before moving away from the fallen man on the table. It was all too much for Erika, who started to shudder with emotion.

*Why did you bring me here, mother?*

There was no reply.

The children gave way to four bearded men carrying an empty wooden casket, which they set down beside the table. One of the women in the room re-wrapped the deceased body in fresh linen while the other appeared to fasten its feet together. She accomplished this by interlacing the dead man's two large toes with string. Next the four men placed the body into the open coffin. Erika watched in disbelief as one of the apparent pallbearers used a pair of large black nails to hammer his fallen comrade's feet into the base of the casket. While this was being done, the other three men used primitive pick axes to knock down parts of the longhouse's inner wall. Erika squinted at the sudden burst of sunlight streaming through the newly created exit.

*What are they doing mother? Why did they nail down and tie his feet together, or break down the wall?*

Another pause.

*It's for his own safety... and theirs.*

Mother and daughter watched as one of the local women placed a set of iron scissors on the body's chest. The men then raised and lowered the casket three times in various directions, before carrying the body-laden box out through the destroyed wall, feet first. Erika peered through the opening as the deceased was placed atop a wooden funeral pyre, built along the rocky shoreline. An elderly man in long, battered robes offered a few words in an unfamiliar language. Then, as roughly a dozen villagers looked on, the stack of wood was set alight using tar-covered torches. The little blonde girl from Erika's dreams stood closest to the rising flames, her cheeks swollen from tears.

Star moved beside her daughter. She placed her hands on Erika's shoulders, the red glow of the flames outside glinting against their faces. She urged her thoughts into her daughter's mind.

*Take heed of what you see, cub. These rituals were performed long ago. They were done to prevent what they called aptrgangr. For those laid to rest improperly, or who died in anguish...* her words trailed off.

There was growing panic in Erika's mind as she sensed her dream was ending.

*Mother, wait, is aptrgangr a Norse word? Is this a Viking ritual?*

As the image of Star faded, her daughter was aware of a new group of people surrounding her.

*Please mother, what does it mean?*

She tried desperately to focus on her mother's face as Star sent out one last impulse.

*Those who walk again.*

Erika snapped out of her daydream, finding herself still crouched beside the ornate sea chest. Along with her father and Jordan, a tall uniformed woman stood beside her with the nametag *Matthews* on her chest. Erika's hand held her precious amulet firmly inside the ancient container's lock. Somehow, she felt she was in trouble.

"What are you doing?" Major Matthews asked nonchalantly enough.

"It wanted me to..." Erika stopped herself. "I was trying to open the case with my good luck charm."

Liam picked up on his daughter's apprehension, stifling his urge to demand an explanation from her in front of Major Matthews. The army officer seemed polite but distracted. She looked familiar to Liam, probably from one of the daily update briefings he'd attended.

"I doubt your key would open this thing," she said. "It's probably been rusted shut for over a century."

Liam examined the sea chest, his eyes widening as he recognised a number of the intricately etched symbols along its sides.

"Major, where did you find this?" he asked curiously.

"Eleanor is fine, and you wouldn't believe me in a thousand years," she laughed. Liam looked back at her, suddenly quite serious.

"Eleanor, your choice of words is more appropriate than you realise, because that's probably how old this thing is, a thousand years."

The major peered at Liam in silence as Erika stood up beside her father. Her mind was still cloudy from her daydream. What exactly had Star tried to explain, and what were the chances her amulet would unlock the rusted sea chest? She shook her head, trying to concentrate as Liam spoke.

"These markings appear to be Old Norse, the same as those found on ancient rune stones throughout Scandinavia."

Eleanor examined the professor's expression, half-trying to ascertain if he was being serious. She had some idea of his academic credentials, but nothing specific. Her commanding general let him into her HQ, so he must know something about what he's talking about.

"Please, Eleanor," Liam continued, "where did you find this?"

"We found a ship frozen in the pack ice about sixty miles from shore, out in the Davis Strait," she allowed. "By *found*, we literally fell on top of it. My signaller was banged up pretty bad, when the snow under our feet gave way. We figured it's an early nineteenth century whaling ship, based on what we saw."

Liam was fascinated, focusing on Eleanor intently. "Please, what *did* you see? I need you to be specific. Tell me everything that happened."

"You really want to know? Well, we landed on its deck, which was made of pine or birch. Either way, the wooden boards looked to have been infested sometime before freezing, maybe termites? There was also a bunch of storage barrels that smelled like tar, a few old sacks and a single sailing mast in the centre of the vessel. Bits of the original sail were still hanging from the spar. The ship also had at least a dozen oars scattered about, which I assume were used for chasing a whale up close. In the middle of the storage area was this fancy looking chest."

"Eleanor, are you absolutely certain about what you saw?" Liam insisted.

"Of course, I even filmed parts of it."

Liam's mind was alight, rapidly processing the evidence as it was presented to him. Could this really be what it appeared to be? Erika moved alongside her father. She knew when Liam's brain was in "the zone" as he called it, trying to deduce some new academic theory or prediction. The whole series of events seemed too far-fetched to be real. She looked over at Jordan, who appeared utterly confused.

"Who were the Norse anyway?" Eleanor asked after a few moments.

Without thinking, father and daughter answered together.

"Vikings."

Rikke looked about at the faces in the general's office. Their expressions ranged from indifference to contempt. It reminded the doctor of her early days in medical school, having to stare down the condescending glare of her instructors. She had prevailed by sticking to the facts, not letting emotion cloud her convictions. At the moment, the only one in the room to show genuine interest in her findings was the person in charge, Brigadier-General Katherine Tremblay. The general leaned back in her chair as she revisited the data before her.

"Dr Larsen, you're absolutely sure about the carbon dating results?" Katherine asked.

"Yes ma'am," Rikke asserted confidently. "After the initial scan, I ran a complete diagnostic test three times to make sure the system was working. The results were the same. The metallurgy of whatever killed the helicopter pilot from the USS *Samuel Ronaldson* was dated at 996 CE."

"This proves nothing," the J2 intelligence officer protested. The general looked over at the American, urging him with a hand gesture to continue. "Ma'am, there is no serial killer out on the ice, hunting people down. It's clearly the Russians, it has to be. Now they've even gone so far as to use archaic weapons, probably taken from the Hermitage museum, to mess with our heads." Rikke noted the man's sarcastic tone as he continued. "I'm telling you, the submarine *Volkov* is still out there and this is all a sophisticated psychological operation against us. The very fact we continue having these conversations is proof enough their disinformation tactics are working."

"That may be," Katherine allowed, "but it doesn't explain the on-going atmospheric interference, nor the death markings carved into those French sailors recovered in June by the *Rasmussen*..."

"Which are the same type of symbols found on several dead German submariners from the Second World War," Rikke added bluntly.

All eyes were back on the Danish doctor.

"What are you talking about?" the J2 asked dismissively. Rikke ignored him, turning her attention back to his boss.

"Please, General, you need to speak with Dr Liam Holstrom," she pleaded. "I know he misrepresented himself to you, but..."

"You mean lied to me," Katherine interjected sharply. Rikke paused in order to regroup her thoughts before continuing.

"Ma'am, I met with him this morning. He came across an old German autopsy report from the war. The dead *U-boat* sailor in question had been part of a clandestine mission to the far north in 1943. He evidently perished the exact same way as the deceased French crew I examined earlier this summer. The blown-out ribcage, lack of any internal organs or entry wounds, even the triangular incision marks behind the ear were identical, but they were inflicted almost a century apart."

None of this made any sense to Katherine. Not only did the various findings only add to her confusion, it did nothing to address the emerging political crisis developing over the loss of yet another Russian aircraft. How on earth would she explain this to her commanders, let alone her own daughters someday?

"All right Rikke," Katherine relented, "let's hear what Dr Holstrom has to say."

Erika was helping her father and Eleanor load the Norse sea chest onto Jordan's four-wheeled ATV when a camouflaged jeep pulled up to the airfield. Two military police constables emerged from the vehicle, quickly giving Eleanor a salute before one of them addressed Liam.

"Dr Holstrom, Brigadier-General Tremblay would like to see you at her command centre soonest please. Major Matthews, you're obviously free to join."

Erika had returned the amulet back around her neck. It again glowed warmly under her sweater. She glanced over at Liam, who looked at her knowingly. At times, her father was nothing short of awesome.

"I'm only going if my daughter Erika can join us," he stated, causing the two MPs to look at each other. "She is my research assistant and I need her with me." Erika and her dad stood side by side, trying to look defiant.

Eleanor broke the tension in an instant.

"What's with you guys?" she said to Liam and Erika, before pulling rank. "Sergeant, Dr Holstrom and I will ride in your vehicle, his daughter can follow us on the ATV with her boyfriend."

Erika's cheeks flushed bright red. She glanced over at Jordan who was equally embarrassed.

"Uh, he's not... he's not my boyfriend."

"Whatever," Eleanor grinned. "Let's go."

The military jeep pulled away from the airfield, followed by Jordan and Erika on the ATV, the rusted sea chest strapped to its front cage. The drive to the community centre took only a few minutes. Their route brought them past Erika's grandparents' wooden lodge. Her roommate Sandra, and Jordan's little sister Amber, were still playing out front when the vehicles drove past in a cloud of dust. Sandra gestured questioningly behind them as the ATV sped along; Erika's arms were wrapped around Jordan's waist. She pressed her head against his muscular back. Despite her earlier embarrassment, there was no denying it felt good to be this close to him.

The oddly matched vehicles came to a stop in front of the community centre, Liam and Eleanor emerging from the back of the jeep.

"Are you serious?" she was asking the professor.

"What else could it be?" Liam said. "Most of the evidence points towards the same conclusion, as odd as it sounds."

Eleanor vouched to the front guards for Liam, Erika, and Jordan as they carried the ancient sea chest into the unclassified section of the temporary command centre. This was the same room where the frustrated

Russian defence attaché, Colonel Borishov, was often sent by the general to cool his heels. At the moment, he was nowhere to be found, which was probably a good thing. Erika and Jordan set the rusted container down in the middle of the room, surrounded by giant television screens and collapsible wooden tables. Various official-looking people scurried about as Erika took in the sights before her. A woman in her forties with a Danish flag on her shirt walked up to Liam with a big smile. They shook hands, causing Liam to blush slightly. Her father's reaction was completely out of character, which instantly made Erika protective of him.

"Hi, I'm Doctor Holstrom's *daughter*, Erika," she interjected, thrusting her hand out towards the smiling Dane.

The woman pivoted to Erika. "I'm Dr Larsen, but please call me Rikke. I only met your father this morning, but I'm very familiar with his incredible research, especially about climate change in the Arctic. You must be very proud?"

"Uh-huh," Erika answered dryly, clearly unimpressed.

"Is this your boyfriend?" Rikke asked, offering her hand to Jordan.

"We're not... he's not my boyfriend," Erika said awkwardly, her cheeks once again red.

The friendly banter stopped when an impressive older woman in a military uniform entered the room, followed by several staff officers. Erika had never met a general before, but she was pretty sure the commanding presence before her had to be one. She watched as Eleanor shook hands with the woman, before discreetly whispering to her. The general, if that's what she was, shot a look at the trio of civilians before specifically approaching Liam.

"I don't like being deceived, Dr Holstrom," she started, her tone a mixture of scorn and genuine hurt. "I'm all for intellectual curiosity, but there are far better ways to seek it than through deception. You could have just asked me to grant a security waiver, professor."

*What the hell?* Erika thought as she watched her father bow his head in remorse. Jordan moved next to her. "Geez, what did your dad do?"

Before Erika could answer, the general placed her hand firmly on Liam's shoulder as if to say, *Don't let it happen again.*

Next she turned her attention towards Erika. "You must be the professor's daughter. Your father has told me a great deal about you." The general was a giant, towering above Erika. She tipped her head down, looking directly into Erika's eyes as only a mother could. "I'm so very sorry for your loss. The community elders said your eulogy to your mom was beautiful."

Erika instantly choked up, unable to respond. To everyone's surprise, the general leaned in and hugged her.

"Brigadier-General Tremblay, I'm sorry to interrupt," a man wearing an American uniform interjected, Erika felt somewhat rudely. "Ma'am, we've received encrypted flash traffic from the United Nations HQ in New York. The message was garbled, but we've decoded most of it."

The general stood up, acknowledging her intelligence officer. "All right, let's have a look at what Major Matthews found trapped in the ice, first," she directed, peering down at the intricate sea chest. She then turned to Liam. "Dr Holstrom, the good Dr Larsen recommends I listen to what you, and I presume your daughter, have discovered?"

"Yes, ma'am," Liam said, "it's quite fascinating actually..."

The general cut him off with a hand gesture, her demeanour once again that of a career professional.

"Let's take this conversation into the primary conference room so we can examine the sea chest along with the film footage collected by Major Matthews from the sea ice. Dr Larsen, please have your autopsy reports ready. I want to cross reference them with what Dr Holstrom evidently dug up from 1943, and then compare it with the black box data from the downed *Poseidon* aircraft."

There was a flurry of activity following the general's direction. For the first time in Erika's life she was getting to glimpse what her father had been up to all these years in the north. She wasn't quite sure how much help she could be, after all her dad knew way more than she did. All she'd done was listen as Liam explained what he had unearthed in her grandparents' attic. She had nothing to offer, except maybe the details of her *conversations* with Star. Should she reveal what she had learned from her mother? After all, they were just dreams. The longhouses, the *skraeling*, or the burial ritual she had witnessed. What about the visions she kept having while awake, or the treasure-seeking amulet, or her... abilities? Suddenly Erika felt very alone, and craved the companionship of her friends.

*My friends!* she thought at once. Sandra, Nicole and Michelle must be worried sick about her by now. She glanced over at Liam and Eleanor as they carried the ornate sea chest towards a side room, Rikke following close behind. Jordan was still standing in the main foyer, trying not to get in anyone's way. Erika was about to move towards him when the general interjected.

"OK, Erika, I need to listen to what the UN sent us," she said. "Let's head over to the conference room, and feel free to bring your boyfriend."

# CHAPTER 22

The sound was unmistakable. Katherine pressed her eyes shut, concentrating on the recording. The distant noise had been captured a month earlier by one of the United Nations' global monitoring stations in Greenland. Originally deployed in the 1990s to enforce the UN's comprehensive nuclear test-ban treaty, the international array of sensors had a vast range. The sensitive instruments could distinguish between naturally occurring seismic activity, and an unauthorised atomic detonation. As a consequence, they were also able to detect acoustic anomalies such as submerged volcanoes or, in this case, an underwater implosion.

"Play it again please," Katherine ordered quietly. A junior technician complied as the J2 intelligence officer stood by grimly. For all his scepticism these past few weeks, even he had to accept the latest findings before them.

"Beginning playback at the sixteen hour and twenty-two minute mark, ma'am."

Once more Katherine closed her eyes and listened intently through a sonar headset. After a few seconds of ambient background noise came what sounded like a large metal drum being crushed. Katherine intuitively knew she was hearing how ninety Russian submariners had perished in an instant.

"New York is confident of the tape's accuracy," the J2 allowed. "It's the same type of sonic pattern detected in 2017 when the Argentine submarine ARA *San Juan* was lost. The remote listening site in Greenland is auto-archived once a month, which is why we're only now hearing these recordings." The American bowed his head. "I'm sorry I doubted you, General. I should have been more open minded and... more loyal."

"No need for apologies, J2," Katherine answered. "This hasn't exactly been a typical summer in the Arctic. The fact that we were even able to receive this transmission in the first place, given all the on-going atmospheric interference, is a small miracle."

Katherine stood up within the confined space of her temporary HQ's communication room. "Has Colonel Borishov heard this?"

"Unlikely, ma'am, but we've sent a runner to the guest house where the Russian defence attaché team is staying."

"Moscow must have known their sub was lost weeks ago, but chose to keep it quiet. This will definitely upend their President's image," Katherine said to her American colleague. "What do we expect the Kremlin's reaction to be?"

The intelligence officer shrugged. "Unknown, General," he sighed, hanging his head in defeat. His commander gave him an encouraging look.

"It's no secret you can be a real patronizing jerk sometimes, J2," Katherine said. "But I've never once doubted your competence. Draft up an acoustic assessment summary as soon as you can, including coordinates. I then want you to cross-reference Dr Larsen's medical report on the recovered French fishermen, with the historic autopsy records Dr Holstrom brought us from that German *U-boat*."

Katherine looked directly at her colleague, ensuring he clearly understood her meaning and intent. "J2, as unorthodox as it sounds, I want you to explore any hypotheses, no matter how far-fetched. Don't just think outside the box, instead pretend the box never existed, got it? Now, off you go."

The intelligence officer acknowledged the general and set about triangulating the precise location of the *Volkov's* implosion on a digital map of the Davis Strait. Katherine stood up, stretching her arms in the air and letting out a yawn. She was tired, but quietly encouraged by this latest turn of events, however sombre and unsettling the details.

*At least one piece of this summer's many mysteries seems solved*, she thought. *Now if we could just figure out why the Volkov sank.*

"You're drawn to my granddaughter, aren't you?"

Michelle looked back at Erika's grandmother in disbelief at what she was asking. She placed down the food she'd been preparing in the kitchen, and scanned to see if anyone else was around. Her teammate Nicole sat oblivious in the living room, using a smartphone and headset to listen to a pre-downloaded podcast. Outside in the front yard, Michelle could hear Sandra and little Amber happily playing ball hockey, while Erika's grandfather had left earlier in the day. The elderly woman sensed Michelle's discomfort and moved to reassure her.

"There is nothing to hide in being two-spirited," she said calmly.

"I'm sorry, being what?" Michelle hesitated, still unsure how to react.

"Two-spirited, those that are drawn to others of the same mould in a special way."

*This is getting way too weird for me*, Michelle thought in a panic.

"My granddaughter is also very special, but perhaps in a different way than you are, Michelle. You are free to love her as you see fit; but please do not be hurt if the love she returns towards you is not the same, for now. She has been through much recently."

Michelle wasn't sure what shocked her more. The fact that a revered matriarch whom she barely knew was so understanding of her choices in love, or that this same person was confirming Erika wasn't ready to reciprocate her affection. Getting shunned by Erika was one thing; having it confirmed by her grandmother was something else. Michelle dropped her shoulders. It was all too much. Grandma moved in and gave Michelle a reassuring hug, as the younger of the two quietly sighed.

"I'm so sorry," Michelle said. "I just wish things were different. I know Erika isn't ready, but I can't hide how I feel. Still, I should have been more supportive of her during the memorial service, and..."

"All will be good in time," the elderly woman encouraged. "Like many things in life we cannot control, you will find meaning from this."

Michelle looked into her wise old eyes and pondered the lifetime of experiences they must have witnessed. She smiled back at Michelle reassuringly.

Suddenly Erika's grandmother became very tense, almost fearful. Michelle immediately picked up on her mood change.

"What is it?"

"Where are the others?"

"Nicole's in the living room, and the rest are outside..."

Before Michelle could finish, grandma moved to the front entrance with amazing speed, far faster than a person of her advanced age should.

"Sandra, Amber, come inside please," she said firmly while opening the front door. With a gleeful cheer, Amber came running into the lodge, followed by a smiling Sandra.

"She's a handful," Sandra confessed. "By the way, did you see Erika and her dad go driving by with a bunch of army dudes a while back? I wonder where they were headed?"

Sandra's question was met with silence. The elderly woman peered past her at the dark green clouds forming on the horizon. She softly whispered a prayer in a language the others did not understand.

"What's wrong?" Sandra asked.

Grandma stood motionless.

"Something... terrible."

"Rewind that part again," Rikke blurted out.

The excited Danish doctor was seated next to Major Eleanor Matthews in the main conference room of the Pond Inlet community centre. They were both hunched over a laptop, watching Eleanor's footage from the ice cavern she'd unwittingly discovered. A few curious military personnel looked on from nearby.

"It's a *knarr*," Rikke said in amazement. "It has to be."

Eleanor looked back at her confused. "A what?"

"A *knarr*, it's a type of longboat used by Norse sailors during the Viking age. My God, Eleanor, do you have any idea the significance of what you've found?"

She admitted to her Danish colleague she did not.

"Roskilde," Rikke said excitedly, "the town where I work during the winter. It has a Norse ship museum with one of the few surviving examples of an eleventh century *knarr*. I can tell you it's nowhere near as well preserved as what you've found trapped in the pack ice."

It was clear to Eleanor that Rikke's mind was racing. She wished to join in her excitement, but couldn't. After a difficult summer in the north that had already cost her the lives of two soldiers to a freak of nature, joy was an emotion beyond Eleanor's reach. Her sombre thoughts were interrupted by a serious question from Rikke.

"Did you find any human remains?"

Eleanor shook her head. "No, but I only stayed down there for about thirty minutes until my guys were able to haul us out. Should there have been?"

"It depends on what happened to the ship," Rikke allowed. "Did the crew abandon it before it got caught in pack ice, or was it intentionally set adrift? Who knows?"

Rikke looked back at the laptop monitor and zoomed in on the square-shaped cargo hold at the base of the longboat's mast. She noticed several barrels, which Eleanor explained were filled with tar, probably used to coat the ship against parasites. Rikke paused the footage as the Old Norse sea chest they'd brought back to Pond Inlet appeared on camera.

"Captain's log..." she breathed in astonishment. Rikke leapt from her chair and started moving towards the room where Liam and Erika were examining the ancient storage locker. She was stopped by Eleanor forcefully grabbing her arm.

"Doctor," she said sternly, "please tell me what the hell you are talking about."

"I'm sorry, I'm sorry. I got carried away." Rikke looked at her Canadian colleague, still unable to hide her excitement.

"Eleanor, you have likely made one of the greatest maritime discoveries in human history. Right up there with the *Mary Rose* or the *Titanic*, if not more important. If we can figure out who owned this ship, and where it sailed, we can likely rewrite our entire understanding of the early European exploration of North America. I bet that old sea chest next door contains the logbooks or navigational charts of an actual Viking crew and its voyages. This is huge, Eleanor. Nobel prize-winning huge."

With that, Rikke closed the laptop and left for the examination room where her newly found friends were trying to open the rusted container in question. Eleanor slowly followed her in stunned silence.

The cold northern wind of the Davis Strait cut across Ujurak's face as he tried to see his peers. The guide adjusted his snow goggles, unable to comprehend how such a thick fog bank could linger in gale force winds. As far as he could tell, he currently stood a hundred metres from the ice cavern Major Matthews had accidently discovered. Sergeant Major Bernard had placed two sentries at the entrance to make sure no curious soldiers went scavenging for souvenirs. Ujurak had already heard the rumours circulating among the troops he was supporting. They gossiped about everything from finding lost treasure to the missing Russian submarine. His intuition told him better. Instead of excitement, he felt utter dread.

"Ujurak, where are you, tabarnak," yelled a familiar French-Canadian voice.

He watched as the sergeant major emerged from the mist, a pair of night vision goggles strapped to his wool hat.

"This fog is insane," Bernard complained. "But here, try these NVGs. We had a couple stored in the quartermaster's toboggan. Didn't think we'd need them in the land of the midnight sun, but voila."

Ujurak was often dismayed by his southern counterparts' constant reliance on technology to solve their problems. He felt it disconnected them from their natural roots. Instead of embracing Mother Earth, the southerners tried to master it. He sighed. If growing up in the Arctic had taught him anything, it was that the balance of the natural world should be respected, not conquered. The early teachings were ripe with tales of lost souls that did not heed nature's warnings. Sometimes to move forward, one must embrace the past, he thought. Perhaps climate change was Mother Earth's revenge.

"Go ahead, mon ami, have a look," the sergeant major encouraged. Ujurak held the night vision goggles to his eyes and scanned the horizon from right to left. The NVGs were on a heat setting, which depicted the various members of Bernard's unit as dark thermal blobs, spread out across the floating ice shelf. He glanced at the cavern's entrance, and was rewarded by the sight of two human-sized shapes standing guard. He then looked for signs of the adolescent polar bear he'd detected following them yesterday, but found none. Lastly, he zoomed in on the large heat bloom emanating along the horizon of the open ocean to their south.

"That's the Russian frigate *Khabalov*," Bernard said, following the direction of Ujurak's gaze. "It's been out there stationary for a while now, probably socked in by the same sea ice as the *Rasmussen* and *Samuel Ronaldson* over the horizon, never mind this latest fog. It doesn't help that the *Khabalov* lost its only helicopter - not that it could fly in this weather."

Ujurak nodded and continued scanning the massive ice floe on which they stood. Through the NVGs, the distant snow mounds and frozen pressure ridges appeared as gentle silhouettes. This optical illusion masked the actual danger of their razor sharp edges, some rising several metres into the air. Ujurak was about to return the goggles to Sergeant Major Bernard when he glanced back at the ice cavern's entrance. He adjusted the zoom feature on the device as best he could, unnaturally leaning forward in a subconscious effort to improve his sight. He stayed that way for several seconds, whispering a few inaudible words in Inuktitut. Bernard was about to make a snide remark when he noticed the deadly serious expression on the older man's face.

"Qu'es qu'il y a, Ujurak?" The sergeant major asked with concern in French.

"Your two guards... they're gone."

"Here Dad, try this," Erika said, handing her father another can of cleaning solution. She and Jordan hovered over Liam as he gently sprayed the anti-corrosive along the seams of the Norse sea chest. The ancient container sat atop a table in a temporary medical room, surrounded by halogen lights. Two soldiers recorded the professor's efforts using encrypted smartphones. Slowly, the orange rust surrounding the sea chest's lid dripped away, revealing a beautifully ornate silver box. Next, Liam placed a sheet of white paper along the sides of the chest, rubbing it with charcoal he'd collected from a fire pit outside. Slowly, the *futhark* hieroglyphics of the Old Norse language appeared across the paper.

As Erika watched her father in amazement, the amulet around her neck started glowing. She slowly lifted the artifact from under her sweater so as to avoid the earlier, awkward episode that led her to the airport. Subtly but firmly, she held the amulet against her chest, suppressing its evident desire to be reunited with the ancient container. Erika knew her pendant could unlock the sea chest, but the layers of surface corrosion had kept it sealed shut. She waited until her father had removed the last rust stains before trying once more. She was about to offer Liam assistance when a very excited Dr Larsen entered the room with Major Matthews.

"Rikke, what is it?" Liam asked, his face suddenly alight. Erika couldn't help feeling a pang of protectiveness at his familiarity towards the doctor.

"Eleanor found a perfectly preserved *knarr* trapped in the pack ice." The words could not escape Rikke's lips fast enough.

"Wh...What?" Liam mumbled, visibly taken aback by the news.

"You heard me, a real longboat from the Viking age," Rikke said with a grin. "And we think the sea chest you've got may contain the ship's logbooks."

"This is incredible," Liam said. "Well, the rust has pretty much been removed. All that's left now is for Erika to..." He looked over at his daughter, who clutched her amulet. Without a word she moved forward and removed the glowing artifact over her head. She then slid it into the lock, located on the front of the sea chest. Just like at the airport, it unlocked with ease as she turned her prized possession to the right. Now, however, the lid lifted slightly, emitting a sucking sound at the release of several centuries' worth of trapped air. Erika stepped back from the unlocked container, allowing Liam to gently lift open the lid using a pair of latex gloves.

Rikke closed in beside him, peering into the chest at objects not seen by human eyes in a millennium. Inside were several rolls of parchment, held together by brittle pieces of yarn. Liam gently lifted them from the container and placed them on a sterile table, usually reserved for treating medical patients. Next he pulled out a hoard of what felt like coins, the small leather pouch sewn shut at the top. Lastly he produced what appeared to be a pocket-size notebook, with various futhark words etched into the leather cover.

"Its Old Norse," Rikke whispered, the intensity of the moment creating a hushed silence no one wanted to disturb.

"What does it say?" Liam asked Rikke, his hands visibly trembling as he placed the book on the table beside the rolled-up parchment.

"I think it says, The Helluland Sagas of Bjarni Grimolfsson, the Icelander..." Rikke stopped, pointing at the symbol imprinted under the notebook's title.

"But that... that can't be."

Ivan knew he had to leave. If his ship the *Nikolay Khabalov* stayed on station much longer, the frigate's hull would likely get trapped in sea ice. Still, he ached to remain, desperate to know what happened to his beloved brother Sergei and the rest of the missing submarine *Volkov's* crew. He was convinced the Western forces operating in the region knew something, though they were likely as blind as him at the moment. The deteriorating weather over the past few hours, coupled with the rapidly dropping outside temperature, had worsened an already difficult situation. The *Khabalov* would have to manoeuvre using dead reckoning, with none of the ship's navigational or communications equipment functioning properly, thanks to the persistent atmospheric interference. Add to that the thick green fog that had rolled in, which prevented Ivan launching the lone observation drone the frigate carried - a lesser substitute for the helicopter they'd lost to the damn Yankees. He had no clue how a fog bank could persist in such strong winds, nor how a mass of sea worms had somehow wiggled their way into the frigate's propeller shafts.

"Are the outer deck sentries in place?" Ivan asked the ship's chief petty officer.

"Aye, sir," came the gruff reply. "Both lookouts are manning their posts and report increasing ice build-up along the lower hull."

Ivan moved to the starboard side of the bridge and peered out the main window at the deck below. He could just discern two sailors near the forward railings, dressed in several layers of protective winter clothing with yellow glow sticks on their backs.

"Very well, come about to a new heading of one seven zero," Ivan ordered calmly. "Helm, make your speed no more than three knots."

The nervous helmsman complied with Ivan's order. Most of the *Khabalov*'s crew were terrified of their unpredictable acting captain, this young sailor being no different. Ivan sensed their fear. In fact, he relished in the power it garnered him. Only his stubborn old chief seemed to take Ivan's obtuseness in stride. Slowly, the *Khabalov* moved, gently turning on the spot as chunks of ice grazed its hull.

"That's it, steady as she goes," Ivan said, for once in an almost reassuring tone. His plan was to sail well south of the current storm front and try to reach Northern Fleet Command via a secure uplink in order to finally figure out what the hell was going on in the world. The last garbled news he'd had from Moscow indicated they were going to perform an aerial show of force in the region using Tu-160 *Blackjack* bombers. This was to demonstrate Russia's displeasure at the perceived lack of information sharing by the North Americans regarding both the *Volkov* search, and the recent loss of a *Bear* surveillance aircraft. Even though they were only a few nautical miles away, he couldn't even intercept the radio signals from the Canadian and American troops located on the enormous ice shelf to the *Khabalov*'s north. Ivan shook his head. So this is what it must have been like to sail in the dark ages.

"Chief, what's the latest from the lookouts?" Ivan demanded. The veteran petty officer tried several times to reach the sentries located on the forward deck. He was using the ship's internal copper cable phones, specifically to get around the on-going electromagnetic interference. Again nothing.

"Sir, I can't raise them," the chief reported, more annoyed than alarmed.

Ivan moved back towards the bridge's starboard window, peering through the Arctic fog at the location of the forward sentries. All he could see was a lone yellow glow stick, rolling about the slightly pitching deck.

Squadron Leader Kendra Livingstone returned her Eurofighter alongside the lead Russian *Blackjack* bomber, allowing her wingman to depart and refuel after several hours in the air. She had just come back from topping up her wing tanks, courtesy of a nearby *Voyager* refueller loitering east of Greenland. She was fortunate to have pre-assigned fuelling points, especially since their long-range communications equipment seemed to be unreliable. Having a pre-determined rendezvous location was standard air force practice, specifically in case of a communications failure. Kendra had passed on to the *Voyager* crew the latest location of the two *Blackjacks* they were escorting, in the hope they could relay the info back to NATO's air operations centre in Germany. Though Kendra had very robust rules of engagement, they seemed unnecessary as the pair of Russian aircraft were staying well east of Greenland's airspace, north of Iceland.

She first noticed the green flashes emitting from the front canopy of the second Russian bomber. They grew into pulsating jade lights that surrounded the massive swing-wing aircraft, causing its fuselage to shudder. Soon the adjacent *Blackjack* was also encircled with the same green stocks of lightning. The highest concentration of the energy waves appeared to emanate from the flight decks of both aircraft, where the pilots were located. The brightness of the static energy reached such intensity that even with her sun visor down, Kendra had to shield her eyes.

*Is this what the Norwegian pilots were talking about?* she wondered, referring to the crashed *Bear* bomber from the week before. Within seconds of the green energy enveloping the two Russian aircraft, they both dipped their starboard wings and banked rapidly to the west.

*Bloody hell.*

"Lion leader to lion two," Kendra called to her wingman as she matched the *Blackjacks'* manoeuvre, the increased gravity pushing down on her body. "Lion leader to lion two, break from your refuelling run and return to my location, over?" Her calls were met with static, as she expected.

*Dammit*, she thought. The squadron leader with the famous last name was very much on her own.

The pain in her abdomen returned with a vengeance. Kendra screamed in agony as the kidney stones she'd tried to ignore made their way along her urinary tract. She doubled over and for a moment thought she was going to vomit into her oxygen mask. Her fighter dropped several hundred feet before she was able to recover it. Kendra could sense she was in danger of blacking out due to the pain, but was determined to fulfil her mission. Through watery eyes she glanced at the pair of *Blackjack* bombers visible in her heads up display, increasing her own thrust rate to catch up. Her nimble fighter closed the distance with the lead Russian aircraft, which had already accelerated well past Mach one.

More calls to her wingman went unanswered as Kendra observed the lead bomber begin to shudder. On closer inspection, she realised the bomb bay doors of both Russian aircraft were now open. No sooner had she noticed this clearly hostile act, than the doors from the lead *Blackjack* were ripped away. Apparently they were not designed to be opened at such speeds. Kendra's reactions were superb, but she only just managed to avoid the pieces of flying debris.

Again the pain.

This latest bolt of agony caused Kendra's right hand to reach for her stomach, while her left hand slammed against the canopy. Wave after wave of the piercing torture shot through her torso. It was all too much for her body, and the dedicated aviator began to lose consciousness. In a daze, Kendra managed to increase the oxygen output to her facemask, the shot of O2 briefly reawakening her thoughts. In the end, however, it was no use. The crack pilot, a pioneer of her generation, slowly passed out as her multi-million dollar aircraft fell towards the Greenland coast. With blackness consuming her, Kendra didn't notice the packet of cruise missiles being launched from the Russian bombers.

The deadly projectiles chased the Arctic sun as they raced off to the west.

# CHAPTER 23

Erika burst into the community centre restroom, frantic for one of the open stalls. She lifted the toilet seat and started dry-heaving over the bowl. The amulet around her neck dangled precariously as Erika's stomach muscles rebelled against her desire for calm. The throbbing between her temples was excruciating. Her futile gagging efforts complete, she fell backwards onto the tiled floor.

*Get out of my head!*

Erika knew she was conscious, yet her thoughts were overwhelmed by a cacophony of images from her nightmares. Visions of barbarians, grotesque flying spirits, and worst of all, her mother Star in pain, flashed before her watering eyes. She screamed, but no one from the Arctic headquarters heard. She turned over onto all fours, crouching as a predator would before pouncing. Next, Erika was atop the restroom counter, her feet propped up like a cat between two sinks.

*What do you want from me?*

The response was terrifying.

*Everything.*

Suddenly, all was calm. Erika looked about from her tabletop perch. She was drenched in her own sweat, but the pain was gone. Slowly she climbed down from the collection of sinks, scanning the room. She was alone, both in body and spirit. She quickly turned on a tap, allowing cold water to spill over her hands before splashing it against her face. Erika repeated this gesture several times until she noticed a slight hissing sound. On inspection, she realised steam was rising from the amulet around her neck as it was hit by water. Her beloved jewellery was that hot.

*What is happening to me?*

She glanced up at the mirror and for an instant, a very brief instant, she swore her eyes had been glowing bright yellow.

Erika's instincts told her grave danger was approaching.

The cluster of cruise missiles screamed low across Greenland's snowy terrain. The Russian Kh-101s were designed to fly a few metres above the ground, just shy of the sound barrier. A by-product of the Cold War, they used an inertial guidance system to zig-zag between geographic features in order to avoid detection. Despite the best attempts of the Soviet-era engineers, their assembly efforts were not always successful. A pair of the three-ton projectiles veered off and crashed into the side of a remote glacier. The twelve remaining missiles continued on their deadly westerly course, each emitting the same greenish glow as they sliced through the Arctic air.

Colonel Borishov removed the sonar headset and looked over at the gathered northern command personnel. A military veteran with three decades of service to his mother Russia, he sadly recognised what he'd just heard. The *Volkov* was gone. All hands were lost. He stood up as Brigadier-General Katherine Tremblay approached, offering her hand.

"Oleksandr, I'm so very sorry for your nation's loss," she sympathised.

"Spasiba, General. This is most upsetting news," the defence attaché said, clasping his host's hand in return.

"I'm afraid there's more, my friend." Katherine gestured at the unlikely collection of military, academic, and medical colleagues she'd assembled, each of whom would weave one piece of an elaborate tale.

First came a situational update briefing from the general's intelligence officer, including the latest weather and atmospheric forecasts, which were not good. This was followed by a Danish ship's doctor, who described the uncanny similarities of autopsy findings conducted decades apart, yet with identical post-mortem markings. Next, came an assessment of the metallurgy recovered from the remains of a downed American pilot, which showed the weapon used dated to the tenth century. An initial crash investigation report was then presented, detailing what brought down an American surveillance plane, including photo evidence of the same markings carved into the side of the crashed *Poseidon*. A Canadian major then outlined how her troops had been attacked by a stampeding herd of wild caribou, before explaining what she'd uncovered frozen in the Davis Strait.

"Are you serious?" the Russian asked in amazement.

The response came from Dr Liam Holstrom, whom he recognised, regarding the discovery of the Viking-era ship trapped in ice. They explained the condition of the vessel, where it was found, and most intriguing of all, where it may have sailed. Finally, he was shown the logbook from the ancient longboat, its cover written in Old Norse.

"Have you read through it?" the colonel asked, clearly impressed.

"Not yet," Liam replied, "the pages are stuck together. We'll try to dehumidify the book in a lab down south so as not to damage the paper." It was then that Liam drew a basic symbol on a notepad and handed it to Colonel Borishov.

"Should I recognise this?" the Russian asked.

"I doubt it," Liam said, "but we do. It's from the Old Norse runic alphabet known as *futhark,* and usually means birch, or birch tree. That in itself is not of significance, but this is." The professor pulled out a series of photos, some post-mortem. He laid them out in front of the defence attaché, who was once again seated.

"Here is the symbol found on the Viking ship's logbook, so roughly a thousand years old," Liam said, "and here is the same symbol found carved into dead German submariners in the Canadian Arctic back in 1943." The Danish doctor then moved forward in support of Liam, with additional photos on a smart tablet.

"Here is the symbol on the bodies of French fishermen recovered earlier this summer," Rikke explained, "and again on the side of the crashed P-8 *Poseidon* aircraft in Pond Inlet from last month. Here it is on the deceased American helicopter pilot we mentioned. Lastly, here it is marked on the side of a young polar bear killed during that caribou stampede in July."

"I don't understand?" Colonel Borishov pleaded.

"That's the problem," Katherine chimed in, "neither do we. Yet in each case, whether during the war or now, the symbols were carved into their victims after death. That means someone or," she paused unintentionally, "something, has a fixation with branding dead souls, and has apparently been doing it for quite some time."

The Russian defence attaché noted how eerily quiet the room was, despite the number of people present. His mind was racing. Did his superiors know this, and what did it all mean? If this was some kind of a grandiose deception effort on the general's part, it was certainly convincing. He needed to get a message to Moscow, but how?

Just then, Dr Holstrom's daughter burst into the room, looking dishevelled and panicked.

"Dad, we need to leave here now!"

Magnus had just entered the bridge of the *Knud Rasmussen* when the first signs appeared that all was not right. His ship was located in the northeast search zone of the Davis Strait, roughly forty nautical miles east of the Russian frigate *Nikolay Khabalov*, and a further sixty from the American destroyer USS *Samuel Ronaldson*. With most of his vessel's radar and sonar systems still frustratingly inoperative, Magnus was forced to deploy lookouts at all four points of the ship. Their task was both overwatch for aircraft, and surface watch for floating ice or, heaven forbid, submarine debris. It was the starboard sentry who noticed them first.

"Captain, low flying objects approaching rapidly from the east," the junior sailor called out.

"What?" Magnus protested. "We're not expecting any..."

The first cruise missile sliced past the *Rasmussen's* bow, missing it by a few metres as it raced west. The next three flew behind the Danish vessel, as its captain yelled the codeword for an incoming missile into the ship's intercom: "Vampire, vampire, vampire, brace for impact!"

One of the forward sentries was literally knocked over by the jet exhaust from a passing Russian projectile while he scrambled for cover. Magnus counted a dozen contrails race by, all at low altitude, but none hitting the *Rasmussen*. He watched as the exhaust flames from the last of the missiles faded from view.

"Action stations," he ordered, "helm, bring up the ship's power output to full capacity and be prepared to engage evasive manoeuvres on my mark." Whoever launched this attack, Magnus was sure there was more to come.

Adrenaline pumping through his veins, he moved to his captain's chair and called for the weapons control officer.

"Where did they go?" Sergeant Major Bernard protested, before yelling down into the ice cavern. "I swear, if you two are down there looking for souvenirs, I'll have you both on outdoor polar bear watch for the next month!"

There was no reply. Somehow Ujurak knew what had happened to the pair of sentries, and it wasn't good. A sense of unease swept over him. He'd not felt like this since the day of the tragic caribou stampede. The only good news was that the lingering green fog had lifted somewhat, allowing him to see the rest of the Arctic troops he was escorting. Past the white figures on the ice floe, Ujurak could just see the deck lights of the Russian frigate *Khabalov* on the horizon. It appeared to be slowly sailing away, much to the dismay of his colleagues. He always found it odd how the sight of a ship, any ship, brought the troops comfort, but not him.

He was about to call for the acting company commander, Captain

Janet Simmons, when the first of three distinct explosions caught his attention. The deep booming sounds echoed from the south. Both Ujurak and the sergeant major watched in amazement as a series of green and white contrails shot towards the *Khabalov* in the distance. Most sailed past the Russian warship, but at least three detonated just shy of hitting the vessel. A series of puffy clouds drifting towards the sea were all that remained of the fearsome weapons.

"Jesus!" the sergeant major exclaimed. "Those are missiles. Someone is shooting missiles at the Russians."

"And us!" Ujurak yelled, throwing himself on top of the burly French-Canadian. The Kh-101 impacted fifty metres past the two men, the lethality of its warhead dampened by the deep snow. Still, the explosion was tremendous, throwing sheets of ice several hundred metres into the sky. More missiles soared overhead, but none landed, continuing instead on their deadly journey westward.

"Ujurak, are you all right?" the sergeant major bellowed, his ears ringing from the violent concussion. The guide nodded as he got up, brushing the snow from his parka. He could hear Captain Simmons yelling for the company to stand-to. There didn't appear to be any casualties from the near miss, but two of their sentries were still unaccounted for from earlier. Sergeant Major Bernard bounded back towards his troops, hobbling as quickly as his snowshoes would carry him.

Ujurak then looked with dismay at the ice cavern entrance. It was covered by several tons of collapsed ice.

"How many, how many?" Ivan demanded, his two missing lookouts now an afterthought.

"Captain, we count three detonations off the rear port quarter, plus one to our north on the pack ice," the *Khabalov's* radar operator stated anxiously. "The remainder are heading west, away from us."

"But whose are they?" Ivan raged. "Chief, why didn't the counter-measures engage?"

The gruff chief petty officer was already wearing a helmet and flak jacket as he reviewed the footage from the ship's deck cameras.

"Stand by," he said calmly. The sensors on the *Khabalov* were not as sophisticated as on most NATO ships, but they were still effective. Within a few seconds, the chief had isolated an image of one of the passing projectiles, and zoomed in. Despite his years of experience, even he was surprised but what he found.

"Sir, they're ours," he sighed.

*That can't be*, Ivan protested in his mind. He moved over to the console where the chief was seated. There, clear as day, was the distinct body and winglets of a Kh-101 cruise missile, complete with Cyrillic markings.

"That explains why they didn't hit us," the chief dryly observed.

"What are you talking about?" Ivan said dismissively.

"The missiles must have been equipped with friend or foe sensors, meaning when they detected their target was a Russian ship, they self-destructed."

"But why didn't the other missiles detonate?"

"I can only suppose we were not the intended target for the remaining weapons. Either way, based on the numbers, my Captain, this looks like an opening salvo."

Ivan stared long and hard at his chief. He instinctively knew the man was right. Both the doctrine of his nation and that of its adversaries advocated for the use of overwhelming surprise when initiating hostile action. Ivan tried to make sense of it all.

*But why target one of your own ships, and who else were the intended targets?*

A partial answer came just beyond the western horizon from a series of enormous crimson flashes.

Blanketed in fog and starved of digital communication, there was no warning. The initial pair of cruise missiles punched through the forward super-structure of the USS *Samuel Ronaldson*, disintegrating everything in their path. The extreme heat created by the warhead detonations quickly overpowered the automated fire suppression systems onboard the American ship. The second set of missiles pierced the destroyer's hull near the waterline. The massive explosions caused the warship to lift from the

water slightly, resulting in a huge crack shooting up the side of the wounded grey beast. As more missiles approached, a lone white dome near the
ship's flight deck belatedly chirped to life. The automated defensive weapon system began spewing hundreds of rounds a second at the approaching
danger, blasting two invaders from the sky with deadly accuracy. It was
soon silenced by a secondary explosion from within the *Ronaldson,* sending parts of the stern crashing into the sea. The last of the missiles finished
what the others had started, slicing their way deep inside the American
destroyer, before exploding near the engine room.

The wounded ship heaved to port, then split into three uniform
pieces. The centre portion containing the bridge and crew quarters sank
immediately, while the bow and stern sections lingered on the surface.
Next, the rear of the ship, with its ruined flight deck, slipped below the
icy waves. Lastly the bow section of the mighty destroyer, the number *142*
clearly emblazoned near its anchor port, rose vertically from the ocean,
before disappearing into the depths.

The rumbling noise grew in intensity from the west. Erika's grandmother
slowly moved from her front porch onto the dusty road in front of her
wooden lodge. In the distance, just past the Pond Inlet airport, an enormous cloud of dust rose towards the heavens. The ground under her feet
began to shake.

"What's happening?" Sandra called out from the front porch, Michelle and Amber by her side. Grandma did not say a word, instead motioning for the women to stay put. She'd heard of these occurrences in
her youth, but had never actually experienced it herself. The elders spoke
of bad omens, unexplained natural disasters that seemed to plague every third or fourth generation. Sometimes it came in the form of a bru-
tal winter; at other times it was drought, or a lack of fish and seal meat.
In all instances, people perished, either immediately, or as a result of the
lingering impact. Until recently, both her generation and that of her late
daughter had been spared. Now, however, it seemed her granddaughter's
generation was being made to suffer.

The noise grew with such intensity that the women in the doorway had to yell to be heard. A very confused-looking Nicole Gibson joined the others, the massive vibrations having snapped her out of her headphone-induced oblivion. Amber started to cry and held onto Sandra's leg, the big goalie trying to shield her young friend from looking outside. From the airport came several crashing sounds, as enormous metal antennas were knocked over like match sticks. Erika's grandmother watched as the tops of the towers disappeared behind a series of trees, their branches waving from side to side.

"Is this an earthquake?" Michelle hollered.

"Sure feels like one," Nicole agreed.

Just then, a wall of brown fur thundered into view. Hundreds, perhaps thousands of crazed caribou stampeded down Pond Inlet's main road. Erika's grandmother held her ground, closely eyeing individual animals as they approached from half a kilometre away.

"Oh my God, come inside, please!" Sandra yelled.

Grandma did not move. It was only when she realised the enraged beasts were mounted, that her wrinkled eyes widened. As if from a nightmare, grotesque forms clung to the backs of several animals, yelling and hollering as they approached. On closer inspection, they resembled decomposing barbarians, half-wrapped in leather and metal garments. Some clearly held bladed weapons and what appeared to be circular shields. They rode their mounts like possessed cowboys. The lead monstrosity straddled a large bull caribou, its gauntlet-covered arms raised to the sky in twisted adulation. It locked eyes with the elderly woman standing her ground, and lowered a rusted spear at its intended target. It cried out at a debilitating pitch, causing the women in the front doorway to cover their ears. The first of the beasts and their devil riders were almost upon the elder when she seemed to disappear. Before the others realised it, she was at Sandra's side.

"The basement," she yelled. "Hurry, everyone, this way!"

Grandma pushed aside a polar bear rug in the centre of the living room floor, revealing a metal trap door. She quickly released the sliding lock, then pulled at the closed entrance. *Help me*, she willed the others without them realising. First Sandra, then Michelle joined in and with an enormous heave, lifted the heavy door open.

*Downstairs, all of you.*

Nicole, Amber, Michelle, and Sandra all clambered down into the darkness, just as the first of the lodge's outer walls came crashing down. Grandma half-slid, half-fell into the basement entrance, the metal door slamming shut above her. The five women huddled in pitch-blackness as the terrifying destruction continued above. The sound of glass and ceramic shattering was mixed with the noises of hundreds of hooves galloping across the basement's ceiling. Walls that had stood for decades flew apart in a physical tornado of animals and monsters. The cast iron stove in the centre of the living room was upended, spilling its molten hot embers onto the stone floor. Immediately the debris surrounding the oven caught fire, a few of the rabid caribou crying out in distress as they charged by. The flames caused the stampeding animals to form a tear-dropped opening around what was left of the living room, as they avoided the unwanted heat. The fire spread quickly to the remaining rooms, until soon the entire pile of debris that was once a loving home, was engulfed. The five women huddled together in their darkened dungeon sanctuary, petrified but safe.

"What the hell are those things?" Nicole burst out at no one in particular.

"The ones who cannot rest." Grandma sighed, as the noise above their heads subsided to a low rumble. Sandra tried to feel her way up the stairs to the closed metal door, but retreated once her skin made contact with its hot metal.

"That was one messed up rodeo," she said, trying to lighten the mood. No response.

"My son-in-law's ancestors once called them *aptrgangr*, or again walkers, but they are supposed to be a myth, from the time of the Vikings," Grandma explained.

"The Vikings?" Michelle protested. "They looked pretty damn real to me!"

"*Apt... aptr...* Jesus, do they have another name?" Sandra complained.

"The early Norse people also knew them as *draugar*," came the sombre reply. "But in English, one might as well describe them for what they are."

"And what's that?" Nicole asked as she hugged Amber.

"The undead."

# CHAPTER 24

Run my cub

Mother?

You must flee

Mother, I don't understand

It is not you they seek

Please mother, what do they want?


Erika grabbed at her father's arm like a possessed child, begging him to leave. The others in the room were silenced by her antics, Erika's outburst disrupting their earlier deliberations. Brigadier-General Katherine Tremblay and the rest of the assembled group looked over at Liam, who quickly moved his daughter aside. He brought her into an adjacent room within the community centre that served as the general's temporary northern headquarters. Jordan dutifully followed Erika and her father, unsure of how to react.

"Erika, what's gotten into you?" Liam demanded in a hushed voice.

"Daddy, please, we need to go, right now."

"C'mon, cub, we can't leave now, not after what we've discovered. Think of the historical significance of finding a Viking age ship trapped in ice…"

"To hell with your work," Erika snarled, staring directly into her father's eyes. Liam was taken aback by his daughter's uncharacteristic tone. She continued, the amulet around her neck radiating energy.

"Dad, I love you very much, but we need to leave now." Her eyes started to glow. "She said danger is approaching and we need to escape."

"Who... who said danger is approaching?" Liam asked, shaken.

"Mother did, just now."

*Too late.*

The outer retaining wall of the community centre buckled at the first impact of the enraged beasts. There was a pause, followed by a horrendous galloping noise as the stampede outside made another run at the side of the structure. While the building's concrete support beams stood firm, the aluminium siding walls didn't stand a chance. The first of the caribou and their demon riders burst through a sidewall, spilling into the main conference room next door. Two startled technicians were immediately cut down by one of the massive creatures, their entrails spilling onto the linoleum floor. A military police officer drew his side arm, firing several rounds into the side of a snarling caribou. The animal collapsed, throwing its hideous-looking mount to the ground. The leather-clad creature quickly recovered and raised its arms at the mortified constable, whose vital organs were suddenly blown from his chest. A scientist off to the right screamed, before he too was cut down by the enraged attackers.

"Eleanor, take Rikke and the others with you," Katherine ordered, hearing the awful commotion next door. "Colonel Borishov, J2, you're with me."

"No, General," the J2 intelligence officer insisted. "Ma'am, you're far too valuable to be playing hero soldier. Please go with the others, we can hold them."

The entire south wall of the examination room where they stood came apart, flying pieces of debris knocking everyone to the floor. The J2 regained his composure first, then lunged at the closest form that approached him. The massive figure swatted the American aside like an insect, sending his shattered body into a series of television monitors. Katherine was the next to recover, followed by Rikke and Colonel Borishov. Eleanor was nowhere to be seen, likely buried under a series of collapsed tables. There were now at least eight of the ashen monstrosities standing in the room, their skin a sickly hue of greyish green. A few additional brave souls tried to confront the invaders, all quickly meeting the same fate as their colleagues. Katherine held her ground off to the side of the room, with Rikke and their Russian counterpart right beside her. For some reason, the grotesque attackers seemed to ignore them.

"Who... or *what* are they?" Katherine breathed, her eyes fixed on the lead creature, only ten metres away.

"It can't be..." Rikke trembled, causing Katherine to glance questioningly at her.

It was soon clear the invaders had no interest in the unarmed people off to their right. The lead creature moved forward, throwing several tons of debris aside like cardboard. Under the last bit of rubble, it found the Norse sea chest, its contents scattered across the floor. While the others looked on, it crouched down. Using its skeletal arms, it collected the rolls of parchment Liam had examined earlier. The entity gently placed the items back into the ancient container, before slamming the top down firmly. It then turned and hissed at one of its fellow creatures, which moved forward in a bow. The two then began to communicate, their deformed jaws moving while emitting a series of distorted words. Rikke grabbed Katherine's arm.

"Its Old Norse..." she whispered in disbelief. "It sounds like a primitive version of Norwegian or Icelandic, but they are definitely speaking Old Norse." Rikke tried to suppress her anxiety and listen to what was being said, Katherine and Colonel Borishov by her side. "Uh... something about things, or items," she said. "And... maps or charts of *Helluland*, and returning... returning to a ship, I think?" Rikke closed her eyes in concentration, not fathoming what she was hearing.

"*Knarr*. They just mentioned a *knarr*."

"A what?" Colonel Borishov asked confused.

"It's a Viking longboat," Katherine quickly explained. "Like the one we found trapped in the ice."

Rikke shook her head, not sure if she had heard correctly.

"General, I think these things have come for the sea chest and intend to return it to their ship," Rikke deduced.

Out of nowhere, Eleanor swooped down from one of the building's rafters, slamming a flat-screen TV against the head of one of the monsters. Her blow landed with such force it decapitated the creature, the remainder of its torso collapsing to the ground beside its severed head. Eleanor rolled along the floor, her legs absorbing the impact of her landing. She readjusted herself into a crouching position, ready to make a run for the exit. The others watched in shock as her body was suddenly encased in a green glow, her feet lifted off the ground by an unseen force. Unable to move her limbs, Eleanor floated towards the lead creature, its decomposed face coming into view from under a dark hood.

*Kvinna…* the figure seethed, its lips not moving. It eyed Eleanor from top to bottom, not quite sure what to make of the woman warrior that had just felled one of its kin. Eleanor closed her eyes as a rancid tongue emerged from behind stained teeth, licking at lips that barely existed. Its hands moved towards her uniform, with what was left of its fingers, covered in seaweed.

*Bruor…*

"Oh no," Rikke whispered from the side of the room. "I think it wants her as a hostage, or a prize." Katherine and Colonel Borishov exchanged looks, not sure what to make of anything they were currently witnessing.

*Let her go.* The command was clear. Several of the creatures looked around, unsure where it had come from.

*I said, let her go.*

The voice was female, but very deep, almost baritone. The trio watched in amazement as Erika Holstrom entered the room, her eyes glowing brightly as she moved towards the lead apparition. The massive creature towered over Erika, yet she stood her ground, her eyes focused like lasers on the perceived leader of the gruesome clan.

*Take what you want, but leave her.*

The monster crouched down as if to smell Erika, when it noticed the amulet around her neck. It let out a horrendous roar, then reached with one hand for Erika's throat. She seemed to know it would, dodging its advance with ease. Twice more it lunged, but Erika nimbly avoided its efforts. The creature pulled back, canting its head at the insolent youngster. Erika remained standing: defiant, confident, and strong. She dangled the necklace at the decomposing form, almost teasing it.

*You want this?*

Again it hollered, this time raising some kind of deformed battle-axe and slammed it into the ground. The impact released huge amounts of electrical energy. As if hit by a lightning bolt, Erika was thrown across the room, knocking over Colonel Borishov, while Katherine and Rikke scattered. Liam and Jordan had just entered the room when they saw Erika's limp form sail in front of them.

*Skraeling...* the monster salivated in disgust towards a stunned Erika. Then, before anyone could react, the creatures were off, soaring away through the shattered opening they'd created. The others watched helplessly as Eleanor and the ancient sea chest where sucked along with them. Even the corpse of the headless demon was taken. Then, all was quiet.

For several minutes no one dared move, nor say a thing.

After a while, Katherine slid over to Rikke, whose jaw was trembling in shock.

"They're *draugar*," Rikke said without prompting. "I don't understand how this is possible. They only exist in Viking lore, in a few old texts and legends. They can't be real!"

"Doctor, those things are gone," Katherine said in a reassuring tone, masking her own fears. "But we need your help. There are many people hurt that will require medical attention."

Liam moved to Erika's side as Colonel Borishov brushed himself off.

"We need to figure out if they've actually gone back to their ship, and fast," Katherine said to the assembled bunch. "Those things took Eleanor."

She then looked about, realising more immediate concerns needed her attention. The general glanced over at Erika, who was stirring, her father and Jordan supporting her. Erika moaned, her hand grasping the amulet around her neck.

"I guess they got what they came for and left," Liam said bitterly.

"Not everything," Rikke interjected quietly. From under her jacket, she pulled out the Old Norse logbook before continuing. "Liam, did we really just see what I thought we saw? I mean, this isn't some elaborate hoax or a psychological trick being played against us by...by..."

Before Rikke finished her insinuation, all eyes fell to the Russian defence attaché. For once, Colonel Borishov spoke openly and honestly.

"If you think we had a hand in this, you give us far too much credit. I assure you, my friends, I am just as much at a loss for words as you are." He glanced about the shattered headquarters. "These things are not of this world."

"General, General!" The tension was broken as a group of heavily armed soldiers emerged through one of the partially destroyed doorways. "She's over here," a relieved troop yelled back outside. "And there are other survivors with her."

Katherine knelt, speaking quickly but succinctly to her rag-tag crew. "I need to go deal with the carnage these things have created," she said. "Liam, Rikke, I want a no-bullshit assessment of what attacked Pond Inlet, and I need it quickly. More importantly, I have to know how to fight these creatures, or whatever they are. Colonel Borishov, you're with me, please." With that, Katherine stood up and started delivering orders to the growing number of military and medical personnel entering the destroyed community centre.

Rikke moved to Erika's side and performed a tertiary medical assessment. She seemed fine, with just a few bruises, but Erika's breathing was very rapid. Rikke took her pulse, which was racing. Before Rikke knew it, her patient's eyes opened. Erika started flailing her arms as if fighting off an unseen foe. Her father moved in, trying to calm her, while Rikke offered a few soothing words. Erika accidently kicked Jordan as he leaned over to help Liam, then she sat up.

"Where'd they go?" she gasped, looking about.

"Easy, cub, you got thrown pretty hard," Liam said, before Erika cut him off.

"Dad, I'm fine, but the *aptrgangrs* took Major Matthews!"

"We know, cub, the General is working on it. What did you call them?" Liam asked confused.

"The undead, that's what mother calls them: again walkers."

"Or *draugar*," Rikke interjected. "A revenant from Old Norse mythology."

None of this made any sense to the rational minds around the room, except for Erika. It all came together in her mind as she realised what these creatures were, and where they came from.

"Did you say mother told you?" Liam asked hesitantly.

Erika gave her father a sympathetic look. "It's a long story, Dad. I swear I'll explain everything when we have time." She stood up, suddenly very much in command of the situation.

"Where can we find more information about these *draugar*?" she asked Rikke and her dad. "We've got zero Internet access and none of our smartphones work."

"The attic," Liam said. "Remember, cub, the Norse sagas I showed you at your grandparents' home? It's as good a place as any to start."

"Erika!" a grizzled voice called out. "Cub, are you in here?"

Erika turned to find her grandfather moving about the rescue personnel, long rifle slung across his back. She waved at him, and he quickly moved to his granddaughter. He and Erika hugged, before he turned to Liam.

"They will return," he said grimly. "This was just a warning. It's their way of telling us not to meddle where we don't belong. My own grandparents spoke of such evil spirits. Those that had unfinished business in this world would often return from the other side and haunt the living. We have disturbed their home."

"The Viking ship," Erika agreed. "Their home is the *knarr* trapped in the ice."

"Have you got your vehicle nearby?" Liam asked his father-in-law, who nodded. "We need to get back to the lodge."

Grandpa led Liam, Erika, and Jordan outside, while Rikke briefly conferred with a nearby doctor and several medics. They promptly waved her off, allowing her to run outside and join her colleagues. She jumped inside the back of the SUV.

As they drove away, the full extent of the damage to Pond Inlet became apparent. A huge swath of buildings and trees, several hundred metres wide, had been flattened by the stampede. The group drove down the bumpy main road, its smooth surface churned up by a thousand angry hooves. As they turned the corner, they realised the destruction led all the way to the airport, and right past...

"No!" Grandpa blurted out, stunned.

The SUV pulled up in front of his shattered wooden lodge. What had once been a loving home was now a mammoth collection of charred timbers and shredded furniture. Erika was the first out the car door, yelling desperately for her grandmother and friends. Liam and Rikke followed her sombrely. It was painfully clear to them that no one inside could have survived. Jordan emerged last, his normally calm demeanour replaced by anguish for his lost sister.

"Nicole! Michelle! Sandra!" Erika hollered. "Grandma!"

Liam moved to be with Erika, but was gently held back by his father-in-law. The two men looked at each other, and for the first time in their lives they embraced, the magnitude of the family loss slowly setting in.

"Quiet," Rikke demanded, the harshness of her voice taking everyone by surprise. After a brief moment, there was a distinct but muffled sound of banging.

"The cellar!" Grandpa suddenly cried. "They must have hidden down there. Now where's the damn door?"

He and Erika scrambled about what remained of the living room, their boots covered in grey ash. Following the sounds, Erika discovered they were coming from under the remains of the cast iron stove.

"Help me," she urged the others. Her grandfather and Liam moved to assist her, the cracked oven still warm to the touch. As much as they tried, it would not move. More noise from below. Someone was alive. Again the trio heaved at the enormous stove, but it was no use.

"We'll need a crane," Liam suggested.

Erika had had enough. Between the loss of her mother, the destruction of her grandparents' home, her incessant nightmares, and her confusing new abilities, she was at her wits' end. Her eyes glowed like the sun as she reached under the cast iron frame, the amulet around her neck pulsating with energy. With a single strained effort, she lifted the stove just enough to move it off to the side.

The banging noise was now very clear, directly below Erika's feet. Together with Liam's help, she kicked aside the burnt remains of the living room, until the outline of a metal trap door was in view.

"Hello," Erika yelled. "Can you hear me?"

"Of course we can," came the muffled reply. "Now open the damn door!"

It had to be Sandra, there was no mistaking her voice. With her grandfather and Liam in support, they raised open the trap door to find Sandra's enormous smile beaming back up at them.

"You know what, Holstrom?" she said. "You have a serious problem with some very weird undead dudes in this town."

Sandra made way for the others to climb out of the cellar first. Amber emerged from the darkness, immediately running towards the safety of her older brother. Next came Nicole, her hair a complete mess, to which Erika smirked. Then it was Michelle, her tattooed arms visible under torn sleeves. She looked over at Erika, who was filled with an immense relief. Before she knew it, she'd grabbed Michelle in a tight hug. She quickly extended the embrace to include a rather rigid Nicole, but not before Erika felt a fierce and affectionate squeeze from Michelle. Then came Erika's grandmother. She bounded up the stairs like a teenager, moving to her husband's waiting arms once she was on the surface. Rikke smiled at the sight of the elderly couple, gently rubbing their noses together. Lastly came Sandra the cellar gatekeeper, light grey ash clinging awkwardly to her dark skin.

Rikke gently gave each woman a quick once over, making sure there were no injuries. They were all alive, and safe, for now.

"What happened?" Nicole asked, still bewildered from their experience.

"Dude, you heard Erika's Nana," Sandra exclaimed. "We got rolled up by a bunch of undead zombie Vikings, that's what happened."

There was some nervous laughter at the absurdity of Sandra's statement.

"I found it," Liam declared from the far side of the rubble. The heavy old storage chest he'd kept in the attic had somehow survived.

*They sure don't build luggage like this anymore*, he thought, brushing away some soot. He opened the singed case just as Erika and Rikke joined him. Liam pulled out his battered copy of *The Sagas of the Icelanders,* quickly flipping to the glossary.

"Now, let's see how one slays these *draugar*."

THE
ARCTIC REGIONS
OF
NORTH AMERICA
BY
EDW WELLER, F R G S
PARRY ISLAND
MELVILLE ISLAND
BATHURST Isld
CORNWALLIS ISLAND
Melville Sound
Pr of Wales Land
Pr. Albert Land
BANKS LAND
Minto Inlet
Pr Albert Sound
Wollaston Land
VICTORIA Land
King William Land
Booth
Arctic Circle
Great Bear Lake

# CHAPTER 25

*"The oxen which had been used to haul Thorolf's body were ridden to death by demons, and every single beast that came near his grave went raving mad and howled itself to death. The shepherd at Hvamm often came racing home with Thorolf after him. One day that fall neither sheep nor shepherd came back to the farm."*

The three helicopters rose from the football field adjacent to the smashed Pond Inlet airport. Two massive *Chinook* aircraft and a lone *Seahawk* circled once over the pulverized community, before banking east towards the harbour and open ocean of Baffin Bay. The late Arctic summer sun was masked by the green northern lights. The larger pair of flying machines carried a mixed collection of soldiers, hunters, scientists, and other local volunteers. Brigadier-General Katherine Tremblay had assembled the desperate bunch, cut off from the outside world by forces they were only just beginning to understand. The general sat near the flight deck of the lead *Chinook*, reviewing the Old Norse sagas she'd been given by Dr Holstrom.

*"And the many draugar entered the dreams of the living, cursing their victims as they bent day into night. For they were immune to all forms of earthly weapons, with only the noble strength of a hero being able to counter such powerful forces. Their motivation was envy, both in protecting their tomb, and a longing for the life they once led, while their appetite was insatiable."*

Katherine contemplated the ad hoc team she had put together. Even the youngest of the volunteers understood the seriousness of their task, especially Erika with her special abilities. Katherine knew Erika was unique, composed of both Inuit and northern European blood. Her father Liam was also along, since he understood the *draugar's* mythology through the ancient legends Katherine now read. In addition, Dr Rikke Larsen had joined for her medical prowess and grasp of early Scandinavian languages. They were flying into battle, most for the first time, in defence of what the *draugar* called *Helluland*, the land of flat stones. Most of Katherine's volunteers simply called it home.

*"For Einar knew his neighbour would return as a draugr, as he had not perished horizontally. In the nights that followed, the livestock began to disappear, for the recently departed had not met with a good death. Though on the darkest nights he was not seen, he was heard, his anguished soul imploring for a proper burial."*

The helicopters racing across the frigid ocean would first try to establish contact with any friendly vessels in the area they could find. Next they were to land on the floating ice, in proximity of the *draugar's* snow-covered tomb. If any of the original Arctic troops on the pack ice were still alive, Katherine would rally them for a final assault against the undead. She glanced back at the thirty souls seated in the cargo bay of the vibrating *Chinook*.

*"They were powerful, with the will to draw the animated spirit back into a deceased body. The again walker was known as a dra-ugr, with a clan called draugar. But the dead could die anew, if*

*they were burned, dismembered, or otherwise destroyed. The wits of a mighty hero must be noble and pure, for any weakness would be exploited."*

"Hey, Holstrom," Sandra yelled at Erika over the roar of the rotor blades. "My ears are clogged. You got any gum?"

Erika checked inside her leather purse and shook her head. Sandra shrugged, turning her attention to Nicole seated next to her.

"Yo, Gibson, you got any gum?"

Another negative response. "Ask Lavoix."

Michelle Lavoix looked at Sandra, raising her palms in defeat.

Erika watched her three friends huddled across from her in red-netted seats. Even with all they had been through since arriving in Pond Inlet, the sea worm incident on the water, a near miss with a polar bear, and almost getting crushed by demonic caribou, they still volunteered to join Erika, despite the danger. Perhaps this was due to a sense of adventure on their part, or the sombre realisation that, as the general put it, this was the only option they had. *We either drive these things back into the sea, or die trying.* Brave but scary words. There were not even enough modern weapons to go around. The military arsenal located in the community centre had been completely destroyed by the creatures, including most of the northern forces' rifles and ammunition. It was hoped that some of the lethality aboard the warships at sea could be harnessed, assuming the monsters had not already sunk the vessels. Erika looked over at Rikke, who was poring through a book on combat casualty care. The Danish doctor wore the cap of her home ship, the *Knud Rasmussen.*

*I hope your shipmates still exist.*

A hand reached over and took Erika's. She looked up at her father, who was strapped in beside her, and smiled. Liam stared back with a pained expression.

"I'm so sorry I got you into this, cub," he said over the noise.

"What are you talking about, Dad? This was my choice."

"But it was me that gave you the amulet, me that let you bring your friends up north, and me that dragged you into this whole mess."

"Yeah, like you knew all along Grandpa's boat would get eaten by sea worms," she countered sarcastically. "Or that Pond Inlet would get overrun by zombie Vikings. Way to go, Dad!" She smiled back at him with two thumbs up.

Just then, Katherine approached from the flight deck. She wore a headset and microphone, handing a similar pair each to Liam and Erika. The two donned the listening devices, as Katherine plugged their cables into intercom sockets attached to the ceiling.

"Can you hear me?" she asked. Both nodded.

"Erika, I want you to explain to me again your abilities," she said. "Don't be shy about it, just tell me what you think you can do, it's important."

Katherine held on to a roof railing, fixated on her young prodigy as the cabin interior shuddered through mild turbulence. Erika pulled the amulet out from under her clothes, holding it up towards the general.

"I don't know how much of what I can do is me, and how much is because of this necklace, but even before my dad gave me the jewellery, I had started to see things just before they happened."

"How do you mean?" Katherine encouraged her.

"Like on the ice, when playing hockey, I somehow always know where the puck is going to be just before it actually moves. Or once, when driving with my friends, we would have hit a moose if I hadn't foreseen the danger and told them to stop the car."

"Is that how you were able to avoid that monster's lunges when it tried to grab you back at the HQ?"

"I guess so," Erika shrugged.

"You guess so, or you know so, this part is critical," Katherine persisted. "I need to know every tool I've got in my toolbox when we go up against these things - that includes your special powers."

It felt strange yet somehow comforting to hear another person acknowledge Erika's abilities, even need them. After months of confusion, she was not a freak of nature after all, but instead a valued member of this impressive commander's team.

"Your eyes," Katherine continued. "When you went up against that creature your eyes were almost on fire, what's that all about?"

Erika shook her head. "I don't know, that's a recent thing, like in the last few days. I don't know what it means."

"Maybe you can fire optical laser beams, like in the comic books," Liam said encouragingly. Both women gave him a look of contempt.

"Sorry," he sighed sheepishly, sinking in his seat.

"Can you fly?" Katherine asked, half-disbelieving her own question.

"No."

"Control the elements, like water, wind?"

"No."

"Do you have enhanced strength? Can you lift heavy things?"

"Sometimes, I think so, but I don't know if it's my abilities or just adrenaline."

Katherine paused, unable to think of what else to ask. Erika looked up at her, pointing to her own temples.

"I think I can communicate with my mind."

"Telekinetically?" Katherine said, her eyes widening.

"What does that mean?"

"It means you can move stuff with your thoughts," Sandra yelled all excited from behind Katherine. "Like that space ninja dude in the sci-fi movies!"

Erika hung her head. "No."

Katherine crouched down, her gloved hands resting on her knees.

"Can you communicate with other creatures, like animals, or those *draugar*?"

"Yes!" Erika said confidently. "Yes, I can. Remember how I told it to let Eleanor go? I just kind of think it and they hear. I even tamed a polar bear."

"Most amazing thing I ever saw," Michelle chimed in, staring warmly at Erika.

"General," a female voice interrupted over the intercom. "There's something up ahead you should come and see."

Katherine acknowledged the pilot, then leaned towards Erika.

"No matter what happens down there, I want you and your friends to stay close to me. I know you're all legally adults, but just barely, and you've had no military training, so no unnecessary risks, understood?"

Katherine shook both Erika and Liam's hands, before moving back towards the flight deck of the *Chinook* helicopter.

"You're a real life oracle, my friend," Rikke called out to Erika with a smile. "A living seeress, amazing."

Erika recoiled slightly. Her mother used to say the same thing when reading Erika childhood bedtime stories. The Dane's use of Star's words, however unintentional, felt too close to home. It also didn't help that Rikke seemed to have taken a shine to her father. Erika rubbed the amulet around her neck and closed her eyes.

Up front, Katherine followed the pilot's hand as she pointed out several small plumes of smoke on the horizon.

"How far out is that?" Katherine asked.

"Ten nautical miles and closing," came the reply. "Ma'am, it's in the vicinity of the USS *Samuel Ronaldson*'s last known position."

Both women looked soberly out the front window as the pilot brought her flying machine lower to the sea ice. With the other two aircraft in the formation keeping their distance, Katherine's *Chinook* flew low over the water. They circled the debris floating among the ice floes at least three times in order to be sure. Given the number of uniformed bodies in the water, as well as the size of the burning oil slick on the surface, it had to have been the *Ronaldson*. There didn't appear to be any survivors.

They again took up the lead position within their flying formation, as the three helicopters continued east.

*If these things can sink a destroyer*, Katherine pondered, *maybe that's what happened to the Volkov.*

She pulled out a field message pad from her tactical vest, flipping to the last marked pages. Her initial plan had been largely dependent on harnessing the *Ronaldson's* considerable firepower against the creatures' floating lair. The only other allied vessel in the vicinity was the *Knud Rasmussen*, if it still existed. The Danish patrol ship carried a single deck-mounted auto-cannon, insufficient for what she had in mind. Her only option was to go with plan B, as risky as that sounded. In reality, she had little choice.

Katherine noticed the *Chinook's* forward-looking radar display was covered in grainy static.

"Can we see or communicate with anyone?" she asked, already knowing the answer.

"Negative," came the response. "The atmospheric interference means we can only speak to the other helos in our flight, that's it."

"Roger. Patch me through to Colonel Borishov in the *Seahawk*." Soon a familiar Russian accent filled Katherine's headset. "Oleksandr, we'll have to go with contingency plan bravo, and hope the *Nikolay Khabalov* is still in one piece."

"My General," came the garbled response, "if I were you, I'd be more concerned if the *Khabalov* does indeed remain afloat, given the unpredictability of its current captain. At least that's what I've heard."

Katherine couldn't tell if her Russian counterpart was trying to be funny or morbid. Either way, their collective fate would soon be at the mercy of a certain temperamental acting captain named Ivan Egorov.

"All right, Oleksandr, good luck," Katherine encouraged. "We'll keep our distance until we've got confirmation you've made positive contact with the Russian frigate, either with three blue flares or over the radio, if it works."

She watched as the *Seahawk* helicopter with Danish markings broke off from the pair of *Chinook*s. The nimble flying machine dropped down to fifty metres above the icy wavetops and engaged both its landing lights and halogen search lamp. They did not want to surprise a character like the *Khabalov*'s skipper, so made themselves as visible as possible. Colonel Borishov was located in the centre jump seat, slightly behind the flight crew. He could see the co-pilot trying to use the *Seahawk*'s side-scanning radar, with little success. All were now convinced the atmospheric interference across the region this past summer had something to do with the creatures they now hunted. And here the normally desk-bound defence attaché had thought his adventurous field days were over.

"Colonel," the pilot signalled, "surface lights visible ahead. Their disposition matches that of an *Admiral Gorshkov*-class frigate, so it must be the *Khabalov*."

*Now how in the hell could you tell that?* Colonel Borishov thought, rather impressed with the Dane's ship recognition skills.

"Releasing flares," the pilot said calmly, again in an effort to have their helicopter recognised as non-threatening.

Colonel Borishov squinted as the first of the bright red decoy flares shot out from the side of the *Seahawk* helicopter. Next the co-pilot indicated their radio was set to the standard maritime frequency used by the Russian navy.

"*Nikolay Khabalov, Nikolay Khabalov*, this is Colonel Oleksandr Borishov, Russian Army, do you read me?"

The Danish flight crew gave each other a knowing glance. By now, virtually everyone knew the colonel worked for Russian intelligence and not the army, though it mattered little at the moment. Colonel Borishov kept repeating his message, both in his mother tongue and English. His efforts were met with static, as the frigate's outline slowly came into view. It was clear the ship was steaming south, away from the pack ice.

Two white flares shot into the sky from the mid-section of the ship. The pilot eased his aircraft into a hover, not sure if the *Khabalov*'s response was welcoming or a warning. He turned the *Seahawk* ninety degrees to the right, parallel to the Russian frigate, while his crew chief slid open the left side door. With the chief's assistance, Colonel Borishov moved a massive signal light into the open doorway. Using the lamp's shutters, he signalled to the *Khabalov* with Morse code, another skill the colonel had thought he would never again need.

"What are you telling them?" the crew chief asked.

"That we're friendly," the colonel said, "and a little something only we Russians would recognise."

"A deck lamp is active," the pilot reported. "Starboard side, near the bridge."

Colonel Borishov breathed a sigh of relief at the response they received. Within minutes, the *Seahawk* was lining up with the stern flight pad of the *Khabalov*, the pilot trying to avoid what was left of the frigate's own disabled helicopter. As soon as the front wheels touched down, Colonel Borishov was outside, two of the ship's sailors quickly escorting him below deck. Without hesitation, the Danish aircraft was again airborne, moving to a loitering position eight hundred metres away.

Several kilometres back in the lead *Chinook*, Katherine watched through a pair of binoculars for the signal that the *Khabalov*'s acting captain had agreed to support their plan. Without the firepower of the Russian warship, they didn't stand a chance against the undead. She shook her head. Katherine had never been a superstitious person, or ever believed in ghosts. Her only understanding of such subjects was what she occasionally read in her daughter's fantasy novels. Still, she surmised there were likely many unexplained phenomena in this world, yet to be defined by science. Her security clearance allowed her to read about the intercept missions her air force counterparts sometimes flew, chasing unknown objects that possessed incredible manoeuvrability and speed. As a teenager in the late 1970s, she often watched a mystery documentary series narrated by a famous science-fiction celebrity. It explored everything from the Yeti and the Loch Ness Monster, to the Bermuda Triangle. Of course none of it was true. Or was it? Katherine had observed helplessly as one of the creatures killed her intelligence officer with the flick of its wrist. As unworldly as the concept of the *draugar* seemed, there was no denying they were real, and deadly. Something was wrong with the natural order of things in the north, and Katherine feared things would only get worse, unless...

"General," the pilot reported excitedly. "I have a visual on three blue flares, just fired from the surface contact."

*Well done Oleksandr, you sly dog,* Katherine thought triumphantly.

She quickly turned around, moving back towards the civilians in the rear of the *Chinook* as it accelerated under her feet. In less than ten minutes they would be dropped onto the pack ice where she hoped the remainder of Eleanor's Arctic troops were still located.

*Eleanor*, she reflected quietly to herself. Katherine had watched the missing major grow from a young, wide-eyed platoon leader into a decorated company commander. Now Eleanor was a hostage to these ancient ghouls - if she was even alive.

*We're coming, my friend.*

Katherine stopped in front of Erika, looking hopefully at the young prodigy with the pixie haircut and magical amulet. She motioned for Erika to put her headset back on. Liam did the same.

"You mentioned you tamed a polar bear?" Katherine asked.

"Yeah," Erika said. "I didn't want to hurt it, but it had taken my friend's sister. I assumed it was just hungry, probably even starving, so I helped it figure out where food would be."

"Can you communicate with several animals at the same time?"

"I don't know."

"How about ones underwater?"

# CHAPTER 26

"One minute," the pilot announced over the intercom. Erika reached down and felt for her trusted leather purse. She then tucked the amulet around her neck into the white parka she'd been given before leaving Pond Inlet. The mighty *Chinook* bucked as it initiated a rapid descent towards the enormous ice shelf floating below. Erika and her friends were seated near the back of the helicopter's cargo compartment, a few soldiers and local hunters standing between them and the rear ramp door. Brigadier-General Katherine Tremblay had instructed the young students, along with Erika's father and Dr Rikke Larsen, to wait until everyone else had disembarked from the flying behemoth before exiting. Perhaps Erika should have felt apprehensive, even scared with what loomed ahead, but she did not. Instead she felt serene.

For the first time in her life, Erika had clarity, both in her sense of purpose and convictions. After years of trying to fit in, and more recently the terrible confusion as her abilities awakened, her mental puzzle was at long last coming together. Erika was an emerging warrior, a competitor, a champion, and a natural leader in the making. For whatever reason, her bloodline had endowed her with exceptional powers, while her upbringing had instilled her with a strong moral compass. She was compassionate and resilient, physically fit and empathetic, the very best her generation had to offer. Whatever these twisted creatures on the ice were, Erika felt she was ready for anything they could throw at her. She sensed her late mother would have approved.

Erika's personal reflections were rudely interrupted as Sandra threw up across Nicole's boots. Sandra had never been good with flying, as was again evident.

"Dude!" Nicole cried out in disgust.

"Sorry," Sandra said hesitantly, covering her mouth. "The sooner we get off this thing, the better for all of us I think."

"Amen," Michelle added, looking back across at Erika.

"Thirty seconds," came the intercom warning.

"Remember," Erika yelled, "we stay put on the chopper until everyone else is off." Her friends nodded their understanding. Erika's father actually looked the most concerned of them all. Maybe Liam knew more about the monsters below then he was letting on. Erika squeezed his leg in support. Two red lights on the roof signalled everyone to get ready. Erika sensed the prevailing emotion of the other adults onboard - that of fear.

The rear ramp of the *Chinook* dropped down. A howling wall of white swirled outside, caused by the rotor blades' downwash against the snow. The blast of cold air signalled the temperature on the pack ice was much cooler than in Pond Inlet.

"Go!" hollered the flight crew chief, as the two signal lights turned green. The collection of Arctic troops and local hunters scrambled out of the helicopter, some nudging each other in encouragement. From the flight deck, Katherine emerged wearing her tactical fighting equipment and carrying an issued rifle. There was no denying Erika was in awe of the general, and trusted her implicitly.

"Follow me," Katherine instructed her civilian cohort. They unfastened their seatbelts and stood up. While Erika wasn't scared for her own safety, she was genuinely worried about her teammates. All three of them had been given the chance to stay behind in Pond Inlet, but had declined without reservation. Only their local friend Jordan had opted to stay back for the sake of his little sister, Amber. It was the right decision. The amulet glowed warmly against Erika's chest as she moved down the rear ramp.

The barren ice was hard under her boots, the top snow blown aside by the pair of helicopters now lifting off behind her. To Erika's front, she noticed several of her fellow passengers conferring with a group of uniformed individuals who had greeted their arrival. Erika and her peers formed a loose circle. She watched as Liam and Rikke moved forward with Katherine towards an American officer.

"Morning, General," Captain Simmons said. "Are we glad to see you."

"It's Janet, correct?" Katherine asked, receiving an affirmative nod. "How far are we from the ice cavern entrance that Major Matthews discovered?"

"About a click away, near the southern edge of the ice shelf, but the opening collapsed last night after we got hit by what we're pretty sure was a missile attack. We think two of our personnel are trapped inside, but it's covered under several tons of ice. Our guide, Ujurak, can show you."

Katherine noted the unease in the American's voice. It reinforced to her that they needed to act quickly, lest there be more *missing* by nightfall.

"Captain, please gather your sergeant major and platoon commanders," Katherine ordered, "as well as any other local guides you may have with you. I have some extremely important information to pass on."

Captain Simmons sent off a runner to collect the requested leadership before turning back to Katherine, somewhat confused.

"General, where's Major Matthews?"

Ivan's blood boiled as he watched the pair of transport helicopters lift off from the pack ice in the distance. His emotions were consumed by inner turmoil. After days of limited communication with Moscow, exacerbated by multiple confusing and tragic events, the *Nikolay Khabalov's* acting captain had received the worst news imaginable. His beloved brother Sergei, his mentor and best friend, was dead. The details were delivered by a pompous Russian defence attaché, whom Ivan assumed was GRU. The colonel was currently conferring with the ship's chief petty officer, the two discussing the sea worms infesting the *Khabalov's* propeller shafts. In the end, Ivan had agreed to support Colonel Borishov's ridiculous plan, but for his own ulterior motives. Ivan wanted revenge, of any kind, and he would unleash his fury when the opportunity presented itself. If he had to suffer in silence, then so would everyone else. Ivan had heard some far-fetched cover stories before, but this one was absurd, even for Moscow. His intellect felt belittled while his pride was deeply offended.

*Patience, Ivan, patience.*

"Captain," the starboard deck sentry called out. "Sir, two times *White Swans* approaching from the north-east."

Ivan, the chief, and Colonel Borishov watched in amazement as the pair of Russian *Blackjack* bombers swooped in low over the ice. Their massive swing-wings were extended, while both aircraft emitted a translucent green glow. They passed between the *Khabalov* and the Arctic troops gathered on the ice shelf. The planes then banked north, exposing their scarred underbellies towards the Russian frigate.

"The bomb bay doors are missing," the chief observed, confused.

Ivan peered through his binoculars at the majestic flying machines. Sure enough, there were signs of considerable structural damage to the bottoms of both aircraft.

"They're empty," Ivan said dryly, "the bomb bays are empty." He hung his head. "So they're responsible for launching the cruise missile salvo that tried to sink us."

"Shoot them down," Colonel Borishov instructed urgently.

Both Ivan and the chief looked at the older Russian officer in disbelief.

"They are not what they seem," the colonel continued. "If you do not destroy them, countless more will perish, just like on the *Volkov*."

Ivan raged at the mention of his brother's lost submarine. Who was this glorified embassy bureaucrat giving orders on his ship, never mind suggesting his crew commit an act of treason? Ivan was about to suggest the colonel mind his tongue, when the chief pointed urgently towards the circling bombers.

The first of the two *Blackjacks* descended just above the frozen landscape, bearing down on the departing helicopters still gaining altitude. The Russian bomber's wing sliced off the tail rotor blades of the lead *Chinook*, sending the helicopter crashing onto the pack ice. The second *Chinook* desperately tried evading the Russian warplanes by staying low, but it was no use. As the first *Blackjack* banked away, its left wing severely damaged, the second bomber intentionally collided with the surviving *Chinook*. Both aircraft disintegrated in a shower of sparks, twisted metal, and flames, their wreckage slamming onto the frozen features below.

"Take cover!" Katherine screamed as the enormous fuel-laden fireball approached. Erika and her friends scrambled behind a series of frozen pressure ridges, while Katherine and her uniformed comrades' dove into newly dug ice trenches. The deadly heat consumed several recently arrived ammunition crates left on the ice. The boxes cooked off in every direction, as the wall of flames rose towards the sky. As soon as the explosion dissipated, the remaining *Blackjack* circled into view, preparing for another pass. The nose of the warplane pointed directly at the centre of the Arctic troops cowering on the ice. Despite all her abilities, there was nothing Erika could do to intervene. The attacking white bomber was too fast, seemingly flying itself.

The first air-to-air missile overshot the *Blackjack*, but the second buried itself in the Russian plane's starboard engines before detonating. The force of the explosion separated the *Blackjack's* right wing from the fuselage, sending the bomber cart-wheeling past its intended targets. A spontaneous cheer erupted among the troops, more from relief than joy. The enormous white aircraft crashed near the ice cavern entrance, unsealing it. Shortly after, a lone Eurofighter Typhoon appeared, banking low over the carnage it had created. To everyone's surprise, Katherine's personal radio crackled to life.

"Lion two to unknown ground call sign," the male voice was British. "Lion two to unknown ground call sign, do you copy?"

The general was about to respond, when a silver object streaked up from the ocean's surface towards the circling fighter jet. Katherine and her colleagues watched aghast as the aircraft that had been their salvation, was blown from the sky by a surface-to-air missile. The rocket's smoke trail led back to the *Khabalov*.

"What the hell did you just do?" Colonel Borishov demanded.

"I followed the rules of engagement," Ivan said cynically. "The British fighter jet was a legitimate target after it shot down one of our nation's beloved *White Swans*." He stood up from the *Khabalov*'s weapon control console as the ship's chief watched silently from the corner of the bridge. He noticed the incensed defence attaché was not armed.

"You young fool," Colonel Borishov shouted. "If any of us are to survive this day, we need to work with the Americans and their allies, not attack them. We are dealing with forces far more powerful than any of us can imagine. Call it black magic, or God's wrath for all I care, but the threat we face is horribly real. You are helping the enemy with your belligerent actions."

"My dear Colonel," Ivan stated, unimpressed, "another outburst from you and I will have you removed from my ship, is that clear? As far as I can tell, the enemy is human and out on the ice in front of us, not some fanciful creation from a delusional mind."

Colonel Borishov stood apprehensively on the bridge, his eyes moving from Ivan to the ship's chief and back. The rumours were true. Acting Captain Ivan Egorov was a madman in the making. Despite his own superior rank, Colonel Borishov needed to proceed cautiously with the unhinged man before him, lest Brigadier-General Tremblay's plan, and their only hope, unravel. He was pondering his next move when a ship's lookout interjected urgently.

"Sir, contact," the sailor reported. "Multiple shots fired on the pack ice to our immediate north."

"Captain, we have troops in contact!"

The young soldier handed his binoculars to Captain Janet Simmons just as the western horizon erupted with small-arms fire.

"Stand to, stand to!" someone called out.

It sounded like the company's entire lead platoon was decisively engaged. Multiple rifle shots echoed across the ice, mixed with short bursts from a heavy weapon. With their radios down, there was no way to directly communicate with the forward troops.

"What the hell are they shooting at?" Janet demanded, looking west. Katherine was located a few metres away and moved to her side.

"You won't believe it until you see it," the general said with a grim tone.

Janet scanned the horizon from right to left, then froze. From a fissure created by the crashed *Blackjack*, the first green apparition emerged some 800 metres away. It effortlessly bounded across the ice, before diving into a snow trench filled with panicked troops. She dropped her binos and looked at her general in disbelief.

"You need to counter with a hasty attack," Katherine ordered, snapping Janet from her initial shock. The two women quickly conferred to modify their original plan.

Soon all was chaos.

Erika hid with her friends behind a nearby ice ridge as the carnage unfolded. It was terrifying. She witnessed several newly arrived soldiers cut down by flaming arrows, fired from an unseen bow. Off to her right was the steady clatter of a machine gun, trying to engage the creatures emerging from further down the enormous ice floe. A green energy bolt to her left sent several Inuit hunters scrambling, while a medic raced forward to help the wounded. Beside her, Sandra and Nicole desperately covered their ears while Michelle stared detached at the battle unfolding before them. Erika was experiencing yet another nightmare, but this time her eyes were wide open.

"Liam, Rikke, Erika, you and your friends are with me, and stay low!" Katherine called out. "Captain Simmons, you know what to do."

"Yes, General," Janet said as Katherine and her party dashed off following their guide Ujurak.

"Sergeant Major Bernard, on me," Janet called out. The brawny French-Canadian ran up behind her, several panting soldiers with him. The group flinched as multiple detonations shook the frozen ground where they crouched. The smell of cordite was everywhere. The *draugar's* assault had only just begun, yet already things were not going well for the defenders

"These things are trying to flank us," Janet assessed. "Our rifle rounds fly right through the bastards, but the machine guns seem to at least slow them down. Sergeant Major, I want you to take the heavy weapons detachment and set up a firebase to the south-east of the ice cavern entrance. Try and hit them from the side with high explosives as they surface."

"D'accord, Captain," Bernard acknowledged. "Where is the general?"

Another bolt of green energy shot overtop the gathered troops.

"She went with Ujurak and the civies. They're going to try and get around these things while we keep them occupied."

The sergeant major looked alarmed at the ground between them. "Mon dieu, the general left her weapon."

Before anyone could respond, a flaming arrow flew past their heads, burying itself in the snow behind them. Janet had just missed being hit.

"Shit, that was close! Get going, Sergeant Major, we'll try and cover you." Soon a dozen men and women clad in white uniforms opened fire against a mass of approaching *draugar*. A few of the monsters were knocked down, but quickly regained their footing and charged at the humans.

"Grenade!" someone cried out, followed by a muffled explosion that lifted a creature into the air. It promptly landed on both its deformed legs and continued its advance. Suddenly there was a loud bang off to the left, followed quickly by a deep concussion. Janet watched with satisfaction as one of the *draugar* before her came apart, its dismembered limbs twitching on the ice.

"Reload," the sergeant major ordered.

Two soldiers, one with a steaming *Carl Gustav* rocket launcher on his shoulder, frantically repositioned themselves to fire another shot. They quickly reloaded an 84mm high explosive round into their Swedish designed weapon and engaged a new target. The two disappeared in a cloud of snow as the *Carl Gustav's* back-blast obscured them from view. Another one of the monsters exploded into a revolting green mist.

"How many more Carl G rounds have you got?" the sergeant major hollered.

"Three," came the reply.

He knew it was not enough.

Ivan watched the ground battle taking place just a few hundred metres from the bow of his ship in disbelief. What appeared to be enormous creatures threw themselves at the hapless Arctic soldiers, who desperately tried to fend them off. Behind him, Colonel Borishov pleaded for Ivan to open fire with the *Khabalov's* deck canon in support of the beleaguered ground troops. Ivan had other plans.

"Fire the canisters," he ordered his ship's chief.

The chief looked back at Ivan with concern. "Sir, excuse me?" he said, wanting to make sure he'd understood his captain correctly.

"You heard me, Chief, fire the canisters."

There was a pause as both men stared at each other, a very confused Colonel Borishov looking on.

"No sir," the chief finally said, standing up straight. "I will not."

"What did you say?" Ivan fumed through gritted teeth.

"Sir, those canisters are only to be used in time of war. Even then, they require two levels of authorisation from Moscow, neither of which we have received, my Acting Captain."

Ivan noticed the insubordinate chief's emphasis and drew his sidearm. He levelled the weapon at the older man's head.

"Move aside you insolent rat of a man," Ivan ordered. The grey haired sailor slowly complied as Colonel Borishov looked on apprehensively.

"You're mad," the chief hissed at Ivan.

"Perhaps," he replied, then promptly turned several keys on the bridge's weapon control console before pressing a lone red button. Along the sides of the *Khabalov's* main deck, several small mortar tubes elevated to a forty-five degree angle. This was followed by a series of popping sounds as multiple canisters, each no larger than a soda can, launched towards the massive ice shelf to their north.

The projectiles landed among the lead platoon of Arctic troops, desperately fighting off the advancing monsters. Within seconds, the canisters released their deadly agent, the scent of chlorine filling the air. Soon, the first of the young soldiers dropped to the ice, writhing in pain and unable to breathe. Several were dry-heaving on all fours as the unaffected *draugar* finished them off with bladed weapons from another age.

Sergeant Major Bernard had served in Syria and instantly recognised what was unfolding before him. He scrambled for his gas mask, located in a pouch on his left thigh. He quickly removed the mask from its protective seal. Placing it over his face, he covered the side filter with his hand while blowing out then inhaling, ensuring an airtight seal. Next he yelled as loud as he could from his covered mouth, "Gas, gas, gas!" A few troops around him hesitated before their training kicked in and they too donned their protective kit. Some of the soldiers had ignored parts of their mandatory equipment list. They were soon writhing in agony on the lifeless ice, their gas masks intentionally left behind in Pond Inlet to save weight.

Captain Janet Simmons ran up to the sergeant major, her face covered in rubber.

"Did that come from the *Khabalov*?" she asked in a muffled voice.

"Yes, ma'am," the French-Canadian nodded in disgust. "They probably fired sarin or chlorine canisters at us. I have no idea of our casualties, but the gas seems to have no effect on the creatures." The experienced sergeant major scanned the hopeless struggle unfolding before them. "Ma'am, the monsters will continue to exploit our tactical weaknesses until we're overrun, which at this rate could happen at any moment."

Even through the clouded rubber eyepieces of the man's gas mask, Janet could see the pained look on the sergeant major's face.

"Captain, we need to fall back," he recommended in resignation. "If we haven't given the general enough time by now, then it's too late no matter what we do."

Janet knew he was right, and soon gave the order for their shattered Arctic company to disengage and withdraw.

Throughout the entire battle, the northern horizon continued to dance with green energy waves. It was as though an unseen force of nature was laughing.

Katherine scrambled towards the open water. She led her gaggle of civilians close to the ice floe's southern edge and away from danger. Their assigned guide, Ujurak, had moved ahead to reconnoitre the entrance of the creatures' ice cave. Katherine was taking an awful risk. She was relying essentially on teenagers, or one young woman in particular, to try to defeat the ancient *draugar* in their lair. If Liam and Rikke's mythology research was correct, then they needed to get Erika down to the *knarr* longboat trapped in the ice. The *draugar* would not make it easy. She was working on the premise that her adversaries were from a doomed voyage, centuries ago. Dead or undead, they had once been men with medieval prejudices. As a result, and despite her training, she intentionally left her weapon behind. She hoped the creatures would perceive an unarmed woman as harmless. In other words, not worthy of their attention. Maybe this ploy would let Erika get close enough to the prize, while also finding Eleanor and the other missing personnel.

It didn't help matters that Katherine had no idea what Colonel Borishov was up to on the *Khabalov* to their south. The frigate wasn't providing any fire support and worse, it had earlier blown a friendly fighter jet out of the sky. She waited to let the others catch up, glancing back at the Russian ship sitting motionless several hundred metres away on the frigid water. Erika and Michelle were the first to join her, followed by Liam and Rikke, and then Sandra and Nicole. All were out of breath.

"We'll wait here a few minutes until Ujurak gets back from his reconnaissance," Katherine explained. "Then we'll see if we can get Erika down onto the *draugar's* longboat." She paused as several explosions boomed in the distance. The battle between the living and the undead was reaching its climax.

"Erika," she said, "I want you to talk us through the plan again, so everyone is reminded what needs to happen once we get inside the ice cave."

*If we get inside the ice cave*, the general sighed to herself.

As if to underscore her doubts, Ujurak frantically appeared, running towards Katherine and her posse with three enormous *draugar* in pursuit. The putrid creatures, covered in leather and chainmail, floated effortlessly towards them. The guide turned and raised his hunting rifle at the first monster, which snatched it away and snapped it like a rotten branch.

Katherine could tell that the *draugar* were toying with them. Her instincts were correct. The monsters no longer perceived the mostly female, unarmed humans as an immediate threat. It didn't mean they weren't in terrible danger, but her ruse would buy them a few precious moments.

*Men, so predictable. Even dead ones.*

The three *draugar* closed in, pushing Katherine's group back towards the edge of the ice shelf and the deadly cold water below. These creatures intended to cast the living into the sea, where they'd freeze to death in minutes.

"Now, Erika," Katherine quietly ordered.

Erika looked back at her confused.

"Now," the general said again, urgently. "Use your abilities, your powers, quick!"

Erika nodded her sudden understanding just at the monsters surrounded them. She closed her eyes, taking the amulet around her neck into one hand, while placing her other palm down against the ice. Her hair glowed, causing the advancing *draugar* to hesitate. Unseen pulses radiated from Erika's body as wave after wave of mystic signals were released. Katherine and the others watched in total silence.

*Help us.*

Erika opened her eyes, which were as bright as the sun.

*Please.*

A nearby splashing sound signalled their salvation had arrived. The *draugar* held their ground as Katherine waited for Mother Nature to intervene. From the water, a black form flopped onto the ice between the humans and the undead. It rolled onto its front, two flippers propping up its bulbous body.

"WTF, Holstrom," Sandra complained from behind the general. "Are you serious? A seal?"

Katherine watched in utter dismay as the lone harp seal began barking at the green glowing *draugar.* They towered over the obnoxious mammal. It was the most ridiculous thing she had ever seen.

Erika smiled mischievously back at her roommate.

"Remember what my grandparents taught us; where there are seals, there are..."

The front paw of the giant polar bear took the first monster's head clean off, its body dropping to the ice. The other two *draugar* barely had time to react before the mighty northern carnivore removed one of their legs with its powerful jaws. The wounded monster limped backwards as its accomplice moved to confront the attacking bear with a broadsword. The animal avoided the weapon as it swung past its head, nicking the yellow conservation tag dangling from its ear. It barrelled into the creature, its white fur merging with the green aura surrounding its prey. The broadsword fell to the ground as the monster was thrown over the icy ledge and into the ocean below. The polar bear then turned its attention back to the one legged creature, its jaws locking onto the bony neck of the longdead Viking. With an audible snap, its head went sailing through the air, its limp body a mass of frozen goo. The mighty Arctic hunter rose on its hind legs and roared fiercely, then dropped onto all fours. The polar bear briefly glanced back at Erika before trundling off, the lone harp seal still barking away like a circus animal.

"Holy shit, Erika!" Sandra yelled in delight as the others slowly stood up. Katherine moved over to Erika, while her father hugged her in relief.

"Well done, my friend," Katherine said impressed. "But what about the one that fell in the water? Drowning doesn't kill them, does it?"

Erika winked at her, just as a pod of orca killer whales tore the remaining monster apart, limb from limb.

"They've reached the main deck," a panicked voice reported across the ship's intercom before being cut off.

Using the *Khabalov's* interior cameras, Ivan watched speechless as the mass of sea worms from the vessel's propeller shafts multiplied at an astonishing rate. They swelled in size, consuming everything in their path. His mighty ship was dead in the water as deck after deck fell to the ravenous parasites. They had already short-circuited the frigate's mainframe, causing the warship's automated weapon systems to malfunction. A few errant missiles sprung out of their silos at awkward angles, before falling harmlessly into the sea. In desperation, Ivan had ordered the release of poisonous canisters inside the engine room and crew quarters, but with little effect. The Davis Strait was once again the legendary Sea of Worms, exacting its revenge against the morally corrupt.

Colonel Borishov looked from the bridge at the forward deck, just as the auto cannon and anchor chains were consumed. He had already put on a protective immersion suit, as had the ship's chief, realising the end was near. Soon the lights on the *Khabalov* flickered, then darkened permanently. Next the alarms fell silent, as millions of wiggly sea creatures oozed from every open hatch on the frigate. The enormous weight of the worms began to swamp the ship, the frigid waves of the surrounding ocean already lapping over the lower deck railings.

"Sir," the chief implored, "we need to abandon ship!"

Ivan ignored the man, instead firing his pistol out an open bridge window at the wall of worms climbing up the side ladders. Several of the ship's company had already leapt overboard, their bright orange survival suits bobbing amongst the surrounding waves. Colonel Borishov and the chief looked at each other one last time, before both jumped into the icy water below. They knew the ship's commanding officer was far too stubborn to let go, even in the face of total defeat. The last they saw of Acting Captain Ivan Egorov, he was pouring kerosene onto the bridge's floor tiles, just before the *Khabalov* capsized and sank among the sea ice.

# CHAPTER 27

It took them a while to find the ice cavern entrance. The jagged opening was long and narrow. The lingering scent of jet fuel from the downed *Blackjack* that had created the entrance wafted into the tunnel. Erika crawled through the confined space, her amulet acting as an improvised torch. She was the second person to emerge into the vast frozen grotto. The stale air had the unmistakable scent of decay, causing adrenaline to pump through her veins. She linked up with their guide Ujurak, who helped clean the snow off her parka. The man peered into the vast subterranean darkness of the centuries-old floating ice. Erika could tell he sensed danger, though his neutral expression revealed little. Based on her father's estimate, the trapped *knarr* longboat was just a few dozen metres to their front. She closed her eyes and tried to remember the camera footage taken days earlier by Major Matthews.

Katherine was the third to arrive from the tunnel, followed by Erika's three loyal friends, Sandra, Michelle, and Nicole. Last came Liam and Rikke, whose combined historical knowledge and linguistic skills were critical for what they were about to face. The collection of humans was intentionally unarmed. Each knew that if the forces that haunted the Davis Strait were allowed to spread, it could mean the end of the northern hemisphere's natural order. Erika complained to herself that people had already made an environmental mess of the Arctic, and didn't need any assistance from a collection of undead Vikings, thank you very much.

"The prow of the *knarr* should be just beyond the next ice mound," Ujurak whispered. Erika made sure the straps of her leather purse were secure, then crawled forward. The ice under her belly quickly transitioned to solid wood. She inspected the timber planks on which she moved. The brittle lumber showed traces of an infestation, long extinct.

"Sea worms," Ujurak breathed behind her. "The longboat's deck is very faded, but there's no mistaking their trails."

"Is that what happened to the ship?" Erika asked, looking at him.

"Perhaps," Ujurak glanced about, "or something worse."

Katherine slithered in beside them.

"The primary cargo compartment should be in front of us," she said, "near the base of the main mast. If your dad and Rikke's analysis of Eleanor's footage is correct, then that's where you need to do your thing."

Erika acknowledged the general, then looked back over her shoulder. Her three friends moved forward in support. Whether it was their blind faith in Erika's special abilities, or simply naiveté, the trio stayed with their teammate. Liam and Rikke brought up the rear of the crouched group.

"Have we reached *iluraijuaqtut*?" Erika asked Ujurak, struggling with the Inuktitut pronunciation. Liam looked up, recognising the symbolism of his daughter's question.

"Yes," Ujurak smiled back quietly. "We've reached the end of the mourning period for your dear mother. You may proceed with the *naasiivik* ritual at any time."

Erika felt her entire upbringing, both good and bad, came down to this very moment. With the stench of decomposed flesh filling her nostrils, she gave one last look at her loved ones, then moved off towards the centre of the *draugar's* lair. If she could just make it to the cargo hold without being noticed.

The atrophy in her muscles was immediate.

Erika couldn't move as her body was enveloped by the pulsating green force. A wretched cackle echoed through the ice cavern as she was lifted off the ground. Erika felt she could still speak, but nothing more. Her eyes widened in panic as she used her peripheral vision to look for her friends. To her dread, they too were now trapped by the same force field. The four of them slowly rose towards the centre of the ice chamber.

*Pjófur*, a voice echoed in everyone's thoughts.

"Oh no," Rikke gasped, pulling at Liam's arm. "It thinks she's a thief."

"The *draugar* are motivated by spite," Liam said quickly, gripped with dread for his daughter. "They were said to jealously guard their tombs from the living. General, what should we do?"

Katherine knelt with Liam, Rikke and Ujurak, who had apparently not yet been detected. She watched the four young women, who she felt personally responsible for, float helplessly as mid-air prisoners. She glanced at the sides of the frozen walls for something to use as a distraction, but found none. Katherine then stared knowingly into Liam's eyes. His return gaze beckoned her to stay, but it was no use. She was on the move, running as fast as her legs could carry her. Katherine sprinted under the hovering women, her boots thumping against the wooden deck. From her tactical vest she pulled out a red emergency flare, lighting it with a twist. She raised her right hand and prepared to throw it into the darkness.

The arrow cut deep.

It caught Katherine in the right bicep with such force that it spun her around. She fell to the ground, her own body weight snapping the projectile lodged in her arm. The flare fell from her hand, illuminating the surroundings as it rolled deeper into the frigid cavern. She tried to get up, but was immobilised, her body now glowing green as well. The odour that seeped into the frozen chamber was repugnant. Katherine watched as her burning flare came to rest by a massive sheepskin boot. Even under the limited red glow, there was no mistaking the sheer size of the monster before them.

Erika looked down from her elevated position at the creature, recognizing it as the one she had challenged in Pond Inlet. It was clad in layers of wrinkled leather straps and corroded chainmail, its gaunt face hidden under a hood. Close by stood two more similarly dressed *draugar*, one with a quiver of arrows, the other a battle-axe. She detected further movement behind the creatures, but couldn't tell who or what it was. Her amulet felt stone-cold against her chest, its magic gone. The dark energy around her was preventing it from working, like a mobile phone in a lead box. If only she could break through the green energy field, or pierce it somehow, but she was numb – totally unable to move.

Katherine screamed as the lead monster picked her up, releasing her from the green force field's grip. It intentionally held Katherine by her wounded arm. The other creatures hissed with delight as the largest among them taunted the general. Liam and Rikke watched mortified from behind an ice mound, while Ujurak searched for anything to use as a weapon. As the red flare fizzled, its illumination was replaced by the same ambient green aura that had plagued the Arctic skies for months. Erika observed as the jade glow revealed the vastness of the ice chamber. She counted at least ten *draugar*, standing in the middle of the longboat, which was roughly thirty-five metres in length. In the centre were multiple wooden drums that likely contained tar, as well as the monsters' beloved sea chest they had so enviously wanted returned. Behind it were the vessel's main mast and sail, as well as a decrepit wooden table with several parchment sheets unrolled across it.

The lead creature dropped Katherine down beside the table, lifting its crippled finger towards the stained pages. She recognised the sheets as primitive maps, but with names she didn't understand. Katherine thought she could discern Greenland, and perhaps the north-eastern coast of Canada, but the scale and markings were all wrong. Again the hideous monster pointed insistently at the navigational charts.

"I don't understand what you want?" Katherine said defiantly. An unseen force applied more pressure against her wounded arm. She grimaced in pain.

"Read me what it says," Rikke called out, standing up with her arms raised. Liam reached out to pull her back, but fell over, exposing himself to the *draugar* as well.

"Oh, what the hell," he grudgingly whispered to Rikke, as he got up. "I guess we're in this together."

Liam lifted his hands in surrender and slowly moved forward with Rikke towards the aged table. The *draugar* chief sized up the pair and let them approach, sensing they were hardly a threat. Erika continued to watch from her unnatural perch, immobilised and unbearably frustrated. The scenes before her were straight from a nightmare, but very real. Now her own father was risking his life for what increasingly seemed a hopeless cause.

"It's a map," Katherine called out. "It's got Greenland where it's supposed to be, but I don't understand the language used to describe it."

Rikke slowly reached the map table under the glare of the closest monster.

Her eyes widened, before calling out to Liam. "Newfoundland is marked as *Vineland.*"

"That's incredible," Liam said, astonished. "Go on."

"I think Labrador is listed as *Markland,* and Baffin Island as *Helluland.*"

Erika noticed the other *draugar* became agitated at the mention of the last location. Her usefulness finished, the lead creature thrust Katherine's head against the table with such force it cracked the faded surface. She fell back dazed as Rikke looked on helplessly. The same monster traced its finger from *Helluland* along a series of ancient contour lines that led west, gazing directly at Rikke.

"It's the north-west passage," she realised. "They must have been looking for the north-west passage when they became trapped."

"Or were abandoned," Liam said grimly.

The *draugar* surrounding their leader started moving towards Rikke and Liam. One particularly bloated monster slowly unsheathed a rusted long sword, making sure the unsettling sound of metal-on-metal was heard by all.

"Hvao viltu?" Rikke yelled at the primary creature in a language Liam assumed was Old Norse. Rikke's ghoulish audience took several steps back, disoriented to hear words they recognised. After a pause, the chief monster spoke at Rikke, festering saliva dripping from its deformed mouth.

"I don't understand it all," she announced, her hands trembling, "but it translates roughly as it wants revenge, against the *skraeling,* for killing its... for killing its brothers. Uh... Revenge against natural life, for entombing them in ice. They will bring a plague the likes of which no mortal will survive." Rikke was having a hard time keeping up her translation. "Uh...the living creatures of the Arctic will be infected by their spirits and compelled to do their bidding... uh, in order to destroy what's left of humanity in the north. As the Arctic continues to warm... more like them will be freed from their frozen prisons and unleash their wrath. My God..."

"Oh, is that all?" Sandra yelled, exasperated, from inside her energy bubble. "C'mon, Erika, let's show this geriatric troll what the sisters are made of."

Nothing happened.

"Erika, please," Sandra begged.

Again, silence.

Erika floated above the room, powerless. She felt nothing, sensed nothing, was nothing. Now the closest people in her world were going to die, and no one could stop it. As if on cue, the *draugar* chief threw Katherine back against an ice wall, its awful cackle echoing through the dank chamber. The general slumped to the ground, motionless. Erika screamed inside. Next the same monster lifted both Rikke and Liam off the ground, one in each bony hand. It banged them together, allowing their limp forms to fall to the cold floor. There was no way to tell if they were still breathing.

*No, please, no.*

Nicole and Michelle screamed as their bodies were spun in mid-air with such force that they soon passed out from blood loss to the brain. Sandra remained defiant until the end, the green bubble in which she was encased being thrown around violently until she too was silenced.

Erika had never felt so alone. She begged for the amulet around her neck to react. Nothing. She willed her thoughts, calling for assistance in any form, but none came. The undead would defeat the living. Most terribly, they would take their time doing it.

*Mother, I'm so sorry.*

Ujurak knew he had one chance. He leapt from behind his frozen sanctuary and ran directly for Erika. She saw his giant shadow approaching, but could only will him on, her body cemented within the floating green energy.

*Ten steps to go*, he calculated in his mind.

*Five steps...*

*Three...*

*Two...*

Ujurak threw himself in the air towards Erika as the first green-hued arrow pierced his back. A second deadly missile landed between his shoulder blades, hurling him against Erika's energy cocoon. She looked on in anguish as the bloodied face of the guide smiled back at her, crimson liquid streaming from his mouth. The final projectile did what the dying Ujurak had hoped. It punched clean through his torso, its energy pulsating with the same black magic that held Erika. As a result, the arrowhead penetrated her virtual prison without resistance, dissolving the energy field in an instant. She fell to the ground, along with poor Ujurak's lifeless body.

*Now, my cub!*

Erika screamed until her lungs felt they would burst.

Her eyes roared with the brightness of the sun, temporarily blinding all in her sight. The amulet around her neck was molten hot, its reawakened magic from the first millennia merging with her own abilities. Sparks flew in every direction. Again Erika yelled, her pitch so high several of the *draugar* covered what was left of their ears. Static energy swirling about her body as she crouched like a lioness ready to pounce. Erika sensed a new energy trap trying to form around her. This time she was ready, thwarting the black magic with her own electric surge.

She rolled to the right, then again to the left, dodging a series of arrows that flew her way. The *draugar* chief bellowed in anger as its fellow monsters tried to chase the nimble human. Erika was too fast. She antagonised them, bouncing from side to side, her intuition pre-empting their every move. She ran between the legs of one creature, which raised its long sword attempting to cut her down. As a second monster approached, Erika ducked, causing it to be sliced in half by the first attacker's blade. She then threw herself on the deck, just as the archers' next arrows whizzed by, slamming into the undead swordsman. *Two down,* she thought as she sprinted along the centre boards of the encrusted longboat, several creatures in pursuit. Her foresight abilities grew with each fallen monster, as did her confidence.

*Stay focused, cub.*

Erika was holding her own, but needed help if she had any hope of actually defeating the *draugar*. She raced back along the seam of the long-boat, avoiding several battle-axe swings in the process. Near the bow of the ship, she found her three friends, still encased in their debilitating force fields. She ran among the trio, slapping her energised hands against the energy bubbles so that they disintegrated, freeing their occupants. Sandra was the most lucid among them.

"Sandra," Erika yelled as she moved about, "grab Michelle and Nicole, and get the others behind cover."

Sandra scrambled to her feet, attracting the attention of an enraged creature with a studded club. Erika noticed it move for Sandra and pulled herself up the central mast of the ship. She then grabbed the top of the faded main sail and with all her might, threw herself off the spar towards the monster stalking Sandra. The ancient tarp tore away from its davits, covering the creature's head and torso. Erika crashed through the boat's floorboards, allowing no fewer than four arrows intended for her to dispatch the fabric-laden beast.

She landed in darkness onto something soft. Erika had fallen at least two metres through the rotted deck into the ship's hold. She had no time to waste, quickly raising her lit amulet in order to find a way out. It was then she noticed she had landed on what felt like soil, probably used by the Vikings as ballast. To her surprise, the texture of the dirt was no longer frozen, and felt like mud. Erika sank down to her ankles. More crashing sounds above indicated the *draugar* were searching for her. Better her than her friends.

*Movement, to your left.*

She stood absolutely still. Something big was definitely writhing just out of her field of vision. There was a pause, then several more sounds as the unknown form in the darkness began to thrash wildly. Erika turned to face whatever it was that lurked in the shadows. She could see from its silhouette that it was smaller than the other *draugar*, but with a humanoid shape. It made noises, muffled but distinct. Whatever it was, she sensed it was enraged, and yet felt trapped.

Erika's eyes grew bright. Her optic glow lit up the ballast hold where she stood. In the corner, with her mouth and limbs bound, was Major Eleanor Matthews.

*Oh crap.*

Erika moved towards Eleanor, each footstep making a sucking sound in the dark mud. Eleanor stared in disbelief at her liberator, who removed the gag from her mouth. Erika then went to work freeing her hands and legs.

"Thank you," Eleanor gasped, "but what the hell are you doing here? Never mind, we need to escape and fast. I think that big bastard has some kind of twisted courtship ritual planned for me. How large is your rescue team?"

"Still conscious, four," Erika replied.

Eleanor's face fell.

"Actually, you make it five," Erika added, trying to sound positive.

The wooden boards above their heads tore away. Two massive arms reached down, grabbing both women by their shoulders. They were lifted back onto the main deck with such force, the pair were left winded. As Eleanor coughed on all fours, Erika looked up at the *draugar* chief towering over them. It appeared to have grown to twice its original size, obese and rancid. Maggots spilled from several ulcered wounds while it clasped its hands together in anticipation.

The two trapped women looked at each other.

"Any ideas?" Eleanor asked, trying to make light of their hopeless situation.

"You tell me," Erika scoffed. "It's your fiancé."

The creature suddenly fell backwards with a crash as it was knocked off its feet. Nicole and Michelle ran along either side of the fallen beast, having just tripped it using ancient rowing oars. The mammoth form rolled onto its side as the four women dashed to get out of its way.

"Erika! Over here," Michelle yelled, throwing her an oar. "Sandra is waiting up front."

"What's she doing?" Erika asked, hoping she was all right.

Michelle smiled back. "She's in net."

Confused, Erika quickly followed her teammates, as did Eleanor. The four women moved past several destroyed *draugar* before they came across Sandra in the centre of the cargo area. She was holding an enlarged rowing oar, deflecting wave after wave of hungry worms as they slithered towards her. She was protecting the exposed drums of tar, which were critical to the general's original plan.

"The last few zombie freaks took off when these things showed up," Sandra yelled at Erika between swings. "It's just us, that big bad dude, and these worms. They look like the same gross critters that sank your grandpa's boat."

Sea worms, thousands of them, rose up from holes in the exposed deck. The massive bursts of energy, coupled with the rising northern temperatures, must have melted the permafrost mud in the ship's belly, reanimating the ancient life forms. The few surviving *draugar* had disappeared in desperation, trying to avoid the same fate that had doomed their original voyage. Undead souls forever trapped in the Sea of Worms.

Michelle and Nicole jumped down with their oars to help Sandra deal with the growing mass. Erika reached into her satchel purse, then stopped.

*Dad.*

"Come with me," Erika called to Eleanor. Without having time to ask, the major followed Erika to the front of the ship. There they found both Liam and Rikke, unconscious but alive. Next to them lay the crumpled body of Ujurak. Eleanor moved to her fallen guide, rolling him over. The man was clearly dead, yet his facial expression was one of calm, perhaps even satisfaction. The three arrowheads protruding from his chest told Eleanor all she needed to know about his demise.

"Ujurak saved me," Erika said as she turned her father onto his side. "He saved us all."

Eleanor was about to respond when she heard a familiar voice off to her left. She glanced over to find Katherine trying to lift herself off an ice ledge next to the ship. She was covered in blood.

"General," Eleanor shouted, bounding over. She quickly scanned her fallen mentor, then pulled off the belt from her pants. She tightened it as a tourniquet around Katherine's wounded arm so as to stem the bleeding.

"Has... has she done it?" Katherine asked, breathless.

"Has she done what?" Eleanor responded in wonder.

The sound of the twin explosions was earsplitting. Bolts of energy from the remaining *draugar* chief slammed against the frozen wall in front of the trapped longboat, sending ice shards in every direction. A second wave of electricity overflew Erika and the others near the bow, punching deeper into the frigid cavern. A small crack appeared in the ice wall near the site of the blasts. Slowly the rupture grew, until it reached the cavern's roof. More blasts of molten hot energy, all directed at the same location, filled the air with crackling and steam.

"What the hell is it doing?" Eleanor gasped, trying to shield Katherine with her own body.

"I don't know," Erika said, "but please stay with my father and Rikke. I need to get back and help the others. We need to finish this."

"Finish what?" Eleanor protested as Erika ran off without answering. "You know, I'd really appreciate it if someone would tell me what the hell is going on," Eleanor demanded. Katherine looked up at her and gently smiled, too weak to reply.

"Michelle, I'm on your left." Erika grabbed an oar and joined her teammates as they batted away the sea worms.

"Holstrom, we don't have any more time," Sandra pleaded. "You have to do your thing now!"

As if to underscore her point, the enormous *draugar* chief fired several more energy fireballs into the collapsing ice wall to their front. Erika put down her oar and again reached into her purse. She had just found what she was looking for, when all four women were thrown off balance, landing momentarily amongst their slithering opponents. The longboat moved. Ever so slightly at first, but Erika distinctly felt the *knarr* shift under her feet. Another crashing sound near the bow, then a single ray of green tinted sunlight pierced through the frozen mass above. More ice was blown away by the creature, now four times its original size, until Erika could see open sky above her. The boat slid several metres, again knocking the women over. Finally, with a thunderous crash, the entire southern wall in front of them collapsed, revealing the open ocean. Huge ice sheets from the destroyed cave wall floated among the waves.

"Oh my God," Katherine realised, with no strength to intervene.

"That thing is going to try and set sail. Eleanor, you have to get the others off the ship."

Eleanor propped Katherine up against the relative safety of the ice ledge, then ran back to the longboat. First she returned with Rikke, the unconscious doctor slung over her shoulder. Next she went back for Liam. Slightly heavier, Eleanor brought him off using a firefighter's carrying technique. Finally, she hauled Ujurak's lifeless body from the vessel. She rested him down just as the wooden hull of the ancient longboat slid forward toward the open water, taking their four young friends and the *draugar* chief with it. Eleanor and Katherine watched in awe from the frozen ledge as the Viking ship launched onto the Davis Strait, as if resuming the journey it had failed to complete so many centuries ago.

Erika glanced about as they rose in the metre-high swells. The sea worms continued their insatiable mission to devour the longboat as the behemoth behind them redirected its attention towards the troublesome students. The monster pulled a pair of daggers from its mouldy belt. It hesitated, realising that at least one of the humans was not as she seemed. A *skraeling*, yes, but with spirit powers of her own. The creature planned to dissect her fully once it was finished with the others.

"We have to get off this boat," Nicole called out.

"Not until we've done the deed," Erika shouted back. "If we don't do this right, they'll just come back in another form, way more evil than they are now."

"I don't know, Holstrom," Sandra said looking up. "This big one seems pretty evil already."

The creature straddled the centre of the ship. All around it, the green northern sky flickered with a morbid rhythm. The daggers the monster held in its hands were alight with dark energy. There was no place for the four women to go. They would either be cut down by the creature before them, overcome by the ferocious sea worms, or freeze to death in the Arctic Ocean. If this was going to be the end, Erika knew she had to make sure the *draugar* could never again be awakened. If only she could distract the fearsome beast.

The initial projectiles all overshot the longboat. They landed in the water beyond the ancient ship, creating harmless geysers. The next salvo was more accurate. One of the supersonic rounds hit the *draugar* chief's left arm above the elbow. The high explosive shell detonated on impact, unbalancing the massive creature as its severed arm fell into the frigid sea. Another explosion struck its upper thigh, shattering what was left of its rotting femur. It fell to one knee, wounded but still very much in the fight.

Erika looked out across the waves to see a ship flying a Danish flag closing in towards them. The warship held its fire. The giant monster had made for an easy target while standing several stories above the waves. Now, however, it was hunched over, too close to the surviving humans to risk another shot.

It was now or never.

*I love you, Mother.*

Erika pulled from her purse the firestone her grandmother had given her the day of Star's memorial. In older times, the striking of the firestone represented the end of the week-long mourning period for a loved one. In this case, if the Norse mythology proved correct, it also meant their salvation.

The *draugar* chief noticed the human expose the stone from her satchel and instantly realised the threat it posed. It lunged at the wretched *skraeling*. The dagger in its remaining hand embedded into the deck just beside Erika as she ducked, dropping the firestone in the process. It rolled haplessly along the upper deck, in danger of falling into the pool of slithering sea worms. The creature reached for it but fell short.

Nicole was first on the move. Using an oar, she navigated the stone forward along the uneven deck. When the monster grabbed for her, Nicole flicked the rock over to Michelle, who controlled it with her own oar. The *draugar* chief tried to turn around, howling an awful cry in the process. The women were unfazed. Erika was now advancing as well, running up the centre elevated boards, as Michelle made her way up the right. A bolt of energy just missed Michelle as she shot the firestone back to Erika. She in turn hit the rock with her oar and sent it flying towards Sandra near the drums of tar. The monster snarled again, unable to prevent what it knew was coming. Sandra deflected the stone off her paddle and into the air behind her. Erika launched herself. Avoiding the creature's desperate swing, she intercepted the stone and slammed it against the top iron ring of the first drum. The firestone's cryptocrystalline acted as a flint, setting off a series of sparks that fell into the container of tar. The ancient tar of the Viking era was derived from pine and birch, making it an excellent combustible.

All four women scrambled for the front of the ship as the first drum exploded, spilling several gallons of flaming tar onto the wooden deck. The wounded beast writhed in agony as the burning pitch raced up its legs, setting its garments alight. The sea chest, with its priceless artifacts, was vaporised. The second drum detonated, followed by a third, until most of the mid and aft sections of the longboat were ablaze. The last of the *draugar* collapsed into the fire that consumed its ship.

"We need to jump," Erika urged from the bow as the flames approached, roasting millions of sea worms in the process.

"We'll freeze to death," Nicole protested.

"Better freeze than fry," Michelle said, and dove headfirst into the icy water.

Next went Nicole, egged on by Sandra. The latter then joined her teammates in the form of a cannonball as she landed among the frigid swells.

Erika was the last aboard, glancing back at the wall of fire behind her. She could still hear the moans of agony from the defeated monster. She almost felt pity for the creature, until she remembered what it had done to her beloved Pond Inlet. Erika looked up through the fire and smoke to see, for the first time in weeks, a yellow sun shining brightly in a clear blue sky. As the rescue craft from the *Knud Rasmussen* approached, Erika jumped into the freezing water where her loyal friends thrashed about. The ancient longboat continued to burn like a Viking funeral ship until its smouldering hull finally gave way, allowing it to slip below the Arctic waves forever.

# CHAPTER 28

"Holstrom, you're off," Nancy yelled from the Vermont bench. "Lavoix, get going."

Michelle leapt over the boards onto the Gutterson Fieldhouse rink as Erika skated off the ice. She sat down beside their newly promoted captain, Nicole Gibson, and sprayed cool water into her mouth. Unlike Michelle and Sandra, their new team captain had said little in the month since their return from the Arctic. Erika looked over at Nicole, the letter *C* newly stitched onto her jersey. She ignored Erika, staying focused on the mayhem at centre ice. Nicole had even stopped fussing about her hair in recent days, choosing instead to keep it in an uncharacteristically simple ponytail. Whether it was psychological trauma, or mere ambivalence, she had definitely changed.

The opposing team's buzzer went off, signalling Delaware had scored another goal, making it a 3-1 game in their favour. Sandra hit her goalie's stick against the frozen ground in frustration. It was already several minutes into the third period, meaning if the visiting team won the game, they'd win the tournament. Erika's old nemesis number 19 skated past the Vermont bench, mockingly waving at the seated players. Neither she nor Nicole cared much for the Delaware enforcer's antics. They had both witnessed far worse this past summer. Yet to most of the world, it was as though the horrors in the far north had never occurred. What the international media had dubbed the *Davis Strait Crisis,* had lasted less than three news cycles. Moscow had admitted to the loss of two vessels, including the attack submarine *Volkov,* but said little else. Washington had similarly lamented the sinking of an American destroyer as tragic, promising a full congressional inquiry. Even London quickly moved on from the unexplained loss of two fighter jets, while the electromagnetic interference across the north that had lasted months, was passed off as a rare natural phenomena. For Ottawa, the priority was to rebuild Pond Inlet following the damage sustained from thousands of highly unusual migrating caribou. Erika shook her head. At least her grandparents and friends in the remote northern community were safe.

Someone banged on the protective glass beside the Vermont bench. Erika peered over to see Liam cheering her on, complete with a green UVM sweatshirt. If any good had come from their northern experience, it was that father and daughter where now closer than ever. Erika was even grudgingly coming to grips with Liam's new acquaintance, whom he'd been chatting with occasionally online. Maybe it was time to give Dr Rikke Larsen a second chance, but it was difficult. Through no fault of her own, Erika was constantly comparing Rikke with her late mother, even if Liam insisted they were just friends. Erika longed for Star's presence. Her mother had not visited Erika's dreams since the demise of the *draugar.* More concerning, the precious amulet around her neck had permanently ceased emitting its comforting warmth. Perhaps this was a good thing, as it seemed to suggest any danger had passed.

"Gibson, you're in," Nancy ordered, freeing Nicole to storm onto the ice with a vengeance. Always bombastic, Nancy was now the team's head coach and clearly had something to prove as this was her first tournament in charge. Michelle slid in beside Erika, having been swapped on the ice with Nicole.

"Number nineteen is good," Michelle huffed while catching her breath. "Hey, when are we going to see some of the old Holstrom magic on the ice?"

Erika smiled back politely through her face mask. She had made a conscious effort to suppress her abilities since the start of the regular season. Erika wanted to be judged based on her own merits, as an equal, and not reliant on ancient sorcery. Vermont's current two-point deficit was an awkward testament to Erika's new approach to hockey. Michelle gave her a knowing look and went back to observing the game. If Nicole had grown more distant from her friends, Michelle was the opposite. She had thrived since their time in the north, their near-death experience infusing her with a renewed zest for life. The previously brooding local from Burlington had been transformed into a self-assured woman, comfortable with who and what she was in the world. Erika was glad for her friend, and had to admit that Michelle's newfound confidence was attractive.

The referee blew her whistle. An infraction had been given against Vermont. Nancy looked on in dismay as Nicole skated over to the penalty box for her two minutes of penance. Something was clearly amiss with their new team captain, as she rarely received penalties. The home team was now down two points and one player, a situation Delaware was sure to exploit.

"Holstrom," Nancy sighed, bending down beside Erika and Michelle, "it's up to you, my friend. Let's see some of that magic you demonstrated during summer training." Erika and Michelle exchanged a glance, their head coach oblivious to the *double entendre* of her statement.

"I'll do my best, coach," Erika said, and took to the ice. She moved in for the face-off, again against number 19.

*Who was this person?* she thought, as Liam cheered loudly from the stands. It was only then Erika realised that the Gutterson Fieldhouse was packed. Even the team's mascot had been relegated to the bleachers. A whistle blast and they were off, the puck taken by Delaware with a five to four person power play advantage. Erika kept up with number 19, refusing to rely on her foresight abilities she knew wanted to emerge. She was playing to the best of her abilities, or at least the best of her *natural* abilities. Seemingly out of nowhere, another Delaware player body-checked Erika. The hit sent her into the sideboards while her opponent took a slap shot against Vermont's goalie. Sandra was ready. With a backhanded move, she caught the hockey puck in mid-air. Erika got up from the ice as the audience cheered the spectacular save. She looked at the clock: seven minutes to go.

Another face-off, another possession for Delaware. This time, however, one of the attackers tripped, allowing Erika to slip in and take the puck.

"Go, Holstrom!" Nancy yelled, her access badge flailing in front of her as she bounced up and down on Vermont's bench. Erika had always been most comfortable on the offence. She easily evaded two defensive players, and lined up for a shot against Delaware's net. She faked her first shot, then sliced the puck into the bottom left corner of the opposing goal, the buzzer signalling a 3-2 game. The crowd went wild as Erika was surrounded by her teammates.

"Two more, Holstrom," they yelled in encouragement.

A scuffle broke out near Delaware's net. Number 19 and a group of her teammates were having words with their Vermont counterparts. Three referees swooped in to break up the altercation, but not before 19 glanced at Erika, her lips clearly mouthing a less than complimentary phrase. Erika just smiled back and waved, having heard it all before.

It still felt surreal to be back in Burlington. The simplicity of her chosen sport seemed a far cry from the intensity and devastation of their experiences in the Arctic. Before leaving Pond Inlet, Erika had promised little Amber that she would return next summer to see how the girl's hockey skills had progressed. Saying goodbye to her older brother Jordan had been more complicated. He wasn't sure what to make of his childhood friend, half-thinking she may be a witch. Erika tried to explain her inherited abilities to him, passed on from her grandmother's lineage. It had all been too much for Jordan to accept. He even shunned her advances when she tried to kiss him goodbye. Her grandparents passed it off as late adolescent angst, but Erika knew better. In her eyes, he was a responsible, beautiful young man, thrust into an unimaginable situation where he felt utterly powerless. To Jordan, his southern friend represented confusion and danger, something he'd already had enough of in his life. Sandra had tried to cheer Erika up during their flight home, whenever the goalie's face wasn't buried in an airsick bag.

A girl in the stands caught Erika's attention. As the players on the ice reset themselves for the next face-off, Erika stared at the little one's face. She was no older than eight, yet was a spitting image of the blonde Norse girl from Erika's dreams. The child was busy finishing off an ice cream cone while her mother watched. It was a further reminder of the summer's trauma, and the fact her dreams were now silent.

"Holstrom, wake up!" Nancy hollered.

Erika shook her head and moved into position. The familiarity of the little girl was clearly a coincidence. *It had to be.*

The two teams carried on a steady flow of back and forth as the minutes diminished. Nicole was again on the ice, her penalty complete. She tied the game 3-3, only for Delaware's number 19 to make it 4-3, with two minutes remaining. Nancy called a time-out, and gathered her Vermont players near their bench.

"All right ladies," she asserted. "This is it." She pulled out her signature clipboard and drew several scenarios onto the white pages. "We're going to stack the deck. Gibson, I want you and Lavoix to come up the wing and try to make a play for the puck, but pay attention not to get an icing call." Nicole and Michelle nodded their understanding. "Holstrom," she continued, "you're the ace in all this, so stay back behind Lavoix. Once you have all cleared centre ice, whoever has the puck drop it back to Holstrom. Any questions?"

"You can do it Erika," Sandra encouraged, her goalie helmet lifted up on her head, "just like you did with those..." Her three friends shot Sandra a look. She immediately corrected her gaffe. "Those... players from Massachusetts. Yeah, them."

"You'd better not," Nancy protested. "Bruster, we lost that game, remember?"

"Ah, sorry, I was thinking of something else," Sandra said, lowering her eyes. Michelle leaned in beside Erika with a hushed voice. "I know you're trying not to use your special skills, but it's nothing to be ashamed off. This stuff is part of you and honestly, we could really use the help."

Erika looked over at Michelle, her friend staring encouragingly back at her.

"I need to do this my way," she whispered back. "I'm worried if I rely too much on these abilities, they will consume who I really am. Grandma even warned me they should only be used in time of danger."

"Break glass in case of emergency. That sort of thing," Sandra chimed in, eavesdropping. "Dude, I get it, but I'm really with Michelle on this one."

Erika looked over at Nicole, to see if their team captain had any insight. Nicole was passive, which was typical of her lately.

"You do what you want Holstrom," she said flatly, "just don't do it near me. Coach, we done?"

"Yes," Nancy said, clapping her hands several times. "Let's go Vermont!"

"Don't worry about Nicole," Michelle said, skating alongside Erika. "She'll come around. What we saw up north would mess with anyone's head. Just focus on the game. And Holstrom?" Michelle paused for effect. "I trust you."

Erika blushed under her helmet. *At least someone does.*

The puck dropped, with Nicole taking control. Delaware was going to try to run down the clock, which meant Vermont had to be aggressive. Sandra was pulled from net, allowing her team to put a sixth player on the ice. Nicole was in control, the puck dancing between her stick as she advanced. Number 19 zeroed in on her, but not before Nicole launched the piece of rubber over to Michelle. They needed to tie the game so they could go to overtime, otherwise the tournament would end with Delaware as the champions for a third year in a row. Erika was reminded of their final minutes on the sinking Viking ship, how they collectively worked as a team to defeat an unrepentant foe. It was a struggle none of them had wanted, nor ever wished to relive.

"Holstrom, snap out of it," Nicole ordered over her shoulder. Erika's mind was brought back to the task at hand. She moved in behind Michelle, who slipped the puck back to her as planned. There were only a few seconds left when Erika lined up for her shot. Nicole and Michelle kept number 19 at bay as Erika zeroed in on the Delaware net. Her senses screamed to be unleashed, but her conscious self would have none of it. She took the slap shot just before the end game buzzer sounded. Her valiant effort deflected harmlessly off the goal post as the whistle blew.

She had missed.

The Delaware players threw their gloves in the air with delight, swarming around their goalie. A very stunned Gutterson Fieldhouse looked on. Slowly, the Vermont fans applauded quietly out of respect for the opposing team's success. Erika stood alone in the corner of the rink, her chin resting on top of her hockey stick. The other Vermont players made their way back towards their own bench, as Nancy shook hands with the Delaware coach. Liam looked on encouragingly at his daughter from the stands, giving Erika two thumbs up as she'd often done to him. She smiled back softly, making her way over to her teammates to form a handshake line with the victors.

The two varsity teams moved down each other's side, shaking hands and patting one another on the back. Erika was second last in the Vermont line, followed by Sandra. As number 19 approached, she made eye contact with Erika. Her handshake was firm and cold. There was a knowing look in her eye, but she said nothing to Erika, not even the obligatory *good game*. 19 moved on and shook Sandra's hand, then cruised to leave the ice. The tournament trophy ceremony would take place later in the evening. Erika watched as the Delaware enforcer reached the rink side exit. The tall woman took off her helmet, revealing a tight bun of ice-blonde hair. A small family waited to congratulate her. As number 19 hugged the adults, a young girl with them locked eyes with Erika.

*It couldn't be her, could it?*

"Don't let it get to you," Sandra said, jolting Erika from her thoughts. The goalie placed her gloved hand on Erika's shoulder pad. "It's just a game, and no crazy zombies are trying to kill us. Now, you go do your weird sauna thing while I rest my feet in the hot tub."

Erika watched the goalie leave the ice. She knew Sandra was just trying to put things in perspective, even if her example was a bit crude. Erika glanced back at the opposing side of the rink, but the blonde girl was gone.

"Good game, cub," Liam said from above the Vermont bench, the audience stands now almost empty.

"Thanks, Dad," she smiled back up at him. "I'll catch up with you after dinner."

He waved and moved off, replaced by Nancy.

"Holstrom, there's something about you," the head coach observed. "I'm not sure what it is, but you've changed since the summer." Erika looked blankly at Nancy as the coach continued. "You're good, but you could be so much better. I know it, I saw it at training camp. You need to concentrate, my friend." Nancy eased the intensity of her words, realising her young subject was getting visibly upset. "But it's all good, Holstrom. Just keep it up. And by the way, good game." She walked away awkwardly, leaving Erika alone to hobble down the hallway on her blades towards the change room.

Erika unlaced her skates, thinking back to Nancy's words. She was conflicted. She wished she still had that competitive edge, but knew that with it came a whole world of trouble, from nightmares to monsters. Still, winning felt nicer than losing. She sighed, and not for the first time wondered what Brigadier-General Tremblay or Major Matthews would do were they in the same confusing life situation as she was. The last of her hockey equipment discarded, Erika took off her clothes, wrapping her bruised body in a towel. She passed a few of her teammates laughing in the shower room, then moved towards her place of sanctuary. She opened the wooden sauna door, embracing the warm humidity that greeted her. The room was dimly lit, just how she liked it, a lone water bucket and ladle on the lower step. She dropped her towel and moved to the top bench. It was only then that she realised she was not alone. Michelle sat quietly in the corner, her eyes closed as sweat glistened down her tattooed body. Erika said nothing as she sat down, throwing some water from the pail onto the hot rocks of the sauna oven.

"You played really well," Michelle said softly, "and I respect your decision not to use your powers, even if it meant we lost. We all need to be true to ourselves, and if for you that means just being the same as everyone else, that's cool."

"Not the same," Erika quietly interjected, "equal. Those things up north made me realise how trivial so much of our life down south can be. Following the latest fashion trends, worrying about social status, being beholden to an online image. None of it matters when you're gone. What's worse, I don't want to become a slave to my abilities. My grandmother already warned me it could lead to a dark and dangerous place."

She threw more water on the sauna stove. Steam lifted to the wooden roof before rolling back onto the two women.

"What matters to me now is my family and my friends, like you, Sandra, and Nicole. None of you asked to be part of what happened to us in the Arctic, but when it really mattered, you were there." Erika looked down briefly. "Though I think it has really affected Nicole in a bad way."

"I agree," Michelle allowed. "But she'll get over it. Let's hope so anyway."

A few moments of hushed silence passed in the humid room before Michelle opened her eyes and turned towards her teammate. "I'm so very sorry for the loss of your mother," she said. "And if I ever made you feel uncomfortable, I apologise. You're an amazing person, Erika, and I should have been more understanding. Please forgive me."

Erika looked over at her friend. Before Michelle could react, the younger of the two slid across the sauna bench, stopping by her side. Erika gazed warmly into Michelle's green eyes, then leaned forward and kissed her.

The End

THE
ARCTIC REGIONS
OF
NORTH AMERICA
BY
EDWd WELLER, F.R.G.S
PARRY ISLAND
PRINCE PATRICK'S LAND
MELVILLE ISLAND
BATHURST Isld
CORNWALLIS ISLAND
Grinnell Land
North Cornwall
BANKS LAND
Melville Sound
Pr of Wales Land
Peel Sound
Prince Albert Land
Minto Inlet
Prince Albert Sound
Wollaston Land
Victoria Land
King William
Boothia
Great Bear Lake
Arctic Circle

# EPILOGUE

The winter ice formed later and later each year along the eastern shores of Greenland. Where once the massive pack ice lingered year round, now it dissipated for several months each summer. This affected many of the Arctic's diverse species of wildlife, while also allowing for more unwanted human incursions.

The young female Arctic fox sniffed at the cool coastal air. Just over a year old, the scavenger was an epic example of nature's ability to adapt. Born on Norway's Svalbard Islands in the North Atlantic, the tenacious animal had set out across the frozen Arctic Ocean in late March. Within a month she had reached Greenland, her traditional Iceland hunting grounds no longer accessible due to melting ice. The little creature travelled further to Ellesmere Island on Canada's east coast, before returning to Greenland by July. In all, the Arctic fox had covered some 4,000 kilometres in only half a year; an unbelievable journey of endurance. Her primary motivation, as with most living things, was survival and the quest for food.

The scent caught the fox's attention instantly. Though not one of its usual staples, it had the alluring odour of raw flesh. The young female nimbly bounced about the jagged rocks of Greenland's coast as it zeroed in on the enticing smell. Despite the relative remoteness of the region, the fox still paid attention for any potential threats, especially polar bears and the occasional overzealous orca under the thin ice. She stopped several more times along the way, readjusting her route based on the wind direction carrying the unknown scent. The fox paused to drink from a small pond nestled among the rocks, swatting away an annoying insect with its tail. The young animal travelled a further few kilometres before stopping at the top of a rocky outcrop.

The small scavenger did not recognise what it had discovered, moving cautiously towards the centre of the twisted and burnt metal. Occasionally it would stop and chew at melted rubber, only to spit it out in disgust. The young female fox moved about the torn wreckage, looking for the origin of the scent. She passed a billowing mound of white silk, momentarily mistaking the torn fabric for a threat. The animal then found herself under the remnants of a glass canopy, with several words stencilled at the bottom. Of course, it meant nothing to the Arctic fox, who moved further towards the middle of the destroyed flying machine.

The little one hesitated. The mammal seemed very large to the fox, and was covered in a strange skin that it was unable to gnaw through. She made her way towards the creature's lower legs, which had apparently been torn away from the rest of the body. The fox took a few bites from the severed limbs, then spat out the mouthful, the unfamiliar taste less appealing than its scent. She moved up the torso, licking at the exposed face, which still rested in a flight helmet. Across the front of the unsavoury nylon skin was the name Livingstone, the shiny identification patch catching the young hunter's eye. The animal pulled at it briefly with its mouth, before moving on to scavenge different parts of the silver airframe.

As the resilient Arctic fox left the crash site in search of other food, she did not notice the downed pilot's body begin to stir.

# Afterword

At its core, *Helluland* is a work of speculative fiction, embedded in pure fantasy. Having said that, some aspects of the story were inspired by historical events. For example, the prologue's Arctic weather station was real, as was the German submarine that secretly delivered it in 1943 (parts of the station are on display at the Canadian War Museum in Ottawa). In addition, much of the Viking lore was inspired by Old Norse mythology, and will be familiar to the novel's Scandinavian readers.

*Helluland's* intricate storyline could not have been produced without the input of countless subject matter experts from several countries. Amongst them were medieval historians, cultural anthropologists, environmental scientists, and military advisors, as well as one very tenacious hockey coach, all of whom freely offered their insights and guidance. From the creative artists, editors, and translators, to close family and friends who read and re-read multiple drafts, the authors are forever grateful.

A special mention must go to *Helluland's* European and North American literary teams, who made the book possible, as well as spouses and partners for their endless love and support. Finally, and perhaps most poignantly, an immense debt of gratitude is owed to the people of the North, from both sides of the Atlantic, who so willing shared their time, culture, and infectious sense of humour in the creation of this Arctic tale. Thank you seems painfully inadequate.

Sincerely and respectfully,


C.R. Lindström
January 2023

**EERIE RIVER PUBLISHING**

**NOVELS**
**Helluland**
At Eternity's Gate
Beyond Sundered Seas
Path of War
In Solitudes Shadow
Dead Man Walking
Devil Walks in Blood
The Void
They Are Cursed Like You
SENTINEL
NOTHUS
Miracle Growth
Infested
A Sword Named Sorrow
Storming Area 51

**ANTHOLOGIES**
AFTER: A Post-Apocalyptic Survivor Series
Elemental Cycle: Four Book Series Blood Sins
It Calls From The Forest: Volume I
It Calls From The Forest: Volume II
It Calls From The Sky
It Calls From the Doors
It Calls From the Veil
It Calls From Below
Blood Sins
Last Stop: Whiskey Pete
Elemental Series (Anthology Series)
Of Fire and Stars
From Beyond the Threshold

**DRABBLE COLLECTIONS**
Forgotten Ones: Drabbles of Myth and Legend
Dark Magic: Drabbles of Magic and Lore

**COMING SOON**
Chasing the Dragon
Rotten House
A Year of Tarot (Anthology Series)

EERIE RIVER PUBLISHING PRESENTS
THEY ARE CURSED
LIKE YOU
TRAILER PARK WITCHES
BOOK ONE
HOLLEY CORNETTO & S.O. GREEN

THE VOID
BOOK ONE OF THE FANG RIPPER SERIES
NEEN COHEN

EMPIRE OF RUIN
1
IN SOLITUDE'S SHADOW
DAVID GREEN

More from Eerie River

Eerie River Publishing, is a small independant publishing house that is devoted to uplifing Indie Authors and releasing quality dark fiction novels, novellas and anthologies.

To stay up to date with all our new releases and upcoming giveaways, follow us on Facebook, Twitter, Instagram and YouTube. Sign up for our monthly newsletter and receive a free ebook Darkness Reclaimed, as our thank you gift.

https://mailchi.mp/71e45b6d5880/welcomebook

Interested in becoming a Patreon member?
Patreon membership gives you exclusive sneak peeks at upcoming books, early chapter releases, covers art as well as free ebooks and discounts on paperbacks.

https://www.patreon.com/EerieRiverPub